# "I only noticed because I can't seem to take my eyes off you whenever you're around."

And there it was. The acknowledgement of whatever this was. Attraction. Curiosity. Carnality.

"I thought we weren't going to do this," she said softly. She kept her hands folded tightly in her lap to keep them from going where they wanted to go—on him. "I'm only here for a few days."

"Then there's no danger. We both know what's what. We're going in with our eyes wide open."

"Are you seducing me, Rhys?" His thumb toyed with her lower lip and her eyes drifted closed.

"With any luck." He moved closer, leaning forward slightly so she began to recline against the cushions. "We're adults," he stated. "We're both wondering. It doesn't have to go any deeper than that."

Tentatively she lifted her hand and touched his face. "Usually I'm the confident one who goes after what she wants."

He smiled a little, his gaze dropping to her lips. "You don't want this? I could have sworn you did."

"I didn't say that…" she whispered, sliding deeper into the cushions.

"That's what I thought."

His voice was husky now, shivering along her nerve-endings. He leaned closer until he was less than a breath away.

# A CADENCE CREEK CHRISTMAS

### BY
### DONNA ALWARD

First published in Great Britain 2013
by Mills & Boon, an imprint of Harlequin (UK) Limited,
Eton House, 18-24 Paradise Road, Richmond, Surrey TW9 1SR

© Donna Alward 2013

ISBN: 978 0 263 90158 0

23-1113

Harlequin (UK) policy is to use papers that are natural, renewable and recyclable products and made from wood grown in sustainable forests. The logging and manufacturing processes conform to the legal environmental regulations of the country of origin.

Printed and bound in Spain
by Blackprint CPI, Barcelona

A busy wife and mother of three (two daughters and the family dog), **Donna Alward** believes hers is the best job in the world: a combination of stay-at-home mum and romance novelist. An avid reader since childhood, Donna always made up her own stories. She completed her arts degree in English literature in 1994, but it wasn't until 2001 that she penned her first full-length novel and found herself hooked on writing romance. In 2006 she sold her first manuscript, and now writes warm, emotional stories for Mills & Boon.

In her new home office in Nova Scotia, Donna loves being back on the east coast of Canada after nearly twelve years in Alberta, where her career began, writing about cowboys and the West. Donna's debut romance, *Hired by the Cowboy*, was awarded the Bookseller's Best Award in 2008 for Best Traditional Romance.

With the Atlantic Ocean only minutes from her doorstep, Donna has found a fresh take on life and promises even more great romances in the near future!

Donna loves to hear from readers. You can contact her through her website www.donnaalward.com, or her page at www.myspace.com/dalward.

To the Mills & Boon® Romance
authors—my writing family.
You guys are the best.

# CHAPTER ONE

TAYLOR SHEPARD FROWNED as she assessed the lineup of men before her. All five of them were big, burly and, with the exception of her brother Jack, looked irritated beyond belief.

"Come on, Taylor, can't we take these monkey suits off?"

Her oldest brother, Callum, pleaded with her. Along with his best man and groomsmen, he'd spent the past half hour trying on various tuxedo styles. Callum, being her brother and, of course, the groom, was the spokesman for the lot.

"If you want to show up at your wedding in jeans and boots, be my guest. I don't think your bride would appreciate that too much, though."

A muffled snort came from down the line. Her head snapped toward the sound and she saw one of the groomsmen—Rhys, if she remembered correctly—struggling to keep a straight face.

"Keep it up," she warned severely, "and you'll be the one trying on a cravat."

His face sobered in an instant.

"This was supposed to be a small and simple wedding," Callum reminded her. "Not one of your massive events."

"And it will be. But small and simple doesn't mean it

can't be classy." She pinned him with a stare. "Your soon-
to-be wife trusts me. Besides, you need to balance your
look with the wedding dress and flower girl dress for Nell."
She paused and played her trump card. "They're going to
be *beautiful*."

There'd be little argument out of Callum now. All it took
was the mention of Avery and his baby daughter and the
tough ex-soldier turned into a marshmallow. She thought it
was fantastic. He'd needed someone like Avery for a long
time. Not to mention how fatherhood had changed him.
He had the family he'd always wanted.

She examined each man carefully. "I don't like the
red vests," she decreed. She went up to Sam Diamond
and tugged on the lapels of his jacket. "And not double-
breasted. The green vests, like Tyson's here. The single-
breasted jacket like Jack has on, which is much simpler."
She smiled up at her brother, easily the most comfortable
man in the group. Jack wouldn't give her a moment's trouble, not about this anyway. She got to the last body in the
line and looked up.

Dark eyes looked down into hers. A little serious, a
little bit of put-upon patience, and a surprising warmth
that made her think he had a good sense of humor. She
reached up and gave his tie a tug, straightening it. "And
not the bolo tie, either. The crossover that Rhys is wearing is classier and still very Western."

Her fingertips grazed the starchy fabric of his shirt as
she dropped her hand. It was a negligible touch, barely
worth noticing, except the slight contact made something interesting tumble around in her stomach. Her gaze
darted up to his again and discovered he was watching
her steadily in a way that made her feel both excited and
awkward.

Interesting. Because in her line of work she dealt with

all sorts of men every day. Rich men, powerful men, men who liked other men and men who couldn't keep their hands to themselves. She knew how to handle herself. Was never tempted to flirt unless it was a business strategy. She was very good at reading people, figuring out their tastes and wants and knowing what methods she needed to use to deliver them.

So getting a fluttery feeling from barely touching Rhys Bullock was a surprise indeed. And feeling awkward? Well, that was practically unheard of. Of course, it could be that she was just very out of practice. She'd been far too busy building her business to do much dating.

She straightened her shoulders and took a step backward. "Okay, now on to footwear."

Groans went up the line.

She smiled. "Guys, really. This will be the best part. I was thinking black boots which we can get wherever you prefer to buy your boots. No patent dress shoes. Put on the boots you wore here so we can accurately measure your inseam for length. Then we'll finish up your measurements and you're done." She made a dismissive sound. "Honestly, what a bunch of babies."

She was having fun now, teasing the guys. They were good men but not much for dressing up. She got that. Their standard uniform was jeans and boots, plaid shirts and Stetsons. Tuxedo fittings had to be torture.

Still, it didn't matter if this was her brother's wedding or a client's A-list party. Or if she was being paid or doing it as a wedding gift. Avery and Callum's day would be exactly what it should be because she'd oversee every last detail.

And if she were being honest with herself, it was a relief to get out of Vancouver for a while and deal with "real" people. It had been exhausting lately. Most of her clients were rich and used to getting exactly what they wanted exactly when they wanted it. Their sense of entitlement could be a bit much. Not to mention the unorthodox requests. She sometimes wondered what sort of reality these people lived in.

As she looked after the ordering details, one of the alterations staff did measurements. Another half hour and they were all done and standing out in the sunshine again. Taylor pulled out her phone and scanned her to-do list for today. She had to drive back to Cadence Creek and meet with Melissa Stone, the florist at Foothills Floral. The final order was going to be placed today—after all, the wedding was less than two weeks away now. All this should have been done a month ago or even more, but Taylor knew there were ways to get things done in a hurry if needs be. Like with the tuxes and invitations. Both should have been tended to months ago but it had merely taken a few phone calls and it had all been sorted. A little out of Callum's budget, perhaps, but he didn't need to know that. She was good for it. *Exclusive!*—her event planning business—had treated her well the past few years.

Still, there was no time to waste. She closed her calendar and looked up.

The group of them were standing around chatting, something about a lodge north of town and what had happened to the rancher who'd owned it. Jack was listening intently, but Rhys was missing. Had he left already?

The bell on the door chimed behind her, and she turned to see Rhys walking through. He looked far more himself now in black jeans and a black, tan and red plaid shirt beneath a sheepskin jacket. His boots were brown and weathered and as he stepped on to the sidewalk he dipped his head just a little and placed a well-worn hat on top. Taylor half smiled. The hat looked like an old friend; shaped precisely to his head, worn-in and comfortable.

"Feel better?" she asked, smiling.

"I'm not much for dressing up," he replied simply.

"I know. None of you are, really. But it's only for one day. You're all going to look very handsome."

"Is that so?"

Her cheeks heated a little. Rhys's best feature was his eyes. And he was tall and well-built, just the way she liked her men. Perhaps it was growing up the way she had. They'd all been outdoor kids. Heck, Callum had joined the military and Jack had been a pro downhill skier until he'd blown his knee out at Val d'Isère.

But Rhys wasn't classically handsome. Not in the way that Tyson Diamond was, for instance. In this group Rhys would be the one who would probably be overlooked. His cheekbones were high and defined and his jawbone unrelenting, giving him a rough appearance. His lips looked well-shaped but it was hard to tell—the closest she'd seen him come to smiling was the clandestine chuckle while they were inside.

But it was the way he'd answered that piqued her interest. *Is that so?* he'd asked, as if he couldn't care one way or the other if anyone thought him handsome or not.

It was quite refreshing.

"I should get going," she said, lifting her chin. "I've got to be back to town in thirty minutes for another appointment. Thanks for coming out. It'll be easy for you from here on in. Weddings do tend to be mostly women's business." At least with these sorts of men…

"Drive carefully then," he said, tipping his hat. "No sense rushing. The creek isn't going anywhere."

"Thanks, but I'd like to be on time just the same." She gave him a brief nod and turned to the assembled group.

"I've got to go. Thanks everyone." She put her hand on Callum's shoulder and went up on tiptoe to kiss his cheek. "See you soon." She did the same for Jack. "When are you flying out?"

He shrugged. "I'm going to hang around for a few days. I've got to be back in Montana for meetings on Monday, though, and then I'm flying in the Thursday before the wedding."

"Let's have lunch before you go back."

"You got it. Text me."

With a quick wave Taylor hurried across the parking lot, her heeled boots echoing on the pavement. She turned the car heater on high and rubbed her hands together—December in Alberta was colder than on the coast and she felt chilled to the bone all the time.

She was down to twenty-five minutes. As a light snow began to fall, she put her rental car in gear and pulled out, checking her GPS for the quickest route to the highway.

Three weeks. That was how long she had to decompress. She'd take care of Callum's wedding and then enjoy one indulgent week of vacation before heading home and working on the final preparations for New Year's. This year's planning involved taking over an entire warehouse and transforming it into an under the sea kingdom.

It all seemed quite ridiculous. And because it did, she knew that it was time she took a vacation. Even one as short as a week in some small, backwater Alberta town. Thank goodness her assistant, Alicia, was completely capable and could handle things in Taylor's absence.

She turned on the wipers and sighed. Compared to the crazy demands of her normal events, she knew she could do this wedding with her eyes closed.

If that were true, though, why was she having so much fun and dreading going back to Vancouver so very much?

\* \* \*

It was already dark when Taylor whipped out her phone, brought up her to-do list and started punching in brief notes with her thumbs. Her fingers were numb with cold and she'd been out of the flower shop for a whole minute and a half. Where on earth was the frigid air coming from anyway? Shivering and walking toward the town's B&B, she hurriedly typed in one last detail she didn't want to forget. Instead of typing the word "cedar," however, she felt a sharp pain in her shoulder as she bounced off something very big and hard.

"Hey," she growled. "Watch where you're going!"

She looked up to find Rhys Bullock staring down at her, a scowl marking his angular face.

"Oh, it's you," she said, letting out a puff of annoyance.

He knelt down and retrieved her phone, stood up and handed it over. "Hope it didn't break," he said. His tone suggested that he wasn't quite sincere in that sentiment.

"The rubber cover is supposed to protect it. It'll be fine."

"Maybe next time you should watch where you're going. Stop and sit down before you start typing."

"It's too damn cold to stop," she grumbled.

He laughed then, the expulsion of breath forming a white cloud around his head. "Not used to an arctic front? This isn't cold. Wait until it's minus forty."

"Not a chance."

"That's right. You're only here for the wedding."

"If you'll excuse me, I'd like to get out of the cold before my fingertips fall off." She tried to ignore how his face changed when he laughed, softening the severe lines. A smattering of tiny marks added character to his tanned skin. If she had to come up with one word to describe Rhys, it would be *weathered*. It wasn't necessarily a bad thing.

He took a step closer and to her surprise reached into her pocket and took out her gloves. Then he took the phone from her hands, dropped it in the pocket and handed over the gloves. "This will help."

She raised an eyebrow. "That was presumptuous of you."

He shrugged. "Ms. Shepard, I'm pretty much used to keeping things simple and doing what has to be done. If your fingers are cold, put on your gloves."

She shoved her fingers into the fuzzy warmth, her temper simmering. He spoke to her as if she were a child!

"Now," he said calmly, "where are you headed? It's dark. I'll walk you."

Her temper disintegrated under the weight of her disbelief. She laughed. "Are you serious? This is Cadence Creek. I think I'll be safe walking two blocks to my accommodations." Good Lord. She lived in one of the largest cities in Canada. She knew how to look out for herself!

"Maybe I just want to make sure you don't start texting and walk out into traffic," he suggested. "You must be going to Jim's then." He named the bed and breakfast owner.

"That's right."

He turned around so they were facing the same direction. "Let's go," he suggested.

She fell into step because she didn't know what else to do. He seemed rather determined and it would take all of five minutes to walk to the rambling house that provided the town's only accommodation. To her mind the dive motel out on the highway didn't count. She watched as he tipped his hat to an older lady coming out of the drugstore and then gave a nod to a few men standing on the steps of the hardware. He might be gruff and bossy and not all that pretty to look at, but she had to give Rhys one thing—his manners were impeccable.

The light dusting of snow earlier covered the sidewalk and even grouchy Taylor had to admit that it was pretty, especially in the dark with the town's Christmas lights casting colored shadows on its surface. Each old-fashioned lamppost held a pine wreath with a red bow. Storefronts were decorated with garland on their railings and twinkle lights. Christmas trees peeked through front windows and jolly Santas and snowmen grinned from front yards.

Cadence Creek at the holidays was like one of those Christmas card towns that Taylor hadn't believed truly existed. Being here wasn't really so bad. Even if it was a little…boring.

They stopped at a crosswalk. And as they did her stomach gave out a long, loud rumble.

Rhys put his hand at her elbow and they stepped off the curb. But instead of going right on the other side, he guided her to the left.

"Um, the B&B is that way," she said, turning her head and pointing in the opposite direction.

"When did you eat last?" he asked.

She fought the urge to sigh. "None of your business."

Undeterred, he kept walking and kept the pressure at her elbow. "Jim and Kathleen don't provide dinner. You need something to eat."

She stopped dead in her tracks. Rhys carried on for a few steps until he realized she wasn't with him then he stopped and turned around. "What?"

"How old am I?"

His brows wrinkled, forming a crease above his nose. "How could I possibly know that?"

"Do I look like an adult to you?"

Something flared in his eyes as his gaze slid from her face down to her boots and back up again. "Yes'm."

She swallowed. "You can't herd me like you herd your cattle, Mr. Bullock."

"I don't herd cattle," he responded.

"You don't?"

"No ma'am. I work with the horses. Especially the skittish ones."

"Well, then," she floundered and then recovered, ignoring that a snowflake had just fallen and landed on the tip of her nose. "I'm not one of your horses. You can't make me eat just because you say so."

He shrugged. "Can't make the horses do that, either. Trick is to make them *want* to do what I want." He gave her a level stare. "I'm pretty good at that."

"Your ego isn't suffering, I see."

His lips twitched. "No, ma'am. Everyone has a skill. Smart man knows what his is, that's all."

God, she didn't want to be amused. He was a bullheaded, overbearing macho cowboy type who probably called women "little lady" and thought he was all that. But she was amused and to be honest she'd enjoyed sparring with him just a little bit. At least he wasn't a pampered brat like most people she met.

She let out the tension in her shoulders. "Where are you taking me, then?" She'd seriously considered ordering a pizza and having it delivered to the B&B. It wasn't like there was a plethora of dining choices in Cadence Creek.

"Just to the Wagon Wheel. Best food in town."

"I've been. I had lunch there yesterday." And breakfast in the dining room of the bed and breakfast and then dinner was a fast-food burger grabbed on the way back from the stationery supply store in Edmonton.

The lunch had definitely been the best meal—home-made chicken soup, thick with big chunks of chicken, vegetables and the temptation of a warm roll which she'd left behind, not wanting the extra carbs.

Her stomach growled again, probably from the mere thought of the food at the diner.

"Fine. I'll go get some takeout. Will that make you happy?"

He shrugged. "It's not about me. But now that you mention it, I think tonight is pot roast. I could do with some of that myself." He turned and started walking away.

Reluctantly she followed a step behind him. At least he didn't have that darned proprietary hand under her elbow anymore. Half a block away she could smell the food. The aroma of the standard fare—fries and the like—hit first, but then the undertones touched her nostrils: beef, bread and baking.

Her mouth watered as she reminded herself that she had a bridesmaid's dress to fit into as well. Pot roast would be good. But she would absolutely say no to dessert.

It was warm inside the diner. The blast of heat was a glorious welcome and the scents that were hinted at outside filled the air inside. Christmas music played from an ancient jukebox in the corner. The whole place was decorated for the holidays, but in the evening with everything lit up it looked very different than it had yesterday at noon. Mini-lights ran the length of the lunch counter and the tree in a back corner had flashing lights and a star topper that pulsed like a camera flash. The prevalence of vinyl and chrome made her feel like she was in a time warp.

Two-thirds of the tables were filled with people, all talking animatedly over the music. Rhys gave a wave to a group in a corner and then, to her surprise, slipped behind the cash register and went straight into the kitchen.

Through the order window she saw him grin at an older

woman in a huge cobbler's apron who laughed and patted his arm. Both of them turned Taylor's way and she offered a polite smile before turning her attention to the specials menu on a chalkboard. Takeout was definitely the way to go here. This wasn't her town or her people. She stuck out like a sore thumb.

She was just about to order a salad when Rhys returned. "Come on," he said, taking her elbow again. "Let's grab a seat."

"Um, I didn't really think we were going to eat together. I was just going to get something to take back with me."

"You work too hard," he said, holding out a chair for her and then moving around the table without pushing it in—polite without being over the top. "You could use some downtime."

She shifted the chair closer to the table. "Are you kidding? This is slow for me."

He raised his eyebrows. "Then you really do need to stop and refuel."

He shrugged out of his jacket and hooked it over the top of the chair. She did the same, unbuttoning the black-and-red wool coat and shoving her scarf in the sleeve. She wore skinny jeans tucked into her favorite boots—red designer riding boots—and a snug black cashmere sweater from an expensive department store in the city. She looked around. Most of the men wore thirty-dollar jeans and plaid flannel, and the women dressed in a similar fashion—jeans and department store tops.

Just as she thought. Sore thumb.

When she met Rhys's gaze again she found his sharper, harder, as if he could read her thoughts. She dropped her gaze and opened her menu.

"No need for that. Couple orders of pot roast are on their way."

She put down the menu and folded her hands on the top. While the rest of the decorations at the diner bordered on cheesy, she secretly loved the small silk poinsettia pots with Merry Christmas picks. "What amusement are you getting out of this?" she asked. "From what I can gather you don't approve of me but you do enjoy bossing me around."

"Why would you think that?"

"Oh, I don't know. Because so far you've found fault with everything I say or do?"

"Then why did you come with me?"

"You didn't leave me much choice." She pursed her lips.

"You always have a choice," he replied, unrolling his cutlery from his paper napkin.

"Then I guess because I was hungry," she said.

He smiled. "You mean because I was right."

Oh, he was infuriating!

"The trick is to make them want to do what I want." He repeated his earlier sentiment, only she understood he wasn't talking about horses anymore. He'd played her like a violin.

She might have had some choice words only their meals arrived, two plates filled with roast beef, potatoes, carrots, peas and delightfully puffy-looking Yorkshire puddings. Her potatoes swam in a pool of rich gravy and the smell coming from the food was heaven in itself.

She never ate like this anymore. Wondered if she could somehow extract the potatoes from the gravy or maybe just leave the potatoes altogether—that would probably be better.

"Thanks, Mom," she heard Rhys say, and her gaze darted from her plate up to his face and then to the woman standing beside the table—the same woman who had patted his arm in the kitchen. Taylor guessed her to be somewhere around fifty, with dark brown hair like Rhys's, only cut in an efficient bob and sprinkled with a few gray hairs.

"You're welcome," she said, then turned to Taylor with a smile. "You're Callum's sister. I remember you from the christening party."

Right. Taylor had flown in for that and she'd helped arrange a few details like the outdoor tent, but she'd done it all by phone from Vancouver. "Oh, my goodness, I totally didn't put two and two together. Martha Bullock… of course. And you're Rhys's mother." She offered an uncertain smile. Usually she didn't forget details like that. Then again the idea of the gruff cowboy calling anyone "Mom" seemed out of place.

"Sure am. Raised both him and his brother, Tom. Tom's been working up north for years now, but Rhys moved home a few years back."

"Your chicken tartlets at the party were to die for," Taylor complimented. "And I had the soup yesterday. You're a fabulous cook, Mrs. Bullock. Whoever your boys marry have big shoes to fill to keep up with Mom's home cooking."

Martha laughed while, from the corner of her eye, Taylor could see Rhys scowl. Good. About time he felt a bit on the back foot since he'd been throwing her off all day.

"Heh, good luck," Martha joked. "I'm guessing groomsman is as close to the altar as Rhys is gonna get. He's picky."

She could almost see the steam come out of his ears, but she took pity on him because she'd heard much the same argument from her own family. It got wearisome after a while. Particularly from her father, who'd never taken her business seriously and seemed to think her sole purpose in life was to settle down and have babies.

Not that she had anything against marriage or babies. But she'd do it on her own timetable.

"Well," she said, a bit softer, "it seems to me that getting married is kind of a big deal and a person would have to be awfully sure that they wanted to see that person every day for the rest of their lives. Not a thing to rush, really."

Martha smiled and patted Taylor's hand. "Pretty *and* wise. Don't see that very often, at least around here." She sent a pointed look at a nearby table where Taylor spied an animated blonde seated with a young man who seemed besotted with her.

"Well, your supper's getting cold." Martha straightened. "And I've got to get back. See you in a bit."

Taylor watched Rhys's mother move off, stopping at several tables to say hello. Her full laugh was infectious and Taylor found herself smiling.

When she turned back, Rhys had already started cutting into his beef. Taylor mentally shrugged and speared a bright orange carrot with her fork.

"So," she said easily. "How'd a nice woman like your mother end up with a pigheaded son like you?"

## CHAPTER TWO

TENDER AS IT WAS, Rhys nearly choked on the beef in his mouth. Lord, but Callum's sister was full of sass. And used to getting her own way, too, from the looks of it. He'd noticed her way back in the fall at the christening, all put together and pretty and, well, bossy. Not that she'd been aggressive. She just had one of those natural take-charge kind of ways about her. When Taylor was on the job, things got done.

He just bet she was Student Council president in school, too. And on any other committee she could find.

He'd been the quiet guy at the back of the class, wishing he could be anywhere else. Preferably outside. On horse-back.

Burl Ives was crooning on the jukebox now and Taylor was blinking at him innocently. He wasn't sure if he wanted to be offended or laugh at her.

"She only donated half the genetic material," he replied once he'd swallowed. "Ask her. She'll tell you my father was a stubborn old mule."

Taylor popped a disc of carrot into her mouth. "Was?"

"He died when I was twenty-four. Brain aneurism. No warning at all."

"God, Rhys. I'm sorry."

He shrugged again. "It's okay. We've all moved well beyond the shock and grief part to just missing him." And he did. Even though at times Rhys had been frustrated with his father's decisions, he missed his dad's big laugh and some of the fun things they'd done as kids—like camping and fishing. Those were the only kinds of vacations their family had ever been able to afford.

They ate in silence for a while until it grew uncomfortable. Rhys looked over at her. He wasn't quite sure what had propelled him to bring her here tonight. It had been the gentlemanly thing to do but there was something else about her that intrigued him. He figured it was probably the way she challenged him, how she'd challenged them all today. He'd nearly laughed out loud during the fitting. He could read people pretty well and she had pushed all the right buttons with Callum. And then there was the way she was used to being obeyed. She gave an order and it was followed. It was fun putting her off balance by taking charge.

And then there was the indisputable fact that she was beautiful.

Except he really wasn't interested in her that way. She was so not his type. He was beer and she was champagne. He was roots and she was wings.

Still. A guy might like to fly every once in a while.

"So," he invited. "Tell me more about what you do."

"Oh. Well, I plan private parties and events. Not generally weddings. Right now, in addition to Callum and Avery's details, I'm going back and forth with my assistant about a New Year's party we're putting together. The hardest part is making sure the construction of the giant aquariums is completed and that the environment is right for the fish."

"Fish?"

She laughed, the expression lighting up her face. "Okay,

so get this. They want this under the sea theme so we're building two aquariums and we've arranged to borrow the fish for the night. It's not just the aquariums, it's the marine biologist I have coming to adjust conditions and then monitor the water quality in the tank and ensure the health of the fish. Then there are lights that are supposed to make it look like you're underwater, and sushi and cocktails served by mermaids and mermen in next to no clothing."

"Are you joking?"

She shook her head. "Would I joke about a thing like that? It's been a nightmare to organize." She cut into her slab of beef and swirled it around the pool of gravy. "This is so good. I'm going to have to do sit-ups for hours in my room to work this off."

He rolled his eyes. Right. To his mind, she could gain a few pounds and no one would even notice. If anything, she was a little on the thin side. A few pounds would take those hinted-at curves and make them...

He cleared his throat.

"What about you, Rhys? You said you work with horses?" Distracted by the chatting now, she seemed unaware that she was scooping up the mashed potatoes and gravy she'd been diligently avoiding for most of the meal.

"I work for Ty out at Diamondback."

"What sort of work?"

"Whatever has to be done, but I work with training the horses mostly. Ty employs a couple of disadvantaged people to help around the place so I get to focus on what I do best."

"What sort of disadvantaged people?" She leaned forward and appeared genuinely interested.

Rhys finished the last bite of Yorkshire pudding and nudged his plate away. "Well, Marty has Down's syndrome. Getting steady work has been an issue, but he's very good with the animals and he's a hard worker. Josh is a different story. He's had trouble finding work due to his criminal record. Ty's helping him get on his feet again. Josh helps Sam's end of things from time to time. Those cattle you mentioned herding earlier."

Taylor frowned and pushed her plate away. She'd made a solid dent in the meal and his mother hadn't been stingy with portions.

"So what are your plans, then?"

"What do you mean?"

She wiped her mouth with a paper napkin. "I mean, do you have any plans to start up your own place or business?"

"Not really. I'm happy at Diamondback. Ty's a good boss."

She leaned forward. "You're a take-charge kind of guy. I can't see you taking orders from anyone. Don't you want to be the one calling the shots?"

Calling the shots wasn't all it was cracked up to be. Rhys had seen enough of that his whole life. Along with being the boss came a truckload of responsibility, including the chance of success and the probability of failure. His own venture had cost him financially but it had been far worse on a deeper, personal level. Considering he now had his mom to worry about, he was content to leave the risk to someone else from here on in. "I have a job doing something I like and I get a steady paycheck every two weeks. What more could I want?"

She sat back, apparently disappointed with his answer. Too bad. Living up to her expectations wasn't on his agenda and he sure wasn't about to explain.

Martha returned bearing two plates of apple pie. "How was it?" she asked, looking at Taylor expectantly.

"Delicious," she had the grace to answer with a smile.

"I was trying to be good and avoid the potatoes and I just couldn't. Thank you, Martha."

"Well, you haven't had my pie yet. It's my specialty."

"Oh, I couldn't possibly."

"If it's your waistline worrying you, don't. Life's too short." She flashed a grin. "Besides, you'll wear that off running all over town. I heard you're kicking butt and taking names planning this wedding. Everyone's talking about it."

Apparently Taylor found that highly complimentary and not at all offensive. "Well, maybe just this once."

Martha put down the plates. "Rhys? The faucet in my kitchen sink at home has been dripping. I wondered if you could have a look at it? Consider dinner your payment in advance."

He nodded, knowing that last part was for Taylor's benefit more than his. He never paid for meals at the diner and instead looked after the odd jobs here and at his mother's home.

It was why he'd come back to Cadence Creek, after all. He couldn't leave his mother here to deal with everything on her own. She'd already been doing that for too many years. It had always been hand to mouth until this place. She still worked too hard but Rhys knew she loved every single minute.

"I'll be around tomorrow before work to have a look," he promised. "Then I can pick up what I need from the hardware and fix it tomorrow night."

"That sounds great. Nice to see you again, Taylor. Can't wait to see your handiwork at this wedding."

Rhys watched Taylor smile. She looked tired but the smile was genuine and a pleasant surprise. She had big-city girl written all over her but it didn't mean she was devoid of warmth. Not at all.

When Martha was gone he picked up his fork. "Try the pie. She'll be offended if you don't."

Taylor took a bite and closed her eyes. "Oh, my. That's fantastic."

"She makes her own spice blend and doesn't tell anyone what it is. People have been after her recipes for years," he said, trying hard not to focus on the shape of her lips as her tongue licked a bit of caramelly filling from the corner of her mouth. "There's a reason why the bakery focuses on cakes and breads. There's not a pie in Cadence Creek that can hold a candle to my mom's."

"You seem close," Taylor noted.

She had no idea. Rhys focused on his pie as he considered exactly how much to say. Yes, he'd come back to Cadence Creek to be nearer his mom after his dad's death. She'd needed the help sorting out their affairs and needed a shoulder. He'd been happy to do it.

But it was more than that. They were business partners. Not that many people were aware of it and that was how he wanted it to stay. Memories were long and his father hadn't exactly earned a stellar business reputation around town. Despite his best intentions, Rhys had followed in his footsteps. Being a silent partner in the restaurant suited him just fine.

"We are close," he admitted. "Other than my brother, I'm the only family she's got and the only family here in Cadence Creek. How about you? Are you close with your family?"

She nodded, allowing him to neatly change the subject. "I suppose so. We don't live so close together, like you do, but it's close enough and we get along. I know they were very worried about Callum when he came back from overseas. And they thought he was crazy for buying a dairy farm." She laughed a little. "But they can see he's happy and that's all that matters."

"And Jack?"

She laughed. "Jack is in Montana most of the time, busy overseeing his empire. We don't see each other much. Our jobs keep us very busy. Running our own businesses is pretty time-consuming."

"I can imagine." Rhys had met and liked Jack instantly, but like Taylor, he looked a bit exhausted. Running a big sporting goods chain was likely to have that effect.

Which was why Rhys was very contented to work for Diamondback and spend some of his spare hours playing handyman for the diner and his mother's house. It was straightforward. There was little chance of disappointing people.

Angry words and accusations still bounced around in his brain from time to time. Failing had been bad enough. But he'd let down the person he'd trusted most. And she'd made sure he knew it.

The fluted crust of Taylor's pie was all that remained and she'd put down her fork.

"Well, I suppose we should get going."

"I'm going to have to roll back to the B&B," she said ruefully, putting a hand on her tummy.

"Not likely," he said, standing up, but their gazes met and he was certain her cheeks were a little redder than they'd been before.

He took her coat from the back of the chair, pulled the scarf from the sleeve and held it so she could slide her arms into it. They were quiet now, he unsure of what to say and his show of manners making things slightly awkward. Like this was a date or something. He stood back and grabbed his jacket and shoved his arms in the sleeves. Not a date. It was just sharing a meal with…

With a woman.

Hmm.

"I'm putting my gloves on this time," she stated with a cheeky smile.

"Good. Wouldn't want your fingertips to fall off."

They gave a wave to Martha before stepping outside into the crisp air.

It had warmed a bit, but that only meant that the precipitation that had held off now floated lazily to the earth. Big white flakes drifted on the air, hitting the ground with a soft shush of sound that was so peculiar to falling snow. It draped over hedges and windows, painting the town in fairy-white.

"This is beautiful," Taylor whispered. "Snow in Vancouver is cause for chaos. Here, it's peaceful."

"Just because the wind isn't blowing and causing white-outs," Rhys offered, but he was enchanted too. Not by the snow, but by her. The clever and efficient Taylor had tilted her head toward the sky and stuck out her tongue, catching a wide flake on its tip.

"I know it's just water, but I swear snow tastes sweet for some reason," she said, closing her eyes. Another flake landed on her eyelashes and she blinked, laughing as she wiped it away. "Oops."

Rhys swallowed as a wave of desire rolled through him. Heavens above, she was pretty. Smart and funny, and while an absolute Sergeant Major on the job, a lot more relaxed when off the clock. He had the urge to reach out and take her hand as they walked through the snow. Odd that he'd have such an innocent, pure thought when the other side of his brain wondered if her mouth would taste like apples and snowflakes.

He kept his hand in his pocket and they resumed strolling.

It only took a few minutes to reach the bed and break-fast. Rhys paused outside the white picket gate. "Well, here we are."

"Yes, here we are. What about you? You walked me back but now do you have to walk home in the snow? Or are you parked nearby?" She lifted her chin and Rhys smiled at the way the snow covered her hair with white tufts. She looked like a young girl, bundled up in her scarf and coat with snow on her head and shoulders. Definitely not like a cutthroat businesswoman who never had to take no for an answer.

"I live a few blocks over, so don't worry about me."

"Do you—" she paused, then innocently widened her eyes "—live with your mother?"

He laughed. "God, no. I'm thirty years old. I have my own place. I most definitely do not live with my mother."

Her cold, pink cheeks flushed even deeper. "Oh. Well, thanks for dinner. I guess I'll see you when we pick up the tuxes, right?"

"I guess so. See you around, Taylor."

"Night."

She went in the gate and disappeared up the walk, her ruby-red boots marking the way on the patio stones.

He had no business thinking about his friend's sister that way. Even less business considering how different they were. Different philosophies, hundreds of kilometers between them… He shouldn't have taken her elbow in his hand and guided her along.

But the truth was the very thing that made her wrong for him was exactly what intrigued him. She wasn't like the other girls he knew. She was complicated and excit-ing, and that was something that had been missing from his life for quite a while.

As the snowfall picked up, he huddled into the collar

of his jacket and turned away. Taylor Shepard was not for him. And since he wasn't the type to mess around on a whim that meant keeping his hands off—for the next two weeks or so.

He could do that. Right?

Taylor had left the planning for the bridal shower to Clara Diamond, Ty's wife and one of Avery's bridesmaids. Tonight Taylor was attending only as a guest. In addition to the bridal party, Molly Diamond's living room was occupied by Melissa Stone, her employee Amy, and Jean, the owner of the Cadence Creek Bakery and Avery's partner in business.

In deference to Clara's pregnancy and the fact that everyone was driving, the evening's beverages included a simple punch and hot drinks—tea, coffee, or hot cocoa. Never one to turn down chocolate, Taylor helped herself to a steaming mug and took a glorious sip. Clara had added a dollop of real whipped cream to the top, making it extra indulgent. Taylor made a mental note to start running again when she returned home.

"I hope everything's okay for tonight," Clara said beside her. "It's a bit nerve-racking, you know. I can't put on an event like you, Taylor."

Taylor had been feeling rather comfortable but Clara's innocent observation made her feel the outsider again. "Don't be silly. It's lovely and simple which is just as it should be. An event should always suit the guests, and this is perfect."

"Really?"

Indeed. A fire crackled in the fireplace and the high wood beams in the log-style home made it feel more like a winter lodge than a regular home. The last bridal shower she'd attended had been in a private room at a club and they'd had their own bartender mixing custom martinis. She actually enjoyed this setting more. But it wasn't what people expected from her, was it? Did she really come across as…well…stuck up?

Taylor patted her arm. "Your Christmas decorations are lovely, so why would you need a single thing? Don't worry so much. This cocoa is delicious and I plan on eating my weight in appetizers and sweets."

She didn't, but she knew it would put Clara at ease. She liked Clara a lot. In fact she liked all of Callum's friends. They were utterly devoid of artifice.

Clara's sister-in-law Angela was taking puff pastries out of the oven and their mother-in-law Molly was putting out plates of squares and Christmas cookies. Jean had brought chocolate doughnut holes and Melissa was taking the cling wrap off a nacho dip. The one woman who didn't quite fit in was Amy, who Taylor recognized as the young woman from the diner the night she'd had dinner with Rhys. The implication had been made that Amy wasn't pretty *and* smart. But she looked friendly enough, though perhaps a little younger than the rest of the ladies.

She approached her casually and smiled. "Hi, I'm Taylor. You work for Melissa, right? I've seen you behind the counter at the shop."

Amy gave her a grateful smile. "Yes, that's right. And you're Callum's sister." She looked down at Taylor's shoes. "Those are Jimmy Choos, aren't they?"

Taylor laughed at the unconcealed longing in Amy's voice. "Ah, a kindred spirit. They are indeed."

"I'd die for a pair of those. Not that there's anywhere to buy them here. Or that I could afford them."

Her response was a bit guileless perhaps but she hadn't meant any malice, Taylor was sure of that. "I got them for a steal last time I was in Seattle," she replied. She leaned forward. "I'm dying to know. Why is it that everyone else is over there and you're over here staring at the Christmas tree? I mean, it's a nice tree, but…" She let the thought hang.

Amy blushed. "Oh. Well. I'm sure it was a polite thing to include me in the invitation. I'm not particularly close with the Diamond women. I kind of, uh…"

She took a sip of punch, which hid her face a little. "I dated Sam for a while and when he broke it off I wasn't as discreet as I might have been about it. I have a tendency to fly off the handle and think later."

Taylor laughed. "You sound like my brother Jack. Callum was always the thinker in the family. Jack's far more of a free spirit."

"It was a long time ago," Amy admitted. "It's hard to change minds in a town this size, though."

"You haven't thought of moving?"

"All the time!" Amy's blond curls bounced. "But my family is here. I didn't go to college. Oh, I must sound pathetic," she bemoaned, shaking her head.

"Not at all. You sound like someone who simply hasn't found the right thing yet. Someday you will. The perfect thing to make you want to get up in the morning. Or the perfect person." She winked at Amy.

"I'm afraid I've pretty much exhausted the local resources on that score," Amy lamented. "Which doesn't exactly make me popular among the women, either."

"You just need an image makeover," Taylor suggested. "Do you like what you're doing now?"

She shrugged. "Working for Melissa has been the best job I've ever had. But it's not exactly a challenge."

Wow. Amy did sound a lot like Jack.

"We should meet up for coffee before I go back to Vancouver," Taylor suggested. Despite the fact that Amy was included but not quite included, Taylor liked her. She just seemed young and without direction. Heck, Taylor had been there. What Amy needed was something to feel passionate about.

"I'd like that. Just stop into the shop. I'm there most days. It's busy leading up to the holidays."

The last of the guests arrived and things got underway. Taylor was glad the shower stayed on the sweeter rather than raunchier side. There was no paté in the shape of the male anatomy, no gag gifts or handcuffs or anything of the sort. They played a "Celebrity Husband" game where each guest put a name of a celebrity they had a crush on into a bowl and then they had to guess which star belonged to whom. The resulting laughter from names ranging from Kevin Costner who got Molly's vote to Channing Tatum—Amy's pick—broke the ice beautifully.

The laughter really picked up during Bridal Pictionary, which pitted Taylor against Angela as they attempted to draw "wedding night" without getting graphic. After they took a break to stuff themselves with snacks, they all returned to the living room for gifts.

Taylor sat back into the soft sofa cushions and examined the woman who was about to become her sister-in-law. Avery was so lovely—kind and gentle but with a backbone of steel. She was a fantastic mother to her niece, Nell, who was Callum's biological daughter. Taylor couldn't have handpicked a nicer woman to marry her brother. It gave her a warm feeling, but also an ache in her heart, too. That ache unsettled her a bit, until she reminded herself that she was simply very happy that Callum had found someone after all his troubles. A love like that didn't come along every day.

Her thoughts strayed to Rhys for a moment. The man was a contradiction for sure. On one hand he was full of confidence and really quite bossy. And yet he was satisfied with taking orders from someone else and moving back to this small town with very few options. It didn't make sense.

It also didn't make sense that for a brief moment earlier in the week, she'd had the craziest urge to kiss him. The snow had been falling on his dark cap of hair and dusting the shoulders of his jacket. And he'd been watchful of her, too. There'd been something there, a spark, a tension of some sort. Until he'd turned to go and she'd gone up the walk and into the house.

She hadn't seen him since. Not at the diner, not around town.

Avery opened a red box and a collective gasp went up from the group. "Oh, Molly. Oh, gosh." Avery reached into the tissue paper and withdrew a gorgeous white satin-and-lace nightgown. "It's stunning."

"Every woman should have something beautiful for their wedding night," Molly said. "I saw it and couldn't resist."

Taylor watched as Avery stood and held the long gown up to herself. The bodice was cut in a daring "V" and consisted of sheer lace while the satin skirt fell straight to the floor, a deep slit cut to the hip. It blended innocence with sexy brilliantly.

She took another sip of cocoa and let her mind carry her away for a few blissful seconds. What would it be like to wear that nightgown? She would feel the lace cups on her breasts, the slide of the satin on her thighs. She'd wear slippers with it, the kind of ridiculous frippery that consisted of heels and a puff of feathers at the toe. And Rhys's dark eyes would light up as she came into the room, their depths filled with fire and hunger…

"*Helloooo,* earth to Taylor!"

She blinked and focused on the circle of women who were now staring at her. "Oh. Sorry."

"I was just going to say thank you for the bath basket, but you were in another world." Avery was smiling at her.

"You're welcome! Goodness, sorry about that. Occupational hazard. Sometimes it's hard to shut the old brain off." She hoped her flippant words were believable. What would they say if they knew she'd been daydreaming about the only groomsman who wasn't married or a relative?

"Right," Amy said with a wide grin. "I know that look. You were thinking about a dude."

Damn her for being astute. Who had said she wasn't smart, anyway?

Melissa burst out laughing. "Were you? Come on, do tell. Do you have some guy hiding away in Vancouver?"

"No!" The word was out before she realized it would have been the most convenient way out of the situation.

Avery came to her rescue, though. "We're just teasing. Seriously, thank you. It's a lovely gift."

She reached for the last present on the pile and removed the card. "Oh," she said with delight. "It's from Martha. I wonder if she's going to part with her coconut cream pie recipe." Everyone laughed. Martha Bullock never shared her pie recipes with anyone. Even Rhys had mentioned that at dinner the other night.

Avery ripped the paper off the box and withdrew a plain black binder. Opening the cover, she gasped. "It *is* recipes! Look!" She read off the table of contents. "Supper Dishes, Breads and Muffins, Cookies, Cakes, Salads, Preserves." She lifted her head and laughed. "No pies."

Excited, she began flipping through the pages when Amy interrupted again. "That's it!" she called out, causing Avery's fingers to pause and the rest of the group to stare at her in surprise.

"That's where I saw you last," Amy continued, undaunted. "It was at the diner. You had dinner with Rhys!"

Six more sets of eyes swiveled Taylor's way until she felt like a bug under a microscope.

"It wasn't a date. We both ended up needing to eat at the same time. We just met outside on the sidewalk and, uh, sat together."

"It sure didn't look that way," Amy answered, a little too gleeful for Taylor's liking. "Now that is news. Rhys hasn't shown up anywhere with a date since…"

She suddenly blushed and turned her gaze to something over Jean's shoulder. "Well, it doesn't matter how long since."

It was uncomfortably quiet for a few moments until a small giggle broke the silence. Clara was trying not to laugh and failing miserably. Angela and Molly joined in, followed by Jean and Melissa. Even Avery's mouth was twitching. Taylor frowned a little, wondering what the joke could be.

Amy had the grace to look chagrined. "Okay, I know. My track record sucks."

Angela spoke up. "Honey, Rhys Bullock is one tough nut to crack. Someday the right guy's gonna come along."

Amy's eyes glistened. "Just my luck I won't recognize him when I see him."

Everyone laughed again.

Then Avery spoke up. "That's what I thought, too, Amy. Don't give up hope. You just never know." She looked at Taylor. "And I know for a fact that Rhys is smart and stubborn. Sounds like someone else I know. Keep us posted, Taylor."

"Yeah," Clara added, her hand on her rounded stomach. "The old married women need some excitement now and again."

"I swear I bumped into him outside. Literally. Ran smack into him and nearly broke my phone." She brought her hands together in demonstration of the collision. "It was dark, it was dinnertime and we had pot roast. End of story."

But as the subject changed and they cleaned up the paper and ribbons, Taylor's thoughts kept drifting back to that night and how she'd almost reached out to take his hand as he walked her home.

It was such a simple and innocent gesture to think about, especially in these days of casual hookups. Not that hooking up was her style, either. That philosophy combined with her long hours meant she hadn't had time for personal relationships for ages. Not since the early days of her business, when she'd been seeing an investment planner named John. He'd wanted more than a girlfriend who brought work home at the end of a twelve-hour day and considered takeout a sensible dinner. After a few months in, he'd walked. The thing Taylor felt most guilty about was how it had been a relief.

She balled up used napkins and put them in the trash. Time kept ticking. A few days from now was the rehearsal, and then the wedding and then Callum and Avery would be away on their honeymoon and Taylor would move out of the B&B and into their house until Boxing Day, where she planned on watching movies, reading books and basically hibernating from the outside world. It was going to be peace and quiet and then a family Christmas.

Complications in the form of Rhys Bullock would only ruin her plans.

## CHAPTER THREE

IT WAS TAYLOR'S experience that if the rehearsal went badly, the wedding was sure to be smooth and problem free. A sentiment which boded well for Callum and Avery, as it turned out, because nothing seemed to be going her way.

First of all, everything was an hour late starting thanks to a winter storm, which dumped enough snow to complicate transportation. The minister had slid off the road and into a snowbank. The car wasn't damaged but by the time the tow truck had pulled him out, the wedding party was waiting and quite worried by his absence. Then Taylor opened the box that was supposed to contain the tulle bows for the ends of the church pews to find that they'd been constructed of a horrible peachy-yellow color—completely unsuited for a Christmas wedding!

The late start and the road conditions also meant canceling the rehearsal dinner that had been organized at an Italian place in the city. Taylor was just about ready to pull her hair out when she felt a wide hand rest on her shoulder.

"Breathe," Rhys commanded. "It's all fine."

She clenched her teeth but exhaled through her nose. "Normally I would just deal with stuff like this without batting an eyelid. I don't know why it's throwing me so much."

"Maybe because it's for your brother," he suggested.

He might be right. She did want everything just right for Callum's wedding. It wasn't some corporate dinner or celebrity party. It was personal. It was once in a lifetime.

God, there was a reason why she didn't do weddings.

"What can I do to help?"

She shrugged. "Do you have a roll of white tulle in your pocket? Perhaps a spare horseshoe I could rub for good luck or something?"

He grimaced. "Afraid not. And you rub a rabbit's foot, not a horseshoe. I'm guessing our plans for dinner have changed."

She looked up at him. He was "dressed up" for the re-hearsal—neat jeans, even with a crease down the front, and a pressed button-down shirt tucked into the waistband. His boots made him look taller than ever, especially as she'd decided on her low-heeled boots tonight in deference to the weather. There was a strength and stability in him that made her take a deep breath and regroup. For some reason she didn't want to appear incapable in front of him. "I've had to cancel our reservations."

"I'll call my mom. It won't be as fancy as what you planned, but I'm guessing she can manage a meal for a dozen of us."

"We can't have a rehearsal dinner at a diner."

His lips puckered up like he'd tasted something sour. "Do you have any better suggestions? I guess you could pick up some day-old sandwiches at the gas station and a bag of cookies. You don't exactly have a lot of options."

"It was supposed to be romantic and relaxing and…" She floundered a little. "You know. Elegant."

He frowned at her and she regretted what she'd implied. "What would you do if you were in Vancouver right now?" he asked.

"This kind of weather wouldn't happen in Vancouver."

He made a disgusted sound. "You're supposed to be so good at your job. You're telling me nothing ever goes off the plan?"

"Well, sure it does, but I…"

"But you what?"

"I handle it."

"How is this different?"

"Because it's family."

The moment she said it her throat tightened. This wasn't just another job. This was her big brother's wedding. This was also the chance where she would prove herself to her family. She could talk until she was blue in the face, but the truth of the matter was she still sought their approval. The Shepards were driven and successful. It was just expected. She knew she'd disappointed her dad in particular. He thought what she did was unimportant, and the last thing she wanted to do was fall on her professional face in front of him.

"This isn't Vancouver, or Toronto, or New York or L.A." Rhys spoke firmly. "This isn't a big-city event with a bunch of rich snobs. It's just Cadence Creek. Maybe it's not good enough for you but it's good enough for Callum and Avery and maybe you should consider that instead of only thinking about yourself."

His words hurt. Partly because he was judging her without even knowing her and partly because he was right, at least about things being simpler here. How many times had Avery said they didn't need anything fancy? Taylor had insisted because it was no trouble. Had she messed up and forgotten the singular most important rule: *Give the client what they ask for?*

"Call your mother, then, and see if there's any way she can squeeze us in."

"Give me five minutes."

The words weren't said kindly, and Taylor felt the sting of his reproof. Still, she didn't have time to worry about Rhys Bullock—there was too much left to do. While the minister spoke to Avery and Callum, Taylor fished poinsettia plants out of a waiting box and lined them up on the altar steps in alternating red and creamy white. The congregation had already decorated the tree and the Christmas banners were hung behind the pulpit. The manger from the Sunday School play had been tucked away into the choir loft, which would be unused during the wedding, and instead she set up a table with a snowy-white cloth and a gorgeous spray of red roses, white freesias and greenery. It was there that the bride and groom would sign the register.

The altar looked fine, but the pews and windowsills were naked. In addition to the wrong color tulle, the company had forgotten to ship the candle arrangements for the windows. This would be the last time she ever used them for any of her events!

Her father, Harry, approached, a frown creasing his brow. "What are the plans for after the rehearsal?"

Taylor forced a smile. She would not get into it with her father tonight. "I'm working on that, don't worry."

"You should have insisted on having the wedding in the city, at a nice hotel. Then the weather wouldn't be an issue. Everything at your fingertips."

She'd had the thought a time or two herself; not that she'd admit it to her father. "This will be fine."

He looked around. "It would have been so much easier. Not that the town isn't nice, of course it is. But you're the planner, Taylor." His tone suggested she wasn't doing a very good job of it.

"It wasn't what Callum and Avery wanted," she reminded him. "And it's their day."

He smiled unexpectedly, a warm turning up of his lips

that Taylor recognized as his "sales pitch" smile. "Oh, come now. A smart businessman knows how to convince a client to come around."

Business*man*. Taylor wondered if counting to ten would help. She met her father's gaze. "Callum isn't a client, he's my brother. And he's giving you the daughter-in-law and grandkid you've wanted, so ease up."

Anything else they would have said was cut short as Rhys came back, tucking his cell phone in his pocket as he walked. "Good news. Business is slow because of the weather. Mom's clearing out that back corner and she's got a full tray of lasagna set aside."

It certainly wasn't the Caprese salad, veal Parmesan and tiramisu that Taylor had planned on, but it was convenient. She offered a polite smile. "Thank you, Rhys." At least one thing had been fixed.

"It's no trouble."

With a brief nod, Harry left the two of them alone.

"Everything okay?" Rhys asked.

She pressed a hand to her forehead. "Yeah, it's fine. Dad was just offering an unsolicited opinion, that's all."

He chuckled. "Parents are like that."

"You've no idea," she answered darkly. "I still wish I knew what to do about the pew markers. There's no time to run to Edmonton for materials to make them, even if it weren't storming. And the candles never arrived, either."

"It doesn't have to be perfect. No one will know."

His words echoed from before, the ones that said she was too good for this town. She dismissed them, because she still had a certain standard. "I'll know."

Clara heard the last bit and tapped Taylor on the shoulder. "Why don't you call Melissa and see if she can do something for the pews with satin ribbon?"

"At this late hour?"

Clara nodded. "Worst she can say is no. I have a feeling she'll try something, though. She's a whiz at that stuff. And I might be able to help you out with the windowsills."

Taylor's eyebrows pulled together. "What do you mean?"

Clara laughed. "Just trust me."

"I'm not in the habit of trusting details to other people, Clara. It's nothing personal—it's just how I work."

"Consider it a helping hand from a friend. You're going to be here before anyone else tomorrow anyway. If you don't like what I've done, you can take it out, no hard feelings." She smiled at Taylor. "I'd like to do this. For Avery. She's like family, you know?"

Rhys's hand touched Taylor's back. It was warm and felt good but Taylor got the feeling it was also a little bit of a warning. "I'm sure Taylor's very grateful for your help, Clara."

Dammit. Now he was putting words in her mouth. Perhaps it could be argued that this was "just family" but to Taylor's mind, if she couldn't manage to get the details of one small country wedding right, what did that say about her business?

Then again, in Vancouver she had staff. She could delegate. Which was pretty much what Clara was suggesting. She was just asking her to trust, sight unseen. And then there was the word "friend." She was a stranger here, a fish out of water for the most part and yet everyone seemed to accept her into their group without question. She wasn't used to that.

"Thank you, Clara," she said, but when Clara had gone she turned on Rhys. "Don't ever answer for me again."

"You were being rude."

Now he was judging her manners?

"Look, maybe Callum and Avery are family but I still

hold to a certain standard. This is my job. And it's all carefully planned down to the last detail."

She'd had things go wrong before and it wasn't pretty. She'd been determined never to fail like that again. It was why she dealt with trusted vendors and had a competent staff. She'd pulled off events ten times as complicated as this without a hitch.

Knowing it was like sprinkling salt in the wound.

He put a finger under her chin and lifted it. Considering how abrupt he'd been earlier, the tender touch surprised her. "You don't have to control everything. It'll be fine, I promise. It's okay to accept help once in a while."

"I'm not used to that."

"I know," he said gently. "You're stubborn, strong, bossy and completely competent. But things happen. Call Melissa, trust Clara, pretend to walk down the aisle for the rehearsal and then go stuff yourself with lasagna. I promise you'll feel better."

She didn't like being handled. Even if, at this moment, she suspected she needed it. It was so different being here. More relaxed, laid-back. She was used to grabbing her non-fat latte on her way to the office, not sipping from china cups in a B&B dining room while eating croissants. Maneuvering her SUV with the fold-down seats through city traffic rather than walking the two blocks to wherever. Definitely not used to men looking into her eyes and seeing past all her barriers.

Cadence Creek was a completely different pace with completely different expectations.

"Rhys? Taylor? We're ready for the walk-through," Avery called down the aisle, a happy smile on her face. Despite the wrinkles in the plans, Taylor's soon-to-be sister-in-law was beaming.

Well, if the bride wasn't worried, she wouldn't be, either. She looked up at Rhys. "I'll call Melissa when we're done. But if this goes wrong…"

"I expect I'll hear about it."

The other members of the wedding party joined them at the end of the aisle—first Clara and Ty, then Sam and Angela, Jack and Avery's friend Denise, who'd flown in from Ontario just this morning and thankfully ahead of the storm. Rhys held out his arm. "Shall we?" he asked, waiting for her to take his elbow.

She folded her hand around his arm, her fingers resting just below his elbow as they took slow steps up the aisle. It was just a silly rehearsal, so she shouldn't have a tangle of nerves going on just from a simple touch.

At the front of the church they parted ways and while Taylor slyly glanced in his direction several times, he never looked at her. Not once. He focused unerringly on what the minister was saying, and she found herself studying his strong jawline and the crisp hairline that looked as if his hair had been freshly cut.

The minister spoke to her and she jerked her attention back to the matter at hand, but she couldn't stop thinking about Rhys. It wasn't often that Taylor was intimidated by anyone, but she was by Rhys. She figured it had to be because he found her distinctly lacking in…well, in something.

What she couldn't understand was why on earth his opinion should even matter.

The Wagon Wheel was lit up, the windows glowing through the cold and very white night. Hard flakes of snow still swirled through the air, biting against Rhys's cheeks as he parked his truck in front of a growing drift.

They'd all bundled up and left the church a few minutes ago, the procession of vehicles crawling through town to the diner. There was no way they would have made it to the city for dinner. Even with the roads open, visibility was bad enough that there was a tow ban on. The smart thing was to stay put.

Taylor "Bossy-Pants" Shepard hadn't been too happy about that, though. He'd taken one look at her face and seen the stress that came from dealing with things gone wrong. It was a prime example of why he liked his life simple. If things went wrong out at Diamondback, he might get called to work but the worry belonged to Ty and Sam. Besides, his mother kept him plenty busy with things at the diner when she needed help. There were days he wished she didn't own the place. That she'd stayed on as a cook rather than buying it from the last owner. There was too much at stake, too much to lose.

Frigid air buffeted him as he hopped out of the truck and headed for the door, his head bowed down as far into his collar as possible. This storm had been a good one. Hopefully it would blow itself out by morning and nothing would get in the way of the wedding. For one, he only wanted to get dressed up in that tuxedo once. And for another, Callum and Avery deserved an incident-free day.

It was warm inside, and smelled deliciously like tomatoes and garlic and warm bread. Rhys stamped off his feet and unzipped his jacket, tucking his gloves into the pockets as he walked toward the back corner. His mom had been right. Other than a couple of truckers waiting out the bad roads, the place was empty.

He stopped and looked at the miracle she had produced in a scant hour.

The Christmas tree was lit, sending tiny pinpoints of colored light through the room. The heavy tables were pushed together to make one long banquet style set up for twelve, and they were covered with real linens in holiday red. The napkins were only paper but they were dark green and white, in keeping with Christmas colors. Thick candles sat in rings of greenery and berries—where had she come up with those?—and the candles lent an even more intimate air to the setting. But the final touch was the ice buckets on both ends, and the sparkling wineglasses at each place setting.

"What do you think?" His mother's voice sounded behind his shoulder.

"You're something, Ma," he said, shaking his head.

She frowned a little. "Do you think it'll be okay for Taylor? I know she must have had something fancier planned for the rehearsal dinner."

"You've worked a miracle on short notice. And if Taylor Shepard doesn't like it, she can…" He frowned. "Well, she can…"

"She can what, Rhys?"

Dammit. Her sweet voice interrupted him. He felt heat rush to his cheeks but when he turned around she was looking at Martha and smiling.

"Martha, how did you possibly do all this in such a short time?"

"It was slow in here and I had some help." She grinned. "Jean from the bakery sent over a cake—they were closing early anyway and she was happy to help with dessert. It's chocolate fudge."

"And wine?" Rhys watched as Taylor's eyes shone. Maybe he'd misjudged her. Maybe she'd just been stressed, because the snooty perfectionist he expected to see wasn't in attendance just now.

Or, perhaps she understood she was in a sticky place and was making the best of it. He suspected that faking it was in her repertoire of talents. His jaw tightened. When had he become so cynical? He supposed it was about the time Sherry had promised him to stick by his side—until things got dicey. Then she'd bailed—taking her two kids with her. Kids he'd grown very fond of.

You got to see someone's true colors when they were under pressure. It wasn't always pretty. Sherry hadn't even given him a chance to make things right.

He realized his mom was still speaking. "I'm not licensed, so I'm afraid it's not real wine. But the bed and breakfast sent over a couple of bottles of sparkling cider they had on hand and I put it on ice. I thought at least you could have a toast."

To Rhys's surprise, Taylor enveloped Martha in a quick hug. "I underestimated you," she said warmly. "This is perfect."

Martha shrugged but Rhys could tell she was pleased. "Heck," she replied with a flap of her hand. "That's what neighbors are for."

The rest of the wedding party arrived, complete with laughter and the sound of stomping boots. The next thing Rhys knew, he was seated at the table next to Avery's maid of honor, Denise, and things were well underway. Drinks were poured and he found himself chatting to Harry, who was on his other side. The senior Shepard was a very successful businessman, sharp as a tack and charismatic. Rhys could see a lot of his acumen and energy in Jack, the younger son, and the strength and reliability in Callum, the eldest. Rhys noticed that while Harry spoke proudly about Callum's military career and Jack's business, he didn't say much about Taylor's successes.

What about Taylor, then? She had the dark looks of the Shepard men rather than the more fair coloring of her mother, who sat across the table. But her lips were soft and full, like Mrs. Shepard's, and the dusting of freckles came from there, too. When he met Mrs. Shepard's gaze, he saw a wisdom there that he'd glimpsed in Taylor, too. Wisdom and acceptance. He guessed that it must have been hard to be a girl growing up in a household of such strong males. Had she felt pressure to keep up? Or were the expectations lower because she was female? He'd only known her a short time but he understood that she would hate to be treated as anything less than equal to her brothers. And then there was the tension he'd sensed between them at the rehearsal.

To his surprise, Taylor didn't sit at all but donned an apron and helped Martha serve the meal. When she put his plate before him, he looked up and met her eyes. "Thank you, Taylor."

"You're welcome."

She turned to move away but he reached out and caught her wrist. "What you said to my mother, that was very nice."

Her eyes met his. "I meant it. I apologize for my mood earlier. I was stressed."

"And here I thought it was because you didn't like to be told what to do."

Her eyes flashed at him for a second before mellowing, and then her lips twitched. "I do believe you're baiting me. Now stop so I can finish serving the meal."

He watched as she helped put the plates around, smiling and laughing. He'd thought her too proud for serving but she wasn't. She'd do what it took to pull off an event. There was lots of talking and laughing and toasting around the table, but Rhys frowned. Wasn't she going to sit and eat? While Martha tended to the few customers at the counter, it was Taylor who refilled bread baskets and beverages. Once he spied her in a corner, talking on her cell and gesturing with one hand. When Callum stood and offered a toast Rhys could see her in the kitchen, slicing cake onto plates.

Maybe it was her job, but it was her family, too. She was part of the wedding party, after all. And no one seemed to realize she was missing out.

When the meal was over the party broke up. Callum and Avery departed with a wave, in a hurry to get home to their daughter who was with a sitter. Mr. and Mrs. Shepard left for the bed and breakfast and Jack, being chivalrous, offered to take Denise with him, since they were all staying there anyway.

Angela and Clara offered to help tidy up, but Taylor shooed them away. "You've got Sam and Ty waiting and the kids at home. Go. This won't take but a minute anyway. I'll see you in the morning."

They didn't put up much of an argument, Rhys noticed. Clara put a hand on her swollen tummy and looked relieved.

As they were leaving, another group of truckers came in, looking for hot coffee and a meal before calling it a night. Martha bustled around, attending to them—Rhys knew that on a night like tonight, the tips would be generous.

Meanwhile Taylor grabbed a plastic dishpan and was loading up dirty plates.

She'd missed the entire celebration and was left to clean up the mess. He was pretty sure this wasn't in the job description, and he was annoyed on her behalf. Her family had been utterly thoughtless tonight.

He went around to the opposite side of the table and began stacking plates.

"What are you doing?"

*Clank, clank.* The flatware clattered on the porcelain as he picked up the dishes. "Helping."

"I got this, Rhys."

He took the stack over to her and put it in the dishpan. "Well, you shouldn't."

"Sorry?"

She looked tired. Tiny bits of hair had come out of her braid and framed her face, and her eyes looked slightly red and weary. "Have you even eaten, Taylor?"

"I'll get something later."

Lord, she was stubborn. "There's no one here now to know that this is your job, because I know that's what you're going to say. And you know what? This isn't your job. For Pete's sake."

"Are you angry at me? Because I'm not leaving all this for Martha. It *is* my job, Rhys. When I plan an event, I sometimes have to chip in and help where it's needed. Even if it's taking out trash or clearing dishes or providing someone with a spare pair of panty hose."

"Not this time. And no, I'm not angry at you."

She lifted her chin. "Then why are you yelling at me? People are staring."

He looked over. Martha was pretending not to watch but he could tell she was paying attention. The truckers weren't so discreet. They were openly staring.

He sighed. "I'm angry at your family. They never even noticed that you didn't sit down. Callum gave the toast without you. And other than Clara and Angela, everyone left without so much as an offer to help clean up. If everyone had pitched in…"

"They had more on their minds." Her posture had relaxed slightly. "It's okay, Rhys. Really."

"Will you go eat, please? Let me look after this."

She sighed. "Tell you what. I'll help clear the tables, and then I'll eat while you put the tables and chairs back to where they normally belong. Deal?"

He could live with that, especially since he figured Taylor wasn't one to generally compromise. "Deal."

With carols playing softly in the background, it only took a few minutes to clear the dirty dishes away. Rhys took them to the kitchen while Taylor stripped away the soiled tablecloths and put the centerpieces in a cardboard box. Together they loaded the kitchen dishwasher and then Rhys put a square of leftover lasagna on a plate, heated it in the microwave and poured Taylor a glass of ice water. When it was hot, he added a bit of salad to the side and grabbed a napkin and utensils.

"That smells delicious."

"Sit. Eat. That's an order."

He knew she was tired when she merely smiled and faked a salute as she sat at an empty table. "Yes, boss."

She'd made a good dent in the lasagna by the time he'd pushed the tables back into place and put the chairs around them. Without a word he went to the kitchen and cut a slice of that chocolate fudge cake she'd missed out on. When he took it to her, she held up her hand. "I couldn't possibly."

"Yes, you can. It's delicious."

"I have a dress to fit into tomorrow."

"Which will look beautiful." He put a bit of cake—complete with fudgy frosting—on the fork and held it out. "Trust me."

"Trust you." She raised one cynical eyebrow so brilliantly he nearly laughed. "As if."

He wiggled the fork. She leaned forward and closed her lips around it, sucking the frosting off the tines.

His body tensed simply from the intimate act of feeding her, feeling the pressure of her lips conducted through metal, the way she closed her eyes at the first rich taste. He enjoyed bantering with her. Matching wits. That didn't happen often around here. But it was more than that. There was an elemental attraction at work. Something indefin-able that was more than a physical response to her unusual beauty. She was the most capable woman he'd ever met. So why did she seem particularly vulnerable? Especially around her family?

"That's good," she murmured, licking a bit of choco-late from her upper lip.

"I know." His voice was hoarse and he cleared his throat. "Have another bite."

"I shouldn't."

In response he put more on the fork and held it out. She took it, and then he took a bite for himself, feeling adoles-cently pleased that his lips followed where hers had been. The room seemed more silent now, and he suddenly real-ized that the last few customers had gone, the music had stopped and Martha was turning out lights.

"Oh," Taylor said, alarmed. "We should go."

Martha peered through the kitchen door. "Was every-thing all right, Taylor?"

"It was lovely, Mrs. Bullock. Thank you so much."

"Don't thank me. You were the workhorse tonight." When Taylor moved to stand up, Martha flapped a hand. "Take your time. Rhys will lock up, won't you Rhys?"

"Sure thing, Ma." He never took his eyes off Taylor as he answered. They were going to be alone—truly alone—for the first time. Eating cake by the light of the Christmas tree in the corner. The back door through the kitchen shut, echoing in the silence.

"I didn't mean to…"

He shook his head. "I have keys to the place. It's okay. I've locked up plenty of times."

"No, what I mean is…"

She stopped talking, looked into his eyes and bit down on her lip.

She was feeling it, too. There was something. Something that had been lit the moment that she'd threatened to make him wear a cravat. She meant they shouldn't be alone.

She was probably right.

Instead he gazed into her eyes, unwilling to end the evening just yet. "Do you want some milk to go with your cake?" he asked.

# CHAPTER FOUR

SHE SHOULD NEVER have had the cake. Or the milk. Or sat around actually enjoying Rhys's company as the night drew on and on and it was close to midnight and she was still so wired the thought of sleep was ludicrous.

Rhys was bossy and annoying and, at times, growly. He was also the only person to have noticed how she was excluded tonight. When she was working a job she tried to be invisible, behind the scenes. Maybe she'd done her job a little too well, then. Because she'd sure been invisible to her family this evening.

It had stung. In her head she knew she was just doing her job but in her heart it had hurt a little bit, that no one had at least asked her to pause and join the celebration. Not even for the toast.

Except Rhys had noticed.

She was getting used to the sight of his face, rugged and far less refined than most of the men she was accustomed to. Rhys wasn't pretty. But as she looked into his eyes across the table, with the lights of the tree reflected in the irises, she realized a man didn't have to be pretty to be sexy as hell.

"It's getting late. I should get back. Tomorrow's a long day." She balled up her paper napkin and put it on her dirty plate.

"You're probably right," he agreed. "I'll just put these things in the sink."

She followed him to the kitchen. "Rhys. Thank you. I know I blew it off before but it did kind of hurt. That they didn't notice, I mean."

He rinsed the plate and left it in the sink since the dishwasher was already running. "No problem."

She gave a short laugh. "Well, at least being away from the table meant I avoided the 'why aren't you married with a few kids yet' speech."

Rhys gave the kitchen a final check. "Why aren't you, by the way? Or aren't you interested in those things?"

She shrugged. "I like kids. My dad tends to think in lines of traditional roles, like who the breadwinner is and who does the nurturing."

"And you don't?"

She lifted her shoulders. "I don't. I think as long as a couple has a division of labor that works for them, then who am I to criticize? I suppose I'll settle down someday, when I have the time. After I've proved myself."

"And how will you know when you get there?"

She looked up, startled. "What do you mean?"

"I mean, how do you measure that? What do you need to check off on a list to consider yourself a success?"

She floundered. There was no list. "I guess I'll just know."

"Or maybe you'll never know. Let me hit the lights."

She thought about his words as she put on her coat. What was her "yardstick" for success? A dollar amount? Number of employees? Acceptance from her family?

She was so afraid of disappointing any of them, she realized. Callum was a decorated soldier. Jack had been an elite athlete before he'd become a businessman. She loved her brothers but it was hard to compete with their overachievements.

It was a bit of a shock to realize that she'd picked a business where she was behind the scenes, out of the limelight. Where she was protected just a little bit from visibility if she failed.

When had she become so afraid?

Rhys finished up and when they stepped outside she realized just how much snow had fallen—and it was still coming down. Her car was covered and the snowplow had been by, leaving a deep bank right behind her back bumper. She sighed. She didn't even have a shovel, just a brush in the backseat for cleaning off the windshield.

"Come on, I'll take you in the truck," Rhys said, but Taylor shook her head.

"I have to dig it out sometime and I'm due at the golf club by 9:00 a.m. in order to get everything set up for the reception."

"You try driving that little thing out there before the plows make another pass and you're sure to slide off into the ditch." He shook his head. "There aren't even snow tires on it, just all-seasons. I'll take you out there in the morning."

She didn't want to rely on Rhys too much, especially since he seemed very adept at prying into her business. "Jack's rental's a 4x4. I'm sure he'll run me out if the roads are bad."

"Suit yourself." He didn't sound too put out by her refusal, which was a relief. "But for now, you'd best let me take you home."

Home being the B&B. She didn't have a choice. There was no way her car was going to be unstuck tonight and she really didn't feel like walking through the snowdrifts at this hour.

Rhys unlocked the door to his truck and waited while she got in, then jogged around the front and hopped in the driver's side. He started the engine and let everything warm up for a few minutes while Taylor stared at the clouds her breath was making in the air.

The heater kicked in and the air around her feet began to warm. "Gosh, it's cold. I'm so used to the coast. This is full-on winter."

"Complete with whiteouts and a snow removal system that operates at the speed of a slug." Rhys grinned. "Still, with this good dump of snow there'll be lots of sledding happening over the holidays."

"Sledding?"

"Snowmobiles," he confirmed. "Lots of wide-open space here, but a lot of the guys like to go into the mountains and into the backcountry."

"That sounds like something Jack would love."

Rhys grinned. "He might have said something about coming back for a trip later this winter. If he can drag Callum away from his new bride. I get the feeling that Jack's a little more adventurous than Callum."

"Just in a different way," she replied, rubbing her gloved hands together. "Callum got all the adventure he wanted in the army, I think, and he was ready to settle down. Jack's more of a daredevil. Anyway, hopefully this will let up by the morning so nothing interferes with the wedding."

He put the truck in gear. "Right. Well, let's get you home so you can get your beauty sleep."

It took no time at all, even at crawling speed, to reach the B&B. The front porch light was on and white Christmas lights twinkled through the snow that had settled on the porch and railings. Rhys put the truck in Park and left the engine running.

Taylor faced him; saw his face illuminated by the dashboard lights. The snow on his hair had melted, making it darker than usual, almost black. Who was Rhys Bullock anyway? Horse trainer, sure. And clearly devoted to his mother, which was another plus. But what made him tick? What were his thoughts, his views? What went on in that complicated male mind of his? On one hand he claimed he didn't want to be tied down, but there was no doubt in her mind that he'd put down roots in Cadence Creek. What was that about?

Why on earth did she care?

"I, uh, thanks for the drive."

"You're welcome."

"And for making me eat. And…" She wet her lips. "Well, for noticing what no one else did."

There was an awkward pause as if he were deliberating over his next words. "You don't need to prove anything to your family, you know," he finally said quietly. "As long as you're squared away with yourself, that's all that matters."

Her lips dropped open. How could he possibly know that she'd always felt like she came up short? Her dad was always talking about how the boys made him proud. She always felt a few steps behind. There was something in Rhys's voice, too. Something that said that he was familiar with those words. Like maybe he'd said them to himself a time or two. Why?

"Rhys."

She'd unbuckled her seat belt and for several heartbeats the air in the cab held, as if wondering if she were going to stay in or get out. Their gazes met and things got ten times more complicated as neither of them seemed capable of looking away. Somehow they drifted closer. Closer…

She wanted to kiss him. The notion was strange and wonderful and slightly terrifying. Nothing could ever come of this, but he was feeling it, too. He must be, because she saw him swallow as he blindly reached around and undid his seat belt, his dark gaze never leaving hers. Nothing was holding him back now and still the fear and excitement waved over her, amplified in the small space of the truck cab. She didn't do this. She didn't get personal. And still she had the urge to touch, the desire to explore.

"You're going to have to meet me halfway," he murmured, his voice deep and inviting. There was no doubt now, was there? With those words he'd told her that they were on exactly the same page. The air between them sizzled.

"This is probably a mistake," she answered, dropping her gaze, breaking the connection. "I should go inside."

She didn't want to, though. And her pulse leaped wildly as he slid across the seat and reached out with his left hand, curling it around her hip and pulling her across the upholstery. "Hush," he said, and then cupped her cheek in that same hand. "We're both sitting here wondering, so why don't we get this out of the way?"

When his lips came down on hers, it stole her breath. Nothing could have prepared her for the warm insistence of his mouth or the reaction rocketing through her body. One taste and the whole kiss exploded into something wild and demanding. She reached out and gripped the front of his jacket and his arms came around her, pulling her so close she was nearly on his lap. A squeak escaped her lips as he looped one arm beneath her bottom and tugged so she was sprawled across his legs, cushioned by a strong arm as the kiss went on and on, her body ached with trembling need and her head was clouded with sheer desire.

Except somewhere in the fog was the understanding that this couldn't go any farther. She pulled away first, shaking with the intensity of their connection. "Wow," she whispered, their limbs still tangled. Despite the truck being left running, the windows had already fogged up as the sound of their breathing filled the cab.

He let out a soft curse. "I didn't expect that," he said, running his hand over his hair. "God, Taylor."

She had to get some of her bravado back or he'd see exactly how rattled she was. "Too much?" she asked innocently.

"Too much?" He gaped at her for a second, but she wasn't fooled. There was a fire in the dark depths of his eyes that was tremendously exciting.

His voice held a rasp that shivered over her nerve endings. "When I was eighteen I would have been digging for the condom in my wallet by now and heading for the privacy of the gravel pit."

She giggled. He had a condom in his wallet? Or did he mean hypothetically? What was most surprising was how badly she wanted to. Wanted him. That if he'd seriously asked she would have actually considered it even though she totally wasn't into casual anything.

It was too much. Too fast. "That sounds romantic," she replied, the words injected with a healthy dose of sarcasm. She pushed off his lap and back onto the seat of the truck.

"I'm not eighteen anymore," he admitted, letting out a breath. "I'd like to think I've learned some finesse since then. And a quickie in the cab of my truck…" He hesitated, let the thought linger.

Would never be enough. He didn't need to say it for her to hear the words. "I'd better go," she said, sliding all the way over to the door and grabbing her purse. Get out before she changed her mind and crawled into his arms again. "This wasn't such a good idea."

"Because I'm a small-town hick, right?"

She frowned, brought up short. Did he really think she was such a snob? "I didn't say that. It just doesn't make sense to start something when I'm only here until Boxing Day. Then I go back to my world and you stay here in yours. Anything else is just fooling ourselves, Rhys, and you know it."

There was a long, awkward silence. "I'll pick you up tomorrow morning and take you to the club," he offered, but his voice was tight, like she'd somehow offended him.

"Jack will take me."

Rhys let out a frustrated sigh. "Will you call if you need anything?"

She squared her shoulders. "I won't. Thanks for the lift. See you at the church."

She opened the door and hopped down, her boots sinking into eight inches of fresh snow. She wouldn't look back at him. He'd know. Know that if he said the right thing or made the slightest move she'd be in the middle of that bench seat, holding on to his arm as he drove out to the pit or wherever people went parking these days, snowstorm be damned. And she never did things like that. In fact, she hadn't been involved with anyone that way since John. Since he'd said all those hurtful things before slamming the door. She'd put all her energy into the business instead.

Without looking back, she started up the walk to the porch. Rhys gunned the engine the slightest bit—did "Mr. Uptight Pants" have a bit of a rebellious side after all?—and pulled away, driving off into the night.

She tiptoed up the steps and carefully opened the door—a single light glowed from the front window but Taylor expected everyone would be in bed. She'd have to apologize in the morning for coming in so late.

"Aren't you a little old to be parking?" came a voice on her right.

She jumped, pressed a hand to her heart. "Jack. What are you doing up?"

"Big brother was waiting for you. What took you so long?"

She recalled Rhys's criticism of her family and felt her temper flicker. "Someone had to stay and clean up."

"Isn't that the owner's job? What's her name? Martha?"

"Rhys's mother, yes. And considering she was a staff of one tonight and still managed to put on a great dinner for us at a moment's notice, I certainly wasn't going to walk out of there and leave her with a mess. Not that anyone else seemed to mind."

He came forward and frowned down at her. "Touchy," he remarked. "This have anything to do with why you were in Rhys's truck for so long, and with the windows steamed up?"

She didn't want to blush, but the heat crept up her neck and into her cheeks anyway. "That is none of your business."

"Be careful is all I'm saying. He's not your type."

"How would you know what my type is?"

He straightened and it seemed to her that he puffed out his chest. "Oh, I know. You go for the pretty boys who work downtown in two-thousand-dollar suits."

"Men like you, you mean?"

His eyes glittered. "Hardly. You pick guys who aren't a challenge and who don't challenge you. Guys like Rhys Bullock won't let you away with your usual tricks, sis."

She had to keep a lid on her temper before she said something she'd regret. Jack had such a tendency to be cocky and normally she just brushed it off. Tonight it irritated. Could she not do anything right? "Then how convenient for you that he just gave me a lift home after helping me clear away the dishes. Oh, and he reminded me I hadn't had time to eat at the dinner, either, and fixed me a plate. And when we finally went to leave, my rental was completely blocked in by a snowbank so he offered me a drive home. My type or not, Rhys Bullock was very supportive this evening. So you can put that in your pipe and smoke it, Jackson Frederick Shepard."

Unperturbed, Jack merely folded his arms and raised an eyebrow at her.

"I'm going to bed," she announced. "I recommend you do the same. You're taking me to the golf club at eight-thirty so I can be sure it's ready for the reception."

Without waiting for an answer, she swept up the stairs, her pride wrapped around her. It was only when she was settled in her room, dressed in flannel pajamas and curled under the covers that she let down her guard and closed her eyes.

Behind her lids she saw Rhys. And she saw what might have happened—if only they were different people, in a different place and time.

The church was beautiful.

Taylor let out a relieved sigh as she peeked through the nearly closed door leading through the sanctuary. It had taken longer than she'd anticipated, making sure the reception venue was all on schedule and then it had been time to head to Molly Diamond's, where all the bridesmaids were meeting to get ready and have pictures taken. Taylor gave the thumbs-up to the photographer, Jim, who had flown in from Victoria to do the wedding as a personal favor. He was set up at the front of the church, ready for Avery's walk down the aisle.

Taylor's worries about the decorations had been pointless. She wasn't sure how Melissa Stone had managed it, but the end of each pew held a stunning but simple decoration consisting of a red satin bow and a small cedar bough. Not only did it look festive, but the smell was incredible.

And Clara had come through with the sills, too. On each one was a small rectangular plate with three white pillar candles of varying heights. It was incredibly romantic and the warm light radiated through the church. She couldn't have come up with anything more suitable on her own.

With a lump in her throat, she turned to Clara and smiled. "How on earth did you manage that?" she asked. "It's perfect!"

Clara laughed lightly. "I called the owner of the dollar store last night and asked if we could go in early this morning."

The dollar store. Heaven forbid any of her clients ever found out! She gave an unladylike snort and patted Clara's arm. "I swear I need to stop underestimating the women of this town. First Martha with the dinner, then you with the candles and Melissa with the pew markers. I'm starting to feel rather irrelevant."

Avery heard and her face fell with concern. "Oh, don't say that, Taylor! We put this together in such a short time that if it weren't for you we'd be standing in front of the Justice of the Peace and having a potluck. I never dreamed I'd have a wedding day like this. It would never have happened without you."

Taylor's eyes stung. This was so different from anything she'd ever experienced. She hadn't even had to ask for help. Without even knowing her, people had stepped up because it was the right and neighborly thing to do. Maybe Cadence Creek wasn't the hub of excitement Taylor was used to, but never had she ever been made to feel like she belonged so easily. She was starting to understand why Callum was so happy here.

"It was my pleasure, I promise. Now let me check to see what's going on."

Because Avery had no family, they'd decided to forgo

the official ushering in of the parents. Instead Taylor's mom and dad sat at the front, with an adorable Nell, dressed in white ruffles, on their laps. Taylor turned her attention to the side door as it opened and the minister and men came through. At last night's rehearsal it had become glaringly apparent that everyone had an escort up the aisle but the bride. They'd made a quick change of plans, and the women would be walking up the aisle alone with the groomsmen waiting at the front.

Taylor's heart beat a little faster as Rhys appeared, looking so very handsome and exciting in the black tux and tie. The men lined up along their side of the altar, with Rhys positioned right after Jack. The pianist began to play Gounod's "Ave Maria," the signal for the women to begin their walk.

"This is it, girls." Taylor quickly got them in order and then took her place behind Angela. She gave the man at the door a quick nod and it opened, and the procession began.

Clara went first, radiant in dark green, glowing with pregnancy and holding her bouquet in front of her rounded tummy. Then Angela, smiling at her husband at the other end, and then, in the middle of the procession, Taylor.

She stepped on to the white runner, her emerald satin heels sinking slightly into the carpet. She kept slow time with the music, a smile on her face as she winked at her brother who was waiting rather impatiently for his bride. Jack was beside him, grinning like a fool and then…

And then there was Rhys, watching her with an intensity that made her weak at the knees. The smile on her lips flickered until she purposefully pasted it there, but she couldn't deny the jolt that had rushed through her that second their eyes met. Her chest cramped as her breath caught, and then his lips curved the tiniest bit and his gaze warmed with approval. And she was back in the truck last night, feeling his hands on her body and his lips on her lips and she got hot all over.

Then she was in her place, Denise followed and the music changed.

Taylor forgot all about Rhys the moment Avery stepped to the door and on the carpet. Her lace dress was classic and romantic, her solid red rose bouquet perfect. Taylor's throat tightened as she took one quick glance at her brother and found his eyes shining with tears. She couldn't cry. She wouldn't. She never did at these things. But today was different. She knew how Callum had had his heart broken before and how incredible it was that he was even standing here today. Nell stood on her grandfather's lap and everyone chuckled when she bounced and said "Mumm mumm mumm."

Avery reached Callum, and he held out his hand. She took it and they faced the minister together.

The prayers were short and heartfelt, the "I Do's" immediate and clear so that they echoed to the farthest pew. It was when Avery handed her bouquet to Denise and took Callum's fingers in hers that Taylor wished she'd tucked a tissue into the handle of her bouquet.

The vows were simple and traditional, the words solid and true as they filled the candlelit church. "I Callum, take you Avery, to be my wife. To have and to hold from this day forward."

A lump formed in Taylor's throat as she tried to swallow.

"For better or worse, richer or poorer, in sickness and in health."

Taylor took a fortifying breath and told herself to hold it together. But it was so hard, because she could see the look on Callum's face as he gazed into the eyes of his bride. He was so in love. So sure. The promises were the most important he'd make in his life, but they came easily because he loved Avery that much. Taylor had never experienced anything like that. Sometimes she doubted she ever would…if she was actually that…lovable.

Avery's soft, gentle voice echoed them back. "I Avery, take you Callum, to be my husband. To have and to hold, from this day forward."

A single tear splashed over Taylor's lower lashes. She was mortified.

"To love, honor and cherish for as long as I live."

The pair of them blurred as her eyes filled with moisture and she struggled not to blink. The pronunciation was made, there was clapping during the kiss, and then Avery, Callum, Denise and Jack moved to the table to sign the register and wedding certificate. Just when she was sure the tears were going to spill over, a dark figure appeared in front of her and held out a handkerchief.

She didn't need to see the fine details to know it was Rhys. Her heart gave a confused flutter just before she reached out and took the fabric from his hand. The shape of his lips curved slightly before he silently stepped back, and she gave a self-conscious laugh as she turned her head a little and dabbed at her eyes.

She could see again but she didn't dare look at him. A handkerchief—a white one, she could see now, and it smelled like starch and his aftershave. What sort of man these days carried a white handkerchief, for Pete's sake? And why on earth was she charmed by it?

The documents were signed, the minister introduced them as Mr. and Mrs. Callum Shepard and clapping erupted as the bride and groom immediately went to gather their daughter and then swept jubilantly down the aisle.

Taylor swallowed as Rhys offered his elbow. "Shall we?" he asked quietly, smiling down at her.

She tucked her hand in the crook of his elbow. It was strong and warm and she felt stupidly pretty and feminine next to him. "Certainly," she replied as they made their way out of the sanctuary to the much cooler vestibule. They'd form a receiving line there briefly, and then the guests would go on to the golf club for a cocktail hour while the wedding party had pictures taken.

Taylor gave a final sniff and prepared to get herself together. She had the next hour to get through and didn't want smudged makeup or red eyes to mar the photos. The sentimental moments had passed.

What she hadn't prepared herself for was the number of times she'd be forced close to Rhys during the photos; how she'd feel his hand rest lightly at her waist or his jaw close to her hair. By the time the wedding party was dismissed, her senses were so heightened her skin was tingling.

"You want a drive to the club?" Rhys asked, as the groomsmen and bridesmaids gathered by the coatrack.

"Avery said we could all go in the limo that brought us from Diamondback."

"But aren't they doing just some bride and groom photos in the snow first? I guess I figured you'd want to get there and make sure things were running smoothly."

She smiled up at him, making sure to put several inches between them. "You know me too well."

He shrugged. "That part's easy to read. The tears on the other hand? Total surprise." He reached for her coat and held it out so she could slip her arms into the sleeves.

"And yet you were at the ready with a hanky. Impressive." She needed to inject some humor so he wouldn't know how genuinely touched she'd been at the gesture.

He chuckled. "That was Molly's doing. She said that at weddings you never know when a woman might need a hanky. She gave one to all of us."

He brushed his hands over the shoulders of her coat before stepping back. "Didn't think it'd be you, though. You're too practical for that. I guess I figured you'd be thinking two or three steps ahead."

Normally she would have been, and it stung a bit knowing that Rhys only saw what everyone else seemed to see—a woman lacking in sentimentality. But she'd been caught up in the moment just like everyone else. And for the briefest of seconds, she'd felt a strange yearning. Like she was possibly missing out on something important.

"I slipped up," she replied, reaching in the coat pocket for a pair of gloves. "It's just temporary."

She finally looked up into his face. His dark eyes were glowing down at her and whatever other smart reply she'd been about to make fluttered away like ribbons on a breeze. Her gaze inadvertently slid to his lips as she remembered the sound of his aroused breathing in the confined space of his truck. A truck that he was suggesting she get in— again.

This time there would be no funny business. She really should get to the venue and make sure everything was going according to plan. She relaxed her face into a pleasant smile. "I'll accept the drive with thanks. Let me just tell Jack that I'm going on ahead."

"Taylor?" He stopped her from walking away by grabbing her arm, his fingers circling her wrist. "You should slip up more often. It looks good on you."

Maybe he did see more. She wasn't sure if that was a good thing or not. "I'll tell Jack," she repeated.

"I'll warm up the engine," he answered.

She turned around to find her brother and when she turned back again, a cold gust of wind from the just-opened door hit her like an icy wall.

She had to keep her head about her today. Weddings

made people do strange things. It was just as well, then, that she planned on remaining behind the scenes as much as possible.

# CHAPTER FIVE

THE RECEPTION WAS going off without a hitch. When Taylor arrived at the club, the guests were already circulating and enjoying the cocktail hour. Platters of crackers, cheese and cold cuts, shrimp rings, crudités and fruit were set out on tables close to the bar, where people were lined up to be served either punch or hot cider.

The place looked lovely. The centerpieces had been lit—boy, Melissa had really outdone herself with those. White candles enclosed in glass sat on real rounds of wood, surrounded by aromatic greenery and winterberries. Each chair was covered in white fabric, a wide red ribbon around the back with more cedar and a single pinecone adding a festive, homey touch. The pew markers had mirrored the design perfectly. She couldn't have planned it any better. Hadn't, actually. Funny how some things worked out.

Rhys showed up at her elbow and handed her a cup. "Have something hot to drink."

"I should check the kitchen."

"You should relax. Maybe enjoy yourself."

"I'll enjoy myself later." But she took the mug anyway. The sweet, spicy scent of the cider was too tempting to resist.

"You look beautiful by the way," he said quietly.

Her pulse fluttered again. "Thank you," she answered

politely, but inside she glowed. She was used to dressing up, but her style usually ran to the classic and conservative. Tailored fits and solid colors that spoke far more to class, confidence and efficiency than femininity and whimsy. But the dress today made her feel very girly indeed. The bodice was strapless and the lace overskirt to the emerald tea-length gown was far more dainty than she normally wore. Not to mention the gorgeous satin shoes on her feet, or the way her hair was gathered in a low chignon with a few pieces left artfully around her face.

"Do you want something to eat? I can bring you something if you like."

What was she doing? Last night she'd lost her senses, but it was the clear light of day now. Sure, weddings brought out the romantic in anyone but she was smarter than that. This wasn't anything. One kiss in a truck at midnight didn't make them a couple today. Or any day for that matter.

"I can get it myself, you know. You don't have to act like we're a couple just because we're paired up in the wedding party," she answered, making a pretense of scanning the room even though everything was moving along seamlessly.

Her breath squeezed in her lungs as she waited for his reaction. When she didn't get one, she turned to say something only to discover that he'd walked away. He'd gone to the buffet table, and she wondered if he'd stay true to form and simply ignore her wishes. But when he'd put a few selections on his plate, he never even glanced her way. He walked over to the other side of the room, greeting a few guests with a smile.

It made no sense that she felt empty and bereft when he'd done exactly as she'd intended.

Fine. She'd go to the kitchens and check on the dinner

prep, and then make sure the sound system was a go for the emcee. That's where she should be anyway. Not trying to impress a stubborn groomsman.

The words had sat on Rhys's tongue but he'd kept them to himself. At a wedding reception was no place to tell her exactly what he thought of her rude response. But he was plenty put out. He'd only been trying to be a gentleman. Sure, he enjoyed pushing her buttons. But after last night…

Never mind that. Even if that kiss had never happened, he would have been courteous to any woman he'd been paired with for the day. That was just plain manners where he came from. But she was too damned independent. Wanted to do everything by herself. Was it to prove she could? She didn't have to prove anything to him. Anyone with eyes in their head could see she was good at her job. She'd pulled this whole event together in a few weeks. That took organizational skills and long hours and, he suspected, a good amount of money. He felt like saying, "I get it. You're successful and you earned it all by yourself."

The contrast between them was laughable. So why did he bother? He got the feeling she'd never understand his point of view anyway.

He mingled a bit, visiting with neighbors and acquaintances. The Diamonds arrived, and then fifteen minutes after that Avery and Callum followed, along with Denise and Jack and of course, the adorable Nell. His gaze lit on the little girl for a moment, all in ruffles with a tiny green bow in her dark curls. Humph. Taylor probably didn't even want kids. It would take too much time away from her business and important tasks. How much more reminding did he need that she was not for him? Her work was her top priority.

Rhys's heart constricted as he thought of the two little

boys he'd grown so attached to. For a while he'd been so focused on saving the business that he'd neglected the people closest to him. Funny how your perspective changed when you lost what you didn't appreciate in the first place.

So why did he kiss her last night? Why had he made an effort today? And why in hell couldn't he stop thinking about her eyes swimming with tears as he handed her a stupid square of cotton during the ceremony?

Sam took the mic and introduced the happy couple and asked everyone to take their seats. "You, too, Taylor," he added, glimpsing her talking to one of the wait staff by the door. She smiled and gave a little shrug, making people chuckle as she came his way.

Rhys waited. And when she got to his side, he held out his arm.

He could tell her teeth were clenched as she smiled and put her hand on his arm. "You did that on purpose," she accused, smiling brightly.

He smiled back. "Yes, I did. Just to annoy you."

Her eyes sparked. "Why would you do that?"

"Because pushing your buttons amuses me," he replied. "I know I shouldn't." He pulled out her chair with a flourish and noticed her cheeks were flushed. "It's pretty clear where we stand. But I can't resist."

She took up her napkin and gave it a sharp flap before settling it on her lap. "Hmm. I took you for a rule follower. Straight and narrow. Didn't take you as a bit of a scamp."

Once upon a time he'd been far more carefree and less careful. A risk taker. Circumstances had made him grow up in a hurry. "Funny," he answered, taking his seat and retrieving his own napkin. "I never pictured you as the sappy type either, but…"

"Maybe we bring out the worst in each other," she said in an undertone, reaching for her water glass.

"See? We're getting to know each other better. Now I know that you see both fun and sentimentality as flaws."

"You're deliberately twisting my words."

"Be quiet. The minister is going to say the blessing."

He was gratified when she clamped her lips shut—score one for him. After the blessing, Sam took to the mic again, explaining the order of the evening while the salads were served. Even the salads matched the Christmas decor—greens with candied pecans, red cranberries and creamy feta. Her attention to the smallest detail was starting to get annoying.

Staff were on hand at each table to pour the wine, and he noticed that when Taylor's glass had been filled with red, she reached for it immediately and took a long sip.

Maybe he shouldn't bug her so much. She had a lot on her mind today. He didn't need to add to the stress.

Then again, there was something to be said for distraction. And he did enjoy pushing her buttons. It was a nice break from his self-imposed "dry spell."

"Good wine?" he asked, reaching for his glass.

"One of my favorites, from Mission Hill. Do you like it?"

He did, though he wasn't much of a wine drinker. "It's okay."

"What's wrong with it?"

"Nothing. I said it was okay."

A look of understanding lit in her eyes. "You don't drink much wine, do you?"

He shrugged. "Not as a rule." When would he drink wine? It wasn't like he went on dinner dates or was the kind to chill out at the end of the day with a nice chardonnay. At her distressed look, he took pity on her. "Look, I'm a guy. Most of us around here are beer men, that's all. Which would be totally out of place at this dinner."

"Oh, is it too fancy? I tried to keep it fairly traditional. Nothing that people can't pronounce, that sort of thing, you know?"

Gone was the sharp tongue and sassy banter. She was actually concerned. A few days ago he might have taken her comment differently, like maybe she meant the people of Cadence Creek weren't as sophisticated as she was. But that wasn't it. Her brow was wrinkled in the middle. He knew without asking that she'd tried very hard to come up with a menu that people would like.

"What's the main course?" he asked.

"Beef Wellington, Duchess potatoes, green beans and roasted red pepper."

"Sounds delicious."

"Well, Avery approved it, but then she approved just about everything I suggested." Her eyes widened. "Oh, Rhys, did I railroad her into stuff? Did she feel she couldn't say no?"

"Hey," he said, beginning to take pity on her. "Where is all this doubt coming from? You've said from the beginning that this is your thing."

"It is, but…"

He nudged her elbow. "Why did you pick this as the menu?"

She picked at her salad without eating. "Well, I tried to come up with something that was fancy enough for a wedding, something special, while keeping in mind the guest list. This is a meal for ranchers and, well, regular people. Not crazy movie stars or visiting dignitaries who only eat fish and sprouted grains or that kind of thing, you know?"

"So you tailored the food to the guest list?"

"Of course. I always do."

"Then why are you so worried? Know what I think? I think that for most people this is going to taste like a fancy meal out that's not intimidating, you know? Nothing they can't recognize or need to pronounce in a foreign language."

Their salads were removed and the main course put in front of them. Rhys's stomach growled. He'd only managed a few bites of the salad and the beef smelled delicious.

"I swear I'm not usually like this. Not so insecure."

"Is it because it's Callum?"

"Maybe. Then again, I don't usually do weddings. That's the one day everyone wants utterly perfect. There's more freedom with parties. But wedding days?" She took another sip of wine. Was quiet for a moment. "I screwed one up once."

"You did?" Was Taylor actually going to admit she'd made a mistake? It didn't strike him as her style.

She nodded. "The bride was allergic to strawberries. I'd forgotten. You don't mess with a bride on her wedding day, you know? She had a breakfast for her bridal party. I never thought twice about giving the chef dominion over the menu. I trusted him completely." She winced at the memory. "The wedding colors were pink and cream. The chef added strawberry coulis to the pancake batter. She got hives and her face swelled up like a balloon. Four hours before her walk down the aisle."

Rhys was intrigued. "What did you do?"

"We tried cold cloths, creams…it wasn't until the antihistamine shot that she really started to improve. But the 'getting ready' photos never happened, and she still looked rather pink and puffy in the pictures. Not to mention the fact that she nodded off in the limousine on the way to the hotel and reception because the drug made her drowsy. Not my finest moment as an event planner."

She speared her golden-browned potatoes with a somewhat savage poke. "I'm telling you, Rhys, you do not mess with a bride on her wedding day."

She looked so fierce he nearly smiled. But there was something else in her expression, too. She didn't like failure, or anything that would reveal a chink in her perfect armor. He wondered why.

"Have you always been a perfectionist?"

She didn't even take it as a slight criticism. "Yes."

"And doesn't that stress you out?"

She shrugged. "Occasionally. As long as I stay organized I'm fine. And I do work best under pressure. It's just now and again something will crop up and I'll chew antacids for a few days."

He wanted to ask her how that could possibly be fun, but they were interrupted as the speeches began. Mr. Shepard welcomed Avery to the family, and then Avery and Callum stood to speak together, thanking their family and friends. They took a moment to thank Taylor for pulling it all together, and Rhys saw her relax a little in her chair. The day was nearly done. The ceremony had gone without a hitch; the reception was lovely and the food delicious. Perhaps she could actually enjoy herself a little during the dancing.

Dessert was served—pastry baskets filled with chocolate mousse and topped with berries and whipped cream. They were almost too pretty to eat, and Rhys noticed that Taylor had slowed down on the wine and accepted a cup of coffee instead.

He frowned. He shouldn't care. Shouldn't bother him that she was wound tighter than a spring or that she was so deliberate in each choice and move. Except he knew now. He knew that there was a vulnerable side. He'd seen it last night when he'd mentioned how her family had ignored her. Whether she acknowledged it or not, she was desperate for her family's approval.

And he knew there was an unpredictable side to her, too, that rarely had a chance to get out to play. Because he was pretty sure that the heavy kissing they'd been doing in the cab of his truck last night had not been planned out and put on a list of pros and cons. It had been spontaneous. And combustible.

When the meal ended, the wedding cake was rolled in. "Oh, it's stunning," Taylor gasped, leaning forward to see better.

"You didn't know? A detail escaped your notice?"

She laughed. "No one was allowed to see it. Avery's friend Denise did it as a wedding gift. Avery insisted I trust her on this and so I did."

"It bothered you, though, right?"

She tore her gaze away from the cake and slid it up to meet his. "A little," she admitted. "This whole experience has been weird. I've had to give up way more control than I normally do. Usually no detail ever escapes my approval."

"Sometimes it's good to let someone else take the reins."

She chuckled. "Not my style, Bullock."

The cake really was pretty, even Rhys could see that. It looked like three presents stacked on top of each other, each layer turned on a slight angle and alternating red and white. The topper looked like a giant red bow. "What's the bow made out of?" he asked Taylor.

"Fondant," she said, smiling. "Okay, so the only thing to worry about now is the music, and the DJ should be fine, so maybe you're right. Maybe I can relax." She sighed. "And finally get some sleep."

He wondered if her lack of sleep was to do with the wedding or if she'd been like him last night, staring at the ceiling wondering what it would have been like to finish what they'd started.

It had been a long time since he'd come that close. He

certainly hadn't wanted to sow any wild oats here in Cadence Creek. The town was too small. Things got around. And before he knew it he'd be tied down, worrying about what he had to offer a wife, wondering how long it would be before he disappointed her.

No danger of that with Taylor, was there? She wasn't staying long enough for that.

Cheers went up as Avery and Callum sliced into the cake. Nell, clearly exhausted, was curled up in Mrs. Shepard's arms, sound asleep. The wait staff cleaned away the remaining dishes and business at the bar picked up. The show was over. Now it was time for fun.

He looked over at Taylor, who was more relaxed but looking increasingly exhausted. He was starting to wonder if she knew what fun was—or if it was all work and no play with her.

She wasn't sure how much more she could take.

Rhys was beside her every moment. He smelled so good. Like those peel-away cologne ads in magazines only better, because the scent came alive from the contact with his warm skin. He knew how to push her buttons and she'd started to realize he did it intentionally, trying to get a rise out of her. It was sexy as all get-out, like a strange mating dance that sent her heart racing and blood to her cheeks.

Which was all well and good except she kept feeling her control slipping and the balance of power was not in her favor. She found herself admitting things that she'd normally never dare breathe. Like that wedding story. She never shared that. It was too humiliating! At least she'd stopped before she'd said anything about how that day had ended—with John walking out. Professional and personal failure in one twelve-hour period. Talk about overachieving…

She didn't quite know where she stood with Rhys. It was partly exhilarating and mostly maddening and now, at the end of a very long day, she was feeling a bit off her game.

She decided to take a few minutes to chill out. She'd done her job. Everyone was doing theirs. It would be okay to relax for a bit. Especially when she could watch her brother and brand-new sister-in-law take to the dance floor for their first waltz.

Rhys disappeared momentarily to the bar and she let out a breath. Avery and Callum swept across the parquet as everyone watched, but her gaze slipped away from the floor and to Rhys, who stood chatting to the bartender while he waited for his drink. She swallowed. His tux fit him to perfection, the trousers showcasing long, lean legs that led to a gorgeously tight bottom. He'd taken off the jacket, and the tailored vest over the white starched shirt accentuated the breadth of his shoulders. He wasn't classically handsome, but his physique was as close to perfect as she could imagine.

When he turned back from the bar he caught her staring. She gasped a little as heat snapped between them, even from across the room. Maybe his face would never be in a magazine, but there was an intensity to it, a magnetism, that she couldn't deny.

He was holding two glasses in his hands.

When he got back to the table, he held one out to her. "Here," he said, taking his seat. "You look like you could use this."

"Champagne?"

He grinned, and it lit her up from the inside. "They managed to have a couple of bottles back there."

"You're more of a beer guy."

"It depends on the occasion. And you—" his gaze traveled over her for about the tenth time today "—look like a girl who needs champagne in her hand."

She took the glass.

"To a job well done."

She raised her glass to touch his but he wasn't done.

"And some well-deserved R&R."

That's right. After tonight she was on vacation for a whole week. She wasn't sure if it was a blessing or if it was going to drive her stir-crazy. She wasn't used to being idle.

She sipped at the champagne, the bubbles exploding on her tongue. A waitress stopped at the table, offering small pieces of cake. What the heck. Taylor took one, and so did Rhys. She took a bite. Not straight up chocolate… She closed her eyes. It was lavender. "Holy cannoli," she whispered, taking another sip of champagne, which only intensified the flavors on her tongue. "That is some serious cake."

"You," he said in a low voice, "are killing me here."

She held his gaze. Put a bit of cake on her fork and held it out while the events of the previous night leaped to the front of her mind. "What's good for the goose," she said lightly, offering the cake. "I promise you, this cake is a life-altering experience."

He took it from the fork. "I don't think it's the cake," he answered, reaching out and circling her wrist with his fingers. "Taylor, what are we doing?"

Clapping erupted as Avery and Callum finished their dance. "Now could we have the wedding party on the floor, please?" the DJ called.

Their gazes clung for a brief second as the words sunk in. For all her "you don't have to act like we're a couple" bit, the truth was they *had* been seated together for the reception and they *were* expected to dance together. The other bridesmaids and groomsmen seated along the head table were getting up from their chairs. Rhys held out his hand. "That's our cue."

She put down her fork. For heaven's sake, it was one dance at a wedding. Nothing to get in such a lather over. She'd put her hand in his, the other on his shoulder, and stare at the buttons on his shirt. It would be fine.

Except the moment they hit the parquet, he pulled her close in his arms and the scent that had teased her earlier enveloped her in a cloud of masculinity. Even in her heels—and she wasn't a short girl—he had a few inches on her. His palm was wide and warm and her plan to simply put her other hand on his lapel was a total fail because she remembered he'd removed his jacket and the flat of her hand was pressed simply to his white shirt. And the hard, warm wall of muscle beneath it.

"For goodness' sake, smile," he commanded as their feet started moving to the music.

She looked up into his eyes. He was smiling down at her but rather than feeling reassured she got the feeling that she was looking into the face of the Big Bad Wolf.

# CHAPTER SIX

WHOEVER DECIDED THAT slow, angsty songs were appropriate for weddings needed to be shot.

Taylor made her feet move, determined to keep her distance from Rhys as best she could, which was a rather daunting task considering they were slow dancing. It might have been easier if the song choice had been a wedding standard, something she was used to hearing time and again over the years and could dismiss as cliché and trite. But this was something new and romantic, and an acoustic version to boot that only added to the intimacy. Rhys's hand rode the small of her back, fitting perfectly in the hollow just below the end of her zip. The warmth of his touch seeped through the lace and satin to her skin.

During the planning, a wedding party dance had sounded nice. Since Avery didn't have any family, the traditional Groom/Mom of the Bride, Bride/Father of the Groom dances couldn't happen for the second dance of the night. This was Avery's idea of including everyone. Little had Taylor known that something so innocuous sounding would create such havoc.

"This isn't so bad, is it?"

His breath tickled the hair just above her ear and goose bumps popped up over her skin. How could she say how she really felt about it? That it was pure torture being in his arms this way, determined not to touch, wanting to desperately, knowing she couldn't with such an audience watching their every move?

"Not so bad I guess," she answered.

More shuffling steps. Was she imagining it or did his hand tighten against her back, pulling her closer? She swallowed heavily, the nerves in her stomach swirling with both anxiety and anticipation. Oh, God, now his jaw was resting lightly against her temple and his steps were getting smaller.

Her fingers slid over his shoulders as she imagined the smooth, muscled skin beneath the pure white fabric. Each breath caught for just a moment in her chest, making it hard to breathe as the song went on interminably. His fingers kneaded gently at the precise spot of the dimple at the top of her…

They had to stop this. And yet she lacked any will to back away, to put space between them. What she really wanted was to tilt her head so that his jaw wasn't riding her temple but closer to her mouth.

Holy Hannah.

"What are you doing to me, Taylor?"

If he kept talking in that husky voice she was going to have a meltdown right here on the dance floor.

"Nothing," she replied. "I'm not doing anything."

But she was and she knew it. And he wasn't exactly backing off, either.

"You…" Fear crowded her breath. She was getting in way too deep. "You don't even like me. You criticize everything."

"You're not the only one who enjoys a challenge," he replied, his thumb making circles against her tailbone. "You know as well as I do all that baiting was just foreplay."

Melt. Down.

"You're forgetting," he said softly, "who was with you in that truck last night."

She finally braved a look at him. His dark eyes glittered at her and she knew in a heartbeat where this would lead if she let it. The big question was did she want to?

Her body said yes. Her brain was another matter entirely. And while it was a close-fought battle, her brain was still in charge. By a very narrow margin.

"Not going to happen," she said, sounding far more certain than she felt.

"You sure? No gravel pit required. I have my own house, with a nice big bed in it."

Oh. *Oh.*

While that was a temptingly delicious thought, Taylor knew one of them had to be sensible. "I haven't had that much champagne, Rhys. If you're looking to hook up with someone, maybe you can find someone local. I'm sure there are some pretty girls in town who'd be interested."

He lifted his chin and his hot gaze slid away. "I don't date town girls."

"Ever?"

"Ever," he confirmed tightly.

Well. There was a story there, she was sure. But she wasn't about to ask. The farther away from Rhys she could manage the better. She did not want to get involved. A couple of stolen kisses were one thing. Start to probe into his personal life and it was going to get intimate.

"So I'm what? Not hanging around after Christmas, which makes me convenient?"

He let out a short laugh, dropped his gaze to her lips and pulled her close. Her breath came out in a rush as she found herself pressed against his hard length. "Trust me. You are anything but convenient."

The contact rippled through them both until suddenly

he released his hold and stepped back. The song ended and a new one began. Other guests crowded the floor as a popular, upbeat song thumped through the speakers.

Taylor stepped back. "Thank you for the dance."

Before he could say anything else, she turned her back on him and went to their table, ready to pick up her purse and go. Except she hadn't brought a vehicle, had she? She'd gone to the church in the limo and to here with Rhys and now she'd have to beg a ride back to the B&B. Which she'd planned to do with Jack, but she caught sight of him dancing with Amy Wilson, having a good time.

She grabbed her champagne glass and drained what was in it.

Callum and Avery stopped for a moment, happy and glowing. "Taylor, we can't thank you enough," Avery said. "Today was just perfect."

She was relieved to have something to think about other than Rhys. "It was my pleasure. And I did have some help you know. Your florist is a gem and your cake was out of this world. Not to mention Clara saving the day with the church candles." She looked up at Callum. "You've landed in a very nice place, brother."

He winked at her. "I know it. Sure you don't want to hang around a little longer?"

She shook her head. "A nice diversion but not my style. The week of relaxation that I'll get housesitting for you is enough small-town for me, thanks."

"You sure? Seems to me you've made a friend." He raised his eyebrows.

"I'm a big girl. And that's going nowhere, so don't you worry your head about it."

"That's not what Jack says. He said you were necking with Rhys in his truck last night."

This was what she didn't miss about having brothers

underfoot. They always thought it was okay to stick their noses in her business under the guise of "looking out for their sister." All of it was a pain in the butt.

"Callum," Avery chided softly, elbowing her husband in the ribs.

"Well, they weren't exactly discreet on the dance floor, either."

Taylor's cheeks burned. "Rhys Bullock is a bossy so-and-so who likes to push my buttons. I'm no more interested in him than…than…"

A hand appeared beside her, reaching for the other champagne glass. She turned on him. "Could you please stop showing up everywhere I am?"

He lifted his glass in a mock toast, totally unperturbed. "I'll disappear somewhere more convenient," he said.

He did, too. Right back to the dance floor. The DJ had put on a faster number and Rhys snagged Amy from Jack and swung her into a two-step. He turned her under his arm and she came back laughing.

"You're jealous," Callum noted.

"I most certainly am not."

"You're no better at lying now than you were when we were kids. Dad always said the poker face gene passed you by." Callum grinned, but he couldn't possibly know how much the words stung. Another criticism. She never measured up. She was always one step behind her brothers as far as her dad was concerned. One of these days she was going to show her father her accounts and watch his eyebrows go up. Those "frivolous" parties she planned brought in a boatload of cash.

Funny how the idea of that future moment had always seemed so sweet in her mind, but lately it had lost a little of its lustre. It was only a bank statement after all. There had to be more, right? Something more satisfying than the account balance?

"Don't you have cows to milk or something?"

He laughed. "I hired someone to do that today." His eyes twinkled at her. "And you won't have to worry about any farm work, either, while you're at the house. It's all taken care of."

"Good. Because you used to enjoy mucking around in the barns but I'd rather keep my boots nice and clean."

He laughed, then leaned forward and kissed her cheek. "We'll be gone tomorrow before you get to the house. I'll leave the key under the Santa by the door. Make yourself at home and we'll see you on the twenty-third."

She relaxed and kissed him back. "Love you, Callum."

"I love you, too, brat."

They moved off to visit with other guests. Taylor took a turn on the floor with Ty, and Sam, and even once with her father. True to form, he complimented the wedding but in such a way that it made her feel inconsequential.

"You planned a nice little party," he said, smiling at her.

Her throat tightened. Eighty guests, wedding party, church, venue, catering, flowers and all the other tiny details it took to put a wedding together in a ridiculously short amount of time. And it was "little"?

"Thanks," she said, deflated but unwilling to rise to any bait tonight. Not on Callum's day.

"When are you going to stop playing and start putting that business degree to good use?" he asked.

"I am putting my degree to use," she returned, moving automatically to the music. "Just ask my accountant."

"Planning parties?"

"I know you've never understood that. You wanted me to be a fund manager. I'd be bored to death, Dad."

She made herself look into his face as she said it. For

a moment he'd almost looked hurt. How was that even possible?

Conversation dropped for a minute or so before Harry recovered and changed the subject, talking nonstop about Nell and how it was wonderful to have a grandchild to spoil. The dance ended just in time—she was starting to worry he was going to ask her when she was going to do her duty and provide some more grandchildren. Her father's opinions were clear enough and pretty much paralleled with what John's had been. Personal and professional failure. And if not failure, at the least disappointment.

When the dance was over Rhys gave her a wide berth and she attempted to perk up her mood by spending a half hour with the pregnant Clara, chatting about Angela's charity foundation Butterfly House, and the other initiatives the Diamonds were involved in. It was all quite fascinating and before she knew it, the call went up for the single women to gather on the floor for the throwing of the bouquet.

She was not going to do that. Not in a million years.

Except Avery put up the call and every eye was on her. "Come on, Taylor, you, too!" Taylor spied Rhys standing against a pillar, his arms folded smugly as his eyes teased her, daring her to take part in the silly custom. She lifted her chin and ran her hands down her skirt before joining the half-dozen or so women ready to do battle for the mythical status of the next to be married. She wouldn't give him the satisfaction of backing out. Not that she'd actively try to catch it…

When Avery let the bouquet fly, Taylor had a heart-stopping moment when she realized it was heading right for her. Without thinking she simply reacted, raising her hands. But just before the ribbon-wrapped stems reached her, another hand neatly plucked it from the air.

Cheers went up when Amy Wilson held up the bouquet in a sign of victory.

Taylor was really ready to leave now. As she backed off the dance floor, she looked over at her mother, smiling from the sidelines, still cradling a sleeping Nell in her arms. Taylor wondered if her mom knew how much Taylor admired her. It was always her dad in the spotlight, but Taylor knew how hard her mom worked to keep the ship on course. Once, when she'd been about ten years old, she'd discovered her mother in the kitchen, making lists for an upcoming party they were hosting. That was when Taylor understood how, when everything seemed smooth and effortless on the surface, it was because of a well-oiled, well-organized machine running things behind the scenes. The machine, in that case, had been her mother, who handled everything from start to finish and still found time to run the kids to sports and especially Jack to his ski meets.

Maybe her dad was the one with his picture in the business magazines, but it was her mother Taylor truly admired. Her mother was the reason she'd chosen event planning as her career. Taylor hated how her father minimized the hard work she did, so why did her mother not resent his attitude? Why had it never been an issue for them?

There was another loud shout and Taylor lifted her head to see a stunned Rhys holding the bridal garter. According to tradition, Amy then took the chair in the middle of the dance floor while Rhys slid the garter on her leg. Taylor stifled a laugh. He didn't look too happy about it, especially when the DJ announced that the next dance was for the "lucky couple." Served him right.

As the music started, she headed toward her parents. "I don't suppose you're heading back to the B&B anytime soon, are you?" she asked, kneeling by her mom's chair.

"As a matter of fact, I was just suggesting to your dad

that we should take Nell and go. She's staying with us tonight so Callum and Avery can have the place to themselves before they all fly out tomorrow. Poor little mite's had enough excitement for today."

"So has this big mite. I'm beat. Mind if I catch a lift?"

"Of course not, but don't you want to stay at the party?"

Taylor saw Rhys and Amy out of the corner of her eye. For all he said he didn't date local girls, Amy sure was snuggled close to him, her arms wrapped around his ribs and her head nestled into his shoulder. "I'm sure. I've had a long few days and this will pretty much run itself now."

"Get your things then. You did a beautiful job, sweetheart. Proud of you."

The words warmed Taylor's heart. "Thanks, Mom. I had a good teacher."

"Oh, go on."

But Taylor took a moment to press her mother's hand in hers. "I mean it. I don't know that you were appreciated enough for all you did to keep things running smoothly. I should have said this before, but when I started my business you were the inspiration behind it."

"I didn't know that."

"Well, it's true."

Taylor went to pull away but her mom held tight to her hand. "Mind if I give you a little extra food for thought?"

Surprised, Taylor paused. "Sure."

Susan looked into Taylor's eyes and smiled. "None of it would have meant a thing without your dad and you kids. I know sometimes it looked like I played the dutiful wife…"

"You worked hard."

"Yes, I did, and I enjoyed it. Still, I would have missed out on so much if I hadn't had you kids. I could have gone on and done anything I wanted, you know? And I don't regret my decision for a second. Work is work, but family is forever."

"Didn't it ever bother you that Dad, well, took you for granted?"

Susan laughed. "Is that what you think? Oh, heavens. He wanted you kids, too. Honey, you get so wound up and defensive about this division of labor expectation, but it goes both ways. We did what worked for us. Being home with you three was my choice to make."

"Is this leading to a speech about settling down?"

Susan smiled and patted her hand. "I know better than that."

Taylor let out a breath. "Phew." But after a moment she looked at her mother again. "Mom, maybe I will settle down. When I find the right guy."

"That's a good answer," her mother replied. "Now, let's get going. I want to spend a little more time with my new granddaughter tonight."

Taylor got her coat from the coat check, snagged her purse and checked in with the staff one last time. Her mother was making sure they had all of Nell's stuff—including her car seat—while her dad went to warm up the car. She was just pulling on her gloves when Rhys came up behind her.

"You were just going to leave without saying goodbye?"

She held on to her purse strap. "It's been a long day and I'm catching a ride with my folks."

"That didn't answer my question."

She frowned. "What do you care? You've amused yourself with me a bit for the last few days but the wedding's over, we're not paired up anymore and we can both go about our business."

Rhys stared at her quizzically. "Really?"

"Is there some reason why we shouldn't?"

He looked like he wanted to say something, but held back. She wondered why. And then got a bit annoyed that she kept wondering about Rhys's state of mind at all. She blew air out her nose in an exasperated huff. "What do you care anyway? You seemed to enjoy having Amy Wilson plastered all over you."

"Jealous?"

She snorted. "Hardly."

He stepped forward until there was barely an inch between them. "Amy Wilson is the last woman on earth I want to be with!"

Silence rang around them, and then, almost as one, they realized someone had heard the entire outburst. Amy stood not ten feet away, her creamy skin stained crimson in embarrassment as humiliated tears shone in her eyes.

"Amy…" Taylor tried, taking a hesitant step toward the woman.

But Amy lifted a hand to halt Taylor's progress, and without saying a word she spun on her heel and disappeared into the women's powder room.

Rhys sighed heavily, let out a breathy expletive.

"Good night, Rhys."

"Taylor, I'm…"

But she didn't listen to the end. She turned and walked, quickly, toward the exit. She could see the headlights of her dad's rental car as it waited by the front door, saw him helping her mom in the passenger side. She went outside and was met by a frigid wall of arctic air. As she climbed into the backseat, she made a promise to herself.

Tomorrow she was going to stock up on groceries, wine and DVDs. Then she was going to go to Callum's house and as God as her witness, she wasn't going to venture out into the icy cold for the entire week. She was going to be a hermit. No work. No worrying about freezing her tail off.

And especially no men!

# CHAPTER SEVEN

TAYLOR ROLLED OVER and squinted at the sunshine coming through the bedroom window. Why hadn't she thought to close the blinds last night? Her first full day of vacation and she'd looked forward to sleeping in. She checked her watch. It was only eight-fifteen!

She burrowed into the warm blankets and closed her eyes. Maybe if she breathed deeply and relaxed, she could fall back asleep. But after just a few minutes she knew she might as well get up. She was awake for good now. Besides, just because she was up didn't mean she had to actually "do" anything. She could lounge around in her fuzzy pajamas, drink coffee, read one of the paperbacks she'd brought along.

Come to think of it, that sounded pretty darn good. Especially the coffee part. It was going to be awesome having some peace and quiet. No ringing phones, no buzzing email, no wedding plans and especially no Rhys Bullock to get in her way now that the wedding was over.

She was terribly afraid she was going to be bored to tears within forty-eight hours.

She rolled out of bed and shoved her feet into her favorite sheepskin slippers. On the way to the kitchen she pulled her hair back into a messy ponytail, anchoring it with a hair elastic that had been left on her wrist. While the coffee was brewing she turned up the thermostat and chafed her arms. Even the soft fleece of her winter PJs was no protection against the December cold.

She poured her first cup of coffee and, in keeping with the celebratory nature of the week, substituted her usual cream with the festive eggnog she found in the refrigerator.

She was halfway through the cup when she chanced a look out the front window. The mug paused inches away from her lips as she stared at a familiar brown truck. What on earth was Rhys doing here?

As she stared, the man in question came out of the barn. Even with the hat pulled low over his head, she'd recognize that long-legged stride in a heartbeat.

Irritation marred her idyllic morning and before she could think twice she flung open the door and stepped to the threshold. "What on earth are you doing here?"

His head snapped up and even though he was too far away for her to see his eyes, she felt the connection straight to her toes. Stupid girl. She should have stayed inside. Pretended she wasn't home. Not risen to the bait, except Rhys seemed to get on her last nerve without trying. She swallowed thickly, feeling quite foolish but standing her ground as a matter of pride. He hadn't actually baited her at all. He hadn't done *anything*.

Except show up.

"Well?" she persisted.

"I'm doing the chores." His tone said, *What does it look like I'm doing?*

She frowned. Callum had said at the reception that someone had looked after the chores and would continue to do so during his absence. He couldn't have meant Rhys. Rhys had been occupied with the wedding all day on Saturday. She would have noticed if he'd slipped away.

"Why?"

He came closer, walking across the yard as if he owned the damned place. "Well, I would suppose that would be because Callum hired me to."

"He did not. He hired someone else."

Rhys was only twenty feet away now. "He told you that?"

The wrinkle between her eyebrows deepened. Was that exactly what Callum had said? "He said he hired someone to do the chores during the wedding and during his absence, too."

Rhys stopped at the bottom of the steps to the veranda. "He hired Keith O'Brien on the day of the wedding, because I was in the wedding party."

Oh, hell.

"Why didn't he just hire him for the whole time, then?" She gave a huff that went up in a cloud of frosty air.

"Because Keith left yesterday to go to Fort McMurray to spend the holidays with his family."

"So you're…"

He shifted his weight to one hip, a move that made him look unbearably cocky. "Here for the week," he finished for her, his whole stance screaming *deal with it*.

And then he smiled, that slow grin climbing up his cheek that was at once maddening and somehow, at the same time, made her whole body go warm. His gaze slid over her pajamas. "Penguins? Seriously?" he asked.

Her mouth dropped open as she realized she was standing in the doorway still in her nightwear. Jolly skiing penguins danced down the light blue pant legs. The navy fleece top was plain except for one more penguin on the left breast.

She stepped back inside and slammed the door.

It was eerily quiet for the space of five seconds, and

then her heart beat with the sound of his boots, heavy on the steps, then two more as he crossed the narrow porch.

He was just on the other side of the door. Less than two feet away. He didn't even have the manners to knock. It was like he knew she was standing there waiting for him because he said, in a low voice, "Aren't you going to ask me in for coffee?"

"Humph!" she huffed, taking a step backward and fuming, her hands on her hips. As if. Presumptuous jerk!

"Come on, Taylor. It's cold out here. A man could use a hot cup of joe. I can smell it, for Pete's sake."

"I hear the coffee is good at the Wagon Wheel. Price is right, too."

Was that a chuckle she heard or had she just imagined it?

Softer now, he answered, "But the company isn't nearly as good."

She shouldn't be persuaded or softening toward him at all. He was used to getting his own way and she wouldn't oblige.

Then he said the words she never thought he'd ever utter. "I'm sorry about the other night."

Damn him.

She opened the door. "Come in then, before you let all the heat out. It's like an igloo in here."

He stepped inside, all six-feet-plus of him, even taller with his Stetson on. She wasn't used to seeing him this way—he looked like the real deal with his boots and hat and heavy jacket.

"You smell like the barn."

"My grandfather would say that's the smell of money."

"Money?"

He grinned. "Yeah. Anyway, sorry. Occupational hazard. Me smelling like the animals, that is. Though usually I smell like horses. They smell better than cows."

She didn't actually mind. While she wasn't interested in getting her own boots dirty, she did remember days on her uncle's farm. The smell was familiar and not too unpleasant.

"Just take off your boots if you're coming in for coffee."

While he toed off his boots she went into the kitchen to get a fresh cup. "What do you take in it?" she called out.

"Just cream, if you've got it," he answered, stepping inside the sunny kitchen.

She handed him the cup and then took a plastic container from a cupboard. "Are you hungry? Avery left a mountain of food, way more than I can eat in a week. This one is chocolate banana bread."

"I couldn't turn that down."

She cut several slices and put them on a plate. "Come on and sit down then."

Before Rhys sat down, he removed his hat and put it carefully on a nearby stool. She stared at him as he sat, pulled his chair in and reached for his coffee cup.

"What?" he asked, pausing with the cup halfway to his lips.

She shrugged. "You can be very annoying. But you have very good manners."

He laughed. "Blame my mom, I guess. So, enjoying your vacation?"

"Well, I've only officially been on holiday for a few hours. Yesterday I slept in, then spent last night hanging with my family. My mom and dad booked a place in Radium for the week and are coming back on the twenty-third for Christmas with Callum and the family. And Jack flew back to Montana this morning for a meeting of some sort. Lord only knows what deal he's cooking up this time.

Anyway, I'll probably enjoy my vacation for a few days. And then I'll start going stir-crazy."

Rhys reached for a slice of cake. "You strike me as one of those ambitious, type A personality people."

"You mean I'm driven? Yeah, I guess." She sighed. "I might as well 'fess up. I like being my own boss. Sometimes it's stressful because it's all on me, you know? But I don't like being told what to do."

He began coughing, crumbs catching in his throat. When he looked up at her again his eyes had watered and he was laughing. "Sorry. Stating the obvious shouldn't have been that funny."

"Hey, I know how you feel about it. You think I'm crazy. Most guys are intimidated by it."

"Most guys have a hard time with a woman who is smarter than they are."

She nibbled on her cake. "Careful, Rhys. That almost sounded like a compliment."

He laughed.

"So why aren't you?"

"What?" He tilted his head curiously. "What do you mean?"

"Why aren't you intimidated?"

He smiled again and the dark depths of his eyes warmed. "Oh. That's easy. I said that most guys have a problem with women who are smarter than they are…"

"And you're not most guys?"

"I never said you were smarter than me."

Without thinking, she kicked him under the table. Her toe hurt but he barely even flinched. "You are an infernal tease!"

"And you love it. Because you like a challenge."

How did he possibly know her so well? It was vastly unsettling.

She picked at her cake another moment or two before putting it down and facing him squarely. "What do you get out of this, Rhys? You and me. We're doing this dance and I'm not sure I see the point of it."

"You mean because we're so different and all?"

She lifted one shoulder. "That's only part of it. We both know that on Boxing Day I'm headed back to my life, so why bother?"

Taylor lifted her gaze to meet his. Something curled through her insides, hot and exciting. This simmering attraction they had going on made no sense. They were as different as water and air. But it was there just the same. This chemistry. Rhys Bullock was exciting. A small-town farmworker who hadn't the least bit of initiative and she couldn't stop thinking about him.

And yet, maybe the attraction stemmed from his confidence, a self-assurance that he knew who he was and was exactly where he wanted to be. While she didn't quite understand his choices, she had to admit she was the tiniest bit jealous that he'd gained that understanding while she was still trying to figure it all out. He didn't need accolades. Rhys Bullock had the confidence to know exactly who he was. He was comfortable in his own skin the way she'd never been.

"Why you?" He leaned forward a little. "Beyond the obvious fact that you're crazy hot and my temperature goes up a few degrees when you enter the room?"

She suppressed the urge to fan herself. "Rhys," she cautioned.

"You asked. And for what it's worth, I'm not looking for ties and commitments."

"Funny, because you're a pretty grounded guy. I'd kind of expect someone like you to be settled down with two-point-five kids and a dog, you know?"

Something flickered across his face. Pain? Anger? It disappeared as fast as it had arrived. "Start dating in a town this size and suddenly the town gets very, very small. Especially when things go wrong."

"Ah, like that old saying about…doing something where you eat."

He chuckled. "Yeah. Exactly like that. Look, you're a novelty, Taylor. An adventure. A safe one, because in a week's time you're going to be gone."

"So I'm a fling?"

His gaze sharpened. "A couple of kisses hardly constitutes a fling." He took a calm sip of his coffee. "You're an anomaly. You intrigue me. You know how to keep me on my toes."

"I'm glad I'm so amusing."

"Don't act like your feelings are hurt. We both know that the last thing you want is to be ordinary."

"Yeah, well, not everyone appreciates the alternative."

"That's because you highlight every single one of their flaws. You're not always right, but you're committed." He put his hand over hers. "That kind of commitment can take a toll. I can see you need the break."

"Don't be silly. I'm perfectly fine." She looked away, unexpectedly touched by his insight. How could he see what everyone else did not? The whole wedding she'd felt like she was losing her edge. Normally she'd be fired up and excited about the New Year's job, but instead she was dreading it. What on earth was wrong with her?

He squeezed her fingers. "Oh, Taylor, do you think I don't recognize burnout when I see it?"

She pulled her hand out of his grasp and sat back. "I'm not even thirty years old. I'm too young for burnout. Besides, what would you know about the pressures of running a business, with your 'put in your shift and go home' attitude?"

Silence rang in the kitchen for a few seconds. "Okay then." He pushed out the chair, stood and reached for his hat. "I should get going. I have some work out at Diamondback before coming back tonight to do the evening chores. Thanks for the coffee and cake."

She felt silly for going off on him like that—especially when he was right. At the same time, she didn't need to have it pointed out so bluntly. And the way he'd spoken so softly and squeezed her fingers? Argh! The sympathy had made her both angry and inexplicably tearful.

"Rhys, I…"

"Don't worry about it," he said evenly, going to the door and pulling on his boots. "I'll see you later."

He was gone before she had a chance to do anything. To take back the snippy words. She'd judged him, when she knew how it felt to be on the receiving end of such judgment.

She turned her back to the door and leaned against it, staring at the Christmas tree, fully decorated, standing in the corner. She couldn't even muster up a good dose of Christmas cheer.

Maybe Rhys was right. Maybe she was a little burned out. But she couldn't just take off and leave things. She had clients and commitments. She had employees who were counting on her for their livelihoods.

One week. Somehow she needed to recharge during this one week. With a heavy sigh, she went to the kitchen, retrieved her coffee and headed back to the bedroom. Coffee and a book in bed was as good a start as she could come up with right now.

Rhys was glad of the physical labor to keep him going. He'd been up early to head to Callum's for chores, then to

Diamondback, and now back at Callum's for the evening
milking. Plus he hadn't been sleeping well. He'd had Taylor on his mind. Something had happened between them as
they'd danced at the wedding. Then there was this morning in the kitchen. Lord, how he loved bantering with her.
She was quick and sharp and it was like a mating dance,
teasing then pulling away. Except that when it got a little
too honest she ran scared and the game was over.

It was fully dark outside as he finished tidying the milking parlor and went to the stainless sink to wash his hands.
What was she doing now? Having dinner? A bubble bath?
His fingers paused for a moment as that idea saturated
his consciousness, crowding out any other thoughts. He
imagined her long, pale limbs slick with water and soap,
tendrils of hair curling around her face from the steam
rising from the bath.

Not dating came with a price. It was like anything else,
he supposed. Deny yourself long enough, and temptation
was nearly too much to bear. And Taylor Shepard was
tempting indeed.

But he knew what she really thought of him. That fact
alone would keep him from knocking on her door again.

He shut off the tap. He knew a damn sight more about
running a business than she thought. His livelihood and his
mother's future were tied up in the diner. And he knew the
pain of failure, too. It wasn't even a matter of his savings.
It was a matter of trying to make things right for employees. Creditors. Putting himself last, and scraping the bottom of the barrel to keep from declaring bankruptcy. The
unfortunate part was that he hadn't just messed things up
for himself. It had messed up Sherry's life. And by exten-
sion, that of her kids.

He rubbed a hand over his face.

Never again. Punching a clock made for a lot less stress in the end. Taylor had no right to judge him for it.

He shoved his gloves on his hands and stepped outside into the cold. His feet crunched on the snow and he was nearly to his truck when the front door to the house opened.

"Rhys?"

He turned. His breath formed a frosty cloud as he saw her standing in the circle of porch light, her arms crossed around her middle to keep warm. Her long braid fell over her shoulder again, neat and tidy. Just once he'd like to take that braid apart with his fingers and sink his hands into the thick softness of her hair.

"You need something?" he called out.

There was a slight hesitation. "I… Do you want to come in for a few minutes?"

Hell, yes. Which was exactly why he shouldn't.

"It's been a long day, Taylor." He put his hand on the door handle.

"Oh."

That was all she said. Oh. But he was just stupid enough to hear disappointment in her voice as well as a recognition that it wasn't about the long day at all.

He closed his eyes briefly. This was very likely going to be a big mistake. Huge.

"Maybe just for a minute."

She waited for him, though she had to be nearly freezing by now. She stepped aside as he climbed the steps and went inside to where it was warm. He heard the door shut behind him and fought the urge to turn and kiss her. The desire to take her in his arms was so strong it was nearly overwhelming. Whatever differences they had, the connection between them was undeniable. It made things very complicated.

"Did you need something?" he asked. "I'm pretty handy if something needs fixing."

Taylor slid past him into the living room. He noticed now that the tree was lit up, a beautiful specimen glowing with white lights and red and silver decorations. A few presents were beneath it, wrapped in expensive foil paper with precise red and green bows. "Tree looks good."

"Avery did it before she left."

"I didn't notice it this morning."

She met his gaze and he'd swear she was shy. "It looks different when it's lit up."

"So do you."

He shouldn't have said it. Keeping his mouth shut had never been much of a problem for him before. But there was nothing usual about Taylor, was there? She provoked all kinds of unexpected responses.

"About this morning," she said quietly. "I asked you in tonight because I owe you an apology."

He didn't know what to say. Taylor didn't strike him as the type who apologized. Or at least—came right out and said it. He recalled the night of the rehearsal dinner, and how Taylor had told Martha that she'd underestimated her. She'd expressed the sentiment in a roundabout way when talking to Rhys. But not a full-on apology.

She came forward and looked up into his eyes. "I was overly sensitive this morning, and I said something I shouldn't have. It's not up to me to judge your life choices. Everyone makes their own decisions for their own reasons and their own happiness. I don't like it when people do it to me, and I shouldn't have done it to you."

He'd respected her intelligence before, admired how capable she was. But this was different. Taylor had a lot of pride. Making a point of saying she was sorry took humility.

"It's a bit of a hot-button with me," he admitted. "I tend to be a bit sensitive about it."

"Why?" She cocked her head a little, and the motion made him smile.

"It's a long and boring story," he said lightly.

"I bet it's not. Which is why you're not talking."

He couldn't help it, he smiled back. It might be easier to stay away if he didn't actually *like* her—but he did. She was straightforward and honest and made him laugh.

"Listen," she said, her voice soft. "I made cannelloni for dinner and there's enough to share. Have you eaten yet?"

Her lips had some sort of gloss on them that didn't add much color but made them look shiny and plump. He swallowed and dragged his gaze from her mouth back to her eyes. "Um, no."

"Take your boots off, then, and come inside. I promise that I won't poison you."

She said it with one eyebrow raised and her lips curved up in good humor.

He questioned the wisdom of hanging around, and then his stomach rumbled. As Taylor laughed, he took off his boots and left them by the door.

"Bathroom's through there, if you want to wash your hands. I'll dish stuff up."

When he arrived back in the kitchen, the scent of tomato and garlic seduced his nostrils. "That smells so good," he commented, pausing in the doorway.

She'd only left on the under-counter lighting, which cast a warm and intimate glow through the room. A cheery red and green plaid tablecloth covered the table, and she'd lit a couple of stubby candles in the middle.

Suddenly he wondered if he'd fallen very neatly into a trap. And if he actually minded so very much.

"Do you eat like this every night?" he asked casually, stepping into the room.

Taylor blushed. "Confession time, I guess. I planned dinner a little late because I was hoping you'd say yes." She placed a glass casserole dish on a hot mat on the table, then added a bowl of salad and a bottle of white wine. "I thought I'd have some wine, but if you'd prefer something else?"

"Wine is fine. Just a single glass, though." He was trying to decide what he felt about her admission that she'd planned dinner with him in mind. "You wanted me to come to dinner, and yet this morning you were pretty mad about seeing me here."

She hesitated, wine bottle in hand. "You complicate things for me. But I was here today at loose ends, no work to do, no one to talk to. It seemed lonely to eat here alone and I didn't want to go into town again."

"So I'm a chair filler."

"I decided to stop being annoyed with you and enjoy your company instead." She finished pouring the wine.

When she was seated he sat, and reached for the cloth napkin. "What do you do in Vancouver, then? I mean, at meal times?"

It occurred to him that maybe she didn't eat dinner alone. A beautiful woman like her. It was stupid to think she wasn't taken, wasn't it?

She took his plate and served him a helping of the stuffed pasta. "I usually pick up something on my way home. Or I get home so late I just grab something quick in front of the TV before hitting the bed."

"This pace must be a real change for you."

"A bit. Different, but not entirely unwelcome, actually."

She added salad to his plate and handed it back. "I'm very good at what I do, Rhys. I've built the business from the ground up and I'm proud of it. But sometimes I do wonder if I'm missing out on something."

He nearly bobbled his plate. "You're joking, right?"

"Not really." She sighed. "Of course, it's entirely possible I just need a vacation. I haven't taken any time off in a while."

"Since when?"

She served herself and picked up her fork. "Nearly three years. I took a very brief four-day trip to Hawaii. A few days of sun, sand and fruity drinks with umbrellas."

"Four days isn't much time."

"It was what I could manage. It's not like punching a clock and putting in for two weeks of holiday time."

"I know that." He tasted his first bite of cannelloni. Flavor exploded on his tongue—rich, creamy cheese, fresh basil, ripe tomatoes. "This is really good, Taylor. I never knew you could cook."

"My mom taught me."

"Your mom? Really? She strikes me as a society wife. Don't take that the wrong way," he warned. "Your mom seems very nice. But I kind of see her as someone who, I don't know, has things catered. Who outsources."

Taylor nodded. "Sometimes. But growing up—we weren't hurting for money, but we didn't have household staff, either. Mom kept us kids in line, helped with homework, decorated like Martha Stewart and cooked for her own dinner parties. At least until we were much older, and Dad's firm was on really solid ground." She speared a leaf of lettuce. "I learned a lot about my event planning biz from my Mom. She's an organizational whiz."

"Hmm," he mused. "Seems we have something in common after all. While my old man was out taking care of business, my mom held down the fort for me and my brother. I've never met another woman who could make something out of nothing. She worked at the diner during the day, but she was always helping my dad with his ventures."

"What did he do?"

Rhys shrugged. "What didn't he do? He sold insurance for a while, a two-man operation here in Cadence Creek. When that didn't fly, he was a sales rep for some office supply company, traveling all around Alberta. He sold used cars after that if I remember right."

And a bunch of other jobs and schemes that had taken him away more than he was home, and never panned out as he'd hoped. Time and again he'd moved on to something newer and shinier, and financially they'd gone further and further in the hole.

"Sounds industrious," Taylor commented easily, reaching for the wine and topping up her glass.

"Yeah, he was a real go-getter," Rhys agreed, trying very hard to keep the bitterness out of his voice and not doing such a great job. He'd loved his dad but the legacy he'd left behind wasn't the greatest.

She put the bottle down carefully and frowned. "You aren't happy about that, are you?"

He focused on his pasta. "Dad was full of bright ideas and a little fuzzier on the execution. It was my mom who kept her feet on the ground and really provided for us kids. Problem was, every time Dad moved on to something better, he usually left some damage in his wake. Debts he couldn't pay and employees out of a job. It didn't get him the greatest goodwill here, you know? We were lucky that everyone loved my mom. Otherwise maybe we would've been run out of Cadence Creek."

"Surely it wasn't that bad," Taylor said, smiling.

"I know I wasn't supposed to hear, but one day I was passing by the hardware store and I heard these guys outside talking. They called him 'Big Man Bullock' and not in a nice way."

He couldn't look at her. For some reason that single memory had shaped him so much more than any other from his childhood, good and bad. In that moment he'd decided he would never be like his father. Never. Only for a while he had been. He'd let so many people down. It was his biggest regret.

"So that's why you don't want to own your own business? You don't want to fail like your dad did?"

Rhys nodded and stabbed some salad with his fork. "That's exactly why. You said it yourself—you're responsible and can't just take off on a whim. You have other people relying on you." His throat tightened and he cleared the lump away. "You mess up and it's other lives you're affecting, not just your own. I would never want anyone to speak about me the way they were speaking about him that day. My brother and I both left home after high school. It was two less mouths for my mom to try to feed, to be honest."

Silence hummed through the kitchen. It hadn't turned out to be a very pleasant conversation after all. All it had done was stir up things he'd rather forget.

"Well," she said softly. "You're back in Cadence Creek now, and the diner is the heart of this town, and your mom is fabulous. You're steady and reliable, Rhys. There are worse things." She patted his hand. "You don't have to live down your father's reputation. That was his, not yours. You came back to help your mom. Not everyone would do that."

She seemed so sure that she said the right thing as she smiled again and turned back to her meal.

Rhys's appetite, though, shriveled away to nothing as he picked at his food. She had no idea, none at all. Yes, he'd come back when his father died because Martha had needed him. And he'd gone against his instincts and done what she'd asked of him because she was his mother and he couldn't stand the thought of disappointing one more person. He wondered what Taylor would say if she knew he'd gone from one bad venture into immediately investing in another?

He'd come back to Cadence Creek with his tail between his legs. He was more like his old man than anyone knew.

And he hated it.

# CHAPTER EIGHT

THEY RETIRED TO the living room after dinner. Taylor made coffee and insisted they leave the dishes. She'd need something to keep her busy tomorrow anyway. Besides, Rhys had turned surprisingly quiet. She wondered what that was about.

"You okay?" she asked, offering him a shortbread cookie.

"Sure, why wouldn't I be?" he responded, taking one from the plate.

"I don't know. You got quiet all of a sudden. After we talked about your dad."

She looked over at him. Despite his relaxed pose, his jaw was tight. "Rhys," she said gently, "did you feel like it was your job to look after everyone after he died?"

"Why are we talking about this?" He shoved the cookie in his mouth, the buttery crumbs preventing him from saying more. But Taylor waited. Waited for him to chew and swallow and wash it down with a sip of coffee.

"Because," she finally answered, "it seems to me you could use a friend. And that maybe, since I'm not from Cadence Creek, I might be a logical choice."

Confusion cluttered his eyes as they met hers. "Do I strike you as the confiding type?"

She smiled. "Maybe you could make an exception. This once."

He seemed to debate for a while. Taylor pulled her knees up toward her chin and sank deeper into the cushions of the sofa, cradling her cup in her hands. How long had it been since she'd spent an evening like this, with a warm cuppa in front of a glowing tree? No files open, no cell phone ringing. Just a rugged cowboy and coffee and cookies.

Simple. And maybe it would bore her in a couple of days, but right now it was quite heavenly.

"I had my own business once," he confided, staring into his cup. "I had an office based in Rocky Mountain House. I'd wanted to start something away from Cadence Creek, away from my dad's reputation. I was determined to make a go of it, the way he'd never been able to."

She got a sinking feeling about where this was headed. "What kind of business?"

"Feed supplements," he said simply. "I had an office, a couple of office staff and a few reps other than myself who traveled the area to the various ranches. For a while it was okay. Then I started losing money. It got to a point where I wasn't even drawing a salary, just so I could pay my staff. I fell behind on the office rent and we shifted it to run from my house."

His face took on a distant look for a few seconds, but then he gave his head a little shake and it cleared. "It wasn't long before I knew I had to shut it down or declare bankruptcy. Since I didn't want the mark on my credit rating, I closed my doors. My final accounts owing paid my back rent and wages and I got a job as a ranch hand. I got to bring home a paycheck while my employees had to file for Employment Insurance since I laid them off. They had families. Little kids. Mortgages."

"But surely they didn't blame you!"

He shrugged, but the distant look was back. "A million times I went over what I might have done differently, to manage it better. The jobs I took—working the ranches I used to serve—kept a roof over my head. When my dad died, I quit. Sold the house and moved back here to help my mom."

He opened his mouth and then suddenly shut it again.

Intrigued, she unfolded her legs and sat forward. "What were you going to say?"

"Nothing," he answered, reaching for another cookie from the plate on the coffee table.

"You were going to say something and stopped." She frowned. There was more to this story, wasn't there? Something he didn't want to talk about. Something about coming home.

"You're nosy, you know that?"

She grinned. "I'm a woman. We don't let anything drop."

"You're telling me." He sighed. "Look, let's just say I wasn't a big fan of my mother buying the diner. Running a small business is tough and she's worked hard her whole life. She's over fifty now and working harder than ever."

"You wished she had stuck with working her shift and going home at the end of the day. Leaving the stress behind."

"Yes."

She understood. He'd felt terrible when his own business had failed. He'd seen the bad reaction from people when his dad had failed. He wanted to spare his mother any or all of that. She got it. She even admired him for his protective streak.

"Some people aren't satisfied with that, Rhys. I wasn't. I wanted to build something. I wanted to know I'd done it and done it on my own. But I understand where you're coming from. I'm responsible for my employees, too. It's a big responsibility, not just financially but morally. At least for most people, I think, and if not it should be. People need to look at their employees like people and not numbers. Even if I wanted to make a change, I know I'm not the only one to consider."

"You thinking of changing?"

The question stirred something uncomfortable inside her. "Nah, not really. Like I said—I'm just overdue for a break, that's all."

She liked it better when they were talking about him. She put her hand on his knee. "You help her a lot, don't you? Around the diner. Fixing things and whatever needs to be done."

He looked away. "Of course I do."

"And you don't get paid."

He hesitated. "I'm not on the payroll, no," he said.

"You're a good man, Rhys."

She meant it. The things he said made perfect sense and only served to complicate her thoughts even more. She was enjoying the downtime too much. She hadn't truly loved the work for a while now, and she was finally admitting it to herself. Sometimes it felt pointless and frivolous, but every time she considered saying it out loud, she heard her father's voice proclaiming that very thing. She was just stubborn enough to not let him be right. Damn the Shepard pride.

Every time she thought about making a change, she was plagued by the realization that it wasn't just her who would be affected. Her employees needed wages. Her landlord was counting on her rent. Suppliers, caterers... All of that would trickle down, wouldn't it? Walking away would be just about the most selfish thing she could do.

They were quiet for a few minutes, until Rhys finally spoke up. "This business of yours, you've had to fight hard for respect, haven't you?"

"I'm sorry?"

"With your family. Your father's hugely successful, Jack's running what can only be considered an empire and Callum, while way more low-key, has fulfilled the family requirement for a spouse and grandchild. Must be hard standing next to that yardstick."

"I'm doing just fine, thank you." Indignation burned its way to her stomach, making it clench. She wanted to be able to tell him he was dead wrong. Problem was she couldn't.

"Hey, you don't have to tell me that. You're one of the most capable women I've ever met. But seeing your family at the rehearsal dinner, I got the feeling that you had to work just a little bit harder for the same recognition."

"You're a guy. You're not supposed to notice stuff like that."

She put her cup down on the table and folded her hands in her lap.

His voice was low and intimate as he replied, "I only noticed because I can't seem to take my eyes off you whenever you're around."

And there it was. The acknowledgment of whatever this was. Attraction. Curiosity. Carnality.

"I thought we weren't going to do this," she said softly. She kept her hands folded tightly in her lap to keep them from going where they wanted to go—on him. "I'm only here for a few days."

"Then there's no danger. We both know what's what. We're going in with our eyes wide open."

She looked up at him and was caught in his hot, magnetic gaze.

"Since that night in my truck, I can't stop thinking about you," he murmured, reaching out and tucking a piece of hair behind her ear. "I've tried. God knows I've tried." His fingers grazed her cheek and before she could reconsider, she leaned into the touch, the feel of his rough, strong hand against the sensitive skin of her face.

"Are you seducing me, Rhys?" His thumb toyed with her lower lip and her eyes drifted closed.

"With any luck." He moved closer, leaning forward slightly so she began to recline against the cushions. "We're adults," he stated. "We're both wondering. It doesn't have to go any deeper than that."

Tentatively she lifted her hand and touched his face. "Usually I'm the confident one who goes after what she wants."

He smiled a little, his gaze dropping to her lips. "You don't want this? I could have sworn you did."

"I didn't say that," she whispered, sliding deeper into the cushions.

"That's what I thought." His voice was husky now, shivering along her nerve endings. He leaned closer until he was less than a breath away.

The first kiss was gentle, soft, a question. When she answered it his muscles relaxed beneath her hand and he pressed his mouth more firmly against hers. Her pulse quickened, her blood racing as he opened his mouth and invited something darker, more persuasive. His hand cupped her breast. Her fingers toyed with the buttons of his shirt. He sat up and stripped it off, leaving him in just a T-shirt. She expected him to reach for the hem of her sweater but instead he took it slow, braced himself over top of her and kissed her again. His lips slid along her jaw to her ear, making goose bumps pop out over her skin and a gasp escape her throat.

"I'm in no rush," he whispered just before he took her lips again, and they kissed, and kissed, and kissed until nothing else in the world existed.

Taylor's entire body hummed like a plucked string. Rhys felt so good, tasted so good, and it had been too long since she'd felt this close to anyone. Yearning and desire were overwhelming, and his leisurely approach had primed her nearly to the breaking point. The words asking him to stay were sitting on her lips when he softened his kiss, gently kissed the tip of her nose, and got up off the sofa.

She felt strangely cold and empty without his weight pressing upon her. Maybe he was going to hold out his hand and lead her down the hall, which would suit her just fine. If he could kiss like that, she would only imagine his lovemaking would be spectacular and…thorough. She swallowed roughly at the thought and got up, ready to take it to the next step.

Except he was reaching for his coat.

Her stomach dropped to her feet while heat rushed to her face. "What…? I mean where…?" She cleared her throat, crossed her arms around her middle, feeling suddenly awkward. "Did I do something wrong?"

He shoved his arms into the sleeves but wouldn't meet her gaze. "Not at all. It's just getting late. I should go."

She wasn't at all sure of herself but she lifted her chin and said the words on her mind anyway. "For a minute there it kind of looked like you weren't going to be leaving."

For a second his hand paused on the tab of the zipper and the air in the room was electric. But then he zipped his coat the rest of the way up. "I don't want to take things too fast, that's all."

Too fast? Good Lord, she was leaving in a matter of days and he was the one who'd said he couldn't stop thinking about her. She wasn't innocent. She knew where this sort of make-out session was headed. And he was putting on the brakes without so much as a warning? Just when she thought she understood him, he did something else that made her wonder who the heck he was.

"What happened to 'we're both grown-ups'?"

Now he had his boots on. One moment they were sprawled on the couch and the next he couldn't get out of there fast enough. What in heaven's name had she done wrong?

"Let me take a rain check, okay?"

This night was getting stranger by the minute. "Rhys?"

He took a step forward and pressed a kiss to her forehead. "It's fine, I promise. I'll see you tomorrow."

Right. Because he'd be here twice. Great.

Still dumbfounded, she heard him say, "Thanks for dinner." Before she could wrap her head around what was going on he was out the door and headed for his truck. He didn't even let it warm up, just got in, started it up and headed out the driveway to the road.

What had just happened?

In a daze she gathered up the cups and the plate of cookies and took them to the kitchen. She expended her pent-up energy by washing the dishes and tidying the supper mess, and then went back to the living room to turn off the Christmas lights, still reeling from his abrupt change of mood.

His cotton shirt was still lying on the floor in a crumpled heap. He'd been in such a hurry to leave he'd forgotten to pick it up. She lifted it from the floor and pressed it to her nose. It smelled of soap and man and aftershave, a spicy, masculine scent that, thanks to the evening's activities, now elicited a physical response in her. Want. Need. Desire.

She stared at it while she brushed her teeth and washed her face. And when she went to bed, she left the penguin pajamas on the chair and instead slid into Rhys's soft shirt.

Having the material whisper against her body was the closest she was going to get to Rhys. At least tonight!

But the week wasn't over yet. And she was pretty sure he owed her an explanation.

Rather than drive into Edmonton to shop, Taylor decided to explore the Cadence Creek stores for Christmas gifts. After her conversation with Rhys about running a small business, she felt the right thing to do was to buy local and support the townspeople who made their livelihood here. For Avery and Callum, she bought a beautiful evergreen centerpiece for their table from Foothills Floral. The craft store sold not just yarn but items on consignment, and she bought Nell a gorgeous quilt in pink and blue with patchwork bunnies in each square. The men were a little harder to buy for, but she ended up being delighted at the silversmith, where she purchased both her father and Jack new tie clips and cuff links, the intricate design a testament to the artist's talents.

While she was browsing the handcrafted jewelry, a particular display caught her eye. Beautiful hammered and sculpted silver pendants on sterling chains shone in the morning sunlight. She picked one up, let the weight of it sit on her fingers, a delicate horseshoe with tiny, precise holes where nails would go. She smiled to herself, remembering asking for a lucky horseshoe at the wedding and how Rhys had informed her that a rabbit's foot got rubbed for luck.

He'd amused her, even then when she'd been her most stressed.

She let the pendant go and moved on. She still had her mother's gift to buy and then the groceries for Christmas dinner.

At the drugstore she picked up a gift set of her mother's favorite scent, and hit the grocery store for the turkey and vegetables needed for dinner, loading everything in the trunk of her car. She must have done okay, because the bags nearly filled it to capacity.

The last stop was the bakery, where she figured she could grab something sweet and Christmassy for the holiday dinner and maybe sit and have a coffee and a piece of cake or something.

Anything to avoid going to the Wagon Wheel. She was too afraid of running into Rhys, and she had no idea what to say to him. Sleep had been a long time coming last night. This morning he'd been by early to do the chores, and was already gone when she'd finally crawled out of bed.

The first thing she noticed as she went inside was the welcoming heat. Then it was the smells—rising bread and spices and chocolate and vanilla all mingled together. Browsing the display, she immediately decided on a rich stollen, her mouth watering at the sight of the sugar-dusted marzipan bread. She also ordered a traditional Christmas pudding which came with a container of sauce and instructions for adding brandy.

They were going to have a traditional Christmas dinner, with all of them together for the first time in as long as Taylor could remember.

She was just sitting down to a cup of salted caramel hot chocolate and a piece of cherry strudel when Angela Diamond came in, her cheeks flushed from the cold. She spotted Taylor right away and came over, chafing her hands together and smiling. "Well, hello! I didn't expect to meet you in here this morning."

"I thought I'd do a little shopping before the honeymooners get back. It's hungry work."

"Amen. I like to cook but my talents can't compare to the goodies in here. Do you mind?" She gestured to the chair across from Taylor.

"Of course not! I'd love the company."

Angela sat and took off her gloves. "God, it's cold. I wish a Chinook would blow through and warm things up a bit. What are you having? It looks good."

Taylor laughed. Angela was quite chipper this morning. "Hot chocolate and strudel."

"I'll be right back. I need something decadent."

Angela returned shortly with a cup of chocolate and a plate holding an enormous piece of carrot cake. "I'll tell you a secret," she confided, leaning forward. "Since Avery joined forces with Jean, the quality has gone way up. The specialty in here used to be bread and that's it. Now it's everything."

"I bought a Christmas pudding," Taylor admitted. "It's the first time we've all been together in a long time. I'm thinking turkey and stuffing and the whole works this Christmas." She took a sip of her hot chocolate.

"When are Callum and Avery back?"

"The afternoon of the twenty-third."

"And when do you head back to Vancouver?"

Taylor sighed. "Boxing Day."

Angela put a piece of cake on her fork. "Sounds to me like you're not too excited about it." She popped the cake in her mouth.

"I should be. I've got a ton of work to do and not much time to do it in. Big New Year's party happening. I've left most of the work to my assistant. She's very capable, thank goodness."

"You're not enjoying the project?"

Taylor brushed a flake of strudel pastry off her sweater. "I've been doing this for a while now. When I started, some of the unorthodox requests I got were exciting. And I really liked being creative and working under the gun. But lately—"

She broke off. She really *was* having doubts, wasn't she? And then there was the conversation with Rhys last night. How could she even flirt with the idea of walking away when so many people depended on her?

"Lately what?" Angela asked.

"I think I'm getting jaded or something. Most of the events seem so extravagant and pointless."

"You're looking to create something meaningful."

Taylor put down her mug. She'd never quite thought of it that way. "I suppose I am. This party on New Year's Eve? It's just some rock star throwing cash around and showing off, you know? And it'll be fun and probably make some entertainment news and then it'll be gone twenty-four hours later and no one will remember. Weeks of planning and thousands of dollars for what?" She sighed. "It lasts for a few hours and then it's gone like that." She snapped her fingers.

For a minute the women nibbled at their treats. Then Angela spoke up. "You don't have to give up the business to make a change. Maybe you just need to switch the focus."

"What do you mean?"

Angela shrugged easily, but Taylor knew a sharp mind at work when she saw one. Angela had single-handedly started her own foundation for helping battered women. She was no lightweight in the brains or in the work department, and Taylor knew it would be smart to pay attention to what Angela said.

"Say, for instance, there's a non-profit looking to hold a fund-raiser. The board of this foundation is pretty on the ball, but organizing social events is not where their strongest talent lies."

"You're talking about the Butterfly Foundation."

Angela smiled. "Well, yes, in a way. But we're small.

We wouldn't have enough work to keep you going. But there's the housing organization that helped build Stu Dickinson's home after they lost their things in a fire. And many others in any part of the country you choose. I think you'd be very good at it, Taylor."

The idea was interesting, and to Taylor's surprise she didn't dismiss it right away. That told her something.

Angela put down her fork. "Look, I was a social worker before I started Butterfly House and the foundation. I was good at my job but I was frustrated, too, especially as time went on. I'm still using much the same skill set, but I finally started doing something I'm really passionate about—helping abused women get back on their feet. Anyway, think about it. We're going to be planning something for later this spring. I'll give you first crack at the job if you want it. Get your feet wet."

"Thanks," Taylor replied, her mind spinning. "But I can't just up and walk away from what I've built, you know?" It certainly wasn't as easy as putting in two weeks' notice and going on her way.

"Of course." Angela checked her watch. "And I've got to go. I'm picking my son up from a play date in twenty minutes. But I'm really glad we ran into each other."

"Me, too."

Angela got up and slid her gloves back over her fingers. "And merry Christmas, Taylor. To you and your family, if I don't see you again."

"You, too. Say hi to Molly and Clara for me."

After Angela was gone, Taylor sat at the table, her hot chocolate forgotten. Angela had been so right. What was missing from Taylor's job was meaning. It was why she'd been so flustered about things not being perfect at the wedding—it had been important to her on a personal level.

Right now she did a job because she was paid good

money to do so. And she had enjoyed the challenges that went along with the position of being sought after. But at the end of the day, all she had left was the satisfaction of a challenge met. She hadn't given anything back. What Angela suggested, an event like that had the power to make ripples throughout communities, a difference in peoples' lives. It would matter; last longer than a single night. Wouldn't that be amazing?

And then Taylor thought of her staff, and her leases, and the fact that they, too, had lives, and bills to pay.

Maybe Rhys was on to something after all. Maybe working nine-to-five was way easier. He'd just learned his lesson faster than Taylor, that was all.

But then, he'd been forced to shut down his company. As Taylor stood and put on her coat again, she let out a long breath. She didn't have that worry. Her company was well into the black. And as long as they stayed there, she was sure she could find an answer.

# CHAPTER NINE

RHYS HOVERED AT the door to the barn, wanting to go to the house, but hesitating just the same. He'd been an idiot last night. It had all been going great. He hadn't even minded talking about the past so much. Maybe Taylor was right. She was an outsider and completely impartial, and it made a difference. She certainly hadn't judged.

But it hadn't just been about talking. Oh, no. Every time he was around her the sensible, cautious part of his brain shut off. The physical attraction was so strong and sitting alone, in front of the tree, with the cozy lighting and the way her eyes shone and her hair smelled…

Yep. He was an idiot. There'd been no room for logic. Just justification for doing what he wanted rather than what was smart.

He'd been ready to take it to the next level when warning bells had gone off in his head. At first it was knowing that he was on the verge of losing control and pushing his advantage, which he made a practice of never doing. Taylor wasn't as ready as she thought she was. It was in the sweetness of her kiss, the tentative way she touched him, the vulnerable look in her eyes. And just like the horses he worked with, he knew she had to be sure. She needed to come to him.

Except she hadn't, not this morning. He'd hung around

for a while, hoping to see her at the window or door, but nothing, and he'd been due for work at Diamondback and couldn't stay forever. Now he'd finished the evening chores and the lights were glowing at the house and still there was no sign of her. His hasty exit had probably hurt her feelings, he realized.

But there'd been a second issue, too, and one equally if not more important. He'd known exactly where things were headed and abruptly realized he had absolutely no protection. He was a guy who was generally ready for any eventuality, and he should have had a clue after the way the passion had exploded between them while parked in his truck. But he hadn't. And if he'd let things go any further, he might have been very irresponsible. Might have lost his head and let his body override his brain. He wanted to think he wouldn't, but he wasn't exactly objective when it came to Taylor, for some reason.

So he'd pulled the pin and gotten out. And not exactly gracefully.

It wouldn't happen again. A condom packet was nestled in his back pocket. He'd driven out to the gas station on the highway to buy it, because this town was so damn small that it would be just his luck that he'd be spotted at the drugstore and the rumors would start.

He told himself that the condom was just a contingency plan. He could get in his truck and go back home, or…

Resolutely he left the barn and latched the door behind him, and with his heart beating madly, took long strides to the house. He made no secret of his approach, his boots thumping on the steps and he knocked firmly on the door. Whether this went further or ended, some decisions were going to be made right now. He had to stop thinking of her like some nervous, inexperienced filly, afraid of her own shadow. Taylor Shepard was the most self-assured, confident woman he'd ever met. She knew her own mind.

The door opened and anything he'd considered saying died on his lips.

She looked stunning. She'd left her hair down, the dark mass of it falling in waves past her shoulders. Her jeans hugged her hips and legs like a second skin and the red V-neck shirt was molded to her breasts, clinging to her ribs and giving her the most delicious curves he'd ever seen.

"It's about time you got here," she said softly, holding open the door.

He didn't need any other invitation. He stepped inside and, with his gaze locked with hers, kicked the door shut with his foot. She opened her lips to say something but he caught her around the waist and kissed her, erasing any words she might have uttered. When he needed to come up for air, he released her long enough to shed his jacket and boots.

"Hello to you, too," she said, her voice rich and seductive. "Not wasting any time, I see."

"I'm done wasting time. Aren't you?"

The moment paused as her gaze held his. "I think I am, yes."

It was all the encouragement he needed. As a saucy grin climbed her cheek, he chuckled. And then he reached out, threw her over his shoulder in a fireman carry and headed for the hallway as her laughter echoed off the walls.

It was still dark in the bedroom but Taylor's eyes had adjusted to it and she could see shadows cast by the moonlight streaming through the cracks in the blinds. The dark figure of the dresser, a small chair, a laundry basket.

Rhys, snuggled under the covers beside her, his hair flattened on one side where he'd rested against the pillow.

Her heart slammed against her ribs just looking at him. Not in her wildest dreams had she been prepared for last night. Any impression she'd had of him as…well, she supposed ordinary was as good a word as any…was completely false. He'd been an exciting lover, from the way he'd taken control and carried her to the bedroom, to how he'd managed to scatter their clothes in seconds, to how he'd expertly made love to her.

She swallowed thickly. It had been more than exciting. It had been much, much more. He'd been physical yet gentle, fun yet serious, and he'd made her feel things she'd never felt before in her life. She'd felt beautiful. Unstoppable. Completely satisfied. And in the end, rather than skedaddling home as she expected, he'd pulled up the covers and tucked her securely against him.

She'd felt cherished. More than she'd ever imagined, Rhys Bullock was turning out to be someone very, very amazing. Someone who might actually have the power to chase away some of the ghosts of the past.

His lashes flickered and his lips curved the tiniest bit. "You're staring at me, aren't you?"

Heat climbed her cheeks but she braced up on her elbow and rested her jaw on her hand. "Maybe."

"I can't blame you. I'm really quite handsome."

Her smile grew. Had she really ever thought him plain and unremarkable? There was a humor in the way he set his mouth, the way his eyes glowed that set him apart, wasn't there? And then there was his body. She'd had a good look at it now—all of it. There was nothing plain about Rhys.

"Your ego knows no bounds."

"I'm feeling really relaxed this morning." He opened his eyes. "Why do you suppose that is?"

She dropped her gaze for a moment. "Rhys…" she said shyly.

"Is it okay I stayed all night?"

Her gaze lifted. "Of course it is." She preferred it. Things had happened so quickly. They'd touched and combusted. At least by him staying she didn't get the feeling it was only about the sex.

Which was troubling because there really couldn't be anything more to it, could there?

His hand grazed her hip, sliding beneath the soft sheets. "It was good."

She smiled, bashful again because they were still naked beneath the covers. "Yeah, it was."

For a few minutes his hand lightly stroked and silence filled the room. Taylor wished she could abandon all her common sense and simply slide into his embrace again, but being impulsive wasn't really her way. Last night she'd waited for him. She'd wanted this. But now? It was how to go on from this moment that stopped her up.

"Listen, Rhys…"

"I know what you're going to say." His voice was husky-soft in the dark. "You're going to say there's only the weekend left and Callum and Avery will be back and you'll be going to Vancouver."

Nervousness crawled through her belly. "Yeah, I was going to say that."

"Since we're both aware of that, the way I see it we have one of two choices."

She couldn't help but smile the tiniest bit. Rhys was used to being in charge. Even now, he was taking control of the situation. When they'd first met it had grated on her last nerve. But now not so much. It was kind of endearing.

"Which are?" she asked.

"Well, I could get out of bed and get dressed and do the

chores and we could say that this is it. No sense going on with something that's going to end in a few days anyway."

"That sounds like a very sensible approach."

"Thank you."

She might have believed him, except his fingers started kneading the soft part of her hip. She swallowed, trying to keep from rolling into the caress. "And the second?"

"I'm glad you asked. The second option, of course, is that we enjoy this for however long it lasts and go our inevitable separate ways with the memory of the best Christmas ever."

"Not as sensible, but it sounds like a lot more fun."

"Great minds think alike."

The smile slid from her face as she turned serious, just for a moment. "Do you think it's possible to do that?" she whispered.

Dark eyes delved into hers. "I'm not ready to say goodbye yet. I don't see as we have much choice."

She slid closer to him until they were snuggled close together, skin to skin. She hadn't counted on someone like Rhys. She'd thought she'd come here, watch her brother get married, recharge, go back to her life. Instead she was…

She blinked, hoping he didn't notice the sudden moisture in her eyes. She would never say it out loud. Couldn't. But the truth was, she suspected she was falling in love. She recognized the rush. The fear. The exhilaration. Something like that only happened once in a while, and it had been a long, long time for Taylor. It wasn't just sex. She had real feelings for Rhys. Saying goodbye wasn't going to be easy.

"Can I ask you something?"

"Sure." He, too, braced up on an elbow, more awake now.

"Why did you leave so fast the other night?"

"Oh, that." He smiled, but it had a self-deprecating tilt to it that she thought was adorable. "Truth is, things were happening really fast. And you caught me unprepared."

That was it? Birth control? She suppressed a giggle, but a squeak came out anyway. "You could have just said that," she chided. "Instead of rushing out like you couldn't stand being near me another moment."

"Is that what you thought?" His head came off his hand.

"Maybe."

He leaned forward and kissed her lightly. "Nothing could be further from the truth. If I was in a hurry, it was because I was in danger of not caring if I had a condom or not."

Her heart turned over. She wondered if he realized how much he truly tried to protect those around him.

"Now, as much as I'd like to repeat last night's performance, I've got cows that need to be milked," Rhys said quietly.

"And then what?" She lifted her chin and looked into his eyes. The dark light was turning grayer as the night melted into day, highlighting his features more clearly.

"It's Saturday. I'm not due at Diamondback. I'm not expected anywhere, as a matter of fact."

"Then come back in for breakfast," she invited. "I'll make something good."

"You got it." He slid out of bed and she watched as he pulled on jeans and a T-shirt. He turned and gave her a quick kiss. "Look, I'll be a while. Go back to sleep."

"Okay."

He was at the doorway when he turned and looked back at her. "You look good like that," he said softly, and disappeared around the corner while her heart gave a little flutter of pleasure.

They had the weekend. She rather suspected a weekend wouldn't be nearly enough.

After breakfast Rhys went back home to shower and grab fresh clothing. In his absence Taylor also showered and did her hair and put on fresh makeup. She vacuumed the rugs and tidied the kitchen and wondered if he'd bring his things to stay the night. When he arrived again midmorning, he carried a bag with him containing extra clothes and toiletries.

Seeing the black case brought things into rather clear perspective. Their intentions were obvious. There was no need for either of them to leave the house now.

After a rather pleasurable "welcome back" interlude, they spent the rest of the day together. Rhys helped Taylor wrap the presents she'd bought the day before, cutting tape, tying ribbon and sticking a red and gold bow on top of her head while making a lewd suggestion. She made soup and grilled cheese and the long awaited Chinook blew in, raising the temperature and softening the snow. They went outside and built a snowman, complete with stick arms, a carrot for a nose, and rocks for the eyes and mouth. That event turned into a snowball fight, which turned into a wrestling match, which ended with the two of them in a long, hot shower to ward off any damp chill.

He did chores. She made dinner. They curled up in front of the television to watch a broadcast of White Christmas while Rhys complained of actors feeling the need to sing everything and Taylor did a fair impression of the "Sisters" song. And when it was time, they went together to Taylor's room.

By Monday morning Taylor's nerves were shredded. The weekend had been nothing short of blissful but in a few hours Callum would be home and her time with Rhys would be over. There was no question in her mind—her feelings for Rhys were real.

But what hope did they have? He would never be happy living in a city like Vancouver, and she could tell by the way he spoke and how he'd acted since they'd met that he wanted to stay close to his mother to look after her. She realized now that his desire to hold a steady job rather than being the boss was all about taking care of his family. What she'd initially seen as complacency was actually selfless and noble. From what she could gather, his need to care for Martha was, in part, a way to make up for the instability in her past. He'd hold things together the way his father never had—no matter how well-intentioned.

Despite Angela's ideas, Taylor couldn't see any way to avoid going home either. She had commitments and responsibilities at *Exclusive!* This was nothing new. She just hadn't expected that even the thought of leaving him would cause the ache she was feeling in her chest right now.

"Hey," he said softly, coming up behind her. She was standing at the kitchen window, looking out over the fields. "You look like you're thinking hard."

"Just sad the weekend's over, that's all."

"Me, too."

She turned to embrace him and noticed his bag by the kitchen door. "You're leaving already?"

"It's Monday. I'm due back at Diamondback, remember? I should have been there an hour ago."

Right. His job. Time hadn't stood still, had it? "You're working today?"

"And tomorrow."

Emptiness opened up inside her. This was really it then. She might not even see him again before her flight out on the twenty-sixth.

"Rhys…"

"Don't," he said firmly. "We both knew what this was from the start."

Dread of losing him sparked a touch of anger. Was she so easy to forget? So easy to leave—again? "And you're okay with that? Just a couple of days of hokey pokey and see you later, it's been fun?"

He gripped her upper arms with strong fingers. "We weren't going to do this, remember?"

"Do what?"

"Get involved."

"I am involved. Up to my neck, as it happens."

"Taylor."

He let go and stepped back, his dark eyes clouded with confusion. He ran a hand through his hair. "I should never have come back. I should have left well enough alone."

"You didn't. We didn't. I don't know how to say good-bye gracefully, Rhys."

To her chagrin she realized tears were running down her face. She swiped them away quickly. "Dammit," she muttered.

He came closer, looked down at her with a tenderness in his eyes that nearly tore her apart. "Hey, we both knew it would come to this. My life's here. Yours is there. You have *Exclusive!* to run."

Yes, yes, the damn business. When had she started resenting it so much? Even a quick check of her email on her phone this morning had made her blood pressure spike. She couldn't ignore reality forever. Didn't mean it didn't stink, though.

"Thanks for the reminder." She stepped back, wished she had something to occupy her hands right now.

Rhys frowned. "Look, Taylor, we both know you're competitive and a bit of a perfectionist. I like those things

about you. I really do. But I also know that the drive and
determination that made you so successful is going to
keep you in Vancouver until you set out to do what you've
wanted to achieve."

"Even if what I'm doing isn't making me happy?"

It was the first time she'd come right out and said it.

His frown deepened. "The only person who can decide
that is you. But I'll caution you right now. Letting go of
that goal isn't easy. There are a lot of things to accept. And
I'm not sure you'd be happy walking away."

"And if I did walk away, would you be here waiting?"

Alarm crossed his features. She had her answer before
he ever opened his mouth, didn't she? Oh, she should have
listened to what he'd said ages ago when they'd first kissed.
She was different from local girls, and she was low risk
because she wasn't staying. The idea of her not going was
scaring him to death.

"Look, Taylor..."

"No, it's okay," she assured him. "You're right. This
was what we agreed and I don't have any regrets." That,
at least, was the truth. She didn't regret the last few days
even if there were mixed feelings and a fair bit of hurt.
They'd been magical when all was said and done. And
Rhys Bullock would be a nice memory, just like he said.

He came forward and tilted up her chin with his finger.
"I know I'm where I belong. I learned my lessons, had my
failures and successes. You're not there yet, that's all."

She pulled away, resenting his attitude. What did he
know? She had her own failures, but she was glad now
that she'd kept the baring of her soul to one messed up
wedding and not the disaster that was her last relationship. "You're leaving anyway, Rhys. I'd appreciate it if
you weren't patronizing."

The air in the room changed. There was a finality to

it that had been absent only moments before. Rhys went to the doorway and picked up his bag. Silently he went to the door and pulled on his boots and jacket. When he was ready he looked up and met her eyes. "I don't want to leave it this way," he said bleakly. "With us angry at each other."

"I'm not angry," she said quietly. "I'm hurting, and the longer you stay, the worse it is."

He stepped forward and pulled her into his arms for one last hug. "Hurting you is the last thing I wanted to do," he murmured in her ear. "So I'll go." He kissed the tip of her ear. "Take care, Taylor."

She swallowed against the lump of tears and willed herself to stay dry-eyed. "You, too, Rhys. And Merry Christmas."

He nodded and slipped out the door. The milder temperatures of the Chinook had dipped slightly and she could see his breath in the air as he jogged down the steps and to his truck.

She shut the door, resisting the opportunity to give him one last wave.

They'd set the ground rules. Leaving was supposed to be easy. It definitely was not supposed to hurt this much.

# CHAPTER TEN

CALLUM AND AVERY arrived back home, happy and tired from their trip and with tons of pictures from Hawaii. Taylor found herself bathing Nell after dinner while Callum checked on the stock and Avery started to make a dent in the mountain of laundry from their luggage. When Taylor suggested she go back to the B&B for the next few nights, Avery insisted she stay. "The couch pulls out. Please, stay. I've missed having a sister around."

Taylor had no good argument against that so at bedtime the cushions came off the sofa and the mattress pulled out. Avery brought sheets from the linen closet. "Sorry it's not as comfortable as our bed," she apologized.

A lump formed in Taylor's throat. Memories she wished she could forget crowded her mind, images of the last few nights spent in the master bedroom. This morning she'd stripped the bed and put the sheets in the washer. Rhys's scent had risen from the hot water and she'd had to go for a tissue.

"Taylor, are you okay?"

"Fine," she replied. "Hand me that comforter, will you?"

Avery handed it over while putting a pillowcase on a fat pillow. "Callum said Rhys did fine with the stock. Did you see him much while he was here?"

Taylor met Avery's innocently curious gaze, watched

as her expression changed in reaction to Taylor's. "What's wrong? Did something happen with Rhys?"

Taylor focused on tucking the bedding around the mattress. "Of course not."

"Taylor." Avery said it with such meaning that Taylor stopped and sat down on the bed.

Avery came over and sat beside her. "I saw you dancing at the reception. And Callum said Jack said something to him about you and Rhys kissing in his truck the night of the rehearsal. There's something going on between you, isn't there?"

"Not anymore," she replied firmly. She wondered if she sounded convincing.

Callum came through to the kitchen carrying an empty baby bottle. "Hey, what's going on?"

Avery looked up at him. "Girl talk. No boys allowed."

Taylor saw her brother's expression as he looked down at his wife. He was utterly smitten. Having someone look at her that way hadn't been so important even a month ago. Now it made her feel like she was missing out on something.

"Who am I to get in the way of my two favorite girls?" he asked, then looked down at the bottle with a stupidly soft expression. "Well, two of my three favorites anyway."

Callum knew where he belonged. He was contented, just like Rhys. So why was it so hard for her to figure out?

"I'll leave you ladies alone, then. Gotta be up early anyway."

When he disappeared back around the corner, Avery patted Taylor's arm. "Wait here," she commanded, and she skipped off to the kitchen. She returned moments later carrying two glasses of wine. "Here," she said, handing one to Taylor. "Sit up here, get under the blanket and then tell me how you managed to fall in love with Rhys Bullock within a week."

"How did you know?" Taylor asked miserably.

Avery laughed. "Honey, it's written all over your face. And as an old married woman, I demand to know all the details." She patted the mattress. "Now spill."

Christmas Eve arrived, along with Callum and Taylor's parents and Jack, back from Montana bearing presents and a strained expression. His trip hadn't gone all that well, as the manager for his corporate retreat business had been in an accident, leaving no one to run things at his Montana property. He was going to have to go back down there right after Christmas instead of taking the break he'd planned.

But nothing kept Jack down for long, and as they all gathered in Callum's small house laughter rang out in the rooms.

"I wish we had room for everyone here," Avery mourned.

"The bed and breakfast is lovely, don't you worry," Susan assured her. "And Harry and I have a surprise for you. We're taking you all out for Christmas Eve dinner."

A strange sort of uneasiness settled in Taylor's stomach. Please let her say it was out of town and not at the diner...

Susan went on happily. "You two just got back from your honeymoon and you're hosting us all tomorrow for Christmas. Tonight someone else is going to worry about the cooking. It's all arranged. Martha Bullock is doing up a prime rib for us and then we'll go to the Christmas Eve service."

Oh, God. The Wagon Wheel? Really?

Taylor pasted a smile on her face. "Surely the diner closes early on Christmas Eve?"

Harry shrugged. "Mrs. Bullock said it would be no trouble, especially for just the six of us."

Avery caught sight of Taylor's face and jumped in. "What a lovely thought. But really, we can have something here. There's no need..."

"Are you kidding?" Jack interrupted. "Prime rib? I've been living on sandwiches for a week. I'm so there."

Avery looked over at Taylor. What could she say? Besides, there was no guarantee that Rhys would be there. It was Christmas Eve after all.

She gave a short nod. "Sounds good to me," she answered, trying to inject some enthusiasm into her voice. This great Shepard family Christmas wasn't going to be brought down by her bad mood.

During the afternoon everyone brought out their presents and put them under the tree, which was a major source of frustration to Nell, who got sick of the word *no* as she crawled through the living room and pulled herself up on the chair next to the decorated spruce. She went down for an afternoon nap and everyone relaxed with a fresh batch of one of Avery's latest creations—eggnog cupcakes—and hot spiced cider. It was supposed to be perfect. Magical. And instead Taylor could only think about two things— the work waiting for her back in Vancouver, and how much she missed Rhys.

Jack pulled up a footstool and sat beside her, bringing his mug with him. "You're awfully quiet today. What's going on?"

She shrugged. "Too long away from the city, I guess."

He nodded. "Can I ask you something?"

"Sure." Jack and Taylor were the most alike in her opinion. He tended to see the big picture in much the same way that she did. And they were the ones still single now, too.

"Are you happy, sis?"

The question surprised her. "What do you mean?"

He raised an eyebrow. "I recognize the look on your face."

Oh, Lord. If he guessed about Rhys she was going to wish for the floor to open up and swallow her.

"I saw it when I first got here, when you were planning the wedding," he continued. "How's business?"

"Booming," she replied.

"And how do you feel about that?"

She met his gaze. "What do you mean?"

Jack hesitated for a minute. "A few years ago, remember when the company expanded? New franchises opened up, and Shepard Sports launched south of the border. It was all very exciting, right?"

"Dad was ready to burst his buttons with pride."

"I wasn't. It was everything I'd worked for and yet…do you know what ended up making me happiest?"

Curious now, she leaned forward. "What?"

"The property I bought in Montana. The corporate retreat and team-building business. The sporting goods, well they're like numbers on a page. Units in and out. Sure, we do some special work with schools and organizations and that sort of thing. But it's just selling. The team building stuff, though, it's about people. I like that. I like meeting different people and finding out more about them. I like seeing groups come in and leave with a totally different dynamic. They come in and push themselves in ways they don't expect, which was the very best thing I liked about competing."

"That's really cool, Jack."

"I know. And because of it, I can look at you and see that what you're doing isn't giving you that same buzz. Something's missing."

"I've been doing some thinking," she admitted. "But you know what it's like. The bigger you get the bigger the responsibility. You can't just pull up and abandon what's already there."

Jack nodded. "There's always a way. And anyway, you've got good people working for you. You've been gone quite a while and everything's run in your absence, hasn't it?"

It had. Sometimes a little too well. Even when trouble popped up, a quick email giving her assistant the green light to solve the problem was all it took.

"Just think about it," Jack said. "Responsibility or not, there's no sense doing something if you're not happy at it."

"Thanks," she answered, taking a drink of cider. She was glad he hadn't assumed her reticence was caused by a man. That would have been a whole other conversation. Then Avery called her to the kitchen to taste Susan's recipe for cranberry sauce and the afternoon passed quickly.

They arrived en masse at the Wagon Wheel at six on the dot. A sign on the door stated that Christmas hours went to 5:00 p.m. on the twenty-fourth and closed on Christmas Day and Boxing Day. Just as she thought, Martha had stayed open for their family and Taylor was a bit upset at her parents for requesting it. Martha had family of her own, probably had plans too.

Inside was toasty-warm and two tables were pushed together to make plenty of room for the six of them plus the high chair for Nell. Nell was dressed in soft red pants and a matching red velour top with tiny white snowflakes on it. After her nap she was energized, tapping a toy on the tray of the high chair and babbling at the blinking tree lights. Taylor was laughing at her antics when a movement in the kitchen caught her eye. It was Rhys, dressed in one of Martha's aprons, taking the roast out of the oven to rest.

He was here. Her stomach tangled into knots and her mouth felt dry. They hadn't seen each other or spoken since the morning they'd said goodbye. From the strained expression on his face, he wasn't too happy about tonight, either. As if he could sense her staring, he looked up and met her eyes across the restaurant. She looked away quickly, turning to answer a question of her mother's about the upcoming event her company was planning.

Martha brought them all glasses of iced water and placed a basket of hot rolls in the center of the table. That was followed by a fresh romaine salad with red onion, peppers and mandarins in a poppy seed dressing that was delicious. Rhys stayed in the kitchen, out of everyone's way. The fact that he seemed to be avoiding her stretched her nerves taut, and by the time the main course was served she was a wreck.

Martha had outdone herself. Glazed carrots, green beans with bacon, creamy mashed potatoes and puffy Yorkshire pudding and gravy complemented the roast, followed by a cranberry bread pudding and custard sauce. By the time the plates were cleared away, Taylor was stuffed to the top. Her father checked his watch. "Seven-fifteen. We'd better get going," he announced. "The church service starts in fifteen minutes."

Everyone got up to leave, reaching for coats and purses and gloves. Everyone but Taylor. They really didn't see, did they? She'd bet ten bucks that Martha and Rhys probably wanted to go to church, too. According to Callum, most of the community showed up at the local Christmas Eve services. And the Bullocks were going to be stuck here cleaning up the mess instead of enjoying their holiday.

"Taylor, aren't you coming?"

"I'll be along," she said lightly. "You go on without me."

Avery gave her a long look, then a secret thumbs-up. Taylor returned a small smile, but it was quickly gone once the Shepard crew hit the door.

She went back to the table and started clearing dessert plates and coffee cups.

Martha hustled out from the kitchen. "Oh, heavens, girl, don't you worry about that! You head on to church with your family."

"What about you? Aren't you planning to go to church?"

Martha looked so dumbfounded that Taylor knew she had guessed right. "If I help it'll get done faster and we can all make it."

"Bless your heart."

"Where's Rhys?" Taylor looked over Martha's shoulder into the kitchen.

"He just took a bag of trash to the Dumpster out back. I swear I don't know what I'd do without that boy. He always says we're in this together, but he's got his own job." She handed Taylor the bin of dirty dishes and briskly wiped off the tables. "It was more than enough that he invested in this place for me. He's supposed to be a silent partner, but not Rhys. He thinks he needs to take care of me."

Taylor nearly dropped the pan of dishes. Silent partner? But Rhys was so determined to stay away from owning a business. How many times had he gotten on her case about it? And this whole time he was part owner in the diner and just neglected to mention it?

For the briefest of moments, she was very, very angry at him. How dare he judge her? And maybe he hadn't exactly lied, but he hadn't been truthful, either.

She remembered pressing him for something he'd been going to say. Now she got the feeling he'd almost let his stake in the diner slip while they'd been talking, and caught himself just in time.

"Rhys is part owner of the diner?"

Martha looked confused. "He didn't tell you? I mean, he

doesn't say much about it, but I thought the two of you…"
Her cheeks flushed. "Oh. I've put my foot in it."

Taylor shook her head. "Not at all. We're not…"

But she didn't know how to finish that sentence. They weren't together but they weren't *not* together, either.

"I'm sorry to hear that," Martha said quietly, putting her hand on Taylor's arm. "You've been real good for him these last few weeks. And I think he's been good for you, too. You smile more. Your cheeks have more color. If I'm wrong tell me to mind my own business."

"You're not exactly wrong."

"He's needed someone like you, Taylor. Not that he's said a word to me about it." Her lips twitched. "He's not exactly the confiding type. Bit like his father that way."

Taylor knew that Rhys probably wouldn't like that comparison.

"My husband had his faults, but he always meant well. And he loved his family. I wish you were staying around longer, Taylor. You're a good girl. Not afraid to work hard. And I can tell your family is important to you."

She was perilously close to getting overemotional now. "Thanks, Martha. That means a lot to me. And Rhys is a good man. I know that. I'm sorry things can't work out differently."

"Are you?"

She swallowed. "Yes. Yes, I am."

Martha smiled. "Well, never say never."

The back door to the kitchen slammed and he came back in. A light snowfall had begun and he shook a few flakes off his hair. Their gazes met again and she fought to school her features. She should be angrier that he hadn't been totally honest, but instead all she could think of was how he had said he didn't want his mom to own the place. He'd gone against his own instincts and wishes to make her happy, hadn't he? Did Martha realize what a personal sacrifice he'd had to make?

They couldn't get into this now, if for no other reason than Martha was there and she should talk to him about it in private.

She marched the dishes into the kitchen. "Should I put these in the dishwasher?"

"What are you still doing here?"

"Helping. I thought you and your mom might like to go to the service."

"Then maybe you shouldn't have requested a private dinner after we closed."

Guilt heated her cheeks at his condemning tone. "I didn't know about that until it was a done deal. Avery even suggested they do something at home but my parents insisted."

"Really? It kind of struck me as exactly the kind of thing you'd be comfortable asking for. You know, like when you're planning an event and you just 'make things happen.' Right?"

"Are you really that mad at me, Rhys?" She tried to muster up some annoyance, some justifiable anger, but all she felt was a weary sadness.

He shoved a cover on the roaster and placed it—none too gently—in the commercial fridge. "I don't know what I am. I know my mom is tired and was looking forward to a quiet Christmas Eve. Instead she ended up here after hours."

"None of the staff would stay?"

"She insisted they go home to their families. It's their holiday, too." His voice held a condemning edge that made her feel even worse.

He really was put out and honestly she didn't blame him.

She hurried to put the dishes in the dishwasher while Martha put the dining room back to rights. "So you helped."

"Of course I did."

Yes, of course he did, because this wasn't just Martha's diner but his, too. "I'm sorry, Rhys. My parents didn't think. What can I do now? Can we still make it to the church?"

"Run the dishwasher while I finish up these pots and pans. We'll be a little late, and not very well dressed, but we'll get there."

Martha bustled back into the kitchen, either too busy or simply oblivious to the tension between Rhys and Taylor. "My goodness, you're nearly done in here. Rhys, let's just leave the sweeping up and stuff until Boxing Day. It's always slower then anyway."

"If that's what you want."

Martha grinned. "Well, what I want is to get a good dose of Christmas carols and candlelight, followed by a double dose of rum in my eggnog."

Taylor laughed. "Get your coat while I start this up."

Martha disappeared into the office. Rhys frowned at Taylor. "Why did you stay? You could have gone on with your family and been there with time to spare."

She shrugged. "Because tonight isn't about just my family. There are other people to consider, too." She tilted her head to look at him. "Why didn't Martha just say no when my father asked?"

What little softening she'd glimpsed in his expression disappeared as his features hardened. "Your father offered a Christmas tip she couldn't refuse."

Taylor winced. Her dad, Jack, her—they were all used to getting what they wanted. It simply hadn't occurred to her father that Martha would say no. And it wasn't that he was mean or unfeeling. Of course he would consider it fair to properly compensate Martha for the inconvenience.

But she rather wished he hadn't inconvenienced the Bullocks at all. It would have been more thoughtful.

"I'm sorry, Rhys. Can we leave it at that and get your mom to the church?"

His gaze caught hers for a prolonged moment. In that small space of time she remembered what it was to hear him laugh, taste his kiss, feel his body against hers. It had happened so fast, and now here they were, as far apart as ever. Trying to keep from being hurt any more than they already were.

"You'd better get your coat. You can drive over with us."

She rushed to grab her coat and purse and by the time she was ready Rhys was warming up Martha's car and Martha was shutting off the lights to the diner and locking the door. The parking lot at the church was packed and inside wasn't any better; the only seats were on the two pews pushed against the back wall. Taylor spied her family, several rows up, but the pew was full from end to end. She squeezed in with the Bullocks, sitting on one side of Rhys while his mother sat on the other. As the congregation sang "The First Noel" she realized that while everyone here was dressed up in their best clothes, Rhys wore jeans and Martha wore her standard cotton pants and comfortable shoes from work.

It didn't seem fair.

They turned the pages of their hymnbook to "Once in Royal David's City." It was less familiar to Taylor, and Rhys held out the book so she could see the words better. Their fingers never touched, but there was something about holding the book together that healed the angry words of before. When they finally sat down, Taylor took advantage of the hushed scuffle. "I'm sorry," she said, leaning toward his ear. "I really am."

The minister began to speak and she heard the words "Let us pray," but she couldn't. Rhys was staring down into her eyes and she couldn't look away. Not now. She wanted to tell him how much she hated the way they'd left things. Wanted to ask him why he'd never told her the truth about the diner. Wanted to kiss him and know that she hadn't just imagined their connection. Instead she sat in a candlelit church that smelled of pine boughs and perfume, the fluid voice of the minister offering a prayer of thanks for the gift of Christmas, and wondered at the miracle that she'd managed to fall utterly and completely in love for the first time in her life.

Her lower lip quivered the tiniest bit and she looked away. What was done was done.

And then Rhys moved his hand, sliding it over to take hers, his fingers tangling with her fingers. Nothing had really changed, and there was a bittersweet pain in her heart as she acknowledged the truth of that. At least he wasn't angry at her anymore.

During the sermon Taylor looked around at the people gathered to celebrate the holiday. Her big brother cuddling a sleeping Nell in the crook of his arm. Her parents sat in between with Jack on the other side and Amy Wilson beside him—an odd surprise. There was the whole Diamond clan—Molly, Sam, Angela, Clara, Ty, the kids. Melissa Stone and her fiancé, Cooper Ford, sitting with two older couples she assumed were their parents. Many others she recognized as guests from the wedding. Business people, professionals, ranchers. Ordinary folks. This was real. This was life. Not the glammed-up high-paced craziness she was used to living in. Somehow, between Clara's sunny generosity, Angela's steady advice and Martha's ready acceptance she'd managed to become a part of this town instead of remaining on the fringes, where she usually made it a policy to stay.

She'd changed. And she couldn't find it within herself to be the least bit sorry.

As if she could sense her thoughts, Angela Diamond turned in her seat and caught Taylor's eye. She smiled and turned back around.

For the first time ever that she could remember, Taylor had no idea what to do next.

An usher brought around a box with tiny white candles in plastic holders. As the service ended, the choir started with the first verse of "Silent Night" as the minister went along and lit the first candle on the end of each pew. The congregation's voices joined in for the second verse as Rhys leaned over a little and let the flame from his candle ignite hers. Soon they were all standing with their candles, singing the last verse as the piano stopped playing and there was no sound but two hundred voices singing the age-old carol a cappella.

It was the most beautiful Christmas tradition Taylor had ever seen.

And when the song ended, everyone blew out their candles, the minister gave the benediction and a celebratory air took over the sanctuary.

In the midst of the confusion, Rhys leaned over. "Are you staying at the house or the B&B?"

"At the house." She waved at someone she only half recognized and smiled. "Callum and Avery insisted. I got the sofa bed."

Rhys's dark complexion took on a pinkish hue. She shouldn't have mentioned sleeping arrangements.

"Can I drive you home?"

"What about your mom?"

"I'll take her now and come back for you."

She wasn't at all sure what she wanted. She had no idea where things stood or even where she wanted them to stand. And yet they both seemed determined to play this out for as long as possible.

"I'll wait."

He gave her a quick nod and turned to Martha. The older woman had clearly decompressed during the service, and now she looked tired. It didn't look like Rhys was going to have much fight on his hands, getting her to leave.

There was a lot of socializing happening in the vestibule. Avery and Callum were working on getting Nell into her snowsuit without waking her up and the other three Shepards were putting on their coats and wishing a Merry Christmas to anyone who stopped by and offered a greeting. Susan saw Taylor and frowned. "You don't have your coat on! We're nearly ready to leave."

"I'll be along a little later."

"But you didn't bring your car."

Callum joined the group, a blurry-eyed, half-awake Nell fully dressed and snuggled into his shoulder. "We ready to go? Santa will be along soon."

"I was just telling Taylor to get her coat."

Taylor let out a breath and smiled brightly. "I've got a lift home, actually. No worries. You go on ahead."

"A lift home?"

"Rhys is going to drive me."

"I just saw him leave with his mother."

Taylor resisted the need to grit her teeth. "He's coming back."

Harry stepped in. "Rhys. He was one of Callum's groomsmen, right? Is there something going on there?"

Avery looked panicked on Taylor's behalf and Callum's brows were raised in brotherly interest but it was Jack, bless him, who stepped in, Amy Wilson hanging back just a bit, as if she was uncertain whether to join the group or not. "Hey, Dad, I've been meaning to ask you something about a new property I'm interested in buying."

The topic of a property investment was enough to lure her father away and Taylor relaxed. "Don't worry," she said to her mother. "We'll be right behind you."

"You've got your phone?"

Taylor laughed. "Of course."

"We'll see you in a bit, then." She hurried off in the direction of Jack and Harry. Avery came over and gave her a hug. "We're off, too. Good luck."

"Thanks."

As Avery and Callum walked away, Taylor heard Callum say, "Good luck? What do you know about this, wife?"

The vestibule thinned out until there were just a handful of people left. Jack got their parents on their way and came back for Amy, offering her a lift home. They'd just turned out of the lot when Taylor saw Rhys pull back into the yard in his truck.

Her boots squeaked in the snow as she crossed the parking lot, opened the door and hopped up inside the cab. She wasn't sure what to say now, so silence spun around them as he put the truck in Drive and headed out of the parking lot.

"I'm sorry I was so hard on your family." He finally spoke when they hit the outskirts of town.

"Don't be. You were right. About a lot of things."

"Such as?"

"Such as this is exactly something I probably would have done. Like you said, I make things happen. That's my job."

"I shouldn't have said that, either."

She chuckled then. "Boy, we can even turn an apology into an argument. We're good."

He laughed, too, but it didn't do much to lighten the atmosphere in the truck.

"So you're really going day after tomorrow."

"Yeah."

More silence.

It was only a short drive to the farm. Taylor longed to ask him about the diner but didn't want to get in another argument and she sensed it would be a sensitive subject. Besides, what did it truly matter now? It really didn't change anything.

The damnedest thing was that she did want something to change. And she couldn't figure out what or how. She just knew it felt wrong. Wrong to leave here. Wrong to say goodbye.

"You've got a couple days off from Diamondback?"

"Yeah," he answered. "Actually Sam suggested we all take Friday off, too, so I don't actually have to be back to work until Monday. I thought I'd sneak Mom to Edmonton one of those days, let her take in some of the Boxing Week sales."

"You're good to your mom, Rhys. She appreciates you, you know."

"Someone has to look out for her. She's my mom. She doesn't have anyone else."

It made even more sense now, knowing he had a stake in the Wagon Wheel. "You're very protective of the people you care about."

"Is that a bad thing?" He slid his gaze from the road for a moment.

"On the contrary. It's one of the things I l...like most about you."

Yeah, she'd almost said "love." She took a deep breath.

This would be a stupid time to get overly emotional, wouldn't it?

They turned onto Callum's road. "The thing is, Taylor…"

"What?"

He frowned. "You're competent. Everyone can see that. You're confident and successful and clearly you know how to run a business. I don't know why you feel you have to prove yourself. Why you have this chip on your shoulder."

"Sometimes I ask myself the same thing, Rhys." She turned in her seat. "Remember the time you said that most guys were intimidated by smart women? You had something there. There's a lot I don't know and more I'm not good at, but I'm not stupid. I've never understood why I should hide that fact just because I'm a woman."

"So you push yourself."

"Yeah. I guess if this trip has shown me anything, though, it's that I don't need to try so much. That…" She swallowed, hard. "That there are things more important that I've maybe been missing out on. In the past I haven't paid enough attention to personal relationships." She sighed. "I've made my share of screw-ups."

"Figuring that out is a good thing, right?"

"To be honest, it's been a little bit painful."

They pulled into Callum's driveway. Rhys parked at the far side, giving them a little space away from the house, and killed the lights.

"Sometimes the best lessons we learn are the ones that hurt the most."

She laughed a little. "Helpful."

But he reached over and took her gloved hand in his. "I mean it, Taylor. My mother told me once that we rarely learn anything from our successes, and the best teachers are our failures. It hurts, but I have to believe it always comes out better on the other side." He squeezed her fingers. "I wish you didn't have to go."

She wanted to say "me, too," but it would only make things worse, wouldn't it? Why wish for something that wasn't going to happen?

"Right. Well. Before you go in...I uh..." He cleared his throat. "I saw this earlier in the week and..."

He reached into his pocket and held out a small rectangular box. "Merry Christmas."

"You got me a present?"

"It's not much."

"Rhys, I..."

"Don't open it now, okay? Let's just say good-night and Merry Christmas."

She tucked the package into her purse. "Merry Christmas," she whispered, unbuckling her seat belt.

She looked up into his face. How had she ever thought it wasn't handsome? It was strong and fair and full of integrity and sometimes a healthy sense of humor. Before she could change her mind she pushed against the seat with one hand, just enough to raise her a few inches so she could touch her lips to his. The kiss was soft, lingering, beautiful and sad. It was the goodbye they should have had yesterday morning. It filled her heart and broke it in two all at the same time.

"Goodbye, Rhys."

She slid out of the truck before she could change her mind. Took one step to the house and then another. Heard the truck engine rev behind her, the creak and groan of the snow beneath the tires as Rhys turned around and drove away for the last time.

She took a few seconds on the porch to collect herself. She didn't want her family to see her cry or ask prying questions. She had to keep it together. Celebrate the holiday the way she'd intended—with them all together and happy. And if she had to fake it a little bit, she would. Because she was starting to realize that she'd been faking happiness for quite a while now.

She was just in time to kiss Nell good-night; to sit with her family and share stories of holidays gone by. Jack arrived and added to the merriment. After her brother and parents left for the B&B, she stayed up a little longer and chatted with Callum and Avery before the two of them went down the hall hand in hand. No one had asked about Rhys, almost as if they'd made a pact to spare her the interrogation. But as she finally burrowed beneath the covers on the sofa bed, she let the emptiness in. Because in the end she was alone. At Christmas. And her heart was across town, with Rhys.

# CHAPTER ELEVEN

CHRISTMAS MORNING DAWNED cool and sunny. Taylor heard Callum sneak out just after five to do the milking; she fell back to sleep until Avery got up and put on coffee around seven. With Nell being too young to understand it all, there was no scramble for presents under the tree. Nell slept late after the busy night before, and Avery brought Taylor a coffee then slipped beneath the covers with her own mug.

Taylor looked over at her sister in law. "I think I would have liked having a sister if this is what it's like. Jack and Callum's idea of this would be to count to three and jump on the bed and see if they could make me yell. Extra points if they left bruises."

Avery smiled. "It was like this for me and my sister. I'm really glad you're here, Taylor. It's been so very nice."

"I'm glad I came, too."

"Even though it's bothering you to leave Rhys?"

Taylor nodded.

They sipped for a moment more before Avery took the plunge. "Did you fall in love with him? Or was it just a fling?"

Taylor curled her hands around the mug. "It would be easier to say it was a fling."

"But it wasn't?"

She shook her head.

Avery laughed. "I don't know whether to offer my congratulations or my sympathy."

"What do you mean?" Taylor looked over at her. "Do I look happy about it?"

"Yes. And no. You light up when you talk about him, you know."

No, she hadn't known. Damn.

"Falling in love is a bit of a miracle, don't you think? So that's the congrats part. And the sympathy comes in because I can tell you're confused and that's not easy."

"I live in Vancouver."

Avery nodded. "When I met Callum, I lived in Ontario. My life and job were there."

"But you could quit your job. It's different when you own your own venture. It would be harder for you now, with your bakery business, wouldn't it?"

"Difficult, but not impossible."

Taylor let out a frustrated sigh. "Avery, I get what you're saying. I do. But I've spent years building this business and my reputation. I've known Rhys less than a month."

Avery smiled softly. "I know. If you didn't have the business in the way, what would you do?"

*See where it leads.*

The answer popped into her mind with absolute ease. But it wasn't just up to her. "Rhys never once asked me to stay or hinted at anything past our…"

"Affair?"

Taylor blushed.

Avery finished her coffee. "It's that serious, then."

"Look," she said, frustration in her voice. "Last night he said he wished I didn't have to go but that's not the same thing as asking me to stay or when I'm coming back."

"Why would he ask when he's sure of the answer? Have

you given him any reason to think you would stay? Told him how you feel?"

She hadn't.

"Only because I'm positive nothing could come of it except our being hurt even more. Besides, there's a good chance he doesn't feel the same way. He told me straight out that he liked me because I was a challenge. That I was low risk because I was leaving anyway."

Avery snorted. "Oh, my God, that's romantic."

Taylor couldn't help it. She started laughing, too. "I'll be fine, Avery, promise. I just need to get back to a normal schedule. And first we have a Christmas breakfast to cook. You're the whiz, but I'm happy to be your sous-chef today."

"Deal," Avery said.

Babbling sounded from the second bedroom and Avery grinned. "Let me get the princess changed and fed first."

While she was gone and the house was quiet, Taylor snuck out of bed and got the box from her coat pocket. She didn't want to open it when anyone else was around. Sitting on the bed in her pajamas, she carefully untied the ribbon and unwrapped the red foil paper.

Inside the box was a necklace—the very same horse-shoe necklace she'd been admiring at the silversmith's the other day. She lifted it gently and watched the U-shaped pendant sway as it dangled from the chain. How had he known it was just what she liked? It was simple but beautiful. When she went to put it back in the box, she heard a strange ruffle when her fingers touched the cotton padding. Curious, she moved it out of the box and saw the folded note hidden beneath.

*For all the times you need a horseshoe to rub for good luck. Merry Christmas, Rhys.*

He remembered, but he'd hidden the note, as if he didn't want her to find it right away. As if—perhaps—he'd meant her to discover it after she was home again and it would remind her of the time they'd spent together.

She didn't know whether to laugh or cry.

She tucked the necklace back in the box. She wouldn't wear it today, not when everyone was around. She didn't want any more questions about her relationship with Rhys. She just wanted to keep this one thing private, like a secret they shared. Cherished.

But she thought about it as the rest of the family arrived, breakfast was served, presents were opened. And when there was a lull, she took the necklace out of her bag and tucked it into her pocket, where it rested warmly within the cotton.

An hour or so before dinner, it all got to be too much so she excused herself and bundled up for a short walk and some fresh air to clear her head. She was partway down the lane when a dull thud echoed on the breeze. She turned around to see her dad coming down the steps, dressed in Callum's barn coat and a warm toque and gloves. "Hey, wait up," he called.

She had no choice but to wait.

When he reached her they continued walking, the sun on the snow glittering so brightly that Taylor wished she'd put on her sunglasses. "It's been a good day," Harry said easily, falling into step.

"We haven't all been together like this in a long time." Taylor let out a big breath. "It's been good."

"Yes, it has."

Silence fell, slightly awkward.

"Taylor, I've gotten the impression you're not completely happy. Are you okay?"

Her heart clubbed. "What gave you that idea?"

"Your mother pointed out a few things. And then

there's this Rhys guy. You seem half miserable, half thrilled about it."

She huffed out a laugh. "That about sums it up."

"Is it just this guy? Or is it work, too?"

She frowned. "You don't have to sound so hopeful about it. I know you don't like what I do and you'd love to see me settled with kids like Callum."

There. She'd come right out and said it.

Harry let out a long sigh. "I haven't been very fair. Or put things the right way."

Her feet stopped moving, as if they had a mind of their own. "What?"

She looked up at him, suddenly realizing why his eyes seemed so familiar. They looked like hers.

"I don't hate what you do. I resent it a bit, that's all."

"I don't get it."

Harry started walking again. "Callum joined the military instead of going to college. It wasn't my first choice, but when your son says he wants to serve his country, it's a hard thing to find fault with. Then with Jack…we both knew he couldn't ski forever. But after his accident and after the scandal…" There was a telling pause. "When he came to me asking to help him start Shepard Sports, I couldn't say no. It was good to see the light in his eye again. He could have died on that hill."

"What does this have to do with me, Dad?"

"I built my company from the ground up, Taylor. Neither of my boys were interested in finance. But you… you weren't just my last chance to pass it on to one of my kids. I could see the talent in you. You're good at making money, maybe even better than Jack. And you weren't interested in the least in the market or fund management or anything I do."

"You wanted me to work for you?"

"With me. Eventually."

"I thought you thought what I do is stupid."

He stopped walking again. "I was jealous of it."

"You never said anything."

"I kept hoping you'd come to me. I didn't want to pressure you."

"Instead you just made me feel like a disappointment." She wasn't holding anything back today. Maybe Rhys's way of plain speaking was rubbing off.

"I know. And I'm sorry. The truth is that you should do what makes you happy. I can't put my wishes on you kids. I'm proud of all of you for being strong and smart enough to make your own way."

"Even if it's planning frivolous parties?"

He chuckled. "I've seen your mother work her magic enough times at our small functions to know that a big event takes massive planning. You've got a talent, Taylor. And again, I'm sorry that my selfish pride took away from that."

They turned around and headed back, the house waiting for them at the end of the lane, snowbanks curling along the driveway and the remnants of her snowman listing lazily to one side. Her father's approval meant a lot. But she was also realizing that his validation wasn't everything. Her restlessness and drive wasn't about proving herself. It was about looking for something that was missing. It was about meaning, not accomplishment.

"I wish I could tell you that I could join the firm, but I need something that makes me excited to get up in the morning, Dad. I know fund management isn't it. I'm sorry, too. I wish you'd told me sooner."

"All I've ever really wanted for my kids is for them to be happy. If you're not, I want to know if there's anything we can do to help."

"Oh, Daddy." She stopped and gave him a hug, warmth spreading through her as he put his strong arms around her and hugged her back. "Thank you for that. I've got to figure it out on my own, that's all."

"Well, anything worth having is going to take a lot of work. If it was easy it wouldn't mean half so much. And none of my kids are quitters."

"No, we're not."

"You'll figure it out," he assured her. "Now, let's get back. I'm getting cold and I swear I can smell the turkey clear out here."

Taylor walked beside her father, feeling like a weight had been lifted. And yet a heaviness remained, too. Because their conversation hadn't offered any insight into what she should do about her current situation. So much for her creative, problem-solving mind. All she could see right now was a massive New Year's party that needed finalizing and about a dozen employees who were counting on her to keep their lives afloat. Where could she and Rhys possibly fit into that?

No stormy weather or mechanical failures had the grace to delay her flight, so bright and early on Boxing Day Taylor took the rental car back to the depot and walked into the departures area of the airport. Her feet were heavy and her stomach felt lined with lead as she tugged her suitcases behind her. She should be glad to be going home to her apartment, her regular routine, familiar things. Her muffin and coffee from the café around the corner each morning. Walks in Stanley Park. Warmer temperatures. Shopping. Work.

It would be good. It would be fine.

After she checked her bags she went through security and to the gate, even though she had nearly an hour to spare. She checked her phone, going through the email that was waiting for her attention. There was a rather frantic one from her New Year's client, and Taylor's blood pressure took a sudden spike. It was only five days to the party and the construction of the aquariums was delayed. He'd emailed her on Christmas Day, for heaven's sake. Like she could—or would—have done anything during that twenty-four hour period. People did celebrate holidays, she thought grumpily. Even workaholics.

Her fingers paused over the keypad. Was that what she was? A workaholic?

She scanned through the rest, knowing she should cool off before responding, and saw an urgent reply from her assistant, Alicia. Everything was under control. The aquariums were set to be delivered on the morning of the thirtieth, the fish would come a day later when the tank conditions were at the proper levels, and everything else was on schedule.

Taylor let out a breath. Why had she even worried? Alicia could handle anything their clients dished out. She never panicked and she was incredibly resourceful. Heck, Taylor wasn't even really needed.

She put the phone down on her lap as the thought sunk in.

*She wasn't really needed.*

The truth should have been obvious before. She was great at her job. She knew how to make the impossible happen. It stood to follow that she'd train her staff the same way. Alicia had been her right-hand girl for three years. She'd managed smaller events on her own. This party was probably the biggest challenge they'd had in a while and all Taylor had done was been available by email simply to confirm or approve changes in plan. Alicia had done the grunt work. She and her team had put it together.

And yet Taylor couldn't just walk away. She owned the business after all.

Suddenly her conversations with family came back with disturbing clarity. *What you're doing isn't giving you that same buzz,* Jack had said. *Something's missing.* And he'd gone on to say that what had given him the most fulfillment was his corporate retreat business. That it was more than just buying and selling. That it was about people.

An even bigger surprise was how her father had taken her aside yesterday afternoon. Just before they'd gone inside, he'd added one little addendum to their conversation. "I want you to know that I couldn't have done what I have all these years without your mother. Without all of you. Don't let life pass you by, sweetheart. Build your business with people you trust, but build your life with people you love."

People you trust. People you love.

The solution was so clear she couldn't believe it had taken her so long to put it together.

Even though it was still a statutory holiday, she scanned through her directory and found the number she was looking for. A quick call later and she was heading to the gate desk where two service agents had just arrived.

"I need you to pull my bags, please," she said, holding out her boarding pass.

The first agent came to the desk. "I'm sorry? This is the flight to Vancouver, leaving in forty minutes."

"Yes, and I checked in and this is my seat, 12F. But I'm not going to be leaving on it, so I need you to pull my bags."

"Miss." She checked the boarding pass. "Miss Shepard. We're going to be boarding in about fifteen minutes."

"I'm not going to be on it." She tried to stay calm and

smiling. "And if I'm not on it, you're going to have to pull the bags anyway, right?"

"Yes, but…"

"I don't even care if I take them with me now. I can come back to get them. I don't care if my ticket can't be refunded." Her smile widened even as the agent's expression grew more confused. She leaned forward. "Would it help if I told you I fell in love and decided I can't leave after all?"

The confused look morphed into sentimental amusement. "You're absolutely sure you're not boarding this flight?"

"I've never been more sure of anything in my life."

"It might take a while. You'll have to pick them up at baggage services." She sent Taylor a wink. "I'll call down."

"Thank you! I'm sorry for the trouble. And Merry Christmas!"

"Merry Christmas," the agent returned, picking up the phone. "And good luck."

# CHAPTER TWELVE

RHYS PUT THE BROOM back in the storage closet and began running hot water for the mop bucket. He'd left Martha in bed with a cold; she'd insisted on getting up and coming with him to give the diner a good cleaning but he'd convinced her to stay in bed since she'd be needed when they opened tomorrow. Knowing she'd likely change her mind, he'd made sure to give her a good dose of cold medicine. She'd be asleep for a good few hours, getting some much deserved rest. He could mop the floors and do up the bank deposit without any trouble.

If only he could stop thinking about Taylor as easily. That last kiss she'd given him had been so sweet—a bit shy and a bit sad. He knew he had no choice but to let her go, but it was killing him. She'd awakened something in him that was unexpected and he didn't know how to make it go back to sleep. At least a dozen times in the past thirty-six hours he'd grabbed his car keys, ready to drive over to Callum's and tell her he wasn't ready to let what they had end. But he'd put the keys back on the hook every time. It already hurt to let her go. To prolong it would only make it worse.

Something made him shut off the water, a persistent thump that came from out in the main part of the restaurant. Frowning, he stuck his head out of the kitchen and called out, "We're closed!"

He'd nearly pulled his head back in when he saw the red boots.

His heart gave an almighty *whomp*.

She was supposed to be gone. Her flight was supposed to have left almost an hour ago. Maybe he'd been mistaken about the boots?

He slowly stepped through the kitchen door and into the front of the diner. There was no question, they were red boots. The only red boots like them he'd ever seen in Cadence Creek. Most of her body was hidden by the gigantic pine wreath hanging on the door, but he saw her long legs and the tails of her soft black and red coat.

He smiled as she knocked again, harder.

"Rhys, I know you're in there. Your truck is parked right outside."

His smile widened. God, he loved it when she got all impatient and bossy.

"I said we're closed."

There was a moment of silence. Then her voice came again, mocking. "Don't be an ass. Open the door."

He rather thought he could play this game all day. Except he did really want to see her. And find out why she was still here.

"Rhys!" she commanded. "It's freezing out here!"

He couldn't help it, he burst out laughing, half in surprise and half in relief that he actually got to see her again. He went forward and turned the lock back. Gave the door a shove and then there she was, standing in the snow, her dark hair in the customary braid and her eyes snapping at him from beneath a black hat, one of those stylish things women wore in the winter that wouldn't ruin their hair.

"Hello, Taylor."

She stepped inside, reached up and swiped the hat from her head and shoved it in her pocket. "Hi."

"I thought you were leaving today."

"I was."

He locked the door again and faced her, his pulse leaping as he registered the fact that she'd used past tense. "Wait. Was?"

She nodded.

"Your flight get canceled or something?"

"Nope."

"I don't understand."

For several seconds Taylor remained silent. "Do you have any coffee on or anything?" she asked. "I'm freezing."

She was stalling, and the only reason she'd do that was that she was nervous. "I put a pot on when I got here. Have a seat."

She went to one of the lunch counter stools and perched on it. He added the right amounts of cream and sugar to her cup and handed it over. "It's probably not as good as mom's."

"Where is she, by the way?"

"Home in bed with a cold."

"Oh, I'm sorry to hear that." Her face seemed to relax a bit, though—was she glad they were alone? He was still confused as hell. She was insistent on coming in but now that she was here, trying to get anything out of her was about like working with a pigheaded colt who refused to be bridled. Trying on the patience. Once he got the bit in her mouth she'd be just fine, he realized. It was just figuring out what to use to lure her in, make her explain.

"You're probably wondering why I'm here," she said softly, looking up at him with wide eyes.

Feelings rushed through him as he held her gaze. Pain, because prolonging the inevitable was torture of a special kind and they'd done it twice now. Hope, because for some reason she was here and not crossing thirty thousand feet over the Rockies. And tenderness, because he knew now that beneath the dynamo that was Taylor Shepard was one of the most caring, generous people he'd ever met. At the very least he could admit to himself that he'd fallen for her. Hard.

"The thought crossed my mind," he replied.

"I forgot to give you your Christmas present," she said, reaching into her handbag. "I apologize for the poor wrapping job."

She held out a thin plastic bag that bore the logo of one of the airport gift shops.

Amused, he reached inside and pulled out a key chain with a fuzzy fake rabbit's foot on the end.

"Someone told me that you rub a rabbit's foot for good luck." Her voice was barely above a whisper.

It was then he noticed the horseshoe hanging around her neck, just visible in the "V" of her coat and sweater. She was wearing his Christmas present. That pleased him more than it probably should.

"Do you think I'm in need of some good luck?"

She put down her coffee cup but not before he noticed her hand was trembling the slightest bit. She was nervous. So was he. He had no idea what this all meant but he got the feeling they were standing on the edge of something momentous. Somewhere he'd never wanted to be again. Until now.

"Why don't you try rubbing it and find out?" she suggested.

He felt like a fool, but she was here, wasn't she? He'd indulge her. He rubbed the tiny faux-fur foot.

"Ok, Luck," he said when he was done, spreading his arms wide. "Here I am."

She got up from the stool, went around the counter, and grabbed onto his shirt, just above where he'd fastened the last button. "And here I am," she whispered as she tilted up her head and kissed him.

His arms came around her by sheer instinct, pulling her against his body into the places where she fit so well. There was relief in holding her in his arms again, passion that ignited between them every time they touched. She tasted good and he kissed her back, loving the feel of her soft lips against his, the sleek texture of her mouth, the way she made the tiniest sound of pleasure when he nibbled on her lower lip.

"You're right," he murmured. "It *is* lucky."

She smiled against his lips, but then pulled away a little and simply rested in his arms, her head nestled in the space between his shoulder and neck. A lump formed in his throat. Whatever he'd said over the last few weeks, he'd been a liar. There was nothing easy or casual or temporary about his feelings for her. They were very, very real. It wasn't all physical. The way they were embracing now was much, much more than that. What a mess.

"Why didn't you tell me about the diner?" Her voice was slightly muffled against his shirt but he heard her just the same. It was not what he expected her to say.

"What?"

She pushed back out of his arms and met his gaze. "This place. Why didn't you tell me you were part owner?"

Nothing she could have said would have surprised him more. "Who told you that?"

"Your mother. Though I don't think she meant to. It slipped out the other night."

"It's not a big deal."

"It's a very big deal." She frowned, a cute little wrinkle forming between her eyebrows. "For all your talk about not wanting to own your own business, not wanting to be the boss. Heck, you even said you hadn't wanted your mother to buy this place."

"I really didn't want her to buy it. But she was determined. Once my mother gets something in her head…"

"Sounds like someone else I know. And you invested because?"

He frowned. "If I hadn't invested all the money I'd gotten for my house in Rocky, she would have mortgaged herself to the eyeballs to have it. As it is, this place is free and clear in another four years."

"You did it to protect her."

"Of course I did. I couldn't stop her from taking the risk, but at least I could help cushion the fall."

"You did it thinking that you'd never see your money back."

He remembered the heated discussions he'd had with his mother about taking such a big step. In the end he'd had no choice. Money was just money. This was his mother and Rhys knew he had to look out for her. "I did it knowing that was a very real possibility, yes. And not because I didn't think she could do it. I just know from painful experience how many small businesses fail. She'd already lost enough over her lifetime. Her whole nest egg went into buying it, plus Dad's life insurance money. If the diner went under, she'd lose everything."

Taylor must think him an idiot. He'd made a business decision for reasons that had very little to do with business.

"You did it for your mother."

"I know it was foolish. But she's my mom."

"And the job at Diamondback?"

"Security. The best way to take care of her, to protect her, was to minimize financial risk. At least I bring in a regular paycheck that I, or rather we, can rely on."

Taylor reached out and pressed her hand to the wall of his chest. "You are a dying breed, Rhys Bullock. You protect the people you love no matter what. There's nothing foolish about that. What about your brother?"

"He's been gone too long, I think. He's off doing his own thing. He just said, 'Whatever she wants.'"

It had been Rhys who'd come home and helped his mom through those first days of grieving. Who'd met with lawyers and bankers. There had been no way he was going to let her go through that alone.

Taylor squeezed his hands. "Let me guess, Martha insists on you taking your share of the profits."

"Of course. I draw out the same percentage of profit as I initially invested."

He didn't quite like the keen way she was looking up at him. Like she could see right through him. He wasn't exactly lying…

She lifted one eyebrow. "You use the profits to pay down the loan, don't you?"

Busted. "Perhaps."

"And your house?"

He met her gaze. If she was after the whole picture, she might as well have it. She could probably still catch another flight today.

"Rented." Because by using all his equity he'd had nothing left for a down payment.

"And Martha doesn't know. She thinks you own it?"

He nodded. "That's right. You're looking at a full-time ranch hand with a rented house, truck payment and not a scrap in savings."

"So that's why you didn't tell me? Pride?"

She was here. Things were bigger between them than he'd ever planned. "No, not just pride. There's more. You know I never wanted to be like my dad. I was so determined that I'd do better. That no one would suffer because of my mismanagement."

"But someone did?"

He nodded. "Her name was Sherry. She had a couple of kids. She was my office manager—and my girlfriend."

"Oh, Rhys."

"I let them down so completely," he explained. "She blamed me, too. For losing the business. For putting her out of a job when she had the children to support. For..." He cleared his throat. "For breaking her heart."

"So you carried that around, on top of losing the business?"

"She depended on me. I can't blame her for being angry." He ran a hand over his hair and looked in her eyes, feeling miserable. "So you see I don't have a lot to offer in the way of brilliant prospects."

She took his hand. "That's not true! You work hard and you put the ones you love first. You made your mom's dream come true. You're strong and honest and loyal. You've got two strong hands and the biggest heart of anyone I've ever met." Her smile widened. "Know what else you've got?"

"What?"

"Your ace in the hole. Me."

Taylor gazed up at him, filled with admiration for the man he'd become. He really had no clue, did he? Rhys was self-assured, knew his place in the world. But he didn't understand how extraordinary he was.

"You? Come on, Taylor," he said, pulling away a little. "Look at you. You're successful. Your business is profitable enough to keep you in designer boots and who knows what else. We're as different as night from day."

"Not as different as you think. Just so happens that

we're peas in a pod, you and me. I was in a relationship a while ago, too. At the same time as that wedding story I told you about—remember the bride with the allergy? I was so upset about that. I mean disproportionately freaked out. John accused me of being cold. Of caring more about the business than I did about our relationship. The thing is he was right. And so your little digs about proving myself really hit a nerve. I was at a crisis point and he bailed. You weren't the only one who thought you were incapable of making a personal relationship work, and I really wasn't interested in risking myself like that again, you know?"

"He was an idiot."

She smiled at Rhys's blind loyalty. "No, he was honest. And the truth is, I didn't invest enough in our relationship. Probably because I didn't love him. I loved the idea of him. But not him. The idea of losing him didn't make me lose sleep. It didn't break my heart or make this heavy pit of despair settle right here." She pressed her fist to her stomach. Her voice lowered to a whisper. "Not like it felt about an hour and a half ago while I sat in Edmonton airport wondering how I could ever be happy if I left you without telling you how I feel."

His lips dropped open. He hadn't been expecting that. Neither had she. Neither of them had expected any of this.

"Do you really think I care about your bank statement? Truly? When have I ever given the impression that my goals are about making money?"

He shook his head. "You haven't," he admitted. "It's always been about proving yourself, meeting challenges."

"That's right." She tugged on his hand. "Come sit down. I want to run something by you."

"Me? Why?"

"When we first met, you told me that a smart person knows their strengths, do you remember? My dad taught me that a smart person also sees the strengths in others. I want your honest to goodness opinion about something. Will you help?"

"Of course."

They sat side by side on the stools, swiveled so they were facing each other and their knees were nearly touching. Rhys wasn't just some ranch hand. He had a lifetime of experiences to draw upon and she trusted his judgment. "Do you think I could keep the event planning business in Vancouver going and branch out into something else that excites me personally? Can I do both?"

Possibility hummed in the air. Rhys sat up straight and tall. Neither of them were rushing through to the end of the conversation. They'd been through enough to know that what was said today was constructing the foundation of wherever they went from here. It deserved to be built with care and attention. "It depends. What are you thinking?"

"Angela put the idea into my head before Christmas. I mentioned that I'm getting tired of the here today, gone tomorrow scene. Remember when I was so stressed about the rehearsal dinner and you said it was because the event meant something personal to me? You were right. But you know what? The satisfaction from planning Callum's wedding was greater than I expected, too. She said what I want is to create something meaningful, and suggested I help plan an upcoming fund-raiser for the Butterfly Foundation."

"That's a great idea!" Rhys smiled at her. "The Diamonds have done a really great thing with that charity. I know they'd appreciate the help."

"What if I took it a step further and used my expertise to work for lots of charities and non-profits? I love what I do and I'd still have the challenge of that, but I think I'd feel like I was doing something important, too, you know?"

"How could you do that and still keep the Vancouver business going? You'd be spreading yourself pretty thin."

"By promoting my assistant. She can do it. She's handled this party on her own since I've been here and it's been one of the most challenging projects we've ever done. She's built her own team. I'd still own the company, and I'd still be involved, of course. But in a different way. Kind of like Jack is with his business. He's far more hands-on with his team-building stuff than with the sporting goods."

"Would you set up the new venture from the same office?" he asked. "It would cut down on expenses."

He hadn't put the two together. The two of them and the business change. "This might come as a surprise, but I was thinking about running it from here."

"From Cadence Creek?"

He sounded so surprised she faltered. Had she possibly misread the situation? "Well, yes. It's close to Edmonton, not that far to Calgary, and an easy flight to Vancouver or even Toronto. I have family here. And…" She looked down at her lap. She was so confident when it came to her work and capabilities, but when it was personal she wasn't nearly as sure of herself. John's words—*Incapable of what it takes to maintain a relationship*—still echoed in her head. Even though she didn't really believe them, they'd left their mark just the same. "I guess I thought you might like it if I were around."

"Taylor."

She couldn't read what emotion was in his voice other than surprise. Embarrassment flooded through her as she felt quite ridiculous. The old insecurity came rushing back. What if the problem was really her? What if she wasn't lovable? She'd spent so much time trying to be strong that it had become a shell around her heart.

"Of course, it's okay if you don't. I mean, we did agree

that this was a short-term thing, and I don't want you to feel pressured."

His hand touched hers as it sat in her lap. She stared at it for a long moment, watched as his fingers curled around hers, firm and sure. Her heart seemed to expand in her chest, filled with so much emotion she didn't know what to do with it all. She drew hope from the simple touch. Felt wonder at the newness and fragility of it all. And there was fear, fear that this couldn't all be real and that it would disappear at a moment's notice.

She put her other hand over his, tentatively, until she couldn't bear it any longer and she lifted their joined hands, pressing them to her cheek as her eyes closed, holding on to the moment as long as she could.

Rhys lifted his right hand, placed it gently along the slope of her jaw, his strong fingers whispering against the delicate skin there. "Taylor," he murmured, and she opened her eyes.

He was looking at her the way she'd never imagined any man would ever look at her. Wholly, completely, his lips turned up only the slightest bit, not in jest, but in what she could only think of as happiness. His eyes were warm, and looked on her with such an adoring expression she caught her breath. The pad of his thumb rubbed against her cheek, and he pulled his left hand from her grasp. He placed it along her other cheek, his hands cupping her face like a precious chalice, and he slid closer, so slowly it was sweet torture waiting for his lips to finally touch hers.

She thought the sweetest moment had to be in that breathless second when his mouth was only a fraction of an inch away, and all the possibilities in the world were compacted into that tiny space. But she was wrong. Sweeter still was the light touch of lips on lips, soft, tender and perfect.

"You're staying?" he asked, his voice barely a whisper in the quietness of the diner.

"I'm staying," she confirmed.

He pressed his forehead to hers and she slowly let out her breath as everything clicked into place.

"I tried not to fall in love with you." Rhys lifted his head, smiled, and patted his lap. She slid off the stool and onto his legs, and he put his arms around her, strong and secure.

"Me, too. I kept telling myself it was a fling. But I couldn't get you off my mind. You're bossy and you drive me crazy, but you're loyal and honorable and you…"

She broke off, feeling silly.

"I what?"

He gave her a jostle, prompting her to finish her sentence. "It's corny." She bit down on her lip.

"I don't care. What were you going to say?"

She leaned against his shoulder. "You make me feel treasured."

He tilted his head so it rested against hers. "And you make me feel invincible."

She smiled, the grin climbing her face until she chuckled. "I'm glad."

His smile faded as his face turned serious. "I won't let you down."

"You couldn't possibly."

He kissed her again, more demanding this time, and when he lifted his head her tidy braid was well and truly mussed. "Hey," she said, running her fingers through his hair. "Now that I'm going to be here on a permanent basis, we can take all the time we need to fall in love."

"Honey, I'm already there."

She smiled. "Me, too. But I want to enjoy being this way a little longer. Is that okay?"

"Look at me. I'm in no position to argue."

She kissed him again, thinking that she could happily stay that way forever when he gave her braid a tug.

"Hey," he said. "I know we're taking our time and all that, and I don't mean to rush, but what are you doing New Year's Eve? Do you have plans?"

She nodded slowly. "I do have plans, as a matter of fact."

"Oh." Disappointment clouded his voice.

"I think I'd like to spend it right here, in your arms. If that's okay with you."

"That's more than okay. And the night after that, and the night after that."

She snuggled closer. "I don't know what the future holds. Changes are coming, adjustments and transitions are going to be made. But I know one thing for sure. You're my anchor, Rhys. Somehow you make everything right simply by being. And for the first time, I don't have to have all the details sorted and everything planned to the last item. Things will fall into place. And do you know how I know?"

He shook his head.

"Because I didn't plan for you. And you were the best thing of all."

He kissed her hair. "I love you, Taylor."

"And I love you."

And that was all she really needed to know.

\* \* \* \* \*

## "Marry me, Alice. Say yes."

She put her hand on his chest. "I know you have a heart, Noah. I can feel it beating away strong and steady in there."

"What is that supposed to mean?"

"It means I know what I want now, after years of throwing myself wildly into all kinds of iffy situations." Just like a woman. She knew what she wanted, but she failed to share it with him.

"And what, exactly, is it that you want, Alice?"

"I want it all. I'll have nothing less. I want everything. Not only your strength and protection, your fidelity and your hot body. Not only your brilliant brain and great sense of humor and your otherworldly way with my horses. I want your heart, too. And I know I don't have that yet. And until I do, I won't say yes to you."

**The Bravo Royales: When it comes to love, Bravos rule!**

# HOW TO MARRY
# A PRINCESS

BY
CHRISTINE RIMMER

MILLS & BOON

First published in Great Britain 2013
by Mills & Boon, an imprint of Harlequin (UK) Limited,
Eton House, 18-24 Paradise Road, Richmond, Surrey TW9 1SR

© Christine Rimmer 2013

ISBN: 978 0 263 90158 0

23-1113

Harlequin (UK) policy is to use papers that are natural, renewable and recyclable products and made from wood grown in sustainable forests. The logging and manufacturing processes conform to the legal environmental regulations of the country of origin.

Printed and bound in Spain
by Blackprint CPI, Barcelona

**Christine Rimmer** came to her profession the long way around. Before settling down to write about the magic of romance, she'd been everything from an actress to a salesclerk to a waitress. Now that she's finally found work that suits her perfectly, she insists she never had a problem keeping a job—she was merely gaining "life experience" for her future as a novelist. Christine is grateful not only for the joy she finds in writing, but for what waits when the day's work is through: a man she loves who loves her right back, and the privilege of watching their children grow and change day to day. She lives with her family in Oregon. Visit Christine at www.christinerimmer.com.

For MSR,
always.

# *Chapter One*

On the first Wednesday in September, temptation came looking for Alice Bravo-Calabretti.

And she'd been doing so well, too. For more than two weeks, she'd kept her promise to herself. She'd maintained a low profile and carried herself with dignity. She'd accepted no dares and avoided situations where she might be tempted to go too far.

It hadn't been all that difficult. She'd spent her days with her beloved horses and her nights at home. Temptation, it seemed, presented no problem when she made sure there was none.

And then came that fateful Wednesday.

It happened in the stables well before dawn. Alice was tacking up one of the mares, Yasmine, for an early-morning ride. She'd just placed the saddle well forward on the mare's sleek back when she heard a rustling sound in the deserted stable behind her.

Yasmine twitched her tail and whickered softly, her distinctive iridescent coat shimmering even in the dim light provided by the single caged bulb suspended over the stall. A glance into the shadows and Alice registered the source of the unexpected noise.

Over near the arched door that led into the courtyard, a stable hand was pushing a broom. He was no one she recognized, which she found somewhat odd. The palace stables were a second home to her. Alice knew every groom by name. He must be new.

Gilbert, the head groom, came in from the dark yard. He said something to the man with the broom. The man laughed low. Gilbert chuckled, too. Apparently the head groom liked the new man.

With a shrug, Alice gave the beautiful mare a comforting pat and finished tacking up. She was leading Yazzy out of the stall when she saw that Gilbert had gone. The stable hand remained. He'd set his broom aside and lounged against the wall by the door to the courtyard.

As she approached, the man straightened from the wall and gave her a slow nod. "Your Highness." His voice was deep and rather stirring, his attitude both ironic and confident. She recognized his accent instantly: American.

Alice had nothing against Americans. Her father was one after all. And yet…

As a rule, the grooms were Montedoran by birth— and diffident by nature. This fellow was simply not the sort Gilbert usually hired.

The groom raised his golden head. Blue eyes met hers. She saw mischief in those eyes and her heart beat faster.

Temptation. Oh, yes.

*Down, girl. Get a grip.*

So what if the new groom was hot? So what if just a glance from him had her thinking of how boring her life had become lately, had her imagining all kinds of inappropriate activities she might indulge in with him?

*Nothing inappropriate is happening here,* she reminded herself staunchly.

And then, in an attempt to appear stern and formidable, she drew her shoulders back and gave the man a slow once-over. He wore a disreputable sweatshirt with the sleeves ripped off, old jeans and older Western boots.

Hot. Definitely. Tall and fit, with a scruff of bronze beard on his lean cheeks. She wondered briefly why Gilbert hadn't required him to dress in the brown trousers, collared shirt and paddock boots worn by the rest of the stable staff.

He stepped forward and her thoughts flew off in all directions. "Such a beautiful girl," he said in a tender tone—to the mare. Alice stared, bemused, as he stroked Yazzy's long, sleek face.

Like most of her ancient hotblood breed, Yasmine was a fiercely loyal, sensitive animal. She gave her trust and affection to very few. But the bold and handsome American worked a certain magic on the golden mare. Yazzy nuzzled him and nickered fondly as he petted her.

Alice permitted his attentions to the horse. If Yazzy didn't mind, neither did she. And watching him with the mare, she began to understand why Gilbert had hired him. He had a way with horses. Plus, judging by his tattered clothing, the fellow probably needed the work. The kindhearted head groom must have taken pity on him.

Finally, the new man stepped back. "Have a nice ride, ma'am." The words were perfectly mundane, the tone pleasant and deferential. *Ma'am* was the proper form of address.

The look in his eyes, though?

Anything but proper. Far from deferential.

"Thank you. I shall." She led the mare out into the gray light of coming dawn.

* * *

The new groom had disappeared when Alice returned from her morning ride. That didn't surprise her. The grooms were often needed outside the stables.

Her country, the principality of Montedoro, was a tiny slice of paradise overlooking the Mediterranean on the Côte d'Azur. The French border lay less than two kilometers from the stables and her family owned a chain of paddocks and pastures in the nearby French countryside. A stable hand might be required to exercise the horses in some far pasture or help with cleanup or fence repair at one of the paddocks.

And honestly, what did it matter to her where the handsome American had gone off to? He was nothing to her. She resisted the urge to ask Gilbert about him and reminded herself that becoming overly curious about one of the grooms was exactly the sort of self-indulgence she couldn't permit herself anymore.

Not after the Glasgow episode.

Her face flamed just thinking about it.

And she *needed* to think about it. She needed to keep her humiliation firmly in mind in order to never allow herself to indulge in such unacceptable behavior again.

Like most of her escapades, it had begun so innocently.

On a whim, she'd decided to visit Blair Castle for the International Horse Trials and Country Fair. She'd flown to Perth the week before the trials thinking she would spend a few days touring Scotland.

She'd never made it to Blair Castle. She'd met up with some friends in Perth and driven with them down to Glasgow. Such fun, a little pub hopping. They'd found this one lovely, rowdy pub and it was karaoke night.

Alice had enjoyed a pint or two more than she should have. Her bodyguard, huge, sweet old Altus, had caught her eye more than once and given her *the look*—the one meant to warn her that she was going too far, the one that rarely did any good.

As usual, she'd ignored *the look*. Repeatedly. And then, somehow, there she was up on the stage singing that Katy Perry song, "I Kissed a Girl." At the time, it had seemed like harmless fun. She'd thrown herself into her performance and acted out the lyrics.

Pictures of her soul-kissing that cute Glaswegian barmaid with her skirt hiked up and her top halfway off had been all over the scandal sheets. The paparazzi had had a field day. Her mother, the sovereign princess, had not been amused.

And after that, Alice had sworn to herself that she would do better from now on—which definitely meant steering clear of brash, scruffy American stable hands who made her pulse race.

The next morning, Thursday, the new groom appeared again. He was there, busy with his broom, when she entered the stables at five. The sight of him, in the same disreputable jeans and torn sweatshirt as the day before, caused a thoroughly annoying flutter in her solar plexus, as well as a definite feeling of breathlessness.

To cover her absurd excitement over seeing him again, she said, "Excuse me," in a snooty abovestairs-at-Downton-Abbey tone that she instantly regretted, a tone that had her wondering if she might be trying *too* hard to behave. "I didn't catch your name."

He stopped sweeping. "Noah. Ma'am."

"Ah. Well. Noah…" She was suddenly as tongue-tied

as a preteen shaking hands with Justin Bieber. Ridiculous. Completely ridiculous. "Would you saddle Kajar for me, please?" She gave a vague wave of her hand toward the stall where the gray gelding waited. As a rule, she personally tacked up any horse she rode. It helped her read the horse's mood and condition and built on the bond she established with each of the animals in her care.

But once she'd opened her mouth, she'd had to come up with a logical excuse for talking to him.

And she was curious. Would he work the same magic, establish the same instant comfortable rapport with Kajar as he had with Yazzy?

The groom—Noah—set aside his broom and went to work. Kajar stood patiently under his firm, calm hands. Noah praised the horse as he worked, calling him fine and handsome and good. The gelding gave no trouble through the process. On the contrary. Twice Kajar turned his long, graceful neck to whicker at Noah as though in approval and affection.

Once the job was done, the groom led the horse from the stall and passed Alice the reins. His long fingers whispered across her gloved palm and were gone. For a moment she caught the scent of his clean, healthy skin. He wore a light aftershave. It smelled of citrus, of sun and cedar trees.

She should have said, "Thank you," and led the horse out to ride. But he drew her so strongly. She found herself instigating an actual conversation. "You're not Montedoran."

"How did you guess?" Softly. With humor and a nice touch of irony.

"You're American."

"That's right." He looked at her steadily, those eyes

of his so blue they seemed almost otherworldly. "I grew up in California, in Los Angeles. In Silver Lake and East L.A." He was watching her in that way he had: with total concentration. A wry smile stretched the corners of his mouth. "You have no idea where Silver Lake is, or East L.A., do you? Ma'am." He was teasing her.

She felt a prickle of annoyance, which only increased her interest in him. "I have a basic understanding, yes. I've been to Southern California. I have a second cousin there. He and his family live in Bel Air."

"Bel Air is a long way from East L.A."

She leaned into Kajar, cupping her hand to his far cheek, resting her head against his long, fine neck. The gelding didn't object, only made a soft snuffling sound. "A long distance, you mean?"

One strong shoulder lifted in a shrug. "It's not so far in miles. However, Bel Air has some of the priciest real estate in the world—kind of like here in Montedoro. East L.A.? Not so much."

She didn't want to talk about real estate. Or class differences. And she needed to be on her way. She went as far as to stop leaning on the horse—but then, what do you know? She opened her mouth and another question popped out. "Do your parents still live there?"

"No. My father was killed working construction when I was twelve. My mother died of the flu when I was twenty-one."

Sympathy for him moved within her, twining with the excitement she felt at his nearness. Kajar tossed his head. She turned to the gelding, reaching up to stroke his elegant face, settling him. And then she said to Noah, "That is too sad."

"It is what it is."

She faced the groom fully again. "It must have been horrible for you."

"I learned to depend on myself."

"Do you have brothers and sisters?"

"A younger sister. Lucy is twenty-three."

She wanted to ask *his* age—but somehow that seemed such an intimate question. There were fine lines at the corners of his eyes. He had to be at least thirty. "What brings you to Montedoro?"

He seemed faintly amused. "You're full of questions, Your Highness."

She answered honestly. "It's true. I'm being very nosy." *And it's time for me to go.* But she didn't go. She kept right on being as nosy as before. "How long have you been here, in my country?"

"Not long at all."

"Do you plan to stay on?"

"That depends...."

"On?"

He didn't answer, only held her gaze.

She felt the loveliest, most effervescent sensation. Like champagne sliding, cool and fizzy, down her throat. "You love horses."

"Yes, I do. And you're wondering how a guy from East L.A. learned to handle horses...."

*Tell him that you really do have to go.* "I have been wondering exactly that."

"When I was eighteen, I went to work for a man who owned a horse ranch in the Santa Monica Mountains. He taught me a lot. And I learned fast. He kept warm bloods. Hanoverians and Morgans, mostly."

"Excellent breeds." She nodded in approval. "Strong, steady and handsome. Not nearly so testy and sensitive as an Akhal-Teke." All her horses were Tekes. Akhal-Tekes were called the "heavenly horses," the oldest breed on earth. Originating in the rugged deserts of Turkmenistan and northern Iran, the Teke was swift and temperamental and very tough. Both Genghis Khan and Alexander the Great chose Akhal-Tekes to carry them into battle.

"There is nothing like an Akhal-Teke," he said. "I hope to own one someday."

"An admirable goal."

He chuckled and the sound seemed to slide like a sweet caress across her skin. "Aren't you going to tell me that I'll never be able to afford one?"

"That would be rude. And besides, you seem a very determined sort of person. I would imagine that if you want something strongly enough, you'll find a way to have it." He said nothing, only regarded her steadily through those beautiful eyes. She was struck with the sense that there was much more going on here than she understood. "What is it?" she asked finally, when the silence had stretched thin.

"I *am* determined."

She found herself staring at his mouth. The shape of it—the slight bow of his top lip, the fullness below—was so intriguing. She wondered what it might feel like, that mouth of his touching hers. It would be so very easy to step in close, go on tiptoe and claim a kiss.…

*Stop. No. Wrong.* Exactly the sort of foolish, bold, unprincess-like behavior she was supposed to be avoiding at all costs.

"I…" She was still staring at his lips.

"Yeah?" He moved an inch closer.

She clutched the reins tighter. "…really must be on my way."

He instantly stepped back and she wished that he hadn't—which was not only contrary but completely unacceptable. "Ride safe, ma'am."

She nodded, pressing her lips together to keep them from trembling. Then she clucked her tongue at Kajar and turned for the wide-open stable door.

Once again he was gone when she returned from her ride. That day, she worked with a couple of the yearlings and put one of the show jumpers through his paces. Later she went home to shower and change.

In the afternoon, she met with the planning committee for next year's Grand Champions Tour. Montedoro would host the sixth leg of the tour down at the harbor show grounds in June. Through the endless meeting, she tried very hard not to think of blue eyes, not to remember the deep, stirring sound of a certain voice.

That night, alone in her bed, she dreamed she went riding with Noah. She was on Yasmine and he rode the bay stallion Orion. They stopped in a meadow of wildflowers and talked, though when she woke she couldn't remember a thing they had said.

It was a very tame dream. Not once did they touch, and there was none of the heated tension she had felt when she'd actually been near him. In the dream they laughed together. They were like longtime companions who knew each other well.

She woke Friday morning as usual, long before dawn, feeling edgy and dissatisfied, her mind on the American.

Why? She hardly knew this man. She *didn't* know him. She'd seen him twice and shared one brief conversation with him. He should not have affected her so profoundly.

Then again, there was probably nothing profound about it. He was hot and mysterious, untamed and somehow slightly dangerous. He called to her wild side. She found him madly attractive.

Plus, well, maybe she'd been keeping too much to herself. She wanted to avoid getting wild in the streets, but that didn't mean she couldn't have a life. She'd been sticking *too* close to home. This obsession with Noah was clear proof that she needed to get out more.

And she would get out, starting that very evening with a gala party at the palace, a celebration of her sister Rhiannon's recent marriage to Commandant Marcus Desmarais. It would be lovely. She would enjoy herself. She would dance all night.

She rose and dressed and went to the stables, expecting to see Noah again, unsure whether she *wanted* to see him—or wished that he wouldn't be there.

He wasn't there.

And her uncertainty vanished. She *did* want to see him, to hear his voice again, to find out if her response to him was as strong as it had seemed yesterday. As she tacked up the black mare Prizma, she was alert every moment for the telltale sound of someone entering the stables behind her. But no one came.

She went for her ride, returning to find that he still wasn't there. She almost asked Gilbert about him.

But she felt too foolish and confused—which wasn't like her at all. She was a confident person, always had been. She spoke her mind and had few fears. Yes, she was making a definite effort not to get into situations that might attract the attention of the tabloids and embarrass her family. But that didn't mean she was all tied up in emotional knots. She liked to live expansively, to take chances, to have fun.

She was no shy little virgin afraid to ask a few questions about a man who interested her.

The problem was…

Wait a minute. There *was* no problem. She'd met a man and found him attractive. She might or might not see him again. If she ever did get something going with him, well, it *could* be a bit awkward. She was a princess of Montedoro and he was a penniless American from a place called East Los Angeles.

They didn't exactly have a whole lot in common.

Except that they did. She *was* half American after all. And they both loved horses. And she had so enjoyed talking with him. Plus, he was very easy on the eyes….

She'd made way too much of this and she was stopping that right now. He was only a man she found intriguing. She might see him again.

And she might not. The world would go on turning however things worked out.

At six o'clock, Alice returned to her villa on a steep street in the ward of Monagalla, not far from the palace. Her housekeeper, Michelle Thierry, met her at the front door.

"I thought you'd never get back," the housekeeper chided. "Have you forgotten your sister's party?"

"Of course not. Relax. There's plenty of time."

"You're to be there at eight, you said," Michelle accused.

"Oh, come on. It's definitely doable."

Michelle wrinkled her nose. "What *have* you stepped in?"

"I work all day with horses. Take a guess."

The housekeeper waved her hands. "Don't just stand there. Get out of those boots and come inside. We'll have to hurry. There's so much to do...."

"You are way too bossy."

Michelle granted her a smug smile. "But you couldn't get along without me."

It was only the truth.

In her late forties, Michelle was a wonder. She not only took excellent care of the villa but also cooked beautiful meals and played lady's maid with skill and flair. Michelle loved her work and had impeccable taste. Alice knew she was lucky to have her.

Laughing, she perched on the step and took off her boots, which the housekeeper instantly whisked from her hands.

"The bath," Michelle commanded, waving a soiled boot. "Immediately."

Alice had her bath, did her hair and makeup, put on the red silk-taffeta Oscar de la Renta that Michelle had chosen for her and then sat impatiently, fully dressed except for her shoes, while Michelle repaired her manicure and pedicure and clucked over her for not taking proper care of her hands.

The car was waiting outside when she left the villa at ten of eight. The drive up to Cap Royale, the bluff overlooking the Mediterranean on which the Prince's Palace sprawled in all its white stone glory, should have taken only a few minutes. But the streets were packed with limousines on their way to the party. Alice could have walked it faster—and at one time, she would have simply told the driver to pull over and let her out. But no. The goal was to be more dignified, less of a wild child. She stayed in her limo like everyone else. The car finally reached the palace at 8:28 p.m. Hardly late at all, the way Alice saw it. But her mother would think otherwise. Her Sovereign Highness Adrienne expected the members of her family to arrive promptly at important events.

The guests in their gala finery were still streaming in the red-carpeted main entrance. Alice had the driver take her around to a side door where two stern-faced palace guards waited to let in intimate friends and members of the princely family. She gave her light wrap and bag to a servant.

Then she took a series of marble hallways to another exit—the one that led out to the colonnade above the palace gardens. Alice paused at the top of the white stone stairs leading down to the garden.

Below, a giant white silk tent had been erected. Golden light glowed from within the tent, where dinner for three hundred would be served. The palace, the tent, the gardens, the whole of Montedoro—everything seemed ablaze with golden light.

"There you are." Her sister Rhiannon, five months pregnant and glowing with happiness, clutched the frothy tiered skirts of her strapless ivory gown and sailed up the stairs to Alice's side, her growing baby bump leading the way.

Alice adored all four of her sisters, but she and Rhia shared a special bond. They were best friends. "Sorry I'm a little late. The streets are awash in limousines."

The sisters shared a quick hug and kissed the air by each other's cheeks. Rhia whispered, "I'm just glad you're here. I've missed you…." Flashes went off. There were always photographers lurking around, way too many of them at an event like this.

Alice hooked her arm through Rhia's. They turned as

one to face the cameras. "Smile," Alice advised softly, trying not to move her lips. "Show no weakness."

Rhia braced her free hand proudly on the bulge of her tummy and smiled for the cameras. She had a lot to be happy about. For almost a decade she'd struggled to deny her love for Marcus Desmarais. Now, at last, she and her lifetime love were together in the most complete way. Rhia and Marcus had married in a small private ceremony three weeks ago. They'd flown off for a honeymoon in the Caribbean on the same day Alice had made that fateful trip to Scotland.

The party tonight was in lieu of the usual big wedding. The world needed to see how the Bravo-Calabretti family welcomed the new husband of one of their own.

Rhia's groom had been orphaned soon after his birth. He'd started with nothing—and become a fine man, one who'd gone far in spite of his humble beginnings. The party wasn't just for show. The Bravo-Calabrettis did welcome him.

Alice loved that about her family. They judged a man—or a woman—by his or her behavior and accomplishments. Not by an accident of birth or a string of inherited titles. If Alice were to choose a man with nothing, her family would support her in her choice.

Not that she was anywhere close to choosing anyone. Certainly not a bold blue-eyed American she'd only just met and would likely not see again.

She banished the stable hand from her mind—yet again—as Rhia grabbed her hand and pulled her down the curving staircase. They wove their way through the crowd toward the wide-open entrance to the big white tent. Alice spotted her brother Damien, the youngest of the four Bravo-Calabretti princes, entering the tent, his dark head thrown back as he laughed at something the tall golden-haired man beside him had said....

"Allie?" Rhia turned back to her with a puzzled frown.

Alice realized she'd stopped in midstep at the base of the stairs and was staring with her mouth hanging open. Her brother and the other man disappeared inside the tent. She'd only caught the briefest glimpse of the other man from the back. And then from the side, for that split second when he'd turned his head. "It can't be..."

"Allie?" her sister asked again.

"I could have sworn..."

"Are you all right?" A worried frown creased the space between Rhia's smooth brows.

Alice blinked and shook her head. Lovely. Not only was she obsessing over a near stranger, she was also hallucinating that she saw the same man, perfectly turned out in white tie and tails, chatting up her brother. "Did you see that tall blond man with Dami? They just went inside the tent."

"Dami? I didn't notice."

"You didn't notice Dami, or the man with him?"

"Either. Allie, really. Are you all right?"

"I'm beginning to wonder about that," she muttered.

"You're mumbling. Say again?"

Alice would have loved to drag her favorite sister off somewhere private, where she could tell her all about the scruffy, sexy, unforgettable stable hand—whom she could have sworn she'd just seen wearing a perfectly cut designer tailcoat and evening trousers and sharing a joke with their brother. She wanted a comforting hug and some solid, down-to-earth advice. But now was not the time. She tugged on Rhia's hand. "It doesn't matter. Come on. Let's go in. Marcus will be wondering where you've gone."

The family table was a long one, set up on a dais at the far end of the tent. All their brothers and sisters were there. The married ones had come with their spouses. Even dear Belle, who lived in America now with her horse-rancher husband, Preston McCade, had come all the way from Montana to celebrate with Rhia and Marcus. Only the little nieces and nephews were missing tonight. This was a grown-up party after all.

Rhia whispered, "We never have time to talk anymore."

"I know. I miss you, too."

"Come to our villa at seven Sunday night. We'll have dinner, catch up. Just the two of us."

"What about Marcus?"

"He's dining at the palace with Alex. Something about the CCU." Alexander, Damien's twin, was third-born of their brothers. Alex had created the elite fighting force the Covert Command Unit, in which Marcus served.

"I'll be there," Alice promised.

With a last hug, Rhia left her to join her groom in her seat of honor at the center of the table.

Alice went to greet her parents. Her mother, looking amazing as always in beaded black Chanel, gave her a kiss and a fond, "Hello, my darling," and didn't say a word about her tardiness. Her mother was like that. HSH Adrienne had high expectations, but she'd never been one to nag.

In the past, Alice had crashed a motorcycle in the marketplace, run off with a sheikh for a week in Marrakech, been photographed for *Vanity Fair* wearing only a cleverly draped silk scarf and been arrested in Beijing for participating in a protest march. Among other things.

Until Glasgow, her mother had never done more than gently remind her that she was a princess of Montedoro and expected to behave like one. But after Glasgow, for the first time, Alice had been summoned to her mother's office. HSH Adrienne had asked her to shut the door and then coolly informed her that she'd finally gone too far.

"Alice," her mother had said much too sadly, too gently, "it's one thing to be spirited and adventurous. It's another to be an embarrassment to yourself and our family. In future I am counting on you to exercise better judgment and to avoid situations that will lead to revealing, provocative pictures of you splashed across the front pages of the *Sun* and the *Daily Star*."

It had been awful. Just thinking about it made her feel a little sick to her stomach.

And sad, too. A bit wilted and grim.

*Shake it off,* she commanded herself. *Let it go.*

Alice looked for her place card and found it between her older sister Belle's husband, Preston McCade, and her younger sister Genevra. Genny wore shimmering teal-blue satin and was giggling over something with another sister, the youngest, Rory, who was seated on Genny's other side.

Damien sat at the opposite end of the table. No sign of the man who looked like Noah. Alice considered hustling down there and asking Dami...what?

*Who was that man with the dark blond hair, the one you came in with?*

And what if he stared at her blankly and demanded, *Allie, darling, what man?*

She waffled just long enough that she missed her

chance. Her mother rose and greeted the guests. A hush fell over the tent. Then her father stood, as well. He picked up his champagne glass to propose the first toast.

Allie reached for her glass, raised it high and drank on cue. Then she took her seat. She greeted her sisters and Preston, whom she liked a lot. He was charming and a little shy, with a great sense of humor. He bred and trained quarter horses, so they had plenty to talk about.

There were more toasts. Alice paced herself, taking very small sips of champagne, practicing being low-key and composed for all she was worth. By the time the appetizer was served, she felt glad she hadn't asked Dami about the broad-shouldered stranger with the dark gold hair and perfectly cut evening clothes.

It was nothing. It didn't matter. She would have a fine evening celebrating her dearest sister's hard-earned happiness. And no one else would know that she'd imagined she saw someone who wasn't really there. She accepted a second glass of champagne from a passing servant and picked up a spear of prosciutto-wrapped asparagus—and then almost dropped the hors d'oeuvre in her lap when she glanced over and saw Noah.

He wore the same perfect evening attire she'd glimpsed earlier. And he sat between a stunning blonde and a gorgeous redhead several tables away, staring right at her.

## Chapter Two

Noah was watching Alice when she spotted him. Her mouth dropped open. Her face went dead white.

About then it occurred to him that maybe he'd carried his innocent deception a little too far.

She pressed her lips together and looked away, turning to her younger sister on her right side, forcing a smile. He waited for her to glance his way again.

Didn't happen.

Jennifer, the redhead seated on his left, put her hand on his thigh and asked him how he was enjoying his visit to Montedoro. He gently eased her hand away and said he was having a great time.

She hit him with a melting, eager look and said, "I'm so pleased to have met you, Noah, and I hope we can spend some time together during your stay. I would just love to show you the *real* Montedoro."

Andrea, the blonde on his other side, cut in, saving him the necessity of giving Jennifer an answer. "I love all of Prince Dami's friends," Andrea said. "Dami and I were once, well, very close. But then he met Vesuvia." A model and sometime actress, Vesuvia was often called simply V. "Dami is exclusive with V now," Andrea added. None of what she'd said was news to Noah. Or to anyone else, for that matter. "They're all over the tabloids, Dami and V," Andrea whispered breathlessly. She was mistress of the obvious in a big, big way.

"Or at least, the prince is *mostly* exclusive with V," Jennifer put in with a wicked little giggle. She fluttered her eyelashes at him. "I mean, they *are* always fighting and I notice that V's not here tonight...."

The meal wore on. Jennifer and Andrea kept up a steady stream of teasing chatter. Noah sipped champagne and hoped that Alice might grant him a second look.

If she did, he failed to catch it.

Had he blown it with her, misjudged her completely? It was starting to look that way.

But no. It couldn't be.

She'd assumed he was an itinerant stable hand and all he'd done was play along. He'd thought she would find the whole thing funny.

It hadn't even occurred to him that she might be upset about it. How could he have gotten it so wrong? He'd done his research on her after all. She was bold and curious and ready for anything, the darling of the scandal sheets. He'd never imagined she would freak out when she finally saw him as he really was.

So what did he do now?

He wouldn't give up, that was for damn sure. Not now that he'd met her, talked to her, seen her smile, looked in those eyes of hers that could be blue or gray or green, depending on the light and her shifting mood. Not now that he'd discovered she was *exactly* the woman he'd been looking for—and more.

Somehow he would have to make amends.

The meal finally ended. Princess Adrienne rose and congratulated the newlyweds again. She wished them a lifetime of married bliss. Then she invited the guests to enjoy the moonlit garden and to dance the night away in the palace ballroom upstairs.

Jennifer whispered an invitation in his ear. He turned to express his regrets.

When he glanced toward the dais again, Alice was gone.

Alice slipped out of the tent through the servants' entrance behind the dais.

She'd recovered from her initial shock at the sight of Noah sitting between those two beautiful women, looking as though he belonged there. At least by the end of dinner, she'd become reasonably certain she wasn't hallucinating. He was not a bizarre figment of her overactive imagination. The man who looked exactly like Noah the stable hand really did exist.

That meant she wasn't losing her mind after all—a fact she found wonderfully reassuring.

But *was* he actually the same man she'd first met sweeping the stable floor before dawn on Wednesday morning? Was this some kind of bizarre practical joke he was playing on her? And if so, did that make him a palace groom posing as a guest at the palace? Or a jet-setter friend of her brother's who enjoyed masquerading as the help?

She considered tracking down Dami and quizzing him about that friend of his who looked exactly like the poverty-stricken groom she'd met Wednesday.

But no. Not tonight. Damien might be able to enlighten her, but then he would have questions of his own. She just wasn't up for answering Dami's questions. And it didn't matter anyway. She knew what to do: forget it. Forget *him*.

It was all too weird. It made no sense and she wasn't going to think about it.

She would enjoy the rest of the evening and move on.

A familiar voice behind her said, "Allie, I haven't seen you in ages."

She turned to smile at a longtime friend. "Robert. How have you been?"

"I can't complain." Robert Bentafaille was compact and muscular, with an open face and kind green eyes. The Bentafailles owned orange groves. Lots of them. He and Alice were the same age and had gone through primary and secondary school together. "You look beautiful, as always."

"And you always say that."

"I hear the orchestra." He cast a glance back at the palace, at the lights blazing in the upstairs ballroom. Music drifted down to them. He offered his hand.

She took it and they turned together to go inside.

Alice danced two dances with Robert.

Then another longtime friend, Clark deRoncleff, tapped Robert on the shoulder. She turned into Clark's open arms and danced some more.

After that she left the floor, accepted a glass of sparkling water from a passing servant and visited with Rhia and Marcus for a bit. Rhia was sharing her plans for the nursery when Alice spotted Dami across the dance floor. He was talking to the man who almost certainly was Noah. She stared for a moment too long.

The man who had to be Noah seemed to sense her gaze on him. He turned. Their eyes met. His were every bit as blue as she remembered.

She had no doubt now. It had to be him. Quickly, she

turned away and gave her full attention to Rhia and her groom.

Noah didn't matter to her. She hardly knew him. She refused to care what he was doing there at her sister's wedding party or what he might be up to.

Marcus asked Rhia to dance. They went off together, holding hands, looking so happy it made Alice feel downright misty-eyed and more than a little bit envious.

Her eldest brother, Maximilian, came toward her. The heir to their mother's throne, Max was handsome and magnetic—like all of her brothers. He used to be a happy man. But three years ago his wife, Sophia, had died in a waterskiing accident. Max had loved Sophia since they were children. Now he was like a ghost of himself. He went through all the motions of living. But some essential element was missing. Sophia had given him two children, providing him with the customary heir and a spare to the throne. He didn't have to marry again—and he probably never would.

"We hardly see you lately," Max chided. "You haven't been to Sunday breakfast in weeks." It was a family tradition: Sunday breakfast in the sovereign's private apartments at the palace. She and her siblings were grown now, but they all tried to show up for the Sunday-morning meal whenever they were in Montedoro.

"I've been busy with my horses."

"Of course you have." Max leaned closer. "You did nothing wrong. Don't ever let them crush your spirit."

She knew whom he meant by *them:* the paparazzi and the tabloid journos. "Oh, Max…"

"You are confident and curious. You like to get out and mix it up. It's who you are. We all love you as you are and we know it was only in fun."

"I'm not so sure about Mother."

"She's on your side and she never judges. You know that."

"What I know is that I've finally managed to embarrass her." It wasn't so much that she'd French-kissed a girl. It was the pictures. They came off so tacky, like something out of *Girls Gone Wild*.

"I think you're wrong. Mother is not embarrassed. And she loves you unconditionally."

Alice didn't have the heart to argue about it, to insist that their mother *was* embarrassed; she'd said so. Instead, she leaned close to him and whispered, "Thank you."

He smiled his sad smile. "Dance?" Though Max would never marry again, women were constantly trying to snare him. They all wanted to console the widower prince who would someday rule Montedoro. So he tried to steer clear of them. At balls, he danced with his mother and his sisters and then retired early.

"I would love to dance with you." She pulled him out onto the floor and they danced through the rest of that number and the next one.

Before they parted, he asked her directly to come to the family breakfast that Sunday. "Please. Say you'll be here. We miss you."

She gave in and promised she would come, and then she walked with him to where their youngest sister, Rory, chatted with Lani Vasquez. Small, dark-haired and curvy, Lani was an American, an aspiring author of historical novels set in Montedoro. She'd come from America with Sydney O'Shea when Sydney had married Rule, the second-born of Alice's brothers.

Alice had assumed Max would dance next with Rory.

But he took Lani's hand instead. The music started up again and Max led the pretty American onto the floor.

Rory said, "Well, well."

"My, my," Alice murmured in agreement. For a moment the two sisters watched in amazement as their tragically widowed eldest brother danced with someone who wasn't his sister.

Then a girlfriend of Rory's appeared out of the crowd. She grabbed Rory's hand and towed her toward the open doors to the balcony. Alice considered following them. It was a lovely night. She could lean on the stone railing and gaze out over the harbor, admire the lights of the casino and the luxury shops and hotels that surrounded it.

"Alice. Dance with me."

The deep, thrilling voice came from directly behind her and affected her just as it had when they were alone in the stables. It seemed to slip beneath her skin, to shiver its way along the bumps of her spine, to create a warm pool of longing down in the deepest core of her.

She didn't turn. Instead, she stared blindly toward the open doors to the balcony. She wasn't even going to acknowledge him. She would start walking and she wouldn't look back.

If he dared to come after her, she would cut him dead.

But really, what would that prove? That she was afraid to deal with him? That she didn't have the stones to stand her ground and face him, to find out from his own mouth what kind of game he was playing with her? That Max had been right and the tacky tabloid reporters, the shameless paparazzi, really had done it? They'd broken her spirit, made her into someone unwilling to face a challenge head-on.

Oh, no. No way.

She whirled on him and glared into his too-blue eyes. "It *is* you."

He nodded. He held out his hand. "Let me explain. Give me that chance."

She kept her arm at her side. "I don't trust you."

"I know." He didn't lower his hand. The man had nerves of steel.

And she couldn't bear it, to let him stand there with his hand offered and untaken. She laid her fingers into his palm. Heat radiated up her arm just from that first contact. Her breath caught and tangled in her chest.

*How absurd. Breathe.*

With slow care, she sucked in a breath and then let it out as he turned and led her onto the floor. She went into his arms. They danced.

He had the good sense to hold her lightly. For a few endless minutes, neither of them spoke, which was just as well as far as Alice was concerned. She longed to wave her arms about and shriek accusations at him. Unfortunately, shrieking and waving her arms would attract attention, and that would no doubt land her on the front pages of the tabloids again.

She caught a hint of his aftershave. Evergreen and citrus, the same as before. It was all too disorienting. She'd thought he was one person and now here he was, someone else altogether. She felt shy. Tongue-tied. Young.

And at a definite disadvantage. She needed to take back the upper hand here. She had questions for him. And he'd better have good answers.

The next song began, a fast one. Couples separated and danced facing each other, moving to the beat but not touching. Noah didn't let her go, just picked up the rhythm a bit and danced them out of the way of the others.

"You're angry," he said at last.

"What happened to your two girlfriends?"

"What girlfriends?"

"That sexy redhead and the stunning blonde."

"They're not my girlfriends." He kept his voice low, but he did pull her fractionally closer. She allowed that in order to hear him over the music. "They were seated on either side of me at dinner, that's all."

"They seemed very friendly." She spoke quietly, too. She didn't want anyone overhearing, broadcasting their conversation, starting new rumors about her.

He held her even closer and whispered much too tenderly, "Is that somehow my fault?"

She fumed in silence, refusing to answer. Finally, she demanded, "Who are you, really?"

"I'm who I said I was."

"Noah."

"Yes."

"Do you have a last name?"

"Cordell." He turned her swiftly and gracefully to the music, guiding her effortlessly, keeping them to the outer edges of the floor.

"*Are* you a stable hand?"

"No. And I didn't say I was. You assumed that."

"And you never bothered to enlighten me. Do you live in Los Angeles?"

"No. Not for years. I have an estate in Carpinteria, not far from Santa Barbara. I live there most of the time. I also have a flat I keep in London. And a Paris apartment."

"So you should have no trouble affording that Akhal-Teke you said you want."

"No trouble at all. But it's a specific horse I'm after."

She should have known. "Let me guess. One of mine?"

"Orion."

She drew in a sharp breath. In that foolish dream of hers, he'd been riding Orion. "I'm not selling you Orion." That was a bit petty, and she knew it. Not to mention a bad business move. Alice bred her horses for sale—to buyers who would love them and bond with them and treat them well, buyers who appreciated the beauty and rarity of the breed. Her pool of buyers was a small one, as she also demanded a high price for her Tekes. She might be angry with Noah, but he knew horses and loved them. She'd be smarter not to reject him out of hand—as a potential buyer, anyway. "I don't wish to discuss my horses with you right now."

"You brought it up." The next song was a slower one. He effortlessly adjusted to the change in tempo, all the while gazing down at her, watching her mouth. As if he planned to kiss her—a bold move he had better not try.

She accused, "I brought it up as an example of the way that you lied to me. Not with words, maybe. But by implication. By action. The first time I saw you, you were sweeping the stable floor. Gilbert seemed to know you. What else was I to assume but that he'd hired you?"

"Gilbert was joking with me. He saw me sweeping and asked me if I needed a job. Your brother Damien had introduced us the day before. Dami knows I love horses and wanted me to have a chance to ride while I was here. And I had told him I was hoping to buy one of your stallions. He said I would have to talk to you about that."

"You're great friends, then, you and my brother?"

"Yes. I consider Damien a friend."

She thought again of the blonde and the redhead at

dinner. He'd seemed to take their fawning attentions as his due. "You're a player. Like Dami."

"I'm single. I enjoy a good life and I like the company of beautiful women."

"You're a player."

"I am not playing you, Alice." He held her gaze. Steadily. Somehow the very steadiness of his regard excited her.

She did not wish to be excited. "You've been playing me from the moment you picked up that broom and pretended to be someone you're not."

"Everything I told you was true. Everything. Yes, I've got all I'll ever need now, but I started out in L.A. with nothing. My parents were both dead by the time I was twenty-one. I have one sister, Lucy."

"And you went to work on a ranch when you were eighteen?"

"No. I visited that ranch. Often. My boss took a liking to me. He flipped houses in Los Angeles for a living and he hired me as a day laborer to start. I learned the business from the ground up, beginning on his low-end properties in East L.A."

"You're saying you learned fast?" She wasn't surprised.

"Before the crash, I was buying and selling in all the major markets. I got out ahead of the collapse with a nice nest egg. Now I manage my investments and I do what I want with the rest of my time. Oh, and that second cousin you mentioned, the one who lives in Bel Air?"

"Jonas."

He nodded. "I know him. Jonas Bravo and I have done business on a couple of occasions. He's a good man." He pulled her a little closer again. She allowed that, though she knew that she probably shouldn't. They danced without talking for a minute or two.

Finally, she muttered grudgingly, "You should have told me all of this at the first."

"I can see that now." He sounded so…sincere. As though he truly regretted misleading her.

She tried not to soften. "Why didn't you, then?"

"Alice, I…" The words trailed off.

"At a loss? I don't believe it. Just tell me. Why weren't you honest with me from the first?"

"I don't know, exactly. Because it was fun. Exciting. To tease you."

She started to smile and caught herself. "That's not a satisfactory answer."

"Look. I came early to ride and I saw you there, saddling that beautiful mare. It was still dark out and there was no one else around. I didn't want to scare you. I picked up the broom and started sweeping, because what's more nonthreatening than some guy sweeping the floor? And then… I don't know. You thought I was a groom and you talked to me anyway. I liked that. I got into it, that's all. In a way, the Noah you met in the stables really is me. Just…another possible me. The one who didn't make a fortune in real estate. I thought it would be something we would laugh over later."

The dance ended. For a moment they swayed together at the edge of the floor. She should have pulled away.

She stayed right where she was.

He was getting to her. She was liking him again. Believing the things he told her….

Yet another song started.

He pulled her even closer and whispered, his breath warm across her skin, "I screwed up, okay?" He whirled her around. They danced in a circle along the outer rim of the floor.

"You knew who I was from the first. Before we met. Right?"

He pulled back enough to give her a look. Patient. Ironic. "Please. I'm friends with your brother. He's told me about you—and your sisters and brothers. Also, I want one of your stallions and I know you're quite a horse trader, not only brutal when striking a bargain but particular about whom you'll sell to. I've made it my business to learn everything I can about you."

Which meant he would have seen the Glasgow pictures.

Well, so what? She'd done what she'd done. She'd gone over the top and she'd suffered for it. She was tired of being ashamed. "You know all about me? That sounds vaguely stalkerish."

He shrugged, his muscular shoulder lifting and then settling under her hand. "You could look at it that way, I suppose. Or you could admit that it's just good sense to find out what you can about the people you'll be dealing with."

"So of course you won't mind if I track you down online the next chance I get."

"I would expect nothing less." And he smiled, rueful. And somehow hopeful, too. He was way too charming when he smiled. "And when you find out I've told the truth, do I get another chance with you?"

All at once she was too sharply aware of his hand holding hers, his warm fingers and firm palm at her back, his big body brushing hers. Little arrows of sensation seemed to zip around beneath her skin. "A chance with me? I thought we were talking about your buying Orion."

He eased her closer. His breath touched her hair and his body burned into hers. Her skin felt electrified. And he whispered, "You know we're talking about more than the horse. Who's lying now? Ma'am?"

She liked it too much, dancing so close to him. She liked *him* too much. "Please don't hold me so tightly."

He instantly obeyed, loosening his hold so he embraced her easily, lightly, again. "Better?"

She nodded, thinking that this particular Noah, self-assured and sophisticated in evening dress, was every bit as brash and manly as the one she'd assumed was a groom. And smooth, too. She hadn't planned to forgive him for pretending to be a penniless stable hand—but somehow she already had.

And not only had she forgiven him, she was actually considering letting him have Orion after all. Because she did like him and she'd seen him with her horses. Orion would thrive in Noah's care.

He pulled her closer again. She allowed that. It felt good and she wasn't really afraid of him. She was afraid of *herself,* of her too-powerful response to him. And then there was her basic problem: it had always been so easy for her to get carried away. She would have to watch herself.

Then again, her goal tonight had been to get out and have a little fun.

So all right. It shouldn't be too difficult to do both—to have a little fun and yet not get carried away.

They danced the rest of that dance without talking. When it ended, they swayed together until the next dance began and then danced some more.

"Walk in the garden with me," he said when that song was over.

"Yes. I would like that."

He took her hand and led her from the dance floor.

It was going pretty well, Noah thought as he walked with her down the stone stairway that led to the big tent and the palace gardens beyond. She seemed to have gotten past her fury with him for pretending to be someone he wasn't. But he sensed a certain residual wariness in her. Which was fine. Few things worth winning came easily.

"Something to drink?" he asked.

"I would like that."

So they stopped in the tent, where waiters offered wine and cocktails and soft drinks, too. They both took flutes of champagne and went out the back exit behind the dais into the moonlit garden strung with party lights.

She said, "You implied when we talked in the stables that you were staying in Montedoro indefinitely...."

"Not anymore. It turns out there are a couple of meetings I have to get back for. I'll be leaving Thursday."

"Is your sister visiting with you?"

"No, she's at home in California."

"I assume Dami has you staying here at the palace?"

He shook his head. "Lots of guests at the palace this weekend. I went ahead and took a suite at the Belle Époque." The five-star hotel was across from Casino d'Ambre.

Another couple came toward them. They nodded in greeting as they passed. When it was just the two of them again, Alice said, "I love the Belle Époque. We used to go for afternoon tea there now and then when I was a girl, my sisters and I. We would get our favorite table—on the mezzanine of the winter garden, with that amazing dome of stained glass and steel overhead. I would stuff myself with tea cakes, and the governess, Miss Severly, would have to reprimand me."

"Governess? I thought your brother said you all went to Montedoran schools."

"We did. But after we grew out of our nanny, Gerta, we also had Miss Severly. She tutored us between school terms and tried to drum good manners into us."

"Were you scared of your governess?"

"Not in the least. Once reprimanded, I only grew more determined. At tea I would wait until Miss Severly looked the other way and then try to stuff down as many cakes as I could before she glanced at me again."

"Did you make yourself sick?"

She slanted him a glance. "How did you know?"

He thought of all the tabloid stories he'd read about her. Of course she'd been a girl who gobbled cakes when the governess wasn't looking. "Just a guess."

They came out on a point overlooking the sea. An iron bench waited beneath a twisted cypress tree and an iron railing marked the cliff's edge. Alice went to the railing. She sipped her champagne and stared out over the water at the distant three-quarter moon.

As he watched her, he had the oddest feeling of unreality. It was like a dream, really, being there with her. She was a vision in lustrous red, her bare shoulders so smooth, her arms beautifully shaped, muscular in a way that was uniquely feminine.

Eventually, she turned to him. Her eyes were very dark at that moment. Full of shadows and secrets. "I've never been as well behaved as I should be. It's a problem for me. I'm too eager for excitement and adventure. But I'm working on that."

He moved to stand beside her, and leaned back against the railing. "There's nothing wrong with a little adventure now and then."

She laughed, turning toward him, holding her champagne glass up so he could tap his against it. "I agree. But as you said, *now and then.* For me it's like the tea cakes. I just *have* to eat them all." She sighed. And then she drained the glass. "So I'm trying to slow down a little, to think before I jump, to be less…excitable."

"It's a shame to curb all that natural enthusiasm." He wanted to touch her—to smooth her shining hair or run the back of a finger along the sleek curve of her neck. But he held himself in check. He didn't want to spook her.

"Everybody has to grow up sometime." She leaned in closer. Her perfume came to him: like lilies and leather and a hint of the ocean. He could stand there and smell her all night. But she was on the move again. In a rustle of red skirts, she went to the bench and sat down. "Tell me about your sister." She bent to set her empty glass beneath the bench.

"She's much younger than I am. We're twelve years apart. She's been homeschooled for most of her life. She's sensitive and artistic. She could always draw, from when she was very little, and she carries a sketch pad around with her all the time. And she loves to sew. She's better with a thread and needle than any tailor I've ever used. She makes all her own clothes. And now she's suddenly decided that she wants to study fashion design in New York City."

Alice patted the space next to her. "And you don't want her to do what she wants?"

He went to her. She swept her skirt out of the way and he sat beside her. "Lucy was homeschooled because she was sick a lot. She almost died more than once. She had asthma and a problem with a heart valve."

"Had?" She took his empty champagne flute and put it under the bench with hers. "You mean she's better now?"

"The asthma's in remission. And after several surgeries that didn't do much good, two years ago she finally had the one that actually worked."

"So she's well? She can lead a normal life."

"She has to be careful."

Alice was studying him again, and much too closely. "You're overprotective."

"I'm not." He sounded defensive and he knew it.

"But Lucy thinks so...."

He grumbled, "You're too damn smart." He could almost regret not choosing a stupid princess. But then all he had to do was look at her, smell her perfume, hear her laugh, watch her with her horses—and he knew that no silly, malleable princess would do for him. Alice was the one. No doubt about it.

"I certainly am smart," she said. "So you'd better be honest with me from now on. Tell me lies and I'll find you out."

"I *have* been honest." Mostly.

She shook her head. "Do I have to remind you of your alter ego, the stable hand—again?"

"Please. No." He held up both hands palms out in surrender.

"Oh, my." She pretended to fan herself. "You're begging. I think I like that."

He set her straight. "It was a simple request."

"No, no, no." She laughed. She had a great laugh, full-out and all in. "You were definitely begging." Smiling smugly, showing off the dimples that made her almost as cute as she was beautiful, she asked, "You said Lucy is twenty-three, right?"

He kept catching himself watching her mouth. It was plump and pretty and very tempting. But he wasn't going to kiss her, not tonight. He'd just barely salvaged the situation with her and he couldn't afford to push his luck by moving too fast. "Why are we talking about Lucy, anyway?"

"Because she's important to you." She said it simply. Openly.

And all at once he wanted to be...better somehow. It was bewildering. She stirred him, more than he'd ever intended to be stirred. He started talking, started saying *real* things. "When our mom died, we had nothing. Lucy was nine and sick all the time. I was twenty-one, just starting out, working days for that guy with the horse ranch I told you about, taking business classes at night. Our mom died and Child Protective Services showed up the next day to take Lucy away."

"I am sorry...." She said it softly, the three simple words laden with sadness. For him.

He wanted some big things from her. Sympathy wasn't one of them. "Don't be. It was a good thing."

"A good thing that you lost your sister?"

"I didn't lose her. She went to an excellent foster mom, a great lady named Hannah Russo who made me welcome whenever I came to visit."

"Well, that's good."

"It was, yeah. And that they wouldn't let me take care of my sister was a definite wake-up call. I knew I had to get my ass in gear or I would never get custody of her. She was so damn frail. She could have died. I was afraid she *would* die. It was seriously motivating. I was determined, above all, to get her back with me where I could take care of her."

Her eyes were so soft. He could see the moon in them. "How long did it take you?"

"I got custody of her three years·after our mom died, when Lucy was twelve. I've taken care of her since then. She's my family. Sometimes she doesn't see it, but I only want what's best for her."

"I know you do." She leaned in close again. He smelled lilies and sea foam. "I like you, Noah." She said his name on a breath. And then she leaned closer still. "You're macho and tough. Kind of. But not. You confuse me. I shouldn't like that. But I do. I like *you* far too much, I think."

He whispered, "Good." His senses spun. She affected him so strongly. Too strongly, really. More strongly than any woman had in a long, long time—maybe ever. Above all, he had to remember not to push too fast. Not to kiss her. Yet.

Her red skirts rustled as she leaned that little bit closer. Her breath brushed his cheek, so warm, so sweet.

What now? Should he back off? Did it count as moving too fast if *she* was the one doing the moving?

She whispered, "I promised myself I wouldn't kiss you…."

"All right." It wasn't all right. Not really. And she was too close, making it way too hard to remember that he wasn't going to kiss her. Not now. Not tonight….

"But, Noah. I really *want* to kiss you."

He held very still, every molecule in his body alert. Hungry. He wanted to go for it, to grab her and haul her into his aching arms. He wanted that way too much for his own peace of mind. "Remember," he said on a bare husk of sound, "you have a plan."

"What plan?" Her gaze kept straying to his mouth.

"You promised yourself you would think before you jump." Did he mean to be helpful? Maybe. But somehow it came out as a challenge.

And, as everything he'd read about her had made crystal clear, Her Highness Alice never could resist a challenge. "To hell with my plan."

"Tomorrow you'll feel differently."

"Tomorrow can take care of itself." She swayed that fraction closer. "Right now I only want to kiss you." She lifted those plump, sweet lips to him.

He made himself wait. He managed, just barely, to hold himself in check until her mouth touched his.

Then, with a low groan, he reached out and wrapped his arms good and tight around her.

## Chapter Three

Alice knew very well that she shouldn't be kissing him.

Kissing him, after all, was exactly what she'd said she wouldn't do.

But the scent of him was all around her—like his big strong arms that held her so very tightly. His chest was broad and hard and wonderful beneath the snow-white evening shirt.

And his kiss? Deep and demanding at first, thrilling her. His hot breath burned her mouth; his tongue delved in.

But then a moment later he dialed it down, going gentle, easier. He tempted her all the more forcefully by using tenderness, by taking it slow. His big hands roamed her back, making her shiver with delight. And his lips... Oh, my, the man certainly did know how to kiss. She could go on like this forever, sitting under the moon with the soft sigh of the sea far below them, all wrapped up in Noah's arms.

Then again, anyone might come up on them out here in the open like this. The paparazzi were everywhere. She'd learned that the hard way, over and over again.

If someone got a shot of her now, plastered all over a virtual stranger, soul-kissing him deeper than she had that redheaded barmaid during the karaoke escapade...

With a low moan, she put her hands to his hard chest and pushed him away. He made no move to stop her.

Breathless, still yearning, she faced forward again. Sagging against the iron back of the bench, she stared out beyond the railing at the moonlit sea.

Noah said nothing. She was grateful for that.

Back on the path behind them, a woman laughed. It was more of a giggle, really. A man spoke as though in reply, his voice low and intimate, the words unclear. More feminine laughter, and then the man said something else, the sound of his voice retreating as he spoke. Whoever they were, they had turned and gone back toward the palace.

There was silence. Only the breeze off the sea and the distant cry of a gull.

Alice smoothed her hair and straightened the bodice of her strapless gown. "Sometimes I really disappoint myself."

"Is it possible you're trying too hard to be good?" he asked in that lovely sexy rumble that had stirred her from the first.

She shot him a scoffing glance. "More likely, I'm not trying hard enough."

He caught her hand. Before she could pull away, he pressed his wonderful lips to the back of it. His mouth was so warm, so deliciously soft compared to the rest of him. "You're amazing. Just as you are. Why mess with a great thing?" His words were pure temptation. She wanted only to sigh and sway against him again, to kiss him some more, to give him a chance to flatter her endlessly. She wanted to let him kiss her and touch her until she forgot all the promises she'd made to herself about learning a little discipline, about keeping her actions under control.

Instead, she said, "I would like my hand back, please." He released her. She rose and brushed out her taffeta skirt. "Good night. Please don't follow me." She turned for the trail, glancing back only once before she ducked between the hedges.

He hadn't moved. He sat facing the sea, staring out at the moon.

Alice collected her bag and wrap from the attendant at the side entrance and called for her driver.

Twenty minutes after she'd left Noah staring out to sea, the driver was holding the limo door for her. She slipped into the plush embrace of the black leather seat.

At home she had another bath. A long one, to relax.

But she didn't relax. She lay there amid the lily-scented bubbles and tried not to feel like a complete jerk.

Noah had really stepped up. He'd made an honest, forthright apology for misleading her at the stables. And then he'd gone about being a perfect gentleman. He'd also been open and honest with her about his life, his past. About the tensions between him and his little sister.

He had not put a move on her. She'd made sure that he wouldn't, by going on and on about how from now on she planned to look before she leaped.

After which she had grabbed him and kissed him for all she was worth.

Seriously, now. She was hopeless. She needed a keeper, someone to follow her around and make sure she behaved herself. Twenty-five years old and she couldn't stop acting like an impulsive, greedy child.

Her bath grew cold. She only grew more tense, more annoyed with herself.

Finally, she got out and dried off and put on a robe. It was after two in the morning. Time for bed.

But she couldn't sleep. She kept thinking how Noah had said he had no problem with her looking him up on the internet.

Finally, she threw back the covers, grabbed her laptop and snooped around for a while.

She learned that everything he'd told her that night— and in the stables, for that matter—was the truth. He was quite a guy, really, to have come from a run-down rented bungalow in the roughest part of Los Angeles without a penny to his name and built a real-estate empire before he was thirty. When he was twenty-eight, he'd been one of *Forbes'* thirty top entrepreneurs under thirty. Two years ago he'd been a *People* magazine pick for one of America's ten most eligible bachelors. His Santa Barbara–area estate had been profiled in *House & Garden*.

There were several pages of images. Some of them showed him with Lucy, who had a sweet, friendly smile and looked very young. But most of them were of him with a gorgeous woman at his side—a lot of *different* gorgeous women. He'd never been linked to any one woman for any length of time.

The endless series of beautiful girlfriends reminded her of all the reasons she wouldn't be getting involved with him. The last thing she needed was to fall for a rich player who would trade her in for a newer model at the first opportunity.

It was after four when she finally fell asleep. She woke at noon, ate a quick breakfast, put on her riding clothes and went to the stables.

Noah wasn't there. Excellent. With a little luck, she would get through the last five days of his Montedoran visit without running into him again.

Sunday morning, Alice kept her promise to Max and went to breakfast at the palace. Everyone seemed happy to see her.

Her mother made a special effort to ask her how the plans were coming along for next year's Grand Champions Tour. Alice gave her a quick report and her mother said how pleased they all were with her work. She'd sold two mares, a stallion and a gelding in the past month. The money helped support her breeding program, but a good chunk of it went to important causes. Her mother praised her contribution to the lives of all Montedorans.

Alice basked in the approval. She knew what it meant. Her mother was getting past her disappointment over her antics in Glasgow.

At the table, she ended up next to Damien. He threw an arm across her shoulders and pressed a kiss to her cheek. "Allie. You're looking splendid, as always."

"Flatterer."

Dami shrugged and got to work on his eggs Benedict. He looked a little tired, she thought. But then, he often did. He was quite the globe-trotter. Most people thought he was all about beautiful women and the good life—and he was. But he also held a degree in mechanical engineering and design. He was a talented artist, too. And beyond all that, he loved putting together a profitable business deal almost as much as their second-born brother, Rule. And then there were the charities he worked hard to support.

No wonder he looked as though he needed a long nap.

She was tempted to ply him with questions about Noah. But what was the point? She'd already decided that she and Noah weren't going to be happening, so it didn't matter what Dami might have to tell her about him.

Dami sipped espresso. When he set down the demitasse, he turned to her again and said softly, "I heard you danced more than one dance with Noah Cordell last Friday. After which you went walking in the garden with him...."

Well, all right, then. Apparently, she was going to hear about Noah after all, whether she wanted to or not. "I met him in the stables. He was there Wednesday and Thursday mornings, early. He said you had introduced him to Gilbert."

"That's right."

"We...chatted."

"And danced," he repeated, annoyingly patient. "And walked in the garden."

"Yes, Dami. We did."

"You like him." It wasn't a question. His expression was unreadable.

She answered truthfully. "I do. He's intelligent, fun and a good dancer, as well."

"He's worse with women than I am."

"But you're not so bad—lately. I mean, what about Vesuvia?"

"What about her?" He gave her one of those looks. "We've been on-again, off-again. Now we're permanently off."

"I'm sorry to hear that."

"Don't be. It's for the best."

"But you've settled down a lot. We've all noticed."

He dismissed her argument with a wave. "I'm not a

good bet when it comes to relationships. Neither is Noah. It's always a new woman with him. Take my advice. Stay away from him."

That got her back up. "You ought to know better than to tell me what to do, Dami."

"It's for your own good, I promise you."

She laughed. "You're just making it worse. And you know that. You know how I am. Tell me *not* to do a thing and I just *have* to do it. Or are you *trying* to get me interested in Noah?"

"I'm not that clever."

"Oh, please. We both know you're brilliant."

"Sometimes, my darling, I actually do mean exactly what I say. Please stay away from Noah Cordell."

She really wanted to remind him that he had no right to tell her whom she could or couldn't see. But she let it go. "He wants to buy Orion."

"Do you want to sell him Orion?"

"I told him I wouldn't, but actually, I'm still thinking it over."

"I'll be honest."

"Why, thank you."

"I've been to his California estate. It's a horse farm and a fine one. And he's as good with horses as you are."

Alice had seen how good Noah was with horses. Still, her pride couldn't let that stand. "No one's as good with horses as I am."

"Plus, you're so enchantingly shy and modest."

"Shyness and modesty are overrated."

He turned back to his meal. They ate in silence for a minute or two. Then he said, "Noah's got more money than we do. He would pay whatever price you set for one of your Tekes. And he treats his animals handsomely."

"Then you do think I should sell him the stallion?"

"Yes—but then, I know you, Allie. You're going to do exactly what you want to do."

"I certainly am."

"Just don't let him charm you. Keep your guard up, or you'll get hurt."

*Keep your guard up, or you'll get hurt....*

Dami had only warned her of what she already knew. And she *would* heed his warning. For once, she wouldn't be contrary for contrary's sake. She would take her brother's advice and steer clear of Noah Cordell. Should she happen to meet up with him again, she would treat him with courtesy.

Courtesy and nothing more.

Her resolve got its first test at the stables that afternoon. Noah appeared as she was consulting with the equine dentist who checked the teeth of all her horses twice yearly. She glanced up and there he was out in the courtyard, the September sun gilding his hair, looking way too tall and fit and yummy for her peace of mind. Just the sight of him caused a curl of heat down low in her abdomen.

But no problem. She could handle this.

Alice asked the dentist to excuse her for a moment.

When Noah entered the stable, she was waiting for him, her smile cool and composed. "Noah. I hardly recognized you."

Gone were the old jeans and battered Western boots. Today he was beautifully turned out in the English style: black breeches, black polo shirt and a fine pair of black field boots. He regarded her distantly. "I was hoping to ride." A flick of a glance at the rows of stalls. "How about

Gadim?" The six-year-old black gelding had energy to spare and could be fractious.

But she knew Noah could handle him. "Excellent choice. Shall I call a groom to tack him up?"

"I can manage, thanks." His tone gave her nothing. Because she'd come on so distant and cool? Or because he'd already lost interest in her?

She couldn't tell.

And she wished that she didn't care.

"Good, then," she said too brightly. "Have a pleasant ride."

She returned to her consultation with the dentist, who had a list of the horses needing teeth pulled or filed.

Noah was off on Gadim when she finished with the dentist. She considered lingering until he came back. She wanted to ask him how he'd enjoyed his ride, to let him know that she might be convinced to sell him Orion.

But that would only be courting trouble.

She liked him too much. She could let down her guard with him so very easily. Not that he even cared at this point. He'd seemed so bored and uninterested earlier.

Which shouldn't matter in the least to her.

But it did.

No. Not a good idea to hang around in the hope of seeing him again.

She left the stables for a far paddock, where she spent the remainder of the afternoon working on leading and tying with a couple of recently weaned foals.

"Don't listen to Dami," Rhia said that evening as they shared dessert on the terrace of her villa overlooking the harbor.

Alice had told her sister everything by then. "But what if Dami's right?"

"That the man's a player? Oh, please. As though Dami has any room to talk."

"Well, but I just don't need to get myself into any more trouble. I really don't."

Rhia enjoyed a slow bite of her chocolate soufflé. "How are you going to get into trouble? You said he's filthy rich."

"Whether or not I get myself in trouble has nothing to do with how much money a man has."

"I *mean* you can rest assured that he's no fortune hunter. You're both single. You both love horses. You enjoy being with him. And you happen to be extremely attracted to him. You should give him a chance." She savored yet another bite. "Mmm." She licked chocolate from her upper lip. "Lately, if it's chocolate, I can't get enough."

"The baby must love chocolate," Alice suggested with a smile.

"That must be it—and what was it you once advised me? 'Rhia, be bold,' you said."

"Oh, please. That was about Marcus."

"So?"

"Marcus loves you. He's *always* loved you."

Rhia frowned. "I wasn't at all sure about that at the time."

"Still, my situation is entirely different."

"Why?"

"Because *we're* so different, you and I. You've always been nothing short of exemplary. Well behaved and *good.* You needed to be told to get out there and go after the only man you've ever loved. I don't require any such encouragement."

"On the contrary, it seems very clear to me that you do."

"One, Noah Cordell is not my lifelong love. I truly hardly know the man. And two, if anything, *I* need to be told *not* to be bold."

Her sister reached across the table and touched her cheek. "You like him. He likes you. You haven't been this worked up over a man in forever."

"I am not worked up."

Rhia clucked her tongue and then began scraping the last of the soufflé out of her ramekin. "I don't know what I'm going to do with you."

"Support me. Sympathize with me."

"As though that's going to help you." Rhia shook her head and licked her spoon.

"Even if I took your advice instead of Dami's, I'm afraid it's too late."

"Too late for what?"

"I'm afraid he's not interested in me anymore. Today in the stables, he acted as though he didn't even *care* what I thought of him."

"Was this before or after you treated him like a stranger?"

"I didn't treat him like a stranger."

"Yes, you did. You *said* that you did."

"I was perfectly civil."

"Civil. Precisely. Are you going to eat your soufflé?" Alice pushed it across the table.

Rhia dug right in, sighing. "Oh, my, yes. *So* good. And you do see what's happening here, don't you?"

"What?"

"You are not being you." Rhia paused to sigh over another big bite of chocolate. "And you're making yourself miserable."

"Not being me? Of course I'm being me. Who else would I be?"

"Allow me to explain…."

"Please."

Rhia pointed with her spoon. "You went a little over the top in Glasgow."

"A *little?*"

"That is what I said. You went over the top, and since then, you've decided you need to be *so* well behaved and subdued. It's just not like you at all. You are a brave, bold person, a person who jumps right into anything that interests her, who lives by her instincts. But you're trying to be someone else, someone careful and controlled, someone who plans ahead, who reasons everything out with agonizing care. And as your favorite sister who loves you more than you'll ever know, it's my responsibility to inform you that being someone you're not isn't working for you."

Alice thought a lot about the things Rhia had said to her. She could see the sense in Rhia's advice, she truly could.

But the thing was that she liked Noah *too* much. She hardly knew him, yet she couldn't stop thinking about him.

It scared her. It really did. She'd never been so powerfully attracted to any man before. What if she did fall in love with him?

And then he dumped her for someone else?

Even a brave, bold woman who lived by her instincts should have the sense not to volunteer for that kind of pain.

She didn't see him on Monday. But then Tuesday she went down to the Triangle d'Or, the area of exclusive shops near the casino, to pick up a Balenciaga handbag she'd ordered. She saw him sitting at a little outdoor café sipping an espresso. He was alone and she was so very tempted to stop and chat with him a little.

But she didn't. Uh-uh. She walked on by, quickly, before he could spot her and wave at her. Or worse, ignore her.

He was leaving on Thursday, he'd said. She only had to get through the next day without doing anything stupid. He would go home to his estate in California, to his frail and artistic little sister. And in time she would forget him.

All day Wednesday she kept thinking that tomorrow he would be gone. He never came to the stables that day—or if he did, she missed seeing him. She went home at a little after six.

*Tomorrow he'll be gone....*

She wanted to cry.

It was too much. She couldn't stand it anymore, that he would return to America and she might never see him again.

She did the very thing she knew she shouldn't do. She picked up the phone and called the Belle Époque. She asked for his room and they put her right through.

He answered the phone on the second ring. "Yes?"

"It's Alice. Are you still leaving tomorrow?" Her voice came out husky and confident. She sounded like the bold woman Rhia insisted she actually was.

"Alice. I'm surprised." *He* sounded anything but bored. But he didn't sound exactly happy, either.

"You're angry with me."

"Come on. I got the message when you ran away Friday night—and the other day in the stables when I came to ride. I got it loud and clear."

Her heart sank. "I'm sorry. I... Maybe I shouldn't have called."

A silence. And then, with real feeling, "Don't say that. I'm glad that you called."

"You are?"

"Yeah."

She let out a sigh of pure relief. "So, then, are you leaving?"

"Yes. Tomorrow."

"And tonight?" Her throat clutched. She coughed to clear it. "Are you busy tonight?"

Another silence. For a moment she thought he'd hung up. But then he asked, "What game are you playing now, Alice?"

"It's not a game. I promise you."

"Frankly, it feels like a game, a game I'll never win."

She tried for lightness. "Look at it this way—at least I'm not boring and predictable."

More dead air. And then at last he said, "I'm available. For you."

Well, all right. He definitely sounded like a man who wanted to see her again. Suddenly, she was floating on air. "I want to wear a long dress and diamonds. I want to play baccarat and eat at La Chanson." La Chanson de la Mer was right on the water in the Triangle d'Or and arguably the best restaurant on the Riviera.

"I'll arrange everything. Whatever you want."

Her stomach had gone all fluttery. Her heart was racing. Her cheeks felt too warm. Sweet Lord, she was out of control.

And it was fabulous. "Be in front of the casino, by the fountain," she commanded. "Eight o'clock."

"I'll be there."

Noah was waiting right where she'd told him to be, dressed for evening, feeling way too damned anxious to see her again, when her limo pulled up a few feet away.

The driver got out, hustled around and opened her door. She emerged in a strapless gold dress that clung to every sweet curve and had a slit up the skirt to above the knee. Her hair was pinned up loosely, bits of it escaping to curl at her nape.

And she was on her own, as he'd hoped. No bodyguard. Damien had told him that the princely family only used bodyguards outside the principality. Good. He might actually get a chance to be alone with her.

She saw him. A gorgeous, hopeful, glowing smile curved her lips. They stood there like a couple of lovesick teenagers, just looking at each other, as the driver got back behind the wheel and the long black car slid away.

They both started moving at the same time. Three steps and he was with her, in front of her, looking down into those amazing blue-green eyes.

Again, they just stared at each other. He said, "God. You're so beautiful."

And she said, "You came. I was a little worried you wouldn't."

"Are you kidding? Turn down a chance to spend an evening with you? Couldn't do it." Over her shoulder, he saw a man with a camera. "Someone's taking our picture."

"Behave with dignity," she said. "And ignore them. I'll do my very best to follow your lead. Because, as we both know, dignity was never my strong suit."

"You are more than dignified enough," he argued.

She gave him her full-out, beautiful laugh. "Not true, but thanks for trying."

He wanted to kiss her, but not while some idiot was snapping pictures of them. "Dinner first?"

"Perfect." She reached for his arm.

They turned for the restaurant. It was just a short walk across the plaza.

He'd gotten them a table on the patio, which jutted out over the water. The food was excellent and the waitstaff were always there when you needed them, but otherwise invisible. The sky slowly darkened and the moon over the water glowed brighter as the night came on. The sea glittered, reflecting the lights of the Triangle d'Or and those shining from the windows and gardens of the red-roofed villas that crowded the nearby hillsides.

They talked of nothing important during the meal, which was fine with him. He was content right then just to be with her, to listen to her laughter and watch those sweet dimples appear in her cheeks when she smiled.

After they ate, they strolled back across the plaza to the casino. They played craps and roulette and baccarat. People stopped to watch them, to whisper about them. A few took pictures. Noah had foreseen this and called ahead to speak with the manager so that the casino staff was on top of the situation. They made sure none of the gawkers got too close.

Alice won steadily and so did he. Around eleven he

challenged her to play blackjack, two-handed, in one of the exclusive back rooms.

She looked at him with suspicion. But in the end, as he could have predicted, she refused to walk away from a challenge. "Am I going to regret this?"

He simply offered his arm. When she wrapped her hand around it, he led her into the card room in the back, where the table he'd reserved was waiting for them, cordoned off with golden ropes in its own quiet little corner. She eyed the deck of cards and the equally divided stacks of chips as he pulled back her chair for her.

"I thought we would play for something more interesting than money." He pushed in her chair and went around to sit opposite her.

She cast a glance around the big room. Almost every other table was in use. Leaning closer, lowering her voice so only he heard her, she said, "I am not taking off my clothes in a room full of strangers."

He laughed. "Clearly, I should have ordered a private room."

She tried to play it stern but didn't quite succeed. Her dimples gave her away. "Let's just not go there."

"Fair enough." He shuffled the cards.

She watched him, narrow eyed. "All right, then. If not for money, then what?"

He looked up into her eyes. "Orion."

She stared at him for a count of three before she spoke. "Surely you're joking."

He shook his head. "If I win, you agree to sell him to me."

She looked at him sideways, her diamond earrings glittering, scattering the light from the chandeliers above.

"At my price, then. You're only winning the right to buy him."

"That's right."

"Think twice, Noah. It's an astronomical price."

"Name it."

She did.

He looked at her patiently—and counteroffered.

She laughed, glanced away—and then countered his counter.

"Agreed." He slapped the deck in front of her.

Alice cut the cards. "But what if *I* win?"

He took the deck again. "Name your prize."

"Hmm." She grinned slowly. "I know. I want you to donate twenty thousand American dollars to St. Stephens Children's Home. My brother-in-law Marcus was raised there."

He gave her a wry smile. "So either way, I pay."

She dimpled. "Exactly."

He pretended to think it over. Then, "At least it's a worthy cause. Done."

They began to play.

She was an excellent gambler, bold and focused. And fearless, as well. She kept track of the cards seemingly without effort, laughing and chatting so charmingly as she played.

He was down to a very short stack at one point. But he battled his way back, winning. Losing. And then winning again.

It was almost two in the morning when he claimed her last chip from her.

She leaned back in her chair and laughed. "All right, Noah. You win. You may buy Orion for the price we agreed on."

He got the real picture then. "You were going to sell him to me anyway."

Her smile was downright smug. "Yes, I was—and enough of all this." She held out both hands, as though to indicate the whole of the world-famous casino complex. "Let's go somewhere else."

An attendant showed them to a private office where Noah settled up and they collected what they'd won earlier in the evening. The attendant appeared again with Alice's gold wrap and tiny jeweled handbag. A few minutes later they emerged into the glittering Montedoran night.

"What now?" he asked, even though it was a risk; it gave her an out if she suddenly decided she should call it a night. He was betting she wouldn't. She seemed to be having a great time. And he already knew how much she enjoyed calling the shots.

"Somewhere private." She glanced across the plaza where two men with cameras were snapping away. "Somewhere we can talk and not be disturbed."

Noah chuckled, pleased with himself that he'd read her mood correctly. "As though there's anywhere in Montedoro they won't follow us."

She took hold of his arm again and leaned close. He breathed in her scent. Exciting. So sweet. She said, "I have a plan."

"Uh-oh."

She laughed. "That's exactly what my sister Rhia always says when I come up with a fabulous idea." She faked a puzzled frown. "Why is that, do you think?"

He played it safe. "Not a clue."

"Ha!" And then she leaned even closer. "I am having altogether too much fun."

Her words pleased him no end. "There's no such thing as too much fun."

"Yes, there is. But it's all right. It's your last night in Montedoro after all. And we may never see each other again."

*Wrong.* "I just bought a horse from you, remember?"

"Of course I remember. And you shall have Orion. But you know what I meant."

He decided to let that remark go, but if she thought this was the last evening they would spend together, she didn't know who she was dealing with. "Tell me your plan."

"You're sure? A moment ago you seemed reluctant to hear it."

"I'm sure."

"Well, all right, then." She whispered her scheme in his ear.

## *Chapter Four*

"It just might work," he said, admiring the way the bright lights brought out hints of auburn and gold in her hair.

"Of course it will work."

"All right, then. I'm game." They turned together for his hotel, neither looking back to see if they were being followed. Why bother to look? Of course they were being followed. The paparazzi were relentless. As they entered the lobby, he got out his cell and called his driver.

He led her straight through to the elevators. They got on and rode up to his floor—after which they changed elevators and went back down to the mezzanine level.

They took the service stairway to the first floor again and slipped out the side door, where the car he'd called for was waiting, the engine running. The driver, Talbot, held the door for her. Noah jumped in on the other side.

"Where to?" Talbot asked once they were safely hidden from prying eyes behind tinted windows. Alice rattled off a quick series of directions. The driver nodded and pulled the car away from the curb.

Noah raised the panel between the front and rear seats.

Alice glanced at him and grinned. "Alone at last."

He wrapped his arm around her and drew her closer. "If I kiss you, will you run away again?"

She gazed at him steadily, eyes shining. Then she shook her head. "Not while the car is moving."

He bent closer and brushed his lips across the velvet flesh of her temple. "Remind me to tell Talbot never to stop...."

"It's a tempting idea, being here with you forever...." She tipped her face up to him.

He brushed his mouth across hers, giving her a moment to accept him. When her lips parted slightly on a small tender sigh, he deepened the contact.

She let him in. He tasted the wet, secret surfaces behind her lips, ran his tongue along the smooth, even edges of her pretty white teeth.

Another sigh from her, deeper than the one before.

And he tightened his arm around her, bringing her closer so he could taste her more deeply still.

When she brought her hand up between them and pushed lightly against his chest, he lifted his mouth from hers just enough to grumble, "What now, Alice?"

Her eyes had the night in them. "Dami told me to stay away from you. He says you're a heartbreaker." Bad words scrolled through his mind, but he held them in. She added, "My sister Rhia told me not to listen to Dami."

"I like your sister already." He kissed her again, quickly, a little more ruthlessly than he probably should have. "And I'll talk to your brother."

Her fingers strayed upward. She stroked the nape of his neck. He wished she'd go on doing that for a century or two. "Please don't talk to Dami about me. It's none of his business. He doesn't get to decide who I see or don't see."

Noah had pretty much expected Damien to warn Alice off him. He'd considered explaining his real goal to Dami up front when he'd told Dami he wanted Orion—but he'd decided against it.

Damien wouldn't have believed him anyway. And Alice might be convinced to let him off the hook for a lot of things. But even before their first meeting, he'd known enough about her to figure out that she would never forgive him for telling her brother his real intentions before he revealed them to her.

And come on. He'd never planned to tell her *or* her brother everything. He'd assumed the whole truth wouldn't fly with either of them. The idea had been to meet her, pursue her and win her. To sweep her off her pretty feet.

But now that he'd come to know her a little, he was having second thoughts about the original plan. She was honest. Forthright. And after the near disaster of his playing along when she mistook him for a stable hand, he'd learned his lesson: she expected him to be honest, too.

Which brought him to that other thing, the thing he hadn't been prepared for. The way she made him want to give her everything, to be more than he'd ever been.

It was getting beyond his pride now, way past his idea of who he was and what he'd earned in his life. It was getting downright personal.

She *mattered* to him now, as a person. He didn't really understand it or want to think on it too deeply. It was what it was.

And it meant that he would knock himself out to give her whatever she needed, whatever she wanted from him. Up to and including the unvarnished truth.

So, then. He hadn't decided yet. Should he go there—go all the way, lay the naked truth right out on the table for her?

It was dangerous, a bold move.

Too bold?

Could be. And probably not tonight, anyway. It seemed much too soon....

She laid her soft hand against the side of his face. "Earth to Noah. Are you in there?"

"Forget about Damien." He said it too fiercely, and he knew it. "Kiss me again."

She laughed—and then she kissed him. And then she settled against him with her head on his shoulder and asked, "How did you meet my brother?"

He breathed in the scent of her hair. "I thought we were going to forget about Damien."

She tipped her head up and grinned at him. "You wish—and seriously. How did you meet him?"

"At a party in New York a little over two years ago. We both knew the host. I struck up a conversation with him. We found we had a lot in common."

"Fast cars, beautiful women..."

He shrugged. "I like your brother. We get along—as a rule, anyway."

The car pulled to a stop.

"We're here." She straightened from his embrace. With reluctance, he let her go and lowered the panel between the seats.

"Will you be getting out, sir?" Talbot asked.

"Yes, thanks." The driver jumped out to open the door for Alice. Noah emerged on his side. The car sat on a point near the edge of a sheer cliff with the sea spread out beyond. He could hear the waves on the rocks below. He caught her eye over the roof of the car. "It's beautiful here."

She grinned as though she'd created the setting herself. "I thought you might like it. There's a path down to a fine little slice of beach. A private beach. Is there a blanket or two in the boot?"

There were two. Talbot got them from the trunk. He handed them to Noah and then got back in behind the wheel to wait until they were ready to go.

She'd left her wrap and bag in the car, but her gold sandals had high, delicate heels. Noah eyed them doubtfully. "Are you sure you can make it down a steep trail in those?"

"Good point." She slipped off the flimsy shoes, opened the car door again, and tossed them inside. "Let's go."

Going barefoot didn't seem like a good idea to him. "Alice. Be realistic. You'll cut up your feet."

She waved a hand. "The trail is narrow and steep, yes, but not rocky. I'll be fine." She gathered her gold skirts and took the lead.

The woman amazed him. She led the way without once stumbling, without a single complaint. Halfway down they came out on a little wooden landing with a rail. They stood at the rail together, the breeze off the sea cool and sweet, the dark sky starless, the moon sunk almost to the edge of the horizon now, sending out a trail of shifting light across the water toward the shore.

She said, "We all, my brothers and sisters and me, used to come here together, with my mother and father, when we were children. The observation point above, where we left the car, belongs to my family. The only way down is this trail. The high rocks jut out on either side of the beach, so intruders can't trek in along the shoreline. We've always kept it private. Just for our family, a place to be like other families out for a day by the sea."

"Beautiful," he said. He was looking at her.

She waved a hand, the diamond cuff she wore catching light even in the darkness, sparkling. "But of course, now and then, the paparazzi fly over and get pictures from the air." She sounded a little sad about that. But then she sent him a conspiratorial glance. "Come on." And she turned to take the wooden stairs that led the rest of the way down.

The beach was sandy. He took off his shoes and socks and rolled his trouser legs. They spread one of the blankets midway between the cliffs and the water and sat there together. The breeze seemed chilly now that they were sitting still, so he wrapped the other blanket around her bare shoulders. He put his arm around her and she settled against him as she had in the car, as though she belonged there. For a while they stared out at the moon trail on the water.

Eventually, she broke the companionable silence. "I think I like you too much."

He pressed his lips to her hair. "Don't stop."

She chuckled. "Liking you—or talking?"

"Either."

She laughed again. And then complained, "You're much too attractive."

"I'll try to be uglier."

"But that's not all. You're also funny and irreverent and a little bit dangerous. And a heartbreaker, too, just like Dami said. I really need to remember that and not go making a fool of myself over you."

He put a finger under her chin and lifted her face to him. "I have no intention of breaking your heart. Ever."

She wrinkled her fine nose at him. "I didn't say you would *intend* to do it. Men like you don't go out to hurt women on purpose. They simply get bored and move on and leave a trail of shattered hearts behind them."

He was starting to get a little defensive. "From what I've heard, you've broken a heart or two yourself in the past."

She groaned. "I should have known you would say that. After all, I have no secrets. My whole life is available, with pictures, *lots* of pictures, in the pages of the *National Enquirer* and the *Daily Star*." And then all at once she was shoving away from him, throwing off the blanket and leaping to her feet.

"Alice. Don't…"

"I'm going wading." She gathered up her gold skirts and ran to the water's edge.

He got up and followed her, taking his time about it. Better to give her a moment or two to calm down.

When he reached her, she was just standing there, the foamy waves lapping her slender feet, holding her skirts out of the way. For a moment they stared out at the water together toward the sinking moon on the far horizon.

Then she confessed, "All right, that was a little bit bitchy. Not to mention over the top. Sorry."

He said nothing, only reached out a hand, caught a loose curl of her hair and tucked it behind her ear. He really liked touching her—and he liked even more that she let him. "I was only saying that we're more or less evenly matched."

"But I don't want to be shattered. I don't want to shatter *you*. I want…" Words seemed to fail her.

He ran a finger down the side of her neck. Living silk, her skin. He drank in her slight shiver at his touch. "You want what?"

She gazed out over the water again. "I want to rip off my dress and dive in. Right here. Right now."

A bolt of heat hit him where it counted. Gruffly, he suggested, "Fine with me. I'll join you."

She let her head drop back and stared up at the dark sky. "I can't."

"There's no one here but the two of us."

She lowered her head and turned to him then. "Oh, Noah. That's the thing. I can never be sure, never be too careful. If someone just happened to be lurking back on the trail with a camera and got a shot of me cavorting naked in the waves with you... Oh, God. My mother would never forgive me." She smiled then, but it was a sad smile. "If the paparazzi caught me in the buff now, I don't think I would forgive *myself,* if you want the truth."

"You're being way too hard on yourself. You know that, right?"

"Maybe. I suppose. It didn't used to bother me much. I used to simply ignore it all. I did what I wanted and if the journos had nothing better to do than to take pictures of me and write silly stories about me, so what? But now, well, I feel differently. I'm sick to death of being the wild one, the ready-for-anything, out-of-control Princess Alice."

He had a good idea of what had pushed her over the line. "The pictures from that pub in Glasgow?"

She winced. "You saw them."

"Yeah."

"My mother was pretty upset over them."

He blew out a slow breath. "I thought they were hot."

"More like a hot mess."

"*Hot* still being the operative word."

She turned fully toward him and studied his face, a

deep look, one that made him slightly uncomfortable. And then she said, "I think I really should go home now."

*Uh-uh. Not yet. Not this time.*

He reached out. He couldn't stop himself. He wrapped his fingers around the back of her neck and pulled her into him. "Kiss me."

"Oh, Noah…"

"Shh." He took her mouth. She made a reluctant sound low in her throat—but then she softened and kissed him back. When he lifted his head, he said, "I've got to get you away from here."

She gazed up at him, eyes shining, lips slightly swollen from the kiss. "Away from where?"

"Away from Montedoro."

She frowned. "That's not going to happen. Tonight is our last night and—"

He stopped her with a gentle finger on her soft lips. "I don't want this to be our last night. And I don't believe that you do, either."

Her slim shoulders drooped. "Noah. Be realistic."

"But I am. Completely. And my point is, it's a fishbowl here—beautiful, glamorous, but still. A fishbowl. Whatever we do together here, there will be pictures and stories in the tabloid press." Plus, it was way too easy for her to escape him here on her own turf. He needed to get her onto his territory for a change. He went for it. "Come back to California with me tomorrow. Come and stay with me for a while."

She pressed her lips together. "Oh, Noah. I really don't think that would be a good idea."

He wasn't giving up. Ever. "Why not? You'll love it there. And I want to show you my world. I want you to meet Lucy."

"Noah, really. I can't just run off with you. Didn't I just explain all this? I'm trying to be more...discreet. Trying to behave myself for a change. Trying to stop throwing myself blindly into crazy situations."

"It's not crazy. The Santa Barbara area is a beautiful place, almost as beautiful as Montedoro. And my stables are world-class. You can ride every day."

"Oh, Noah..." She pulled away from him then. He wanted to grab her and hold her to him, but he knew better. She spun on her heel and raced back up the beach to the blanket again.

He forced himself to stay behind, turning back to the water, staring out at the horizon for a while, giving them both a few minutes to settle down.

When he felt that he could deal calmly and reasonably, he turned to her once more. She sat on the blanket, the other blanket wrapped around her, her knees drawn up, staring at him with equal parts misery and defiance.

He stuck his hands into his pockets and went to her, stopping at the edge of the blanket, not sure what to do or say next.

She tipped her face up to him and demanded, "What are you after, Noah, really? What in the world do you want from me? Because if I'm just another of your conquests, no thank you. I'm not looking for a meaningless hookup right now."

He knew then that he had to go for it, to tell her everything. What else could he do? A clever lie would never satisfy her. "You're not 'just another' anything. You never could be."

"Please don't flatter me."

"I'm not. Will you listen? Will you let me explain?"

He waited for her nod before he said, "I've done damn well for myself."

"Yes, you have. But what does that have to do with—"

"Just go with me here. Let me play this out."

She hugged her drawn-up knees a little tighter. "All right. I'm listening."

"I've done well for myself and I'm proud. Too proud, I suppose. But that's how it is."

She guided a few windblown strands of hair away from that mouth he couldn't stop wanting to kiss. "Yes, well, I get that."

"A few years ago I decided it was about time I got married and founded my dynasty."

"Ah. Of course. Your dynasty." She made a wry little face.

He forged on. "To found a dynasty, there has to be… the right wife. Someone young and strong, someone from a large family, for a higher likelihood of fertility."

She made a scoffing sound. "I don't believe you just said that."

"Believe it. It's true—and here's where my pride comes in. I decided I wanted a princess. A real one."

Her mouth dropped open. "Oh. You are so bad. Incorrigible, really."

He didn't disagree with her. "How do you think I've got as far as I have in life? Not through good behavior and political correctness. I decide what I want and I go after it."

"You know this makes you look reprehensible, right?"

He only gazed down at her, unflinching. "Do you want the truth from me or not?"

She fiddled with the blanket a little and then hitched up her chin. "Yes. I do. Go on."

He continued, "So I started looking. I wanted a special kind of princess, a princess who was different from the rest. No one inbred. Someone beautiful and exciting. If I'm going to be with a woman for the rest of my life, she will damn well *not* be boring—and my kids won't be stupid or dull."

She made a small snorting sound. "Or, God forbid, unattractive."

He asked very softly, "Are you getting the picture here, Alice?"

Her mocking look fled. She swallowed. Hard. "You… chose me?"

"Yes, I did. The first picture I saw of you, I knew you were the one. I read about you—everything I could find. All the tacky tabloid stories. The articles in *Dressage Today* and *Practical Horseman.* It really worked for me that you loved horses. I wanted to meet you, to find out if the chemistry might be right—because in the end, I would have to *want* you. And *you* would have to want *me*. So I found a way to approach you by using my connections to meet your brother first. As it turned out, I liked Damien. We got along. I invited him to visit me in California. And after we'd known each other awhile, he suggested I come to Montedoro. Of course, I took him up on that."

"It was part of your plan."

"That's right. Damien invited me and I came to Montedoro and I found a way to meet you—in the palace stables, where you're most at home. I set out to get your attention. And I found out that my original instinct was solid. Every minute I've spent with you has only made me more certain that my choice is the right one."

"Wait a minute."

"What?"

"Are you going to try to tell me that you're in love with me?"

"Would you believe me if I did?"

She studied him for a moment, her head tipped to the side. "So, then. It's just chemistry. Chemistry and your plan."

"That's why I want you to come to Santa Barbara. We need more time together. I want you to give that to me—to *us*."

"Be realistic, Noah. There isn't any *us*."

He scowled at her. "There will be. And you're thinking too much."

"Right. Because I'm not a stupid princess, remember? You wanted one with a brain."

"Damn it, Alice." He dropped to his knees on the blanket before her. She gasped, but at least she didn't scuttle backward to get away from him. "I'm only telling you that you don't have to worry. You're not just some hookup. I will never dump you. I want you to marry me. I want children with you. And I won't change my mind. You're the one that I want, Alice. I want you for my wife."

Alice wasn't really sure what to say to him at that point.

Strangely, she still liked him after his extraordinary confession. She liked him and wanted him even more than before. Which probably said something really awful about her character. She didn't especially mind that he'd picked her out as a horse trader chooses a broodmare, for her good bloodlines, her sterling temperament, her fine health and conformation—and her excellent pedigree.

What she did care about was the truth, that he'd told

her honestly exactly what he was after—and that she believed him.

Should she have been at least a little appalled?

Probably. But she simply wasn't.

Surprised, yes. She'd known that he wanted her— pretty hard to miss that—but it had never occurred to her he might be seeing her as a wife. As a rule, she wasn't the type of woman a man would set out to marry in advance of even knowing her. Her reputation preceded her and most men looked for someone a bit more sedate when it came time to choose a lifelong companion.

"Alice. My God. Will you please say *something?*"

She hugged the blanket around her more tightly. "Well, I'm not sure what to say. Except that I do appreciate your telling me the truth."

"I didn't know what else to do," he grumbled. "There's something way too straightforward about you. I get it, that you want honesty. And I'm willing to give you whatever you want."

"Well. Thanks. I think."

He braced his hands on his thighs and gritted his strong white teeth. "Please come to California with me."

"Oh, I don't think so…."

He swore low, then turned and sat down beside her. Drawing up his knees, he let them drop halfway open and wrapped his big arms around them. He stared at his lean bare feet. "Why the hell not?"

"Because when I get married, it's going to be to a man I love and trust and know I can count on."

"I didn't ask you to marry me. Yet. I just told you what I'm after. Now we need the time for you to *learn* to trust and count on me."

She turned her head and pinned him with an unwavering look. "You keep leaving out love."

He made a low growling sound. "You make me be honest, and then you want me to come on with hearts and flowers."

"No, I don't want you to come on with hearts and flowers. I truly don't. I want you to be exactly who and what you are. I like you. A lot. Too much. I find you smoking hot. If I wasn't trying to be a better person, I would be rolling around naked on this blanket with you right now."

He shut his eyes and hung his golden head. "Great. Tell me in detail what you're *not* going to do with me."

"Stop it." She leaned toward him.

His head shot up and he wrapped his hand around her neck and pulled her close. "Alice..." His eyes burned into hers.

She whispered, "Please don't...."

With slow care, he released her.

They sat for a minute or two without speaking.

And then she tried again. "For me, right now, running off to Santa Barbara with you tomorrow seems like just another crazy harebrained stunt. I would need a little time to think this over."

He slid her a glance. "So you're not saying no."

"Not yes, either," she warned.

"But you'll think about it."

She nodded. "And you should do some thinking, too—about how you're hoping I'm going to learn to trust and count on you."

He scowled at her. "You're getting at something. Will you just say it, whatever it is?"

"Fine. If we can't talk about love, we can at least talk

about monogamy. Because that's a condition for me. If you ever want me to marry you, your days as a lady-killer are done."

He said very slowly, the words dragging themselves reluctantly out of him, "I haven't been with anyone for months. And I can't believe I'm admitting it to you."

"Good. It's a start." She stood. "I want to go now."

He didn't argue that time. Apparently he agreed that they'd said all they were going to say for one night. He got up, shook out the blanket and tucked it under his arm. She turned and led the way up to the car.

The ride to her villa took only a few minutes. They were very quiet minutes. To Alice it seemed she could cut the silence with a dull knife.

When they pulled up at the curb, she turned to say good-night to him, to thank him for a wonderful evening. Because it *had* been wonderful, even the rockiest parts. Wonderful and true and difficult. And real.

He only reached for her and covered her mouth with his. She swayed against him, sighing, and he wrapped her up tight in his powerful arms.

It was a great kiss, one of the best. So good she almost said yes, she would go with him after all. Anywhere he wanted. To the ends of the earth.

If he would only kiss her like that again.

But instead, she took a card from her jeweled min-audière and pressed it into his hand. "Home and cell. Call me."

Gruffly, he commanded, "Come and stay with me soon."

She leaned close, pressed her cheek to his and whispered, "Noah. Good night." The driver pulled her door open.

She grabbed her shoes and her wrap and jumped out before she could weaken. Then she stood there on the walk, barefoot in her gold dress, and watched his car drive away.

## Chapter Five

Noah slept on the plane, but only fitfully. His car and driver were waiting for him at the Santa Barbara Airport when his flight touched down. He'd have one night in his own bed and then in the morning he'd board another plane to San Francisco for meetings with a media firm seeking investors for a TV-streaming start-up.

At the estate, Lucy came running out to greet him. She grabbed him and hugged him and said how she'd missed him. It did him good to see her smile. She seemed to have boundless energy lately. He was pleased at how well she was doing.

They were barely in the front door before she started in on him about college in Manhattan.

He took her by her thin shoulders and held her still. "Lucy."

She looked up at him through those big sweet brown eyes of hers, all innocence. "What?"

"You need to call that school and tell them you won't be attending in the spring."

Her lips thinned to a hard line. "Of course I won't call them. I'm going, one way or another, no matter what."

"Later," he coaxed. "In a year or two, after we're certain you can handle it."

"I *can* handle it. And I'm taking the spring semester. *This* spring semester. You just see if I don't."

Noah tried not to let out a long, weary sigh. She was so completely out there on this—nothing short of obsessed over it. She couldn't go if he didn't write the checks. And he had no intention of allowing her to put her health at risk. "We've been through this. It's too soon."

"No, it's not." She shrugged off his grip. "It's been two years since my last surgery. I am fine. I am *well*. And you know it. It's *not* too soon."

He wanted a stiff drink and dinner and a little peace and quiet before he had to leave again in the morning. He wanted Alice, a lot. But he wasn't going to have her for a while yet, and he understood that. "Please, Lucy. We'll talk more later, all right?"

"But—"

He caught her shoulders again and kissed her forehead. "Later." He said it gently.

She shrugged him off again. "Later to you really means never."

There was no point in arguing anymore over it. Shaking his head, he turned for the stairs.

"I suppose you saw the stories in the *Sun* and the *Daily Mirror*." Alice sipped her sparkling water and poked at her pasta salad.

It was Saturday, two days since Noah had gone back to America. Rhia had come to Alice's for lunch. The sisters sat in the sunlit breakfast room that looked out on Alice's small patio and garden.

Rhia slathered butter on a croissant. "As tabloid stories go, I thought they were lovely."

"Tabloid stories are never lovely."

"In this case, I beg to differ. The pictures were so romantic. Noah looked so handsome and you looked fabulous. Two gorgeous people out enjoying an evening together at Casino d'Ambre. Totally harmless. Nothing the least tacky. Good press for Montedoro and the casino. And you both seemed to be having such a good time together. I don't see what you're so glum about."

She was glum because she missed him. A lot. It didn't make sense, she kept reminding herself, to miss a man she hardly knew. No matter how smoking hot he happened to be. "I sold him Orion. He arranged to have the veterinarian at the stables yesterday for the prepurchase exam and he's already sent the money." He'd wired the whole amount after the exam, before he got the papers to sign. So very, very Noah.

Rhia swallowed more pasta. "You've changed your mind about parting with the stallion, then, and want to back out of the sale?"

Alice scowled. "Of course not. I'm a horse breeder. I can't keep them all."

"Then what *is* the matter?"

"Everything. Nothing. Did you see the flowers in the big Murano glass vase in the foyer?"

"I did. The vase is fabulous. And the lilies... Your favorite."

"Noah sent them—both the flowers and the vase. He also sent a ridiculously expensive hammered-gold necklace studded with rubies."

"You know, I get the distinct impression that he fancies you." Rhia ate more pasta and chuckled to herself.

"What is so funny?"

"Grumpy, grumpy." Rhia was still chuckling.

"He wants me to come and visit him in California."

"Will you?"

"I haven't decided. He also wants to marry me."

Rhia blinked and swallowed the big bite of croissant she'd just shoved into her mouth. Since she hadn't chewed, she choked a little and had to wash it down with sparkling water. "Well," she said when she could talk again. "That was fast."

"You don't know the half of it."

Rhia set down her glass and sat back in her chair. "I'm listening."

"Oh, Rhia…"

"Just tell me. You'll feel better."

So Alice told her sister about taking Noah to the family beach, about his startling confession that he wanted to marry a princess—Alice, specifically. "Is that insane or what?"

Rhia shrugged. "He's very bold. Just like you. And you've admitted there *is* real attraction between you."

"But don't you think it's wildly arrogant and more than a little strange to decide to marry a princess out of thin air like that?"

"I'm not going to judge him. Please don't ask me to. What I think is that you really like him and lately you're not trusting your own instincts, so you think you *shouldn't* like him."

"Oh, Rhia. I don't know what to do…."

Her sister gave her a tender, understanding smile. "I think you do. You just haven't admitted it to yourself yet."

Noah arrived home again from the Bay Area on Saturday afternoon.

Lucy did not run out to greet him. Still sulking over

that damn school she wouldn't be going to, no doubt. Fine. Let her sulk. Eventually, she would see reason and accept that she needed more time at home, where he and Hannah, her former foster mom, who managed the estate now, could take care of her. Maybe at dinner that night, if she wasn't too hostile, he could suggest a few online classes. He needed to get her to slow down a little. There was too much stress and responsibility involved in going to college full-time and living on her own. She needed to ease into all that by degrees.

He thought about Alice. On the plane, he'd read the tabloid stories of their night together at Casino d'Ambre. Just looking at the pictures of her in that amazing gold dress made him want to hop another flight back to Montedoro, where he could kiss her and touch her and take off all her clothes.

She should have come home with him. But she hadn't. He had to be patient; he knew it. He was playing the long game with her. And the prize was a lifetime, the two of them, together.

Unfortunately, being patient about Alice wasn't easy. It made him edgy, made him want to pick a fight with someone like he used to do when he was young and stupid—pick a fight and kick some serious ass.

A ride might lift his spirits a little, get his mind off Alice in that gold dress. He put on old jeans and boots and a knit shirt and went out to the stables, where he greeted the staff and chose the Thoroughbred gelding Solitairio to ride.

He took a series of trails that wound over his thirty-acre estate and on and off neighboring properties. His neighbors owned horses, too. They shared an agreement, giving each other riding access.

An hour after he left the stables, he was feeling better about everything. The meetings with the streaming start-up had gone well. Lucy would see the light eventually and agree to take things more slowly. And in time Alice would be his wife.

Sunday, Alice went to breakfast at the palace with the family. She was a little nervous that her mother might not approve of all the press from her night out with Noah.

But Adrienne only greeted Alice with a hug—and congratulated her on getting such a fine price for Orion. Alice was just breathing a sigh of relief when Damien took the chair next to her at the breakfast table.

He leaned close. "So you sold Noah the horse he wanted."

"I did." Alice sipped her coffee.

"Well." Dami spread his napkin on his knee. "Good enough. And now he's gone back to California where he belongs." She promised herself she was not going to become annoyed with her brother, that he only wanted the best for her. Dami added, "And you won't be seeing him again."

That did it. She turned a blinding smile his way. "Actually, he invited me to come and visit him in California."

Her brother didn't miss a beat. "And, of course, you told him no."

"I told him I would think about it. And that is exactly what I'm doing."

Dami gave her a look. His expression remained absolutely calm. But his eyes shot sparks. "Are you *trying* to get hurt?"

She longed to blurt out the rest of it—that Noah wanted to marry her and she just might be considering that, too. But telling Dami was not the same as confiding in Rhia. Rhia didn't judge. Dami had decided he knew what was best for her. "There's no good way to answer that question, and you know it."

Dami only sat there, still wearing *that* look.

She laid it out for him clear as glass. "Mind your own business. Please."

"But, Allie, it *is* my business." He kept his voice carefully low, just between the two of them. "*I* invited him here."

"What is the matter with you?" She spoke very quietly, too. But she wrapped her whisper in a core of steel. "You'd think I was some wide-eyed little baby, unable to take care of myself. You're way out of line about this. You've already told me what you think I need to know. Now you can back off and stay out of it. Please."

"I think I should talk to him. I should have spoken to him earlier."

"Dami. Hear me. Don't you dare."

Something in the way she said that must have finally gotten through to him. Because he shook his head and muttered, "Don't say I didn't warn you...."

"Stay out of it. Are we clear?"

"Fine. We're clear." He was the one who looked away.

The next day, Alice received another vase—Chinese that time, decorated with cherry blossoms and filled with pink lilies, green anthuriums, plumeria the color of rainbow sherbet and flowering purple artichokes. That night he called her.

"I miss you," he said, his voice low and gruff and way too intimate. "When are you coming to see me?"

She felt an enormous smile bloom and couldn't have

stopped it if she'd wanted to. "The flowers are so beautiful."

"Which ones?"

"All of them—the lilies especially. Both vases, too. And that necklace. You shouldn't have sent that necklace."

"Come and visit me. You can wear it for me."

"Thank you. Now stop sending me things."

"I like sending you things. It's fun. How's my stallion?"

"Beautiful. And a gentleman. I hate to part with him."

"You won't have to if you marry me."

"A telephone proposal. How very romantic."

"It wasn't a proposal. Just a statement of fact. You'll know when I'm proposing, I promise you that. I want you to send Orion on Friday—can you do that?"

"Of course. If you have all the arrangements made?"

"I will. He'll fly into JFK, be picked up in a quarantine van and taken to a beautiful little farm in Maryland for testing." The required quarantine for transporting a stallion from Montedoro to the U.S.A. was thirty days, during which time Orion would be tested for contagious equine metritis. "I'll pay a visit to the farm the day after he arrives to see that he's managed the trip well. And I'll arrange to have him put on a hot walker daily for exercise." During quarantine a stallion couldn't be allowed out to pasture or to be ridden. A mechanical hot walker was a machine designed to cool a horse down after exercise. In this case, the machine would give the quarantined stallion the exercise he needed while in isolation.

She said, "By the end of next month, you will have him."

"Come and visit. You can be here when he arrives at his new home."

"That would be a long visit. I do have a life, you know."

He said nothing for a moment. The silence was warm, full of promise. Companionable. "I don't want to take anything away from you. I only want to give you more. We could live here *and* there in Montedoro. I know your work with your horses means everything to you. You wouldn't have to give that up. However you prefer it, that's how it will be."

"Suddenly we're talking about marriage again—but this isn't a proposal, right?"

"Absolutely not. I told you. When I propose, you won't have to ask if that's what I'm doing."

The next night, Tuesday, he called again. She asked about Lucy.

"She's doing well. Feeling great. And still after me to let her move to New York."

"*Let* her? She's twenty-three, you said."

"So? I told you. She hasn't been well for most of her life."

"But, Noah, she's well now, isn't she?"

"She can't be too careful." His voice had turned flat. Uncompromising.

Alice let the subject go. She'd never met Lucy, didn't really understand the situation. She had no right to nag him in any case. They hardly knew each other. She only *felt* as though she knew him. She needed to remember that.

Wednesday, she sent him a text letting him know she'd taken Orion out during her predawn ride.

Hving 2nd thgts abt selling him. He is 2 fabu.

He zipped one right back.

4get it. He's mine.

Hold the tude.

Come 2 C me.

U R 2 relentless.

Rite away wd b gud.

R U NTS?

They went back and forth like that for at least twenty minutes. She stood on the cobblestones outside the stable door, the sun warm on her back, thumbs flying over her phone. It was so much fun.

And yes, she was starting to think that a visit to California might be a lovely idea.

After that day, they texted regularly. He called every night and sent flowers again on Friday, the day Orion boarded a plane in a special stall-like crate for his flight to America.

Noah flew to Maryland to check on his new stallion and then flew from there to Los Angeles for another series of meetings that would go on over the weekend. They kept up an ongoing conversation in text messages, and he called her each night, which rather impressed her. He always called around eight, a perfect time for her since she was sticking close to home and usually at the villa for the evening by then. With the nine-hour time difference, though, it was eleven in the morning in California when he called. Somehow he always managed to call her anyway.

It pleased her, the way he made a point to take the time to get in touch with her consistently. It pleased her a lot. Maybe too much, she kept telling herself.

On Saturday she was expected at a gala charity auction in Cannes. A driver and her favorite bodyguard, Altus, showed up at seven to take her there. It was nice enough as those things went. She bid on several items and visited with people she'd known all her life and had her picture taken with people whose names she couldn't recall. At the end, she wrote a large check for the decorative mirror and antique side table she'd won.

On the drive home, she felt a little down somehow. For some reason, that made her want to talk to Noah. She got out her phone to text him—and it buzzed in her hand.

A text *from* him.

Still @ auction?

That down feeling? Evaporated.

It's over. Cn U tk?

WCU 1 hr.

She was back at her villa when the phone rang. They talked for two hours. She explained how she'd somehow ended up with a mirror and a side table she didn't even want and he told her all about the movie people he'd met with to discuss a film project he was considering investing in. They laughed together and she felt…understood somehow. Connected. And she couldn't help remembering that dream she'd had right after they'd first met, the dream where they rode through a meadow of wild-flowers and talked and laughed together like longtime companions.

Monday, she found pictures of him on the internet. And yes, it was becoming a habit with her, to look him up online. In the pictures, he was having lunch at the Beverly Hills Hotel with a famous movie producer and a couple of actors she recognized. She teased him about it when they talked that night.

He said, "You're checking up on me." He didn't sound the least bothered by the idea. "How am I doing?"

"So far, so good. Not a single scandal since you left Montedoro. No hot gossip about your newest girlfriend."

"You told me I had to be monogamous, remember?"

She half groaned, half laughed. "If you're only sleeping alone because I told you to, you're missing the point."

"Spoken like a woman. Not only does a guy have to do it your way, he has to *like* doing it your way."

"So you're feeling deprived, are you?"

"Only of your company."

She groaned again. "You *are* good. Too, too good."

"Exactly what I keep trying to tell you."

Tuesday, her mother invited her to lunch at the palace in the sovereign's apartment, just the two of them. Alice wondered what she'd done now. But it was lovely anyway to get a little one-on-one time with her mother in the elegant sitting room where Alice and her siblings used to play when they were children.

They chatted about Alice's plans for the stables and her breeding-and-training program, about how happy Rhia and Marcus were. They laughed over how big Alice's nieces and nephews were getting. Her mother had six grandchildren now, seven once Rhia's baby was born. It was hard to believe that Adrienne Bravo-Calabretti was a grandmother so many times over. She remained slim and ageless, her olive skin seeming to glow from within.

"We missed you at Sunday breakfast," Adrienne said a little too casually when they were sharing a dessert of white-chocolate raspberry-truffle cheesecake.

"I had that thing in Cannes Saturday night." And then there'd been that long, lovely chat with Noah. It had been after three when they'd said good-night. "I didn't make it to the stables for my early ride, either. I was...feeling lazy, I guess."

"Dami got me alone and asked for a word with me," her mother said softly. "He's worried about you."

Alice lost her appetite. She set her half-finished cake down on the coffee table. "I'm going to make a real effort not to roll my eyes right now."

Her mother's smile was patient. "Dami loves you. As do I." Alice kept her mouth shut. She couldn't help hoping that this wasn't about Noah after all. Her mother went on, "Your brother is concerned about your relationship with a friend of his."

So much for her hopes. "Oh, really?" Seriously annoyed and unwilling to make a lot of effort to hide it, she laid on the sarcasm. "Which friend is that?"

"The man from California who bought your stallion Orion. Noah Cordell?"

Alice wanted to grab the small cloisonné vase on the coffee table beside their lunch tray and hurl it at the damask-covered wall. "This isn't like you, Mother."

Adrienne had the grace to look chagrined. "You're right. Your father and I have always tried to stay out of the way, to let our children lead their own lives. But your brother was insistent that I speak with you."

"And since Glasgow, you don't trust me."

Adrienne set down her dessert fork. "That's not so."

"I hope not."

"Please, darling. Don't be upset with me."

Alice let out a low sound of real frustration. "I'm not upset with *you*. Not really. But I think I want to strangle Dami. All of a sudden he's worried for my...what? My virtue? It's laughable—besides being more than a little too late."

"Forgive him. He loves you. And I think he's finally growing up. He's changing, starting to think about his life and his future in a serious way, yet not quite sure how to go about making a change."

"Great. Fabulous. Good for him. But what does that have to do with me?"

"He doesn't want you getting hurt by a man who's just like he used to be, a man you met through him."

"He *told* me he would mind his own business. Instead, he came crying to you. And he has no right to bad-mouth Noah. Noah's never done anything Dami hasn't done. Plus, he and Noah are supposed to be friends."

Her mother raised a hand. "It was nothing that bad, I promise you, only that Noah Cordell is a heartbreaker. Dami just doesn't want you to get hurt."

Alice really did want to break something. "I might have to kill him. With my bare hands."

Her mother reached across and clasped her arm, a soothing touch. "My advice? Let it go. On reflection, I honestly do think that this is more about the changes in your brother than anything else." Adrienne tipped her head to the side, considering. "And I think you do like this man, Noah. I think you like him very much."

Alice had nothing to hide. Why not just admit it? She sat a little straighter. "I do like him. I'm beginning to… care for him. He's tough and competitive and way too smart. He calls me every evening. I can talk with him for hours. He's come a long way in his life and he's very proud and more than a little controlling. But he's also tender and funny and generous, too."

Adrienne's expression had softened. "I see that Dami isn't the only one of my children who is changing, growing more thoughtful, more mature, more capable of truly loving— And how about this? I will speak with your brother again on this subject. I will remind him that your life is your own and I have faith in your judgment."

Her mother's words touched her. "Thank you. Noah's invited me to come and visit him in California."

"Will you go?"

"Yes, Mother. I believe that I will."

## *Chapter Six*

That night when Noah called, Alice told him she would like to come for a visit.

He instantly tried to take over. "Come tomorrow. I'll send a plane for you. I'll handle everything."

She was prepared for that. "Thank you. But no. I'll make my own arrangements. I'll need a little more time."

He made a growling sound. "How long is a *little* more time?"

"A couple of days."

"Thursday, then. You're coming Thursday."

"Friday, actually."

"That's three days. You said two."

"It's so nice that you're eager to see me."

"So, then, you'll come Thursday."

Rather than allow him to keep pushing her when she'd already made it clear she would arrive on Friday, she let a moment of silence speak for her.

"Alice. Alice, are you still there?"

"Right here," she answered sweetly.

"I've been patient."

She couldn't suppress a chuckle. "Oh, you have not."

"Yes, I have. I've waited for you to be ready to come to me. Don't you dare change your mind on me now."

"I'm not changing my mind, Noah."

"How long can you stay?"

"A week?"

"Not long enough," he grumbled. "You should stay for a month, at least. Longer. Forever."

"Let's leave it open-ended, why don't we? We'll see how it goes. I'll have to return by the middle of next month for Montedoro's annual Autumn Faire."

"A fair? That sounds like something you could skip this year."

"I never skip the Autumn Faire. There will be a street bazaar and a parade. I'll wear traditional dress and ride one of my horses."

"Sounds thrilling." His tone implied otherwise.

She held her ground. "I have to return for it. I've already agreed to participate."

He relented. "All right, then—and I have a meeting in San Francisco on Friday," he admitted at last. "No way to reschedule it."

"It's not a problem. I can come later, when you're at home."

"But if you came Thursday, you could fly with me up to the Bay Area. We could—"

"Noah."

"What?"

"Just tell me when you'll be back."

"Never mind," he grumbled. "Come Friday. Lucy and Hannah will be here to welcome you. And I'll be home Saturday."

"Wonderful. I'll see you then."

She took Altus and Michelle with her—Altus because her mother insisted that they all use bodyguards when traveling outside the principality. And Michelle because the housekeeper was an excellent companion who never got flustered by long lines or inconveniences and could pack weeks' worth of gear and clothing in a small number of bags.

With the time difference, they were able to leave Nice Friday morning and arrive at Santa Barbara Airport that afternoon. Altus transferred their bags to the car they had waiting and off they went.

It was a short ride along El Camino Real, less than half an hour from the airport to the gates of Noah's property in Carpinteria. The black iron gates parted as the car approached and they rolled along a curving driveway, past vineyards and orange trees and an olive grove, up the gentle slope of a sunlit hill to the white stucco villa with two wings branching off to either side of the carved-limestone entrance.

Even prettier than the pictures Alice had seen of it online, the house was a beautifully simple Italian-style villa, complete with wrought-iron balconies and a red-tile roof. Four wide arches to the left of the entrance framed a front-garden patio centered around a koi pond and landscaped with tropical flowers and miniature palms.

The coffered mahogany door swung open as Altus stopped the car. A slim pixie-haired young woman in skinny jeans, pink Chuck Taylor high-tops and a pink-striped peplum T-shirt bounded out, followed at a more sedate pace by a taller, older woman with thick black hair parted in the middle and pinned up in back.

The girl had to be Lucy, and she looked so eager and happy to have visitors that Alice pushed open her door and called out, "Hello."

"Alice!" The girl blushed. "Er, I mean, Your Highness?"

"Just Alice. Please." She got out of the car and shut the door. "And you must be Lucy...."

"It's so good that you're here." Lucy ran up and embraced her. Laughing, Alice returned the hug. And then Lucy was grabbing her hand and pulling her toward the older woman. "And this is Hannah. Once she was my foster mom, and now she lives with us. She takes care of us—of Noah and me...."

The older woman nodded. "Welcome, Your Highness."

"Thank you, Hannah. Noah's told me about you, about how much he appreciates all you've done for him and Lucy—and call me Alice, won't you?"

"Alice, then," said Hannah with a warm smile. "Let's get you settled. Come this way...."

An hour later, Alice was comfortably installed in a large west-facing bedroom suite that overlooked the estate's equestrian fields and tree-lined riding trails. She could see El Camino Real and the endless blue Pacific beyond that. Michelle and Altus each had smaller rooms above Alice's, on the third floor.

Hannah had provided an afternoon snack of cheese, fresh fruit and iced tea. Alice and Lucy sat on the small balcony off of Alice's room, enjoying the view and the afternoon sun.

Lucy chattered away. "I'm *so* glad you're here. Noah told me all about you, and of course I had heard of you before. Who hasn't heard of your family? It's such a totally romantic story, isn't it? Your mother, the last of her line, visiting Hollywood and falling in love with an actor. I adore the pictures of their wedding, that fabulous dress she wore, all that Brussels lace, the gazillion seed pearls, the yards and yards of netting and taffeta and tulle…." Lucy sighed and pressed a hand to her chest. "Oh, my racing heart. Like something out of a fairy tale." She plucked a strawberry from the cheese tray and popped it into her mouth. "And they still love each other, don't they, your mother and your father?"

"They do, yes. Very much."

"Wonderful. Perfect. Heaven on earth. My mom and dad were deeply in love, too. But then he died before I was born. And we lost our mom when I was nine—did Noah tell you?"

"Yes, he—"

"Ugh! Noah!" Lucy pretended to strangle herself, complete with the bulging eyes and flapping tongue. And then she laughed. And then she groaned. "Honestly, I love Noah more than anything, but sometimes I wonder if he's *ever* going to let me get out on my own. I used to be sick a lot—he told you that, didn't he? Did he also bother to tell you I'm *well* now? Hello! I am. And that I got accepted to the Fashion Institute of Technology in New York for the spring semester? I did! FIT New York. It's the best fashion and design school in the country. They *loved* my portfolio, and my entry essay was brilliant, if I do say so myself. But I swear, Noah's so careful and so sure I can't handle it. I'm afraid that he won't let me go." She pulled a fat grape off the bunch, ate it—and kept right on talking. "Noah says you're twenty-five. Just two years older than me. But you seem so mature, so sophisticated."

Alice smiled at that. "You're making me feel ancient, you know."

Lucy blinked—and then laughed some more. "Oh, you're just kidding. I can see that."

Alice wasn't kidding, not really. There was something childlike about Lucy. She came across as much younger than twenty-three. But she didn't seem the least bit ill. On the contrary, she bubbled with energy and glowed with good health. "I'm sure Noah only wants the best for you. But on the other hand, every woman needs to get out and mix it up a little, to make her own way in the world."

"Oh, Alice. That is *exactly* what I keep trying to tell him. I mean, he's done *everything* for me, to make sure I had a chance when I was sick all the time, to get me the best doctors, the most advanced surgeries, the care I needed so I finally got well. I owe him everything, and like I said before, I love him so much. But I *am* well now. And one way or another, I have to make him see that I've got a great chance here. And I'm not passing it up just because he won't quit thinking of me as his sickly baby sister. Do you want to see my portfolio? I'm really ridiculously proud of it."

"I would love to see it."

So Lucy jumped up and ran to get it. She was back, breathless and pink cheeked, in no time. She shoved the cheese tray aside, plunked the zippered case down on the balcony table and started flipping through her designs.

"They're fabulous," said Alice. Because they were. They were very much like Lucy. Fun, lighthearted and brimming with energy. She favored bright colors and she freely mixed flowing fabrics with leather and lace. She had skirts made of netting in neon-bright colors combined with slinky silky tops worn under studded structured jackets. And then there were simpler pieces, too. Everyday pieces. Perfect little dresses, tops that would make a pair of jeans into something special.

Lucy chattered on. "I always loved to draw, you know?

And it was something I could do in bed when I wasn't well enough to go anywhere. I used to make up stories to myself of where I would go and what I would do—*and what I would wear*—when I finally got well. So I started drawing the clothes I saw in my fantasies, the clothes I saw myself wearing. I got Hannah to buy me a sewing machine and I taught myself to sew. I started making those clothes I dreamed of."

"Seriously. These are wonderful. You ought to be on one of those fashion-design shows."

Lucy put her hands over her ears and let out a silent squeal of delight. "Oh, you had better believe it, Alice. One of these days I will, just you watch and see." She flopped back into her chair—and then she sat straight up again. "Oh! I heard all about your beautiful horses, your Akhal-Tekes. I'll bet you want to get out to the stables, huh? Meet the guys and the horses. Ride."

"I would love to ride, but maybe I should wait for Noah." Noah. Just saying his name brought a hot little stab of eagerness to see him again. "He might want to show me around himself."

Lucy beamed. "You are so gone. You know that, right? But it's okay. So is he."

A shiver of pure happiness cascaded through her. "You think?"

"Are you kidding me? He was beyond pissed off that he wouldn't be here when you came. He wanted everything to be perfect for you. And he kept nagging poor Hannah about how it all had to be just so, giving her endless new items for the menus, insisting over and over that there had to be Casablanca lilies in your room, as though Hannah doesn't always remember what he asks for the first time."

Alice glanced through the wide-open French doors at the big vase on the inlaid table in the sitting area. "The lilies are so beautiful, and I do love the fragrance of them."

"Yeah. But he was impossible. Hannah finally had to talk back to him. She hardly ever does that, but when she does, believe me, he listens. She told him to back off her case and not get his boxers in a twist."

"No..."

"Yeah. It was so funny I had to clap my hand over my mouth to keep from laughing out loud—because I'm barely speaking to him lately and if he saw me laughing he would start thinking I was giving in and accepting that I'm not going to New York after all." Lucy lowered her voice then and spoke with steely determination. "But I *am* going. You watch me. One way or another. I'm going no matter what."

A few minutes later Hannah bustled in and shooed Lucy out so that Alice could rest after her long flight. "Dinner at seven-thirty," she told Alice. "It will only be you and Lucy, in the loggia off the family room downstairs. Now, you lie down for a little, why don't you? Put your feet up."

Alice stretched out on the bed, just for a minute or two....

When she woke up, the sun beyond the balcony was half a red-gold ball sinking into the ocean, the sky a hot swirl of orange and purple. The bedside clock said it was quarter of seven. She had a quick shower. When she got out, Michelle was in the bedroom laying out a white dress with a square neckline and a pair of high-heeled red sandals for her.

Alice put on the dress and sandals and went downstairs to the family room off the ultramodern kitchen. The doors were open to the loggia and a table was set for two. Alice sat alone for a few minutes, sipping the iced concoction Hannah had served her, enjoying the fire in the outdoor fireplace that pushed back the slight evening chill, admiring the infinity pool just visible from where she sat and appreciating the expanse of the equestrian fields below.

Eventually, Lucy bounced out to join her, wearing the cutest striped top in mustard and yellow with a pair of cropped black silk pants and high wedge sandals.

"Adorable," said Alice.

Lucy fluttered her lashes and pulled back her chair. "I do my best. You're not so bad yourself." She giggled. "This is nice, isn't it? Just us girls."

"Yes, it is. Very."

"Oh, I knew I would like you. I adore Dami, and I always had a feeling I would get along great with all you Bravo-Calabrettis."

"I didn't realize you knew Dami."

Lucy shrugged. "He's come to stay here several times when he was visiting California. He's always funny and so charming. Right away he insisted that he would just be Dami, not His Highness or anything—the same way you did. I love to talk to him. I could talk to him forever. He takes time, you know, to pay attention to me, even if I am just Noah's little sister."

"You are a lot more than just Noah's sister," Alice chided. "And you're right. Dami *can* be a sweetheart." She'd been so annoyed with him lately she'd lost sight of his good qualities, his lightheartedness and generosity of spirit. She made a mental note to remember the good things about her bossy big brother.

Hannah brought the food and Lucy chattered on. After the meal, Lucy led Alice to the media room, where they shared a bowl of popcorn and laughed over a comedy about four sorority sisters lost in the jungle. It was still pretty early when the movie ended, but Alice couldn't stop yawning. Jet lag had taken its toll. She went upstairs, climbed into bed and was asleep five minutes after switching off the light.

Hours later she woke.

For a moment she didn't know where she was. And then it came to her: Noah's house. The clock by the bed said it was ten after two in the morning. She stared up into the darkness and wondered what had awakened her.

Then she heard a light tap on the door.

And she knew: Noah. She threw back the covers and switched on the lamp as she reached for her robe. Tying the belt as she went, she raced to the door and yanked it wide.

She caught him in the act of raising his hand to knock again. "Noah…" He looked so fine he stole her breath. How could he be even hotter than she had remembered?

"Okay. It's true," he said in that wonderful gruff tone that always made her pulse race. "I caught a midnight flight because I couldn't wait to see you." His gaze ran over her, hot and slow, from the top of her head to the tips of her toes. "You look amazing."

"All squinty eyed and half-asleep, you mean?"

"Exactly."

She scraped her hair out of her eyes and resisted the

urge to launch herself at him. "How long have you been standing out here?"

He braced an arm on the door frame and leaned in close. "About ten minutes, knocking intermittently. I was trying to wake you up without freaking you out."

"Ah. Very…thoughtful."

"You're staring," he whispered, and stared right back.

"Oh, I know. I can't seem to stop. It's just so good to see you." The urge to jump on him and kiss him sense-less kept getting stronger.

With slow, deliberate care, he lifted a hand and guided a wild curl of hair off her temple and behind her ear. The light touch struck hot sparks on her skin. "I don't know what's happening to me," he said in a wondering tone. "Standing outside a woman's bedroom door at two in the morning, patiently knocking at measured intervals… It's not really my style."

She yearned to touch him, yet she felt strangely shy. And that had her casting madly about for something at least reasonably intelligent to say. "How did your busi-ness meeting go?"

"It was a success." Those blue, blue eyes tempted her down to drowning. And oh, she wanted to go there with him, to sink beneath the waves of shared desire, to lose herself in the heat and hardness of his body. He whis-pered, "I invested."

"In?"

"A new company. They stream television shows. It's an interesting start-up—though I have to admit, today I could not have cared less. I had a hell of a time concen-trating in the meetings. I kept thinking that you were on your way and then, in the afternoon, that you must be here. I kept wishing *I* was here. I couldn't get back fast enough." He said the last softly, a little bit desperately. "And why am I telling you all this? It's nothing you really need to know."

"Of course I need to know that you're thinking of me, that you want to be with me," she told him sternly. "It's important that I know."

He chuckled then. "Ah. That's it. I'm telling you because you need to know."

She had no trouble understanding his desperation. She felt it, too. "I'm glad you came back early. Glad that you stood here in the hallway patiently knocking until I heard you and woke up...."

"I love this...." He touched her cheek beside her mouth.

She had no idea what he was talking about. "This... what?"

He made a low disappointed sound. "You frowned. Gone."

And then she knew. She smiled. "Dimples. You love my dimples?"

"There they are.... Yeah." He touched each one, a matched pair of quick, sweet caresses. And then his finger strayed. He tapped the tip of her chin and traced the line of her jaw, raising little shivers of awareness as he went.

"I spent the afternoon and evening with Lucy," she said. Her voice came out sounding husky and a little bit breathless. "I love her already."

"I knew you would."

She shook her head and gently scolded, "You know she's not happy with you right now...."

"She'll get over it."

Alice wasn't so sure. "She seems pretty determined to get going on her own life."

Twin lines formed between his brows. "She's not strong enough yet."

"*She* says that she is."

"Wishful thinking. She's always been a dreamer."

"Noah. I believe her."

"She can be convincing, I'll admit."

"No. Honestly, if I didn't know she'd been sick, I never would have guessed that she spent so much of her childhood in bed."

"That's because she's better, a lot better. And all I want is for her to stay that way, not to push too hard and end up flat on her back again. In time, yes, she'll get out on her own. But at this point, she still needs taking care of. And why are we talking about this right now?"

"Because she matters. Because you love her. Because she has a right to her own life—and I saw her portfolio. She obviously has talent, a great deal of it. How can you ask her to miss her chance?"

"Alice, come on." He'd changed tactics; his voice had turned coaxing and his eyes were soft as a summer sky. He put a finger to her lips. "Enough about Lucy."

Alice longed to say more. But maybe not now. Not in the middle of the night, when he'd flown home on a red-eye just to be with her, when she was so glad to see him she felt like a moonbeam, weightless and silvery, dancing on air.

She reached up and laid her hand on the side of his smooth jaw. He smelled of soap, all fresh and clean. He must have showered before he came to find her. That touched her, the way he cared so much to please her. So much so, evidently, that his housekeeper had gotten fed up with his endless demands and been forced to take him down a peg. "I like Hannah, too."

He turned his head enough to breathe a lovely, warm kiss into the heart of her palm. "She's the best."

She let her touch trail lower and tugged on the collar of his polo shirt. "And did I mention it's *so* good to see you?"

"You did." He leaned closer. His warm breath touched her cheek. "And I have a question…."

"Mmm?"

"If you're that happy to see me, how come you haven't kissed me?"

She wrapped her hand around his neck and pulled him down to her. "You're right. I need to fix that…."

His lips were so close. "Do it." It was a command, one she was only too happy to obey.

Their lips met.

Paradise.

She slid her other arm up to clasp around his neck and he reached out and reeled her in. Her breasts pressed against his hard chest, and oh, my, down against her belly, she felt how much he wanted her.

And it was so good. So right.

She really had missed him. Three weeks since that first day when she had mistaken him for a stable hand. In three weeks he had become…special to her. Important. Almost a necessity. Like air and water and her beautiful horses.

Now that she had him in her arms again, now that she had his mouth on hers, she didn't want to stop kissing him. She didn't want to let him go. She wanted his kiss, his touch, the heat of his body so close to hers.

She wanted everything.

All of him.

Tonight.

He deepened the kiss, wrapping her tighter in his powerful embrace. She pressed her body closer to his heat and his strength.

It wasn't close enough.

With a little moan, she surged up closer still. He took her cue and caught her by the waist, lifting her. She responded instinctively, wrapping her arms and legs around him.

She gasped. He groaned. She was all over him like a fresh coat of paint, and it was marvelous. The hardest, hottest part of him pressed insistently against the soft womanly core of her, with only a few layers of clothing between.

He tore his mouth from hers and his eyes burned down at her, blue fire. "Alice?"

She knew exactly what he was asking. And she knew she wanted to answer yes.

At the same time, she hesitated. The new Alice, the more cautious Alice, nagged at her to put on the brakes.

And the old Alice, the *real* Alice, was having none of that.

How could she call this magic wrong? It *wasn't* wrong.

All right, yes, she did realize that they had a long way to go if they hoped to carve out a slice of forever side by side. She had to know him better, trust him more.

And *he* had to learn to trust *her,* to count on her.

They both had to find a way to reach for each other with open hearts, to be guided by each other, to hold on, to share support, to count on each other when things got rough.

*It's too soon.* Her wiser self kept after her. *You know*

*how you are, always leaping before you look*. She needed to be more careful. She needed to keep from getting swept away in the heat of the moment.

But no.

Being more careful was the *last* thing she needed right now. At least, her heart thought so. With every swift, hungry beat, her heart seemed to insist that it wasn't too soon at all.

In the weeks apart, when they'd talked and texted constantly, something had been changing. Being so far away from him had actually brought them closer.

So that now, tonight, when he touched her at last, when she heard his voice so low and tender, something special happened. All her doubts melted to nothing. And she knew a deeper truth.

She knew that it would be wrong to send him back to his own bed. It would be wrong and it would be false.

And cowardly, too.

What was that lovely thing Rhia had said to her?

That she was a bold person, someone who lived by her instincts. Rhia had said that she should stop trying to be otherwise, stop second-guessing and being overly careful, stop working so hard to be someone she wasn't.

"My God." Noah's eyes blazed down at her. His wonderful mouth was swollen from kissing her, his eyes feral with need. "Alice?"

And she did it. She took the plunge, gave him the answer they both longed for. "Yes."

"Alice…" It came out on a groan and he claimed her mouth again, harder and deeper even than before.

She kissed him back. The choice had been made and she was bound to glory in it. She wrapped her legs and arms all the tighter around him, pressing her hips against him, feeling him there, right where she wanted him, tucked so close against the feminine heart of her.

"Alice," he whispered once more, so tenderly now. "Alice…"

And then he carried her over the threshold into the shadowed bedroom, pausing only to kick the door closed before striding straight for the bed.

## Chapter Seven

Noah hardly dared to believe.

Now. Tonight. All night.

Alice, in his arms.

They had far too many clothes on. He needed to deal with that. Fast.

And he did. He took her by the waist and lowered her to the rug by the bed, groaning a little at the wonderful friction as her body slid down the front of him until her bare feet took her weight.

She gazed up at him, eyes lazy and hot, soft mouth parted. "Noah…"

He clasped her waist tighter, not wanting to let go, locking her in place. "Do. Not. Move."

She laughed, full-out as always, and husky, too. The sound played over him, making him hungrier, harder. Even more ready than before. She said, "I'm not going anywhere."

"Good." He let go of her and started ripping off his clothes, shirt first. He bent and reached with both fists over his shoulders, gathering the knit material up in a wad, yanking it off and away.

She remained right where he'd put her, looking like an angel in a white robe that seemed spun of silk and cobwebs, her hair wild on her shoulders, her eyes full of promises he fully intended to see that she kept.

He had his zipper down and his trousers dropped when he realized how he'd messed up. A chain of swear words escaped him.

She laughed again. "Oh, come on, Noah. It can't be all *that* bad."

He bent and yanked his pants back up. "I've got to go get condoms," he confessed with a groan.

"Condoms." She looked at him levelly. Calmly. Regally.

He felt like a complete idiot, a dolt of epic proportions. "I'll run all the way to my rooms. I won't be a minute, I swear."

She reached over, pulled open the drawer by the bed and came up with a box of them. "Will these do?"

The woman amazed him. "You brought condoms all the way from Montedoro?"

She tipped up her chin. So proud. So adorable. "I believe it's best to be prepared and responsible. We've had more than one unexpected pregnancy in my family. Those pregnancies ended well, in good marriages and wanted babies. But still, I prefer not to take that chance."

He felt better about everything. "You *were* planning to have sex with me. God. I'm so glad."

Her chin stayed high. "What I *planned* was to be safe *if* I had sex with you."

He wanted to grab her and kiss her senseless, but he had a feeling he'd be better off at that point to fake a little humility. "Yes, ma'am."

She shook the box at him. "Not that I had any intention of using them so soon...."

"Oh, hell, no. Of course you didn't." *And you damn well better not change your mind now.*

Her dimples flashed. He knew then that it would be all right, that she would let him stay with her. That he would have her, hold her, claim her as his own.

Tonight.

She opened the box, took one out and set it on the nightstand. Then she dropped the box back into the drawer and pushed it shut. "Please. Proceed."

And he did. He proceeded the hell out of getting naked fast. When he tossed away his second sock and stood before her in nothing but a little aftershave, she was all softness and sweet, willing woman again.

"Oh, Noah," she whispered, and she stepped in close. She put her hand on his chest, right over his breastbone. "Oh, my…"

He bent and took her mouth. Incredible, the taste of her. No woman ever had tasted so good.

She was a lot more than he'd bargained for when he went looking for his princess. A whole lot more. And he was absolutely fine with that.

He framed her face in his two hands, threading his fingers up into the tangled cloud of her golden-brown hair. And he went on kissing her, feeding off that tender, wet, hot mouth of hers until he was so hard he started worrying he might lose it just standing there naked at the side of the bed, his mouth locked with hers.

No way could he let that happen.

He got to work getting her undressed, first tugging the tail on the bow that held her robe together. The silken tie slithered off and down to the rug. And the robe fell open, revealing a lacy copper-colored cami and a pair of very tiny matching tap pants. He pushed the robe off her shoulders. It fell with a soft airy sound, collapsing around their feet.

Then he pushed down the tap pants, taking longer about that than he'd intended to. But the feel of her skin under his palms, the glorious smooth curves of her hips, the long, strong length of her flawless thighs....

He kind of got lost in the sheer beauty of her. What red-blooded man wouldn't?

But eventually, she stepped out of the tap pants, and he took the lacy hem of that little camisole and pulled it up over her head and away.

And that was it. They were both naked.

And she was so beautiful he almost lost it all over again. Not fragile, not Alice. Uh-uh. All woman, and strong, a true horsewoman, with more muscle than most, with shapely arms and round, high breasts, a tight little waist and lean hips. And those legs of hers...

He couldn't wait to have them wrapped around him good and hard again.

He scooped her up and laid her down. She didn't argue, only sighed and pulled him down with her, offering that tender mouth up to him once again. He took what she offered and kissed her, a hard claiming kiss.

And he went on kissing her, letting his hands go exploring, loving the feel of her skin, the lilies-and-musk scent of her, those hot little cries she made when he cupped her breasts and teased at the nipples, when he spread his fingers across her belly and rubbed.

It got to him, got to him good, to imagine that tight stomach of hers softening, slowly going round and then turning hard all over again—with his baby. He wanted that, to watch her get bigger with their child. He'd done what he had to do in his life to care for his sister, to make a place in the world that no one could take from him or anyone he claimed as his.

Now he had that place. He had the power and the money to earn what mattered—and more important, to hold on to what he earned, to mold the future for his children and his children's children. He had enough to offer a woman like this one, enough to make her his. To give her everything.

To keep her safe and happy and having his babies.

He let his hand stray lower. He parted the closely trimmed curls at the top of those beautiful thighs. And he dipped a finger in.

Wet. Hot. Silky.

She cried out against his lips and caught his face in her two hands. "Noah…"

He dipped another finger in. "Like this?"

"Yes," she whispered. And, "Yes," again.

"So soft. Hot…"

"Noah. Oh, Noah…"

He liked that. More than anything. The way she said his name like he counted, like she couldn't any more get enough of him than he could of her, like he really was the man he'd worked so hard to become—and that other guy, too. The one in the old jeans and the battered boots, sweeping out the stable, dreaming of the day he might have something to call his own. She liked that guy, too, even if she'd been pissed off at him for misleading her.

She reached down between them, wrapped her fingers around him. And then she started stroking.

He was sure he would die. And he knew it would be worth it.

Too bad he couldn't last if she kept that up. He had to reach down between them and capture her wrist.

Her eyes flew open. "Too much?"

His answer was a hard groan and another deep, hungry kiss. She wrapped both arms around him and held him so close.

He wanted to taste her, in the heart of her, where she was so hot and wet. But it had been too long for him. He feared he wouldn't last long enough to feel her sweet body all around him.

So he groped for the night table and found the condom. He had it out of the wrapper and down over himself in a matter of seconds, and then he lifted up on his hands to position himself.

She gazed up at him, eyes dazed, mouth so soft and willing. And she ran her hands over him, across his shoulders, down his chest. Slowly, she smiled, a knowing, wicked smile, those dimples of hers making naughty little creases in her velvety cheeks.

And then she got her feet braced somehow and she was turning him—turning *them*. She must have seen that she'd surprised him, because another of those throaty killer laughs escaped her.

He found himself on his back, staring up at her. "What?" he asked in a growl, though he had a pretty good idea of what—and he didn't mind in the least.

"I want to be on top, that's all." She folded those muscular legs to either side of his waist and sat up on him.

"Be my guest," he managed on a groan. The view was amazing. He couldn't resist. He cupped her breasts, teased the tight dusky nipples with his thumbs.

And then she lifted up again. She reached down between them and she took him in her hand.

They both groaned as she lowered her sleek, strong

body down onto him. She did it slowly, drawing it out, making him suffer and clearly loving every minute of it.

He grasped her waist, trying to take a little control, trying not to lose it when they were so close.

But she just kept right on at her own pace, slowly claiming him, surrounding him with her wet heat, her silky softness, owning him, taking him in. It went on forever, and every second he knew that he couldn't hold on, couldn't last a second longer.

And yet, somehow, he did hold on. For that second. And the one after that, and even the one after that.

Until she had him fully within her.

She stilled. He followed her lead, holding himself steady, though his whole body ached with the need to move. He stared up at her and she gazed down at him through another sweet, endless space of time. He knew he would explode.

Finally, when he was past the point where he couldn't take it anymore and yet, through some dark miracle, kept on taking it without losing it after all, she started to lift up again.

He still clasped her waist and he grabbed on hard— and pulled her back down. She moaned at that and let her head fall back. So beautiful, her long slim neck straining, her hair falling over her shoulders, her mouth open in another cry, a silent one.

After that he lost track of everything but the pure, perfect sensation of being held tight inside her. She rocked those hard little hips on him and he rocked with her.

It was forever and only a moment. Light exploded behind his eyes, and then he was reaching for her shoulders, pulling her down onto him, tight and close. He let his hands glide along the fine shape of her slender back to grasp the twin curves of her bottom and he held her good and tight and rocked up hard against her.

She took him, she pushed right back. A shudder claimed her and he knew she was almost there. Inside, she closed and opened on him in rhythmic contractions. She cried out.

That did it. He was so ready, and now she was going over. He didn't have to hold out any longer.

He lifted his head enough to claim her mouth. She opened for him, her tongue sliding over his, welcoming him with a keening little sigh as her body continued to pulse around him.

So good. Exactly right. Doubly joined to her, he kissed her and he let it happen, let his climax rise to meet hers. No stopping it now. It rolled up through the core of him, a long wave of heat and energy, spreading outward so that everything—his body, her body, the whole of the world—seemed to shimmer, to open.

He surged up harder than ever into her, still holding the endless kiss they shared. She breathed his name into his mouth. He drank it. Drank *her,* as the end shuddered over him in a spinning-hot explosion of burning, perfect light.

Curled on her side facing the bedside table, Alice woke from a deep, peaceful sleep.

The clock by the lamp said it was almost ten in the morning. Daylight glowed around the edges of the drawn curtains.

She rolled onto her back and eased a hand out, feeling her way across the sheet to the other side of the bed. Empty. Frowning a little, she turned her head.

Gloriously naked, feet planted wide apart on the

cream-colored rug, Noah lounged in one of the sitting-
area chairs, watching her through hooded eyes.

Alarm jangled through her. Was something the matter?

She bounced to a sitting position, instinctively pulling the sheet against her bare breasts, pushing her hair
out of her eyes. "Noah, what…?"

He got up and came toward her. Her heart rate spiked.
He really was one magnificent-looking man, wide shoul-
dered and broad in the chest, with lean, hard arms, a
sculpted belly and sharply muscled legs nicely dusted
with burnished gold hair. She found herself staring at the
most manly part of him. It really was every bit as breath-
taking as the rest of him, even at half-mast.

Halting at the side of the bed, he stood staring down
at her.

She blinked up at him, vivid images from the night
before flashing through her mind. It had been wonderful. They'd used three of her condoms and made love
till near dawn, finally falling asleep wrapped up in each
other's arms. "Um. Good morning."

He held out his hand. "Come here."

She frowned, tipped her head to the side and tried
to figure out what exactly was going on with him. "Is
everything…all right?"

He nodded. He really was looking so very serious.
She kept having the feeling that something terrible must
have happened. But what?

He prompted, "Take my hand." He still had it out-
stretched to her.

And she thought of that night at the palace when she'd
first learned he wasn't a poverty-stricken stable worker
after all, and she'd been so angry with him. He'd offered

his hand to her then. And she couldn't bear not to take it, couldn't leave him standing there, reaching out to nothing. She just had to reach back.

She took his hand. His fingers curled around hers, warm and strong and steady. And her heart gave a little lurch of pleasure. Of hope and happiness. "Last night was so beautiful, Noah."

"It was," he said softly. "Let go of the sheet."

Why not? She'd never been all that overly modest, anyway. And he'd seen every inch of her last night. Plus, he was naked, too. They were naked together. A ragged little sigh escaped her as she let the sheet drop. He tugged on her hand. She swung her bare legs over the side of the bed and stood.

"This way...." He led her across the lustrous mahogany floor to the nearest set of French doors, where he released her hand and drew the curtain back.

Morning light burnished the equestrian fields. Several of his men were out working with the horses. A breeze blew the branches of the trees lining the riding trails. Farther out, the ocean was a perfect shade of blue with a rim of white waves rolling onto the sandy ribbon of shoreline.

She turned to Noah again and saw he was watching her. His gaze seemed approving. And possessive. A delicious little shiver ran up the backs of her bare calves. Butterflies got loose in her belly—and her anxiety eased. He wouldn't be looking at her in that sexy, exciting way if he was about to break some awful bit of news to her.

"I'll tell you what's even more beautiful than last night," he said. "You are, Alice. You knock me out...."

A flush of pleasure warmed her cheeks. She breathed easier still. It was definitely not bad news, then. He wouldn't take time to shower her with compliments if he had something terrible to tell her, would he?

Surely not.

So if not bad news, then what?

"Alice." And he dropped to a bare knee right there in front of her—at which point the situation became all too clear. Oh, she should have guessed. She started to speak, but before she could make a sound, he raised his other hand.

Wouldn't you know? There was a ring in it, a stunning marquise-cut solitaire on a platinum band. The giant diamond glittered at her.

She managed to croak out, "Oh, Noah…"

And then he proposed to her, right there on his knees, naked in the morning light.

"I know what I want, Alice. I've known for certain since that first morning I saw you in the flesh, tacking up that golden mare in the palace stables before dawn. I want *you,* Alice. Only you. Now, tomorrow, for the rest of our lives. Let me give you everything, Alice. Marry me. Be my wife."

## *Chapter Eight*

Alice caught that plump lower lip of hers between her teeth. "Noah, I…" The words trailed off.

Not that he needed to hear anymore. He already knew by the tone of her voice and the way she looked down at him, so sweet and regretful, that she wasn't going for it.

"Crap." He stood. No point in kneeling in front of her stark naked if she wasn't going to give in and say yes.

She stared up at him, those gray-blue eyes soft and maybe a little worried—for him. That ticked him off. He didn't want her concern. He wanted *her*. Beside him. For the rest of their lives.

"You're amazing," she said. "I really am crazy for you."

He took her by her silky shoulders and grumbled, "So why aren't you saying yes?"

"Ahem." She went on tiptoe and kissed him—a quick little peck of a kiss. And then she settled back onto her heels again and suggested gently, "Maybe you forgot? A certain four-letter word seems to have gone missing from your proposal."

He scowled down at her. "Fine. I love you, then. I love you madly. All the way to distraction and beyond. You are my shining hope, my only dream of happiness. Marry me, Alice. Say yes."

She put her hand on his chest, the way she had more than once the night before. "I know you have a heart, Noah. I can feel it beating away strong and steady in there."

"What the hell is that supposed to mean?"

"It means I know what I want now, after years of throwing myself wildly into all kinds of iffy situations."

Just like a woman. She knew what she wanted, but she failed to share it with him.

Patiently, he suggested, "And what, exactly, *is* it that you want, Alice?"

"I want it all. I'll have nothing less. I want everything. All that you have. Not only your strength and protection, your fidelity and your hot body and half of everything you own. Not only your brilliant brain and great sense of humor and your otherworldly way with my horses. I want your heart, too. And I know I don't have that yet. And until I do, I won't say yes to you."

"My heart." He sent a weary glance in the direction of the forged-iron fixture overhead.

"Your heart," she repeated with great enthusiasm. "Exactly."

"I'll play along. What about *your* heart?"

"I get yours, you get mine. That's how it works."

He let his lip curl into something that wasn't a smile. "You're being sentimental. It's all just words, what you're talking about."

"Uh-uh. It's not just words. And until you understand that and give me what I want from you, I'm not going to marry you. It's just not going to happen."

He was tempted to shake her until a little good sense fell out. "Alice. Think about it. I've already offered you everything."

"No, you haven't. But you will." She spoke with confidence. Only the slight tightening around her mouth hinted she might have doubts.

He decided to look on the bright side. She hadn't said no. She'd only said *not yet.* Very few deals were ever finalized on the first offer anyway.

And she did look so beautiful, standing there naked in the morning light. Her skin had a golden cast and the scent of lilies swam around him.

He couldn't resist. He stroked her hair. She didn't object. In fact, she stared at him with shining eyes, even let out a sweet, rough little sigh when he ran the back of his finger along the side of her neck.

"You want me," he reminded her, just in case she might be thinking of telling him that last night had been a mistake. "You want me and I want you."

She answered with no hesitation. "Oh, yes. Absolutely."

He touched the pulse in the undercurve of her throat. It beat fast. Yearning. Eager. "I want to marry you. I'm not giving up."

"Of course you're not." She searched his face. Her voice was gentle, almost tender. He realized he wanted her more than ever right then. "I love that about you, Noah. I don't want you to give up."

He slid his fingers around the back of her neck, up into the warm, living fall of her hair. "If you're not going to say yes to my proposal right now, the least you can do is kiss me."

"Oh, I would be only too happy to kiss you."

Enough said. He lowered his mouth to hers. She swayed toward him, sliding her arms up around his neck.

Her body pressed like a brand all along the front of him. He was fully erect in an instant.

He grasped her waist, the way he had at the door last night, and lifted her from the floor. Those fine legs came around him and she linked her ankles at the small of his back.

They groaned in unison.

He carried her that way to the bed, where he paused long enough to set the ring she'd refused on the night-stand. Then he lowered her down to the tangled sheets.

She made no objections. On the contrary, she went on kissing him eagerly, deeply.

He might not have her promise to marry him yet.

But he *was* in her bed.

An hour later, Alice handed him the fabulous ring, kissed him one last time and then sent him to his room to shower and dress. He was barely out the door when someone tapped on it.

Michelle peeked in. "Good morning." Alice had put on her robe while Noah was getting dressed, but the cami and tap pants lay on the bedside rug where he'd dropped them the night before. Michelle bustled over and picked them up. "Breakfast here in the room or…?"

"I'll go down. We'll grab a quick bite and then I'll get my first look at the stables, followed by a long ride and a tour of the property."

Michelle only stood there, holding the bits of satin and lace, a look of bemusement on her face.

Alice held her hands out to the side, palms up. "What?"

"You look positively…glowing."

Glowing. Hmm. She felt well satisfied, certainly. It

had been a wonderful night. But she didn't feel exactly glowing. That would come later, if things went as she hoped they might.

She smiled at Michelle anyway. "Thanks. I'm working on it." And she turned for the bathroom and a nice hot shower.

"What's going on?" Alice asked Noah when she joined him at the table out in the loggia. Beyond the open French doors to the family room, men and women in white shirts and black trousers bustled back and forth. A big bearded fellow in a chef's hat had taken over the kitchen. Alice had seen the pots bubbling on the giant red-knobbed steel range. It all smelled wonderful.

"We're having a party," Noah said. "Coffee?" He held the carafe above her cup.

"Yes, please—a party *tonight?*"

"A welcome party for you. Just some people I know— neighbors, business associates. Is that all right with you?"

"Of course. It's only that this is the first time anyone's mentioned a party to me."

"I'm sure they assumed I'd told you. And I should have." He attempted to look contrite. "I'm sorry, Alice."

She laughed then—and she leaned close to him to whisper, "You intended to announce our engagement tonight, didn't you?"

He gave her a dark look and dropped the apologetic act. "You're damn straight. You should say yes and not ruin my big plan."

She sat back in her chair and gazed out at the tree-shaded, sun-dappled garden. "I believe you are the most relentless person I have ever known."

"You're right. I don't give up. You should say yes

now. Telling me no is only putting off the inevitable." He said it teasingly. But he wasn't teasing, not really. Alice thought of the night before, of how sweet and eager he'd been to see her. He had so many stellar qualities. But he did have a ruthless side, a side that demanded loyalty rather than graciously accepting it, a side that strove constantly for control.

He might claim her loyalty. But she ran her own life and made her own choices. And with the man she loved, she would be willing to share control. But never surrender it completely.

"Alice!" Lucy hovered in the open doorway to the family room, wearing a gathered red skirt with white polka dots, a red lace bandeau and a jean jacket with big red buttons. She bounced over, grabbed Alice by the shoulders and planted a big kiss on her cheek. "There you are." She took the chair on Alice's other side, grabbed an apple from the bowl in the center of the table and bit into it with gusto.

Hannah came out carrying two plates piled with scrambled eggs, bacon, browned potatoes and golden toast. "I hope scrambled will do." She set a plate in front of Alice.

"Wonderful." Alice beamed at her and picked up her fork as Hannah set the other plate in front of Noah.

"I had my breakfast *hours* ago," Lucy announced, and chomped on her apple. "So what are you going to do today?" she asked Alice, taking great care to ignore her brother. "I mean, besides partying all night with Noah's rich friends."

Alice reached over and put her hand on Noah's. He turned his hand over and laced his fingers with hers. A delicious little thrill skittered through her. He might be ruthless and overbearing at times, but when he touched her, she couldn't help thinking he was worth it. "Noah is showing me the stables and then we'll go riding."

Lucy waved her half-finished apple. "I would go with you, but I don't think I like the company you keep."

"Lucy." Noah sent her a warning frown.

She continued to pretend he wasn't there. "Well, Alice, I'm going to put in a few hours sketching new designs." She jumped up, bent over Alice and placed an apple-scented kiss on her cheek. "Come find me if he gives you a moment to yourself…."

Noah kept a variety of breeds, including Morgans, Thoroughbreds and Arabians. Each horse was a beauty with impeccable bloodlines, well trained and well cared for. And the stables and facilities were top-notch. None of that surprised Alice, but it was lovely to see it all for herself nonetheless. Orion would be happy here.

She met his staff—the two trainers, the grooms and stable hands—and she admired the dressage and jumping areas, the oval-shaped private racetrack and the state-of-the-art hot walker. Once she'd had the tour, they chose their horses. He rode a big black Thoroughbred mare named Astra and she chose Golden Boy, a handsome palomino gelding with a blaze on his forehead and a thick ivory mane. Altus, on a gray gelding, followed them at a discreet distance.

They rode for hours, on the trails around the property and sometimes onto trails that belonged to his neighbors. The horses seemed familiar with the route and comfortable with drinking from the troughs they came upon now and then along the way.

Eventually, he turned onto a trail that went under the

highway and they ended up at the ocean, on the ribbon of golden beach. It was nearly deserted, which surprised her. As they rode side by side on the wet, packed sand at the edge of the tide, he told her that the beach was privately owned by him and a group of his neighbors.

They rode until they reached the place where the rocky cliffs jutted out into the tide, much like the cliffs at her family's private beach in Montedoro. It was all so beautiful and perfect. Too perfect, really.

It had her thinking of the other Noah, the scruffy down-and-out Noah she'd met first. She wondered about his early years, about his life growing up. Really, she needed to know more about the man he'd started out as.

"Alice."

She glanced over at him. The sun made his hair gleam like the brightest gold. He grinned and her pulse kicked up a notch. Really, the man ought to come with a warning label: Too Hot. Contents Combustible.

He lowered his reins, canting slightly forward. She didn't have to hear him cluck his tongue to know what he was up to.

They took off in unison, her palomino as quick and willing as his black. The wind smelled of salt and sea, cool and sweet as it pulled at her tied-back hair. She bent over Golden Boy's fine strong neck and whispered excited encouragements as they raced toward the other end of the beach, where Altus waited, ever watchful.

The race was too short. They ended up neck and neck—and then turned their mounts as one and raced back the other way.

That time, she won by half a length. But of course, he couldn't leave it. A lucky thing she had that figured out ahead of time. Again they turned and made for the other end.

He had the slightest edge on her and won that time. When they pulled to a halt, he sent her a grin of such triumph she *had* to kiss him. She sidled her mount in close. He must have read her look, because he met her in the middle.

She laughed against his mouth as the horses shifted beneath them, pulling them away from each other—and then bringing them together so their lips met again.

"We need to go back," he told her regretfully. "The party starts at eight."

Side by side, they turned for the trail that would take them beneath the highway and back the way they'd come.

At the stables, they let the hands clean the tack but took care of their mounts themselves. They hosed off all the salt and sand. Then Alice gave Golden Boy a nice long rubdown, while Noah did the same for Astra. A groom led both horses away to feed and water them. Noah had a few things to discuss with the trainers, so she left him and went on to the house, with Altus following close behind.

Lucy must have been watching for her. She was waiting at the side door when Alice approached.

"Come on," she said, and grabbed Alice's hand. "Have a cold drink with me. There's plenty of time...."

So they went up to Lucy's room, which faced the mountains and was as bright and eye-catching as Lucy herself, the linens neon yellow and deep fuchsia pink. There were plants in pots everywhere. Lucy's drawings and designs covered the walls, and a fat orange cat lay on the floor between the open doors to the balcony, sprawled on its back, sound asleep.

Lucy scooped up the big cat and introduced him to Alice. "Boris, this is Alice. I like her a lot, so you'd better be nice to her."

The cat looked exceedingly bored, but Alice said hello anyway and scratched the big fellow behind the ears. She got a faint lazy purr for her efforts.

Lucy got them each a canned soft drink from her minifridge and they took comfy chairs in her small sitting area. It didn't take her long to get around to what was bothering her.

"Lately, I have a hard time remembering how much I love my brother and how good he's been to me," Lucy said in a whisper, as though Noah might be standing out in the hallway, his ear pressed to the door. "I swear, most of the time now I never want to speak to him again. But I know I need to try harder to get through to him before I do anything drastic."

Alice didn't like the sound of that. "Drastic. Like what?"

"You don't want to know."

"But, Lucy—"

"Trust me. It's better if you don't know. It just puts you in the middle of this more than you already are."

"All right, now you're scaring me."

"Oh, please. It's nothing that awful." Lucy knocked back a big gulp of ginger ale. "And I'm twenty-three years old. If I want to walk out of here and not look back, he can't stop me. But I don't want to do that."

"You want your brother's blessing," Alice said gently.

"Yes, I do. And that means I'm going to have to talk to him some more. I'm going to have to try again to get him to see that he has to let me go." She waved a hand. "Oh, not tonight. Not with the big party and all, but tomorrow or the next day. And I know, a minute ago I said you shouldn't be in the middle of this. I do totally get that it's not fair to ask you, but will you maybe just think about backing me up?"

Alice had no idea how to answer. She felt a strong sense of loyalty to Noah. But she also sympathized with Lucy. Noah *was* too protective and Lucy deserved her chance at her dream.

Her indecision must have shown on her face because Lucy groaned. "Okay, never mind. It's not your battle, I know that. Like I said, I shouldn't have asked."

And Alice found herself offering limply, "I'll...do what I can."

Lucy jumped from her chair, grabbed Alice's hand and pulled her up into a hug. "Oh, thank you. And whatever happens, I'm so glad you came here—selfishly for me because I like you a lot and you're so easy to talk to. But also for Noah. I'm so glad he found you and I hope you two end up together in, well, you know, that forever kind of way."

Alice eased from Lucy's grip and set her soft drink on the side table next to her chair. Then she took Noah's little sister by the shoulders and gazed into her wide brown eyes. "I can't say for certain yet what will happen between me and your brother. But I *can* say that you are absolutely marvelous."

Lucy giggled. "I try." And then she grew more serious. "I worry about Noah. I do. Before our mom died, he used to be...softer, you know? At least, he always was with me and Mom. I was sick so much and Mom, well, she was so sad all the time. Noah said she missed our dad. I remember him then as so sweet and good to us. He would do anything for us back then."

Alice reminded her, "I think he would do anything for you right now."

Lucy made a scoffing sound. "But you see, the point is, there are things he *can't* do for me, things I need to do for myself."

Alice had to agree. "All right. I see what you mean."

Lucy dropped back into her chair again. She kicked off her shoes, drew up her feet and braced her chin on her knees. "All those years ago? Before Mom died?"

Alice knew she should be getting back to her room to prepare for the evening ahead. Michelle would be waiting, growing impatient. But then again, this right now with Lucy, was a lot more important than primping for a party. She sat down, too. "Tell me."

"Well, Noah also had a wild side then, when I was little."

Alice wasn't surprised. "I believe that."

"Outside the house, he was big trouble. He didn't fit in and he used to get in fights all the time. It got worse as he got older. He didn't make friends easily. He was an outsider. And he never backed down, so every night was fight night. I guess it's kind of a miracle he never got shot. He did get knifed a time or two, though. *That* was really scary. He'd come home all bloody and Mom had to patch him up. He barely graduated high school. And then somehow he got into business college and found this job working for this guy who flipped houses. Mom was pleased he was working and actually getting a little higher education, but every day she worried he'd get kicked out of college for bad grades or lose his job for fighting. She had that sadness inside her, and it got worse because she feared for him, for his drinking, for his being out all night, being out of control. And then we lost her…." Lucy shut her eyes and dropped her forehead down on her knees.

Alice sat in sympathetic silence, hoping that she would go on.

And she did. She lifted her head and straightened her shoulders. She stared toward the open doors to the balcony. "And that was it. After the day Mom died, I don't think he ever got into another fight. He got control of himself scary fast. He started getting straight As at his business school. I never saw him drunk again. I mean, that's good, I know, that he isn't out beating people's heads in, that he's not a drunk. That he's focused and determined and a big success and all that. He's come so far. I get that. I'm proud of him. But he's definitely not as sweet as he used to be back in the day, when it was just us at home. He's not as understanding, not as open-minded." She turned her head, looked at Alice, then. "I've done my best, I promise you, to keep him real, to remind him that he only *thinks* he owns the world. But I really am well now. I'm one of the lucky ones. And I have my own life I have to live, you know?"

"Of course you do…." Alice felt strangely humbled. She'd thought Lucy childlike at first. But today she saw the wisdom in those innocent eyes.

Lucy reached between their chairs and squeezed Alice's arm. "Noah desperately needs a person like you in his life, someone he can't run all over. Someone who isn't the least impressed by his money, someone who really cares about him and who can stand up to him, too."

Alice hardly knew what to say. "You make me sound so much more exemplary than I actually am."

"That's not true. You *are* exemplary. You're the best

thing that's ever happened to my brother, and I only hope he doesn't blow it and not let you into his heart and end up chasing you away."

## Chapter Nine

When Alice got back to her room, Michelle was waiting, tapping her foot in irritation. "What am I going to do with you? Is that hay in your hair? The party starts at eight. Have you forgotten?"

Alice didn't even argue. She headed straight for her bath.

She was ready at a quarter of eight, fifteen minutes before the guests were due to start arriving. She followed the sound of music down to the first floor. A quartet was warming up in the wide curve at the bottom of the stairs—a grand piano, bass, drums and a sultry singer in a clinging blue satin dress, her blond hair pinned up on one side with a giant rhinestone clip, her lips cherry red.

Alice had a look around. In the living room, two full bars had been set up, one at either end. The dining room was one fabulous buffet, set out on the long dining table and on each of the giant mahogany sideboards. She moved on to the family room, where the doors were wide-open on the loggia. Outside, there was more food and yet another full bar.

Noah appeared from the foyer. He was looking cool and casual in an open-collared dress shirt and dark trousers.

He swept her with an admiring glance, head to toe and

back again. "You look incredible in that dress and those shoes." She wore a short strapless black cocktail dress, her classic red-soled patent leather Christian Louboutin stilettos and the hammered-gold necklace he'd bought her. He put an arm around her, drew her close and whispered, "So how come all I can think of is getting everything off of you?"

She laughed and leaned against him, the things Lucy had revealed to her earlier foremost in her mind, making her feel tenderly toward him—and sympathetic, too. He'd been through so much and come so very far. She would try to remember to be patient with him. She teased, "I think I'll keep my clothes on, if that's all right with you. At least until the party's over."

He handed her a glass of champagne and offered a toast. "To when the party's over." They touched glasses, sipped and shared a quick champagne-flavored kiss.

The doorbell rang and the party began.

Alice met a whole bunch of handsome, athletic people, most of whose names she promptly forgot. A lot of them were horse lovers. Many knew of her and her family. And she could tell by the gleam in more than one eye that several of them had read of her exploits over the years. Yes, she did feel a bit like Noah's newest acquisition—a famous painting or a champion racehorse brought out and paraded around, yet more proof of Noah Cordell's enormous success.

But she didn't let it get to her. She'd spent too much of her life with people staring at her to become all that upset if they stared at her some more. She didn't let the ogling bother her, only smiled and tried enjoy herself.

Her second cousin, Jonas Bravo, and his wife, Emma, arrived around eight-thirty. It touched Alice that Noah had thought to invite them. She sat out by the infinity pool with them for over an hour, catching up a little. Emma and Jonas enjoyed a great marriage. They loved their four children and they were clearly blissfully happy together. It always made Alice feel good to be around them. They encouraged her to come visit them at their Bel Air estate, Angel's Crest, anytime she could manage it during her stay. She thanked them and promised she would try.

They went back inside together, the three of them. Alice excused herself to mingle with the other guests. She visited with a couple of minor celebrities who lived in the area and chatted with a lovely older lady about the best local beaches and the fine gardens at Mission Santa Barbara. Then she joined Noah, who was talking horses and polo with three of his neighbors. The nearby polo and racquet club was deep into its fall schedule of polo tournaments. After half an hour of that, she excused herself and went upstairs to freshen her lip gloss.

At the top of the stairs stood a tall, attractive fortyish brunette in red silk. "Your Highness. Hello. I'm Jessica Saunders." Jessica had very angry eyes.

Alice was tempted to simply nod and move on past. But she did want to get along with all of Noah's friends. So she paused when she reached the landing and returned Jessica's greeting.

Altus was below her, following her up, staying close as he always did when there were strangers around. She gave him a quick glance and a slight shake of her head to let him know she was fine. He continued the rest of the way up, passing between her and the other woman, stopping farther down the upper hallway, where he could keep her in sight.

Jessica sighed. "Leave it to Noah to bring home royalty." She delicately plucked the cherry from her Manhattan by the stem and popped it into her mouth. Her red lips tipped upward in a smile that managed to be both lazy and aggressive at the same time.

Alice resisted the urge to explain that her family was not strictly considered royal. Montedoro was a principality, not a monarchy. Her mother held a throne, but she didn't wear a crown. It was a distinction most people didn't get, anyway. Plus, in recent generations, with all the media hype, just about anyone with a title could end up mistakenly being called a "royal." So never mind. Let Jessica call her a royal if she wanted to. "Noah didn't 'bring' me here," she said. "I arranged my own transportation, thank you—and the Santa Barbara area is so beautiful. We rode down to the ocean today. It was fabulous."

Jessica was not interested in discussing the scenery. "Slightly, er, tarnished royalty, however. We've all read so *much* about you...."

Alice kept on smiling. "Tarnished? I'm guessing you must have grown up years and years ago, back when women weren't allowed to be as interesting as men."

Jessica took a large sip from her drink. "Humph. Being royalty, *I'm* guessing *you* know about Henry VIII."

"Well, I did see *The Other Boleyn Girl*. I kind of have a thing for Eric Bana, if you must know."

"I only mean, if you think about it, Noah is a little like Henry VIII, isn't he?"

Alice wished she had a drink in her hand. She could toss it into Jessica's handsome, smug face. "Excuse me?"

"Not that he's ever cut off anyone's head. It's only that he becomes bored with his conquests so easily, wouldn't you say?"

Alice gave up trying to play nice. "I'm sorry, Jessica. Could you try being just a little more direct? Are you telling me that you are one of Noah's 'conquests,' and that he dumped you and now you're bitter and out for revenge because he broke your heart?"

Jessica almost choked on her Manhattan. "No, of course not. It's just what I've heard and what I've observed. I'm a *friend*, a neighbor. I have the next estate over to the north."

"You don't behave like a friend."

"I'm only telling you what I've heard."

"Only spreading ugly rumors, you mean—and trying to cause tension between Noah and me."

Jessica huffed. "As I said, *Your Highness*, it was just an observation. There's no need to get hostile."

"Oh, I'm not hostile. I'm merely disgusted. Now, if you'll excuse me, I see no benefit to either of us in continuing this conversation." Alice started walking. She didn't stop until she reached her room. When she glanced back, Jessica was gone and Altus was right where he'd been a moment before, patiently waiting, ever watchful. She gave him a nod and shut the door.

Once alone, she fell back across the bed and stared at the ceiling and slowly smiled. Her mother would have been proud of her. She'd put Jessica Saunders in her place and then some. And she'd done it without causing her usual scene, without so much as raising her voice.

Later, when all the guests had gone home, Noah did what he'd been waiting all day and evening to do. He took off Alice's black dress and her red-soled shoes and made slow love to her. It was even better than the night before.

She cuddled up close to him afterward, and he stroked

her silky, fragrant hair and thought that even if she hadn't agreed to marry him yet, things were going pretty well between them.

Scratch that. Things were going great.

Then she said, "Tell me about Jessica Saunders." Her tone was a little too careful, too neutral.

He wrapped a thick bronze curl around his finger, rubbed it with his thumb and then let it go. "There's nothing to tell. She's always seemed friendly enough. She's a neighbor, a booster of the new Carpinteria hospital—to which I have written more than one large check. She does like her Manhattans, or so I've been told. And she's divorced. I heard she took her ex-husband to the cleaners. He left her for a twenty-year-old dental assistant from Azusa."

"Ouch. I guess that explains the bitterness. At least to a degree. And she was drinking a Manhattan. Maybe she'd had one too many."

"What bitterness?" He took her chin and tipped it up so he could see her eyes. "What happened?"

She wrinkled up her pretty nose as though she smelled something bad. "Jessica caught me on the stairs and told me that you're like Henry VIII. You quickly get bored with your girlfriends and dump them."

"What a bitch. I never realized." He kept his hand under her chin so he could see her eyes as he told her gruffly, "Not bored. Never dumping you—but didn't I tell you that weeks ago, on my last night in Montedoro?"

"You did. And your dumping me or not isn't really what I'm worried about right now."

"Good." He waited. He wasn't sure where this was going, but he already had a feeling it was in the wrong direction.

She asked, "Are you really *friends* with any of the people who came to the party tonight?"

"Not really, no. But I have a good time with several of them. I enjoy their company. Isn't that enough? Do they need to be people I'd take a bullet for?"

She stacked her hands on his chest and braced her chin on them—and didn't answer his question. "It's beautiful here. I love it."

"So, then, why do you sound like you're leading me someplace I'm not going to like?"

She lifted up enough to plant a hard, quick kiss on the edge of his jaw. "I want to know more about you. I want to know *everything* about you."

He scowled up at her. "Why?"

"Noah, come on. You've asked me to marry you."

"Yeah, I have. And in case you've forgotten, you failed to say yes."

"It's not something a person should enter into lightly. We're talking about a lifetime together. *And* about having children."

"Exactly. So when are you going to say yes?"

She puffed out her cheeks with a hard breath. "A woman with any sense at all needs to know everything she can about a man before she says yes."

"You already know me better than anyone else but Lucy—and maybe Hannah."

"I believe that. And still, I don't know you nearly well enough."

He did love her mouth. He loved it even when she was saying things he didn't want to hear. Idly, he rubbed his thumb across those lush, sweetly shaped lips of hers. "Believe me. You know me well enough."

His assurances failed to shut her up. "No, I don't. And

what I'm trying to tell you is that I need to know more. I want you to take me to Los Angeles. I want to see the street you grew up on, the house you used to live in. I want to meet your childhood friends."

That was not going to happen. "Where did you get this idea?"

She bent her head and pressed the sweetest, softest kiss to the center of his chest. "I was talking to Lucy yesterday. She told me a little about how it was for you before your mom died."

He should have known. "Did she tell you that all I did was fight and drink?"

"More or less, yes. But she also said you had a sweeter side then and that you were more open-minded."

He grunted. Of course Lucy would say that he *used* to be sweeter. And maybe it was even true. Being sweet and open-minded had not gotten him what he wanted and needed in life. "I don't *have* any childhood friends, so there's no one there for you to meet."

"That's all right." She laid her head down, her ear against his breastbone. "I still want to see where you grew up."

He eased his fingers under the warm weight of her hair and settled his hand around the back of her neck. He didn't think he could ever get tired of putting his hands on her. It was another of the many things that made her perfect for him. "It's a neighborhood of small older houses, California bungalows and little stucco Spanish-style homes. Nothing special. You'd get nothing out of seeing it."

"Let me be the judge of that." With her index finger, she traced a squiggly pattern along the outside of his arm. It tickled in a very good way. "You can take me to all the places you used to hang out." She sighed, a tender little sound, and snuggled in even closer. "My sister Rhia met her husband in Los Angeles. Rhia was in college at UCLA and Marcus was on some special military fellowship there. They had a favorite hamburger stand." She chuckled to herself. "I want to go to *your* favorite hamburger stand."

He traced a slow path down the bumps of her spine— all the way to those two perfect dimples on either side of her round little bottom. "No, Alice. I'm not taking you there."

She pushed herself up over him and then brought her face down to his, nose to nose. He could smell lilies. Also, sex. Her nipples were like little pink pebbles against his chest. He started getting hard again. She knew it, too. She smiled in that way she had, all woman and all-powerful. "I wasn't asking your permission."

"Listen to me." He cradled the side of her face and gave her his most uncompromising stare. "No."

"You don't intimidate me, Noah. And you don't get to be the only one in control. If you don't go with me, I'll only go without you."

"What in hell did you and Lucy talk about?" he growled against those fine soft lips of hers.

"I'll never tell." She licked him, just stuck out that clever tongue of hers and ran it in a circle around his lips. He got even harder. And then he opened his mouth and sucked her tongue inside.

The kiss was long and wet and wonderful. Before it was over, he'd flipped her onto her back. And once he had her there, well, he had to kiss her everywhere.

She didn't object. She threaded her fingers into his hair and whimpered encouragements, holding him in place against the wet, slick heart of her sex. He kissed her there until she rolled her head on the pillows and whispered his name, the waves of her climax pulsing against his tongue.

He was sure by then that they were done with the subject of the old neighborhood and he was feeling pleased with himself to have so effectively distracted her.

She smiled at him in a dazed and dreamy way and held down her hand. He took the condom from her and smoothly rolled it on. Then he rose up over her. She didn't even try to gain the top position that time. She simply opened to him, soft and giving and welcoming, more woman than any other he'd ever known.

He lost himself in her. It was perfect. Paradise.

And then, sometime later as they drifted toward sleep, with her arms tight around him, her fingers stroking his hair, she whispered, "Tomorrow, then. We can go to East Los Angeles and after that maybe visit Bel Air and see Jonas and Emma and the children."

In the morning, he told her again that they weren't going to East L.A.

She said, "It's all right, Noah. I'll give you a few days to get used to the idea. And eventually, if you keep refusing to go with me, I'll go by myself."

He decided to leave it at that for now. She'd said she would give him a few days. He was hoping that when those days were up, she'd either have seen the light and realized it was a pointless exercise to try to travel backward into his past—or he would have come up with another, better argument to convince her of why there was no need to go.

He left her for his rooms, where he showered and dressed.

When he got downstairs, she was sitting with Lucy out in the loggia. Their heads were together and they were whispering intently.

Then they spotted him.

They straightened away from each other and smiled at him—both of them, Lucy, too.

His sister hadn't granted him a smile in more than three weeks. He knew her so well, knew what that smile meant. She was mounting a new offensive in her campaign to get him to give her the money to go to New York.

Fine. At least she wasn't acting like he didn't exist. Maybe they could work this out. Maybe this time he would be able to get through to her, get her to see that he only wanted what was best for her.

"Noah," Alice said, too sweetly. "Come join us. Hannah is making French toast with raspberries."

He went and sat down and put his napkin in his lap.

Lucy poured him coffee—buttering him up. Definitely.

Hannah came out with the plates full of food.

Lucy waited until he'd had a couple of fortifying bites of his breakfast before she said, "Noah, I want to try one more time to work this out with you, about New York."

He ate another bite of the French toast. Excellent, as always. And then he took a sip of coffee. "Yeah. I think we do need to settle this." He set down his cup and told her sincerely, "You know I want you to be happy." He slid Alice a quick glance. She was concentrating on her breakfast, staying out of it, which he appreciated. He saw the little twitch of a smile at the corner of her mouth, though, the flash of a dimple. She assumed from what he'd just said that he was rethinking his refusal to send Lucy three thousand miles away.

Lucy had known him a lot longer. She regarded him warily. "If you want to settle it, let me have access to my trust fund so I can get an apartment and get ready for the spring semester."

He set down his fork and said gently, "When you're twenty-five, if you're strong enough."

Alice's faint smile had disappeared. She set down her fork, too, and took a slow, thoughtful sip of her coffee.

Lucy said, "I'm strong enough now." She spoke levelly. He could hear the angry undertone in her voice, but she was controlling it.

So far, anyway.

He said, "Listen. Why don't we compromise?"

Lucy cut a bite of French toast and then didn't eat it. "I want to be flexible, Noah. But with you the word *compromise* only means that we'll be doing it *your* way."

"That's not fair."

"It's the truth."

He'd been thinking it over. And he *was* willing to compromise, willing to let her try more than just the online classes he'd been suggesting. He made his new case firmly. "How about this? One year here. At UC Santa Barbara. The School of Art, the College of Creative Studies. Come on. It's UC. It will be challenging and exciting. You'll learn a lot and enjoy yourself. And you can live at home. We'll see how it goes. Then, after two semesters, we can reevaluate, see how you're feeling, see if you're ready to try New York."

From the corner of his eye, he could see the look on Alice's face. It wasn't a happy one. She just didn't understand. Someone had to make sure that his sister was safe. Lucy wouldn't be realistic, so he had to do it for her.

Lucy came right back at him. "I know UCSB is a great school. But it's not FIT New York. I'll only be treading water there, and I have tread water all of my life, Noah. I've always, forever, been waiting—to get better, to be well, to be like everyone else." Tears filmed her big eyes that were just like their mom's.

If only she would face the truth about herself. "But, Lucy, come on. You're not like everyone else. You have to be careful, you have to—"

"No!" Her fisted hand struck the table. Her plate bounced and flatware clattered. "How many times do we have to go over this?"

Damn it, why couldn't she see? He didn't want this fight any more than she did. "Lucy, I—"

"No. Wait. For once, Noah, won't you please just listen to what I keep telling you? Last year I *wanted* to try UC. You said to wait one more year just to be sure I was strong enough. Well, I have waited. I have waited and waited. My doctors have given me their blessing to live a normal life. I keep up with my blood work and exams and stress tests and everything is stable. When I go, it's not like I'm heading off to the ends of the earth. It's New York. Some of the best cardiac doctors in the world are there. I'll get referrals, you know that, the best of the best. I'll keep up with my checkups. I will be fine."

"Lucy. Come on. No."

Her cheeks flushed hot pink. "Just like that, huh? As always. Just *no*."

He felt like some monster. But he knew he was right and he couldn't back down. "If you would only—"

"Stop. Just stop." Tears pooled in her eyes. Furious,

she dashed them away. "I'm a healthy, normal woman now, Noah. Why can't you see that? Okay, Mom died. And Dad. But that doesn't mean something awful will happen to me, too. Why are you so afraid I'm going to keel over dead if I dare to get out on my own?"

Mom and Dad. Why did she always have to bring up Mom and Dad? And Alice was just sitting there, taking it all in. He should have insisted that he and Lucy do this in private.

He said with slow care, "This has nothing to do with Mom and Dad and you know it."

"Oh, please. Get real. You are lying to yourself and I have no idea how to get you to stop. You *have* to let me go, Noah. I'm all grown up, I'm in good health, and you haven't been my guardian since I turned eighteen. I'm getting the money somehow. One way or another, I'm moving to New York before the start of the spring semester." Lucy shoved back her chair and threw her napkin on the table. "You just watch me and see if I don't." She whirled and took off like a shot.

"Lucy, get back here!"

She didn't glance back, didn't even break stride. She stormed through the open doors to the family room and vanished from sight.

Once she was gone, he picked up his fork again. He ate a couple of bites of his fast-cooling breakfast, chewing slowly and carefully, keeping it calm.

Eventually, he sent a sideways glance at Alice. She caught him at it. Because she was just sitting there watching him. She had her hands in her lap.

He supposed he had to say something. "I'm sorry you had to see that."

She picked up her fork without saying a word—and

then set it back on her plate. "This is the thing, Noah. I happen to agree with Lucy."

What? Now she was going to get on his case, too? "Look, Alice, I don't think you—"

She put up a hand. "No. *You* look. Lucy's a grown woman and she has a right to make her own choices now. You should release her trust fund and help her do what she's always dreamed of doing. Think about it. Try to see it from her viewpoint. Finally, it's her turn to have her own rich, full life. And you just keep telling her no."

He wanted to shout at her to stay out of it, to remind her good and loud that she had no idea what she was talking about. Lucy wasn't *her* sister. But he didn't shout. He had more self-control than that. "Three years ago she was in Cardiac ICU at UCLA Medical Center. She weighed seventy pounds and her lungs were full of fluid. They said she wouldn't make it. They'd said that before. I brought in another specialist with a different approach. She survived, barely."

"That was three years ago. And then she had the surgery that made all the difference, you said."

"Nothing in this life is certain."

"Noah. It's been two years since the surgery. Her doctors say she's fine."

"Do you imagine you're telling me something I don't already know? She needs more time at home. I'm not going to bend on that. I *can't* bend. I have her best interests at heart."

Alice pressed her lips together. For a second he dared to hope she would let it go. But no. "I don't think you were really listening to her. I don't think you see how determined and focused she is, how very much like you she is...."

"Of course I was listening. And I know she's determined."

"If you don't help her, she's going to find a way to get the money somewhere else."

"She's twenty-three with no credit and no job history. No way can she afford to relocate to New York by the first of the year without my help." A really bad thought occurred to him. He pinned the woman next to him with his hardest stare, at the same time way too aware of how much he wanted her, how exactly right she was for him in every way. How sometimes when he looked at her, he found himself thinking that she'd somehow wound herself all around his heart, that he couldn't imagine his life without her in it. But if she betrayed him… "My God. You wouldn't."

She drew in a slow breath. "Don't think I haven't been considering it."

"Damn it." The two inadequate words felt scraped from the depths of him. "Don't do that to me."

And then she sighed, softened. "I won't. I wish I could, but…"

"What?" he demanded.

And her eyes went soft as clouds in a summer sky. "I know you would never forgive me. I don't think I could bear that."

It meant a lot. Everything. To hear her say that. He wanted to grab her in his arms and lift her high and carry her back upstairs to bed.

But he knew she wouldn't go for that. Not now. She might be unwilling to betray him, but she was firmly on Lucy's side about the move to New York.

And when he thought about that, when he thought about his sister, it ruined the mood anyway.

## Chapter Ten

After breakfast, Alice went up to check on Lucy.

She tapped on Lucy's door and Lucy called out in a tear-strangled voice, "Go away, Noah! I don't want to talk to you."

"It's only me," Alice said.

A sob, then meekly, "Alice?"

"Come on, Lucy. Let me in."

Swift footsteps on the other side of the door. And then Lucy flung it wide and threw herself into Alice's arms. "Oh, Alice, Alice, what am I going to do?"

Alice took her to the bed and eased her down. She sat beside her and handed her the box of tissues from the nightstand.

Lucy blew her nose and cried some more and kept insisting over and over, "I'm going. I will find a way. He's not going to stop me. I'm not missing my chance...."

Alice put an arm around her and reminded her softly, "He does love you and he thinks he's doing the right thing for you. You know that, right? He loves you so very much."

"Of course I know." Lucy's breath hitched on a hard sob. "Somehow that makes it all worse. That he loves me so much and he's being so stupid and stubborn and wrong...." Another flood of tears poured out.

Alice hugged her close and made soothing noises and stayed with her until the storm of weeping had worn itself out.

"I'm okay now," Lucy said at the end with a sad little sniff.

Alice smoothed her thick, short, brown hair. "I'll stay with you for a while."

"No, really. I mean it. I'm fine. I think I'll pull myself together and go to my workroom. Patterns to cut, hems to turn. Working always cheers me up."

"You sure?"

"Yeah. And thanks." She gave Alice's arm a fond squeeze. "For coming up, for being here."

"Anytime."

Noah and Hannah were sitting side by side at the top of the stairs when Alice came out of Lucy's room.

Hannah got up. "How is she?"

"Not happy."

"I'll talk to her." She went into Lucy's room and quietly shut the door.

Noah reached up a hand to grab the banister and stood. He looked tired suddenly. Older than his thirty-five years. The sight made Alice's heart ache. "I know," he said glumly. "She doesn't want to talk to *me*."

Alice went to him. She wrapped her arms around his waist and laid her head on his broad, warm chest. Slowly, he responded, pulling her closer, resting his cheek against her hair.

She whispered, "I need to go riding. I think we both do."

He made a low noise of agreement, but then just continued to hold her. She lifted her head to look up at him and she remembered that dream of hers, way back at the beginning, before she knew who he really was. The dream of the two of them, longtime companions, riding together, stopping in a meadow of wildflowers just to talk.

Sometimes that seemed an impossible kind of dream. And then, times like now, as he held her at the top of the stairs after all that awfulness with Lucy, she couldn't imagine herself ever being able to leave him.

"Alice..." He bent his golden head and kissed her, a chaste kiss, a warm firm pressure, his lips to hers. "I'll meet you at the stables."

"I won't be long."

He let her go, and she went to her room to change.

Alice let a full week go by without reopening the subject of a visit to his hometown.

It was a lovely week, all in all. They rode every day, long rides on the eucalyptus-shaded trails and sometimes along the quiet private beach where he'd taken her that first day. There were picnics on that beach, just the two of them, with Altus standing watch. They attended a polo tournament at the club.

And they had each night together.

The nights were unforgettable. Alice adored being wrapped up tightly in his arms.

But there were shadows on the sunny expanse of their pleasure in each other. Alice spent time with Lucy, but Lucy would have nothing to do with her brother. She remained determined that somehow she was moving to New York.

And Noah wouldn't hear a word about letting her go. Alice stayed out of it. She'd told Noah how she felt about the situation that Sunday morning at the breakfast table. She wasn't willing to go against him head-to-head and give Lucy the money she needed, so really, she had nothing else to say about the matter. She left it alone.

Three times during that week, she called Rhia and cried on her shoulder—about Noah's unwillingness to let his little sister grow up and escape his well-meaning control. About love in general. Because she was falling in love with Noah.

She wanted to tell him so. But she didn't.

Her love made her more vulnerable to him. And she'd begun to fear that she wanted more from him than he was capable of giving her. He had his own ideas about the way things ought to be and he was never all that willing to be guided by anyone else. How could they have a partnership of equals if he insisted on believing—and behaving as though—he ran the world?

She'd said she would give him a few days to get used to the idea that they were going to his old neighborhood. But then he'd had that awful fight with Lucy and Alice had backed off. She ached for him and she wanted to give the man a break, not to push him too hard. Those few days she'd said she'd give him to think it over went by, and she didn't bring up the subject of visiting his childhood home. She knew he assumed she was letting it go.

Wrong. She was just waiting for the right moment to try again.

One really lovely thing did happen that week.

Thursday morning, early, Dami called. The first words out of his mouth were, "I called to make amends."

Both pleased and surprised, Alice laughed. "Do go on."

He confessed, "Mother accused me of being a pig-headed ass."

"That doesn't sound like Mother."

"Well, of course, she didn't use those words exactly. But she said that she believed I had it all wrong, that not only are you serious about Noah, he cares for you, too. She said that I, of all people, have no right to judge a man just because he's, er, enjoyed the company of a large number of women."

"Don't you just love Mother?"

He laughed then. "Sometimes I find her much too perceptive. Not to mention right. Why does she always have to be so bloody right?"

"It's a gift."

His voice changed, grew more somber. "I'm sorry, Allie. Noah *is* a good man, and I was an idiot. I hope the two of you will be blissfully happy together."

*I hope so, too,* she thought. She said, "Thank you. And you are forgiven."

"Good. Is Noah there?"

"He is, as a matter of fact." Sitting right there in her bed under the covers with her, his pillow propped against the headboard, same as hers. She caught his eye. He arched a brow.

"Put him on," said Dami.

So she handed Noah the phone and sat back and listened to his end of the conversation. He said yes several times and then, "Believe me, I'm on it." And then he laughed. A *real* laugh.

She knew then that it was okay between the two men and she was glad.

Noah reminded Dami that he was always welcome at the estate. "Come anytime. Now, tomorrow... You know you never have to call. The door's always open. You can see firsthand that I'm taking good care of your sister."

Dami must have asked about Lucy, because Noah said in a carefully neutral tone that Lucy was fine. They started talking about some business deal they were apparently in on together.

Alice shut her eyes then and let her thoughts drift away.

She woke when Noah kissed her.

"Your brother forgives me for seducing you," he whispered against her parted lips. "But he's expecting a wedding, and soon."

She lifted her arms and twined them around his neck. "Nice try. But when I marry you, it won't be because Dami expects it."

"*When* you marry me? I like the sound of that...." He deepened the kiss.

She sighed and surrendered to the sorcery in his touch. The man had his flaws.

But when he made love to her, she had no complaints.

On Sunday night, a week after that big argument with Lucy, when Noah joined her in her bedroom as he did every night, she kissed him once—and then she walked him backward to the bed.

She pushed him down, kicked off the purple flats she was wearing and straddled him.

He laughed. And then he commanded, "Take off your clothes. Do it now."

"In a minute." She bent over him, nose to nose, grasped the collar of his shirt in either hand and said, "I need to talk to you."

A little frown formed between his dark gold brows. "About?"

"The place where you grew up. I want you to take me there tomorrow."

He reached up, wrapped a hand around the back of her neck and kissed her. It was an excellent kiss, as usual. It made her want to go loose and easy, to forget everything but the taste of his mouth, the feel of his hand, warm and firm and exciting, stroking her nape, tangling in her hair.

But that was exactly his plan, and she wasn't falling for it.

She lifted away from him, though he tried at first to hold her close. When he gave in and let her go, she said, "If not tomorrow, then Tuesday. And if you won't come with me Tuesday, just tell me now and Altus and I will go alone."

His eyes had gone flat and his jaw was set. "We already settled this."

"Excuse me. We did not."

"I told you—"

"I remember. You told me no. I said I would go anyway. And I will, Noah. Lucy will give me the address of the house you lived in."

He growled, "Lucy's in on this?"

Gee, this was going so well. She rolled off him and flopped to her back on the bed. "No. I didn't want to get Lucy involved if I didn't have to." She turned her head and met his shadowed eyes. "But I will. If I can't get the information I need from you, I'll ask her. It's that simple."

"You would drag my sister into this?"

"That's a bit strong, don't you think? I wouldn't drag Lucy anywhere. But would I ask her for the address of the house you used to live in? In a heartbeat."

"You're being unreasonable."

Was she? And was she pushing this too far? "Why

don't you want to take me there? Why don't you want me to go there on my own?"

"It's the past. It's got nothing to do with me anymore."

She reached across the space between them to touch his cheek. "I think you're wrong."

He caught her wrist. "Leave it. Please."

It was the *please* that undid her.

And in the end, what was the point of going if he didn't want to take her there, if he didn't want her to go? She would learn nothing about his secret heart by driving alone past some house where he used to live.

She pulled her hand free of his grip and sat up. And for the first time since she'd come to stay with him, she thought of home with real longing. Of her horses, her villa, the life she'd left on hold. Was this whole thing with him just an interlude after all? Just two people trying and slowly failing to be more than a love affair?

"All right," she said wearily. "I give up. If you feel that strongly about it, I won't go."

Tuesday evening after dinner, when Alice was in her room catching up on her email and messaging with Gilbert about various minor issues at the palace stables, she got a call from Emma Bravo.

"Come on out to the house," Emma said in that cute Texas twang of hers, as though she and Jonas and their children lived out on the range somewhere surrounded by tumbleweeds and longhorn cattle instead of at one of the most spectacular estates in the whole of Bel Air. "You and Noah and his sister, too. It's still warm enough for a swim party and a nice barbecue. The weekend is the nicest. We'll have all afternoon. How 'bout Saturday at two?"

Alice said she'd check with Noah and get back to her tomorrow.

Noah came to join her a few minutes later and she told him about Emma's invitation. "She said to bring Lucy, too."

"Sounds great. I'd love to go. Who knows? Lucy might even agree to come along."

"I hope she will."

"You'd better be the one to ask her," he suggested somewhat grimly. "We'll get an automatic no if the invitation comes from me."

"I will ask her."

"Perfect." He pulled her close and kissed her, a slow, delicious kiss.

He'd been so attentive and sweet since two nights before, when she'd agreed to give up the trip to his old neighborhood. Alice tried to enjoy his kiss and not to think that it would always be that way with him, that he would stonewall her until she did what he wanted and then reward her for being such a good girl by treating her like royalty.

Royalty. That was a good one. She chuckled against his mouth.

He broke the kiss and guided a few stray strands of hair away from her lips, his eyes full of heat and tenderness, his expression openly fond. "Share the joke?"

"It's nothing," she lied. And then she kissed him again.

He scooped her up high in his arms and carried her to the bed. They made love for hours. He knew just the things to do to thoroughly satisfy her body.

Too bad he wasn't quite so willing to satisfy her heart.

* * *

Lucy didn't come to the breakfast table the next morning. Ever since the big argument with Noah a week and a half before, she'd been taking the majority of her meals in her room.

Around nine, after they'd eaten and Noah had gone to his study to make some calls, Alice went upstairs to invite Lucy to Emma's barbecue that weekend. Lucy's empty breakfast tray waited on the floor outside her door, where Hannah or one of the day maids would pick it up.

At least she wasn't starving herself, Alice thought with a smile. The only thing left on that tray was a little corner of toast crust. Her door was open a crack. Apparently she hadn't closed it all the way when she set the tray out.

From inside the room, there was a burst of happy laughter. And then, "Oh, I'm so glad…Yes…Oh, I can't tell you…A lot to ask…Hero…And don't blow me off. You *are* a hero and I…" There was more, but Lucy's voice dipped and Alice didn't catch the rest.

By then she'd reached the door. Curiosity got the better of her. Shamelessly, she eavesdropped.

"No. It will be awful. Please," Lucy wheedled. "Why don't we just go, avoid all that?…But I…Well, all right, if you think it's best…Mmm-hmm…" A hard sigh escaped her. "I know, I do, I understand…"

About then Alice reminded herself that she hated eavesdroppers. And now she was one. She tapped on the door and it swung partway inward.

Lucy sat on the bed, a cell phone to her ear. She caught sight of Alice. Her mouth dropped open and her eyes went saucer wide.

No doubt about it. She had a coconspirator on the other end of the line.

A boyfriend, maybe?

Or someone who'd agreed to loan her money for New York?

Lucy pulled herself together and wiped the guilty look off her face. "Alice!" She waved her forward and spoke nervously into the phone again. "Ahem. Yes…Mmm-hmm. That's right. I really have to go." She disconnected the call and set the phone on the nightstand. "Come on in." She patted the spot beside her on the bed.

Alice shut the door and went to sit beside her. "Sorry I interrupted…"

"Oh? What?" Lucy fluttered her hands about. "The call, you mean? It was nothing. Just a friend. What's going on?"

Alice considered asking Lucy the same question. But she hardly knew where or how to begin. And really, she shouldn't have been listening in on Lucy's conversation. "Have you met my cousin Jonas Bravo and his wife, Emma?"

Lucy blinked. "Jonas Bravo, as in the Bravo Billionaire? The one whose brother was kidnapped by their psycho uncle when he was just a baby?"

"That's the one." Amazing. Even Lucy knew the old story. Jonas's younger brother, Russell, had been nicknamed the Bravo Baby. Russell grew up in Oklahoma under a different name, never knowing his real identity until the truth came out years later.

Lucy picked up her cell phone, stared at it for a moment then set it back down. "I've never met them, but Noah knows Jonas Bravo, I think."

"Yes. They've done business together, Noah and

Jonas. Jonas and Emma were here, at the party Saturday before last."

"I didn't meet them. But I only stayed downstairs for an hour or two...."

"Jonas is a great guy. And Emma is a sweetheart. I love her. They have four children, two girls and two boys. I think the eldest is ten or eleven now. And Jonas has an adopted sister, Amanda, who's in her teens. Emma's invited us out to their Bel Air estate for a barbecue and pool party this Saturday afternoon. You're included."

Lucy wore a distant look. Preoccupied. Not quite present. She frowned. "Um. Saturday, you said?"

"That's right. We would leave in time to be there at two."

*"We?"*

"You, me and Noah...."

Lucy sighed. "I don't think so."

Alice put an arm around her. "Come on. Consider it, won't you? It will be fun."

Lucy pulled away. "No, really. You two go on. I have... a few projects I'm working on. I need to keep focused."

Alice dressed for riding, and she and Altus went to the stables. She was tacking up Golden Boy when Noah came to find her. She told him that she'd talked to Lucy about Saturday.

"Will she come with us?" He looked so hopeful it made her heart ache.

She shook her head. "She said something about the projects she's working on...."

His big shoulders drooped a little. He stuck his hands into his pockets. "She spends her life hunched over that damn sewing machine."

She turned back to Golden Boy and cinched up the saddle. "Well, I saw her breakfast tray. At least there's nothing wrong with her appetite. I swear she licked her plate clean."

Noah laughed at that and didn't seem quite so sad. He saddled a big gelding named Cavalier and they rode up into the mountains for the day.

She didn't tell him about Lucy's mysterious phone call.

Yes, she felt a bit guilty for keeping that from him. But she shouldn't have been listening in anyway. And Lucy had a right to a secret admirer.

*But what if she's found someone to pay her way to New York?*

Alice doubted it. It would be a lot of money. Several thousand for an apartment and furnishings, living expenses and tuition, fees, books, supplies and whatever else.

But say, just for the sake of argument, that Lucy did have a generous friend who'd agreed to bankroll her dream....

Alice couldn't help thinking that it wouldn't be a bad thing. True, she couldn't bring herself to write the check that Lucy needed, couldn't bring herself to betray Noah's trust. But Lucy *was* her friend. Loyalty counted with Lucy, too.

So Alice kept her mouth shut about the cryptic conversation she'd overheard that morning.

Saturday, Alice and Noah left for Los Angeles early in the morning. They went in one of Noah's limos, Altus in the front seat with the driver.

The drive only took about an hour and a half.

But Alice wanted to play tourist before the barbecue at Angel's Crest. So they drove down Hollywood Boulevard, past Grauman's Chinese and all the gold stars embedded in the sidewalk. And then they went to Beverly Hills and had coffee at the Beverly Hills Hotel. They drove down Sunset and Alice gawked at all the giant billboards advertising movies and rock groups and lawyers to the stars.

They arrived at Jonas and Emma's right at two. The whole family was there. Alice forgot her worries about Lucy. And Noah seemed more relaxed, too. He laughed often and treated her with open affection. They swam and played Marco Polo and water volleyball with the children. And later they all sat down outdoors to heaping plates of Texas-style barbecue.

At seven Emma started herding her children upstairs for their baths. Alice and Noah changed back into their street clothes. Jonas urged them to stay—overnight, if it suited them. The house was bigger than Noah's, with guest rooms to spare.

But Noah squeezed her hand and she understood that he wanted to get back. That was fine with her. They hadn't planned to stay late anyway. Alice went upstairs to tell Emma goodbye. The kids were running around, the girls and the older boy already in their pajamas. The youngest one, Grady, was still splashing in the tub.

Emma embraced her. "You come back soon...."

The children's voices echoed on the upper landing as Alice went down the stairs. Noah was at the door shaking hands with Jonas.

The car waited right outside, the engine running in the warm twilight.

Altus held the door for her. She ducked in as Noah got in on the other side. He put his arm around her.

She leaned against him. "That was fun...."

His lips touched her hair. "Yeah. A good day...."

Alice felt more hopeful than she had in weeks. Noah *was* a good man. And she wanted to be with him.

Most of the time, it felt so right with him, as though she'd known him all her life—or been waiting to know him. He touched some place deep within her heart that no other man ever had.

Alice sighed, settled her head on his shoulder and thought about how every day she fell more in love with him.

Yes, he had a giant blind spot about Lucy, and serious control issues. And he always seemed to keep something of himself apart from her. Even with all that, she wanted what they shared to last.

She snuggled in even closer, breathed in the wonderfully familiar, deliciously exciting scent that belonged only to him and considered just saying it: *I love you, Noah. I love you very much.*

But then he would only start pushing for a yes on the question of marriage.

And she wasn't quite ready to go that far—not yet, anyway.

The driver pulled up at the foot of the wide steps leading to Noah's front door. Someone had parked a black luxury SUV over by the low wall that surrounded the koi pond.

Noah frowned at her. "Were you expecting anyone?"

"No. Maybe a friend of Lucy's?"

His frown only deepened. They got out. Hannah was

waiting in the open doorway, the light from the foyer behind her silhouetting her tall, slim form. They mounted the wide front steps with Altus close behind.

One good look at the older woman's face and Noah demanded, "What's the matter, Hannah?"

The housekeeper spoke quietly. "Prince Damien is here. He and Lucy are waiting for you in the family room. Lucy has informed me that tomorrow the prince is taking her to New York."

## Chapter Eleven

Noah hadn't cracked any heads in fourteen full years. But he burned to crack one now: Damien's, to be specific.

Hannah saw his expression and got out of his way. He headed for the family room.

Behind him, Alice tried to slow him down. "Noah, wait. Please...."

He ignored her and kept going, through the foyer, down the hallway, past the kitchen, to the family room, with the heels of Alice's sandals tapping in his wake.

They were there, the two of them, just as Hannah had said they would be, sitting in the soft white chairs in front of the arched windows. Lucy popped to her feet at the sight of him. Dami rose, too, but more slowly.

A chain of obscenities scrolled through Noah's mind. He demanded, "What kind of crap are you pulling here, Damien?"

Alice came up beside him. "Noah. Can you please just settle down?"

He hit her with an icy look. "Are you involved in this?"

She stared at him. "Involved? What are you talking about?"

Lucy spoke up then. "Stop it, Noah. Alice had no idea that I talked Dami into helping me. You just leave her alone."

He whirled on his sister. "Are you out of your mind? You can't just—"

She cut him off with a cry. "Yes, I can, Noah. And I will. Dami has a place I can stay and he's loaning me the money I need."

Noah felt a fury so hot and so total, it seemed that the top of his head might pop off. He swung his attention to Damien. "Why? I don't get it. Because of Alice? This is some sick revenge because I want to marry your sister?"

Dami stood there and looked at him as if *he* was the one who'd gone over the line. "Of course not, you idiot. Don't be ridiculous."

"I ought to…" He took a step toward Damien.

Alice grabbed his arm. "Noah, don't…."

At the same time, Lucy tried to step in front of Dami as if she was going to protect him, all ninety-eight pounds of her. "Stop it, Noah. I mean it. You stop it right now."

"It's all right, Luce," said Damien, and he took her by the shoulders and moved her out of the way. His body-guard, who'd been standing by the doors to the loggia, stepped closer. Damien signaled the man back.

Lucy insisted, "I *called* him, all right? I called Dami and I begged him to help me. He's my friend, okay?"

Noah made a low scoffing sound. "Oh. Right. Exactly. Prince Damien is such a hero. The Player Prince only wants to be your *friend*."

"He *is* my friend, Noah! He's my friend, and that's all. Just my friend, and a very good one, thank you. And yes, he's a hero, too. Because he knows how much this means to me and he's willing to help me, willing to go up against *you*. He's not blinded like you are, Noah. By fear and by the things that happened years and years ago. He sees me as I am now, not as I used to be, and he knows how long I've waited, for all of my life so far. He knows it's finally time I came into my own. *He* knows that I'm ready." The tears rose, clogging her voice, making those big brown eyes of hers shine too bright.

About then he started feeling like the monster in the room.

Which was insane. Not true. He was the only one here who understood the risk, the only one determined to keep Lucy safe, to make certain she didn't push herself too far and end up at death's door before he could get there and save her.

"Noah." Alice still had hold of his arm. "Can we just sit down, please? Can we just talk this over like civilized adults?"

"Civilized," he growled at her.

But she had his attention now. She gazed steadily up at him, pleading and determined, both at once.

And from behind them, Hannah said, "Do what Alice says, Noah. Sit down. Lucy will be leaving in the morning, one way or another. Now's the time to make your peace with that."

Noah glanced back at her. She stood next to Alice's bodyguard, and she met his gaze, unflinching. He couldn't bear it. He shut his eyes.

And his father's face rose up, laughing, on the morning of the day that he died. Laughing and grabbing his mother for a hug and a kiss, heading off to work like it was any other day, with no idea that he would never be back again.

He shook his head, blinked away the image—but it only got worse. Next he saw his mother lying on the couch in that cramped run-down bungalow they rented after the bank took their house. His mother, her face sickly pale, clammy with fever sweat, her eyes red and dazed looking, insisting that she was fine, there was no problem. No need for a doctor, it was only a little cold....

Alice still held his arm. And she was nudging him, guiding him to a chair.

He dropped into it, feeling disconnected, as if this was all some weird, awful dream. Alice sat beside him. She took his hand and twined her fingers with his. He let her do that, even held on.

Her hand felt solid, her grip sure and strong. At that moment she seemed the only real thing in the room.

Lucy and Damien sat down again, too. Hannah came over from where she hovered by the kitchen and took the last chair.

He heard himself ask Damien, "When you called to apologize to Alice, were you already planning this?"

Damien shook his head. "Lucy called me a couple of days later."

Alice cleared her throat and asked Lucy, "Was that Dami on the phone Wednesday morning, when I came to your room and asked you to come with us to Angel's Crest?"

"Yes, it was," said Lucy proudly.

*"What?"* He turned accusing eyes on Alice. "You never said a word." He started to pull his hand from hers.

She wouldn't let go. "I was eavesdropping, and it was none of my business. Lucy left the door open a crack or I never would have heard a thing."

"You should have told me," he insisted. He might have been able to stop this madness before it went so far.

"I shouldn't have been listening," she said slowly and clearly, as if maybe he didn't understand English very well. "It was a private conversation."

Lucy chimed in, "Alice kept it to herself because *she* understands that I'm an adult and I have a right to my privacy."

"You damn well don't have the right to go cooking up harebrained schemes that put your life in danger."

"Oh, don't be so dramatic, Noah. My life is not in danger. I'm perfectly fine." She swung her gaze to Damien. "Listen to him, Dami. And you kept telling me I needed to try again to get through to him. Ha. Like that was ever gonna happen."

Noah winced. Was he really that bad? He only wanted her safety, only cared about her well-being.

Dami said gently, "Easy, Luce. Calm down."

Noah swung his gaze on his so-called friend and longed to leap up and punch his lights out. But he stayed in his seat, held on to Alice and reminded himself that he was thirty-five years old and there were better ways to fight than with his fists.

Lucy turned on him again. "At least I finally got Dami to see that *you* were never going to listen to me. I… Well, I admit I just wanted to sneak away, not to have to go through this." She raised both hands as though to indicate the five of them sitting there, the tension so thick it seemed to poison the air. "But Dami said I had to face you. That you had a right to know exactly what was going on."

He sent another furious glance in Damien's direction. The last thing he needed to hear right now was how wise and enlightened Damien was.

Lucy was still talking. "So here we are. Now you know. Dami's flying me to New York. My things are all packed and outside in the car. Our plane leaves at eight in the morning."

Noah just stared at her. His mind seemed to have locked up. He had to stop her. He just couldn't seem to figure out how.

Damien said, "I own an apartment building in NoHo—near Greenwich Village? There's a vacant one-bedroom. Luce will have that."

Alice squeezed his hand and coaxed, "I've been there. It's a lovely old building. And the apartments are roomy, especially by New York standards."

He blinked and looked at her again. "You're all for this, aren't you?" His voice sounded strange, without inflection, to his own ears.

She answered softly but firmly, too, "I think Lucy is ready, yes. If you'll recall, I've been clear on that. But in the end, Noah, it's not what *I* think that matters. And it's not what *you* think, either. It's Lucy's choice. And now she's found a way to make it happen."

*Because of your brother,* he thought, but decided not to say. Yeah, he could beat the crap out of Damien for letting Lucy talk him into this, for sticking his nose in where it didn't belong. But Lucy was the key here.

And she wasn't budging. He couldn't get through to her.

She was going. There was no protecting her from herself anymore. One way or another, she would go to New York.

And somehow he would have to learn to live with that.

He met Lucy's wary eyes. "All right. If there's no way to stop you, *I'll* take you. Give me a couple of weeks to put things on hold here. We'll go to New York, get you a place, get you settled in, get your new doctors and services lined up. I'll arrange to get you access to your trust fund. I'll—"

Lucy put up a hand. "No. You're not doing that. You don't get to go with me and take *care* of me, Noah. The whole point is that you have to let me go, let me stand on my own at last, let me make a life that works for me."

He did turn on Damien then. He couldn't seem to stop himself. "So what, then? *You're* going to take care of her?"

"Of course he's not!" Lucy cried. "How many times do I have to say it? *I'm* going to take care of me. Dami's only going to take me to New York, show me my new apartment, loan me an embarrassing sum of money and then go back to his own life—which, if you think about it, is way more than enough."

Damien said quietly, "I'll make sure she's safe, Noah. I won't leave until she's settled in."

Alice leaned close to him. She didn't say anything, just held tight and steady on to his hand. Hannah sat silent, too, her brow furrowed.

None of them agreed with him. Not one of them took his side in this. They didn't know what he knew, hadn't seen what he'd seen.

He couldn't deal. Couldn't take it all in. Couldn't come up with a way to get even one of them to see the situation as he saw it. He turned to his sister again. Her wide mouth was set, her gaze unwavering. He accused, "You'll do what you want to do, then, no matter the cost."

"I *have* to do it, Noah."

"That's a lie."

Alice chided, "Noah, don't…"

He pulled his hand free of hers. There was nothing more to say. "This conversation is through." He stood. "Good night." And he turned on his heel.

Alice called after him. "Noah. Please…"

He kept walking. He didn't stop or look back. Through the kitchen, down the hallway to the foyer, up the stairs to his rooms.

He went inside and slammed the door.

Alice winced at the sound of the door slamming upstairs. She wanted only to go up there, to be with him, to try to ease his suffering at least a little bit.

But it seemed wiser for the moment to leave him alone.

Hannah caught her eye and echoed her thoughts, "Give him a little time...."

Lucy worried her lower lip. "I knew this was going to be awful. I was so right."

Dami suggested rather sheepishly, "You could always slow down a bit, give the poor guy a chance to get used to the idea that you're going."

Lucy shot him a startled glance. "Are you backing out on me now?"

"No. But if you want to think it over a little more—"

"I don't. We're going," she said sharply. And then, more softly, "Please?"

Dami shrugged. "Well, that settles that." He stood. "Allie, a few words, just the two of us?"

Alice got up and followed him out to the loggia.

"You probably don't believe this," he said when they were alone in the cool autumn darkness, "but I'm honestly not the least happy about causing all this trouble."

"So, then, why are you doing it?"

He stared off toward the garden. "I've seen her designs, and she's shown me the clothes that she's made. She's so talented. It's wrong to hold her back."

Alice phrased her next question with care. "I have to ask. Lucy says you're her friend and nothing more.

I'm going to be backing both of you up with Noah after you go. If the two of you are more than friends, I need to know the truth."

Dami groaned. And then he swore. "How can you ask me that? Lucy's very sweet. But she's like a child. I've never been attracted to the wide-eyed innocent type."

"She's *not* a child, Dami. In many ways, she's quite mature."

He stuck his hands into his pockets and cast a glance at the distant moon. "Please. I swear to you on my honor as a prince of the blood. Luce and I are friends. That's all." Alice had known him all her life and she could tell when he was hedging. He wasn't. Not this time. "Peace?" He held out his arms to her.

Alice accepted his embrace. When she pulled back, she said ruefully, "I only wish Lucy could have found someone else to come to her rescue."

Dami made a low ironic sort of sound. "Her options were limited. And for more than a year she's been trying to get Noah to give her a little independence. But he's been locked up tight, absolutely sure something awful will happen to her if he lets her get out on her own. In the end, I couldn't *not* help her. She's got a fine opportunity and she doesn't want to let it slip through her fingers. She has to make the break."

Alice wrapped her arms around herself against the slight chill in the air. "Noah might never forgive you. He might never forgive any of us."

"I think you're wrong. He loves his sister. When push finally comes to shove, he's going to accept that Luce is a grown-up and that she's also fully recovered after that last surgery she had. He'll realize that he doesn't have to take care of her anymore. He'll see that her leaving was the right choice."

Alice blew out a hard breath. "All right, he'll forgive Lucy. But will he forgive *you?*"

"I think so." Dami grinned then, that charming world-famous grin of his. "He'll want to get along with me. After all, I'm going to be his brother-in-law."

She elbowed him in the ribs. "I haven't said I'll marry Noah."

"You didn't have to. It's written all over your face when you look at him. And even tonight, with all hell breaking loose, it was obvious every time he glanced your way that he's found the woman for him."

*I hope you're right,* she thought. But she decided not to say it. As soon as she did, Dami would ask her why she sounded doubtful. And then what would she say?

That she loved Noah but she hadn't told him so, that for some reason, she couldn't bring herself to say the words? That he kept his heart carefully separate at all times. That he wouldn't take her to the place where he'd grown up and that made her feel that she didn't really have his trust.

She wanted to confide in Dami now, but the timing was all wrong. He'd come to take Noah's sister away. He was in much too deep already. He didn't need her crying on his shoulder, revealing things she ought to be discussing with Noah.

Dami took her hand and wrapped her fingers around his arm. "We'd better go in before Luce gets herself into any more trouble."

They returned to the family room, where Hannah and the two bodyguards waited. Alone.

Hannah sent them a smile that was both wise and

weary. "Lucy went upstairs. She said if *you* two could talk things through, she probably ought to make an effort to work it out with Noah."

Noah expected Alice's soft tap on the door. His pride jabbing at him, he started to bark at her to leave him alone. But his heart wouldn't let him do that.

She infuriated and challenged and thrilled and bewildered him by turns. He was angry at her for not having his back with Lucy, for going so far as to keep crucial information from him. She damn well should have told him about that phone call she'd overheard.

And yet at the same time, in a deeper sense, he knew with absolute certainty that she *did* have his back.

From the first, she'd confused the hell out of him. And she continued to do so.

The soft knock came again.

He left off staring blindly out the sitting-area French doors to go and let her in.

But it wasn't Alice.

It was Lucy.

His gut tightened at the sight of her standing there. "What?" He pretty much growled the word at her and then instantly wished he could call it back.

Lucy surprised him. She refused to let his gruffness send her off in a huff. She stared up at him with her lips pressed together and her eyes full of hope and anxiousness. "Look. You're my brother. I love you so much. And you saved my life. Repeatedly. I know that. I get that. I wouldn't be here without you. I owe you everything. I owe it to you to *do* something with this life I have because of you. I know you're afraid for me and you only want the best for me. I just need you to understand that my going *is* the best thing for me. So please, please, can't you just give me your blessing? Can't you just let yourself be okay with it? Can't you just…let me go?"

*Let her go….*

As he'd had to let their dad go, and then their mom? No. He couldn't do it. He *wouldn't* do it….

"Please, Noah," she said again. "Please."

And the strangest thing happened. He looked into her upturned face and he saw the naked truth.

He'd lost the damn battle. She *was* going. He could get with the program and help in any way she would let him—or he could let his pride win, turn his back on her, shut the door in her face.

And then never be able to forgive himself if anything actually did happen to her if she felt that she couldn't call him for help because he'd sent her away in anger.

He went with the truth instead of his pride. He gave in. "Lucy…" He let his pain and his love for her show on his face. In his voice. "All right. Yes. I get it. You need to go."

"Oh, Noah…" All at once her big eyes brimmed with tears. "See, I knew it. I did. I knew you would come through for me in the end. Because you always do." She threw herself against him.

He caught her and wrapped his arms around her good and tight. She smelled like cherries and Ivory soap and that made him want to hug her all the harder. "Just…be okay, will you? Just stay safe."

"I'll try. And if I ever get worried I'm not going to make it—"

"You'll call me. I'll be there."

"I promise, Noah. I will."

\* \* \*

Alice hoped against hope that Lucy and Noah would come back downstairs together.

She got her wish.

Brother and sister appeared arm in arm and Lucy announced, "It's okay. We worked it out."

Dami said, "Wonderful." He offered his hand to Noah.

And Noah took it. "She still insists on going with you in the morning, but I'll handle her expenses."

"Fair enough."

Then Noah led Lucy away to his study to write her a check, explain about how he would arrange to give her early access to her trust fund, and no doubt provide endless and detailed instructions on any number of important subjects.

Hannah excused herself. Dami and Alice told their bodyguards to call it a night. They sat and chatted for a while about the family, about the goings-on at home. But Dami kept trying not to yawn. Finally, he had to admit he was jet-lagged. He said good-night. He and Lucy would be leaving before dawn.

Alice lingered in the family room, hoping Noah might finish giving last-minute advice to his sister and come and find her. She was feeling a little unsure.

Was he still angry with her for not taking his side about Lucy's leaving? It made little sense that he would be. He'd ended up accepting the inevitable after all. But then there was the phone call she'd overheard. He'd seemed pretty put out with her for not telling him about that.

Seriously, though. At this point, he should be over that, too. Shouldn't he?

She had no idea if he was or not. And it bothered her. A lot.

Everything had happened so fast at the end. Noah had whisked Lucy off to his study without so much as a glance in Alice's direction. Just a look or a quick squeeze of her hand would have done it, let her know that he'd forgiven her, too.

But then, maybe he hadn't.

The minutes dragged by. Hannah asked her if she'd like some tea or a snack. She almost asked for a vodka tonic—and to make it a double.

But drowning her doubts about Noah in alcohol was no kind of solution. She told Hannah good-night and went upstairs, where she considered calling Rhia and decided not to. It would be seven-thirty Sunday morning in Montedoro.

Alice settled on a bubble bath, heavy on the bubbles. The suite had a nice big tub. She filled it and lit the fat white candles waiting on the rim. Then she undressed, pinned her hair up and sank gratefully into the fragrant, bubbly heat.

It felt so good she closed her eyes and drifted. She tried to forget her worries about Noah, to be happy that what had started out so badly had ended up with Lucy and Noah reconciled and Lucy gaining her freedom at last.

"You look so tempting in that tub I could almost forgive you for not telling me about Lucy's plans...."

*Noah.*

He might be mad at her, but he *had* come to find her. Her pulse pounded swift and hard under her breastbone. Even in the scented heat of the bathwater, goose bumps prickled across her skin.

She let her eyelids drift open. He lounged against the door to the bedroom, watching her, still fully dressed in the tan trousers and knit shirt he'd worn that afternoon.

"Didn't anyone ever teach you to knock before entering a woman's private space?" she asked him lazily, waving her hands in a treading motion under the water, enjoying the heat and the wet and the feeling of floating.

Not to mention the look in his blue eyes as he watched her. She could stare into those eyes forever and never get bored. A heated thrill of pure anticipation shivered up the backs of her knees.

He undid his belt. It made a soft whipping sound as he pulled it through the loops and off. "I knocked. You must not have heard me."

"But that's the point. If I don't answer, you don't get to come in."

He reached over his shoulders and got hold of the back of his shirt, gathering it in his fists the way he always did, pulling it over his head and tossing it aside. "I wanted to see you." He really did look much too amazing with his shirt off. She admired the depth and breadth of his chest, the power in the muscles of his long arms, the hardness of his belly. And the gold hair in a T-shape, trailing on down to heaven.

Hair dusted his forearms, too. She liked to rub it, just run her hand lightly above the surface of his skin and feel the silky, subtle brush of it against her palm.

What were they talking about?

Right. She was getting on his case for coming in without her knowing. "Still, you shouldn't have."

He undid his trousers and ripped the zipper wide, slanting her a devil's glance as he did it. "Do you want me to leave?"

Her breath came a little shaky. "No. Stay. Join me."

The corners of his mouth curved up and the blue of his eyes grew somehow deeper. Darker. A bolt of heat zipped along her spine, sharp and sweet, pooling in her belly, spreading out slowly like honey in a spoon.

"Happy to oblige." He shucked out of his shoes, lifted one foot and then the other to yank off his socks.

"Lucy all set, then?"

He straightened, barefooted, bare chested, still wearing the tan trousers, though his fly gaped wide, revealing silk boxers beneath. His eyes had changed, gone darker still. There was still heat in them, but there was anger, too. "As set as she's going to be. And I mean it. You should have told me about the phone call."

Alice sat up and shook her head. "I made the right choice on that. You won't convince me otherwise, won't make me feel guilty. Lucy's not only your sister. She happens to be my friend, too. That phone conversation was between her and Damien. I shouldn't have listened in. But then when I did, the only right thing to do was to keep what I'd heard to myself."

His gaze tracked her eyes, her lips. Lower. "You're distracting me, all those wet bubbles on your shoulders, shining on your breasts, sliding down over your nipples…."

She leaned back again, resting her head on the tub rim, letting the bubbles cover her. "Better?"

He made a low sound in his throat and shook his head. And then, swiftly and ruthlessly, he shoved down his trousers and kicked them aside. The boxers followed, down and off. He was fully aroused.

And that turned her on. *He* turned her on.

A lot.

The man was pure temptation—and she'd known it from that first day. From the moment he raised his golden head and met her eyes.

Oh, yes.

Temptation. Coming to get her, to stir everything up—her body, her mind, her heart. To lure her from her home and her horses, to wreak havoc on the careful, well-behaved existence she'd been trying to make for herself after the Glasgow incident.

He came to her then, covering the distance between the door and the tub in five long strides, stepping in at the opposite end and lowering himself slowly until the bubbles covered the proof of how much he wanted her.

His leg brushed hers under the water. She felt his foot sliding along the inside of her calf. And higher. "All right. I forgive you for keeping that phone call to yourself."

She suppressed a low moan of pleasure. "I would prefer if you admitted that I did the right thing."

He regarded her lazily. "Sit up. Let me see your breasts again. You can probably get me to admit just about anything." Something in his voice alerted her.

Something ragged. Raw.

"Oh, Noah..." She did sit up.

"Alice." He said her name low. Rough. And he reached for her.

She went to him, up on her knees between his open thighs, bubbles and bathwater sliding between her breasts and over her belly. Capturing his face between her two hands, she gazed down at him, into his seeking eyes. "What is it?"

He searched her face as though she held truths he needed to find. "Tell me that *I* did the right thing tonight."

She lowered her mouth to him and kissed him. Soft. Slow. Up close, even beneath the floral fragrance of the bubble bath, she caught his scent: sunshine and that aftershave she loved. He tasted of mint. "You did the right thing," she whispered. "Absolutely. The *true* thing." She kissed him again. "And Lucy *is* ready. She's going to be fine. Watch and see."

"God, I hope so. And it wasn't what *I* thought was right. I didn't see a choice, that's all."

She smiled against his lips. "But there *was* a choice. You could have refused to give in. You could have turned your back on her because she wouldn't do things your way. But you didn't. You made the better choice, the *bigger* choice."

"The hell I did," he whispered roughly. And then he caught her lower lip between his teeth, tugging a little before letting go. "She'd better be safe, be all right, or I'll—"

"Shh." She kissed the sound onto his parted lips. "You're not running her life anymore. She gets to be a grown-up now. You're only there for backup *if* she asks you for it."

He laughed low, in equal parts amusement and pain. "You know you're scaring the crap out of me, right?"

"I get that, yes. You had too many losses as a child. You had to make a new life from the ground up, with only your brains and your will to guide you. You had to take control of yourself and your life when your mom died, absolute control. Letting go of it now is not your best thing."

He smoothed the last of the bubbles down her spine, over the curves of her bottom, cupping her, pulling her closer. "I can let go of control."

"Ha," she mocked, trying really hard not to let the teasing sound become a moan.

He brought those wonderful hands between them, sliding them up over her rib cage, cupping both breasts, and he whispered, "You don't know what you do to me. *You* get me out of control."

It pleased her to no end to hear him admit that. She could almost start thinking they were finally getting somewhere. "I do?"

"Oh, yeah…."

"Show me." She kissed him as he caressed her, teasing his lips with her tongue until he let her in, let her taste him slow and deep, let her have control of the kiss. And while she was kissing him, she slipped a hand beneath the water and wrapped her fingers around him nice and tight.

He jerked against her touch and groaned into her mouth. "Alice…"

She stroked him, long, slow strokes. And then faster. Harder. He gave in to her, let her push him back to rest his head on the tub rim, let her guide his hands out to either side, let her slide around and ease her legs under him, bringing his hips above the water and the slowly dissolving bubbles.

He kept those big arms widespread, letting her have him, letting her do whatever she wanted. The sounds he made, low and urgent, drove her on.

She tasted him at her leisure, bending close and surrounding him by slow degrees, letting him free, only to take her sweet time licking all along the length of him.

"Please," he groaned. "Alice…"

And she lowered her mouth on him again, all the way down, then slowly up and down and up again, creating a building rhythm, stroking him with her encircling hand at the same time.

He called out her name. And she felt him, under her palm, at the base, pulsing. She lifted—and then took him in all the way. He touched the back of her throat as he came, tasting of salt and sea foam. She swallowed him down.

A moment later, he reached for her, guiding her around by the shoulders until he could pull her in front of him. He wrapped his arms around her and she lay against him. With her back to his broad chest, the slowly cooling water buoying her, it seemed she felt him all around her, yet she floated above him, too.

He pressed his lips to her temple, murmured rough and sweet in her ear, "We're good together. You know that we are."

She chuckled, a husky, easy sound, tipping her head back enough that they could share a quick kiss. "Spoken like a recently satisfied man."

"I'm serious." Gruff. A little bit angry, but in such a tender, urgent way.

"All right. Seriously, then. Yes, I agree with you. We *are* good together. Mostly."

"You have complaints?" He bent and nipped at the wet skin of her shoulder.

She moaned. "At this exact moment? Not one."

"Good." He cupped her breast with one hand and idly, possessively, teased at the nipple. With the other, he touched her belly, spreading his fingers wide beneath her rib cage, pressing down a little, bringing her into closer contact with his body, making her burn for him within. "I don't want anyone but you." His voice was gruff and soft at once. "I honestly don't. I've been with more women than maybe I should have. But no more. I'm true to you. I *will* be true to you. It's not a hardship. It's what I want."

She reached back, needing her hand on him, and clasped his nape. It felt so good just to touch him. "I'm glad. So glad."

He caught her wrist, brought her hand to his lips, kissed the tips of her fingers one by one. "I started out to find myself a princess."

"Yes. I know."

"I was an ass."

She agreed with him. Gently. "Well, yes. You were. A bit."

"But then guess what happened?" He curved his fingers around hers and brought their joined hands down together under the water. "I went looking for what I thought I wanted—and I found so much more. I found you."

All at once, her throat felt tight and her eyes were brimming. And she couldn't stop herself, didn't *want* to stop herself. She went ahead and said exactly what was in her heart. "I love you, Noah." It came out in a whisper. She made herself say it louder, owning it, proudly. "I'm in love with you. *You're* the one that *I* want, too."

And then he was taking her shoulders again, turning her so that she faced him, so she was meeting his eyes. "Marry me." He said it low. With heat and longing and coaxing intensity. "Say you will. Say yes this time. Be my wife."

## *Chapter Twelve*

Alice longed to give him what he wanted, to tell him yes.

She did want to marry him. She wanted that a lot.

But somehow she couldn't say it. She couldn't quite make herself put that yes out there. She couldn't quite open her mouth and give him the answer he was waiting to hear.

Instead, she only stared at him, mute, her body yearning, her heart aching.

Her silence didn't go over well. The hot, hopeful look left his eyes. They turned cool. Hard.

And then he lifted her off him. Firmly guiding her back to her own end of the tub, he gathered his feet under him and stood.

The water sloshed over the rim and splashed onto the thick bath mat as he got out. He grabbed a towel from the linen cart and wrapped it around his waist. Without stopping to pick up his scattered clothes, dripping water, he headed for the door.

She let out a cry. "Noah, please don't go...."

He kept on walking. Two more steps and he was through the doorway, out of her sight.

She waited to hear the outer door open and shut.

When it didn't, she felt a tiny bit less awful.

He wasn't happy with her, but at least he hadn't stormed out. Well, not *all* the way out. He'd stayed in the suite.

She climbed from the tub, reached for another towel from the stack and dried off, giving him a little time to settle down before trying to talk to him again. At the beveled mirrors over the twin sinks, she took down her hair and shook it out on her shoulders. And then, knowing she'd probably stalled as long as she dared, she snagged her light robe from the back of the door, stuck her arms in the sleeves and belted the sash.

He was standing at the French doors, still wearing the towel, staring out at the moonlit equestrian fields when she found him. She approached with care and drew to a halt a few feet from his broad bare back. About then she realized she had no idea what to say.

Apparently he got tired of waiting for her to find her voice. He demanded, without turning, "What do you want from me, Alice? Heavy use of the L-word? My heart on a pike?"

She fell back a step. "You're being cruel."

He whirled on her then. She startled, certain he would raise his voice to her. But no. He drew in a slow breath and spoke in a tone as even and low as it was dangerous. "I don't know what more to say to you, what else to do to prove to you that I want this, you and me. I want it to last and I intend to do my part to see that it does. I want to be your husband. I want us to have children together. When I get old, I want to be looking over at you in the other rocking chair."

What he said was so beautiful. Her arms ached to reach for him. But she knew he would only pull away from her touch. So she brought her hands up and folded them, prayerfully, under her chin. "I want that, too, Noah. I meant what I said. I love you. I do. You mean the world to me. It's only…" With a hard sigh, she let her arms drop to her sides again. "It's been barely more than a month since we met. I think we need more time."

"Speak for yourself. I *know* what I want."

"All right, then. Speaking for myself, *I* need more time."

"How much time?"

"Some. A little. I don't really know. But when you rush me like this, it only makes me more certain I need to slow things down."

His face looked haggard suddenly. "You say that you love me. But you don't trust me."

Again, she wanted to reach out, smooth his brow, to swear that she *did* trust him, that in the end it would be all right. But she kept her arms at her sides and told him quietly, "It's not you I don't trust. Not really. It's…me."

He threw up both hands. "Oh, excellent. Like there's a damn thing I can do to fix that."

"I don't expect you to fix it. There's nothing *to* fix, not really. There's just…" She struggled for the right words. "Honestly, what you did tonight, making your peace with Lucy, finally letting her go when she's the last of your family and you have this ingrained need to keep her close where you can protect her…. Well, that was amazing. That was really, truly something. It showed me that you *can* compromise, that you're not all about winning, about doing what *you* think is right. That when someone you love finally draws the line on you, you'll do what you have to do to keep the connection. Also, I did hear the things you said to me a little while ago, about being true to me, about wanting me for myself, not because I fit some idea you had of the perfect trophy wife—and then what you said just now, about you and me and the rocking chairs. All of it. It's good. It's right."

He ran a hand back through his hair. "Great. I'm wonderful. Amazing. I say the right things to you. I've proved that I'm flexible, willing to give in. You're in love with me. I'm the guy for you. And still, you keep putting me off."

She wrapped her arms around herself. "I'm an impetuous person. I told you that at the first. My sister Rhia says I do best when I go with that, when I follow my instincts. I think she's right—as a rule. But I do have to be careful about saying yes to sharing the rest of my life. Ten years from now, I don't want either of us to look back and wonder why we said *I do*."

"That's not going to happen. Not for me."

"I have to be sure, too, Noah."

He was silent, watching her. Then he said, "I think I'll sleep in my room tonight." He started to turn.

"Noah."

"What now?"

"Stay. Please." She held out her hand.

He scowled at it—but then, just when she thought he would turn his back on her, he took it. She pulled his arm around behind her nice and snug, stepping up close and resting her head against his bare chest.

"You don't ask much," he muttered against her hair.

She cuddled closer. "I love you, Noah. Let's go to bed."

Noah let her lead him to the bed. But he'd had enough for the night. Enough of stepping back and letting his sister move to Manhattan where he couldn't protect her.

Enough of having Alice turn him down—even though she claimed to love him.

In bed, she cuddled up close the way she liked to do. He wrapped his arms around her—for a while.

But as soon as her breathing grew even and shallow, he eased his arm out from under her head and slept on his side, turned away from her.

In the morning, they were up before dawn to see Lucy and Damien off. He stood on the front steps with Alice on one side and Hannah on the other, waving goodbye as the black SUV drove away.

Once the car was out of sight, Alice turned to him with a brilliant smile, those gorgeous dimples flashing. He made his lips curve upward in response. But his heart wasn't in it.

They spent the day in the stables and out working with the horses. That night, she asked him if something was wrong.

He shook his head and kissed her. They went upstairs together. He'd been thinking that maybe he'd sleep in his own room. But she kissed him again and he couldn't resist her, so that led where it always led.

Later, as they lay together in the dark, she reminded him that she had to leave on Wednesday. "Next weekend is the Autumn Faire, remember?"

He did remember. "The bazaar and the parade you have to ride in."

"That's it." She settled in closer, pressed her lips to his shoulder. "Come with me. It will be fun."

Was it going to go on like this indefinitely, then, with the two of them constantly together in every way except the one that mattered most to him? "I can't."

"Why not?"

"Didn't I tell you? I have a trip to Amarillo Thursday."

She went very still. And then a small sigh escaped her. "No. You didn't tell me."

He *hadn't* told her, and he knew that he hadn't. In fact, the invitation from Yellow Rose Wind and Solar was open-ended. He'd just that moment decided to go on Thursday. "A West Texas wind farm. I want to have a look before I decide how much to invest."

She rolled away from him, sat up and switched on the lamp. "I'll ask you again." She pulled the sheet up to cover her pretty breasts and settled back against the headboard. "What's wrong?"

He started to insist that there was nothing. But instead, he hauled himself up to sit beside her. "Look. It's hard for a guy. To keep asking and getting told no, all right?"

She kind of sagged to the side and put her head on his shoulder, which felt really good, absolutely right. Damn it. "I'm not saying no. I'm just saying not yet."

He couldn't hold back a grunt of disgust. "Sounds a lot like no to me. And then there's the love thing. You said that you love me."

"Because I do." She clasped his upper arm, squeezing a little. He shifted, easing away from her until she let go, lifted her head from his shoulder and frowned at him. "Is there something wrong with my saying I love you?"

He had no idea why they were talking about this. He never should have let it get started. "It's nothing. It doesn't matter."

"Yes, it does. You know it does."

"It's nothing, Alice."

"That's not true."

"Can you just leave it alone?"

She winced. "You mean it bothers you that I told you I love you and then turned down your proposal?"

It occurred to him that if he said yes to that question, this conversation that made him feel as though poisonous spiders were crawling around under his skin might end more quickly. "Yeah. That's it. It ticks me off. You said you love me—and then you refused to marry me."

She leaned in closer, so their noses almost touched. He wanted to push her away—and he wanted to grab her good and tight and bury his face in her sweet-smelling hair. "How about this? I won't say those dreaded words again until I'm ready to answer yes."

He would prefer that she never said them again. Not ever. But if he admitted that, she'd be all over him, wanting to know what was wrong with him that he had such a big issue with the L-word. The questions would be endless. The spiders under his skin would start biting.

Uh-uh. Not going there.

He said, "It's a deal."

She cradled the side of his face, and then combed the hair at his temples with a fond, gentle touch. "Are you worried about Lucy?"

"Hell, yes."

"She's going to be fine, Noah."

"So everyone keeps telling me."

She kissed him. He breathed in her sweetness. "Reschedule your visit to the wind farm," she whispered. "Come to Montedoro with me."

He shook his head. "You go home. I'll go to Texas. We can't be together all of the time."

"Noah." She held his gaze steadily. "Are you trying to get rid of me?"

"Of course not."

She kissed his chin, his jaw and then nipped at his ear. "Say that again."

"I'm not trying to get rid of you."

"Prove it." Her naughty hand slid down beneath the sheet.

A moment later he flipped her over on her back and showed her just how happy he was to have her around.

Lucy called him the next day. He took the call in his study and couldn't help smiling at the breathless, happy sound of her voice.

"Noah! New York is amazing. The energy here... I could work round the clock and never need to sleep. And my apartment! It's in a beautiful old building. I have tall windows facing the street. There's a claw-foot tub in the bathroom and those old black-and-white subway tiles. The building has seven floors, two apartments per floor, except for the top two floors, which are Dami's for when he's in town. Noah, I'm here just a day and I have so many ideas I can't sketch them fast enough."

He chuckled. "Speaking of fast, have you already moved in?"

"No. Remember? I'm at the Ritz-Carlton for the next few days while I get the place furnished and all that— I mean, at least until I get a bed in and a few basics for the kitchen and bath."

"Good, then." He knew she didn't want to hear it, but he had to caution her, "Don't push too hard. Take care of yourself...."

She laughed. "Oh, I will. I promise you. And I'm feeling great. Fabulous. Never better, I swear."

"How's Damien?"

"He's been wonderful. So helpful and sweet. Plus,

he's easy to talk to and I can ask him anything. He never laughs at me for being so inexperienced and having way too many silly questions."

"Is he…there at the hotel with you?"

"Uh-uh. He's staying at his apartment—the one in my new building?"

Excellent. Noah felt relieved enough to tease her. "Right. *Your* building."

"It *is* my building, because I'm going to live there. Tomorrow he's taking me furniture shopping. But then Wednesday he has to go back to Montedoro." Good. Noah was willing to believe that Dami and Lucy were friends and nothing more, but he would still rest easier when the Player Prince had left New York. Lucy added, "Some festival or something."

"The Autumn Faire."

"That's it. He has to drive a race car in a parade. He's been so sweet, though, Noah. He introduced me to nice Mrs. Nichols across the hall from me. And there's a great building superintendent, Mr. Dobronsky. He takes care of the apartments and fixes anything that gets broken. I met him and his wife, Marie, too. I liked them both a lot."

He couldn't help smiling. "You like *everyone* a lot."

"Mostly, yes. I do." She said it proudly. "And how about you?"

"I'm fine. Perfect."

"Hannah?"

"She misses you already."

"I miss her, too. I'll call her tonight. How's Boris holding up?" Hannah would be taking the cat to her later.

"He'll survive."

"And Alice?"

"Good. Alice is good."

Lucy chided, "You'd better *be* good to her."

A curl of annoyance tightened his gut. "Oh, come on, Lucy. Of course I'm good to her."

"You know what I mean. Treat her right. Take care of her. Let *her* take care of you. Don't close yourself off. Don't boss her around."

"Just what I need." He tried to make a joke of it. "Relationship advice from my baby sister."

But Lucy wasn't kidding. "Someone has to say it. Alice is the one for you. I just don't want you to blow it."

"I'm not blowing anything." *She's the one who keeps turning me down.*

"Oh, I know *that* voice. It's your 'I'm the boss and you're not' voice."

He breathed deep and grumbled, "Lucy. Cut it out."

And she relented. "Okay. Just, you know, try to be open, will you?"

"Open. Absolutely. I will."

"Ha. I love you, Noah."

"Good. Be safe. Don't overdo it."

"I will be fine. I promise. Bye, now."

And she was gone. He set down the phone and thought of all the things he hadn't said: *Watch your back. Hold on to your purse. Stay out of dark alleyways. Set up those first appointments with your new doctors....*

He had so much advice he needed to give her. But she was on her own now. All grown up. And a continent away.

Alice didn't know what to do. Noah was shutting down on her, shutting her out. Whenever she tried to talk to him about it, he denied and evaded.

Maybe he was right. A little time apart wouldn't hurt them. It might do them good.

Or it might just be the simplest way to end it. She would go home; he would fly to Texas on business.

The days would go by, the weeks and the months. Somehow they would never quite get back together again....

She left for Montedoro Wednesday morning.

Noah kissed her goodbye at the front door. "Have a good trip," he said. Nothing else. No urging her to hurry back, not a single word about how much he would miss her or when he might come to her.

His coolness hurt. She longed to tell him she loved him, but she'd promised she wouldn't—not until she was ready to marry him. And how could she be ready when he wouldn't even talk to her about the things that really mattered?

So she kissed him back and whispered, "Take care."

Altus held open the car door and she got in.

And that was that. They drove away.


Noah returned from Texas on Friday. He'd sunk a big chunk of change into Yellow Rose Wind and Solar. And he had complete confidence in his decision to go in and go big.

There were other things he wasn't so confident about. Things like his sister's continued good health and well-being now she'd run off to New York to become a star in the fashion world. And Alice.

Alice most of all.

She'd left him without saying when she'd be back. He was pretty damn furious at her for that.

True, he hadn't *asked* when she would be back. He

hadn't offered to join her in Montedoro. But he felt justified in that. After all, *she* was the one leaving *him*. She should be the one to say when she planned to return.

And she hadn't called or emailed or texted him, either.

Well, all right. One text. To tell him she'd arrived home safely:

@ Nice Airport. Flt smooth. Njoy Texas.

He'd texted back, Thnx, a real conversation stopper. Because he didn't really want to text Alice.

Or talk to her on the phone.

Or correspond via email.

He wanted her with him, where he could touch her and see her smile. He wanted his ring on her finger and her sweet, strong body next to him in bed.

Wanted all that. And wanted it way, way too much.

So much it scared the crap out of him. So much it had him all upside down and turned around inside.

It wasn't supposed to be like this. She was supposed to say yes when he asked her—or at least, if she didn't say yes, he should be able to take it in stride. Patience and persistence were everything. He knew that. You kept your eye on the prize and you never gave up no matter what went down.

He was blowing it. He got that. Blowing it and determined to keep on blowing it.

It made no sense. *He* made no sense.

He was ashamed of himself and pissed off at her. And so lonely for her it made his bones ache.

Saturday, he called Lucy just to see how she was doing. And to give her all the important advice he hadn't managed to impart when she'd called the previous Monday. She chattered away, laughing, sharing way more information about her new life in New York City than he ever needed to know.

And he simply listened. And found himself smiling and nodding and now and then making an encouraging sound. He never did give her all that advice he'd been so anxious to share.

Because he realized she didn't need to hear it.

Somewhere around the time she started detailing how Mrs. Nichols across the landing had invited her over and they'd made cookies together—spice cookies with cinnamon and nutmeg and sugar sprinkled on top—the truth came to him.

Lucy was okay.

Lucy was going to be fine.

If she needed him, she would call him. For now, he'd done all he could for her.

It was her turn to soar, and he really couldn't help her with that.

He was just feeling kind of good for the first time in a week when she asked him about Alice. He didn't know what to say so he answered in single syllables, and she knew immediately that things weren't right. When she found out that Alice had gone to Montedoro and Noah had no idea when she'd be back, Lucy got all over him, calling him his own worst enemy, demanding to know if he'd lost his mind.

Noah let her rant on. What could he say? She was right after all.

When she finally wound down, she pleaded softly, "Go after her, Noah. Do not let her get away."

After that conversation, he felt worse than ever. He

went out to the stables and spent the day with his horses. It helped a little.

But not enough.

Monday, Orion arrived from the farm in Maryland. God, he was beautiful. To see that incredible iridescent coat shining in the California sun, well, that was something. Noah called in the vet to check him over. The vet declared him in excellent health. After the vet visit, Noah tacked him up and rode him. Orion amazed him, so calm and responsive for a stallion, especially a super-sensitive Teke recently cooped up in a trailer for the long ride from Maryland.

He started to whip out his phone and text Alice, just to let her know that Orion had finally arrived safe and well, to give her a hard time for parting with such an amazing animal.

But he didn't call.

What if she didn't answer? He had no idea where he stood with her now.

It had been five days since she'd left him. In some ways, those five days seemed a century. Or maybe two.

That got him feeling down all over again.

Back at the house, he showered and changed and then went down for a drink before dinner. He poured himself a double and drank it, staring out over the equestrian fields. When the glass was empty, he poured another.

Hannah served him his solitary dinner on the loggia.

He sat down and looked at the excellent meal she'd put in front of him and decided he wasn't hungry after all. "Hannah, another drink." He held up his glass to her.

She gave him one of those looks and said, "If you want to get wasted, you can do that on your own." And then she spun on her heel and marched back into the house.

He sat there for a moment after she left, fuming. And then he went after her.

"What the hell, Hannah?" he demanded when he got to the jut of white stone counter that separated the kitchen from the family room. He slammed the heavy crystal glass down. "What is your problem?"

Okay, he shouldn't have asked. He knew that. You didn't ask Hannah Russo what her problem was unless you wanted an earful.

"You," she said low, with a cold curl of her lip. "*You* are my problem, Noah. You, moping around here like someone did you wrong when we all know very well that *you're* the one in the wrong here."

"Now, you wait just a minute here…"

"No. Uh-uh. *You* wait, Noah. When are you going to wake up? You think I can't tell what's happened in this house? You think I don't know that you went out and found yourself the woman of your dreams and then brought her home only to send her away again?"

"I didn't—"

Hannah cut him off with a wave of her hand. "Don't even bother lying to me. I've known you for too long. I know what you're up to. You had some grandiose scheme to get yourself the ultimate trophy wife."

"What the… How did you—"

"*You* told me."

"I didn't—"

"You did. Maybe you didn't know that you did. But you told me all about her, including that she's a Montedoran princess. You said you were going to marry her, and that was before you even met her. I can add two and two and come up with four every time—and where was I? Oh, yeah. You went out to catch yourself a princess and instead you found someone to love you. Someone you love right back. That scares you. Love scares you. Well, you know what? You're not the least special. Everybody's scared. Everybody's afraid that they'll lose what they love the most. Everybody's afraid that they'll end up alone."

"I'm not—"

That time, she slapped her palm flat to the counter for silence. The sound echoed like a shot. "Yes, you *are*. You are afraid. And you are taking yourself way too seriously. You need to get over yourself. And here's a hot flash. Getting snockered on thirty-four-year-old Scotch is not going to give you anything but a headache in the morning. You need to go after her. You need to suck it up and say what's in your heart, Noah. You need to get down on your knees in front of her. You need to tell that sweet girl that you love her. You need to do it right away. Before she does exactly what you're afraid she'll do— which is to decide that you're not worth waiting for."

## *Chapter Thirteen*

Alice was doing her best just making it through one day after another.

In some ways it was good to be back in Montedoro. To share long lunches with Rhia, to spend time with her horses.

The Autumn Faire came and went. She rode Yazzy in the parade wearing traditional Montedoran dress: full pink skirt with black trim, a frothy white blouse, a snug black vest embroidered with twining flowers and a round, flat, wide-brimmed hat with a black ribbon that tied beneath her chin. White tights and flat black shoes completed the ensemble.

Alice waved and smiled at the crowds that lined the narrow streets. A lot of people had cameras pressed against their faces or took pictures with their phones as she rode by. Alice just kept smiling even though she felt vaguely ridiculous. She knew she would end up all over the tabloids looking like a country milkmaid.

Which was fine, she reminded herself. Looking like a milkmaid was a significant improvement over coming off like a refugee from an episode of *Girls Behaving Badly*.

After the parade, she went home to change. Dami showed up and coaxed her out for a coffee with him. They sat in a favorite café and he told her what a delight

Lucy was and then asked her why Noah hadn't come with her for the Faire.

She sipped her espresso and said she didn't want to talk about Noah.

And Dami surprised her by not pressing her to say more. He took her hand and kissed the back of it, and then turned it over and pretended to see her future in her palm. "Great happiness. True love. Horses. Children— lots and lots of children." He faked a look of dismay. "Far too many of them, if you ask me."

She eased her hand away. "You just never know, Dami."

He didn't lose his beautiful smile. "Perhaps *you* don't. But *I* know. You are a ray of boldly shining light in a world that is too often boring and gray. You were born to be happy. And you will be. Just watch."

Alice hoped her charming brother might be right. But as each day went by, she grew more afraid that if there was to be happiness for her, it wouldn't be with Noah.

Michelle clucked over her and whipped up delicious meals to tempt her flagging appetite. Alice ate the wonderful food without much pleasure. Everything seemed gray and sad to her, even Michelle's excellent cooking.

More than once she considered simply hopping a flight and returning to California. But she didn't do it— which was unlike her. She'd always been one to go after what she wanted.

With Noah, though...

It just didn't feel right to go running after him. He'd sent her away alone, though she'd asked him twice to come with her. He wanted her to marry him, but he wouldn't or couldn't say that he loved her. He didn't even seem to want her to say that *she* loved him. It was all too perplexing, and she didn't know what to do about it, didn't know how to get through to him.

So she did nothing.

Rhia gave her a hard time about that. "Waiting. That's what you're doing. You realize that, don't you? Waiting for him to make the first move. It's so...backward of you to wait for a man to make the moves. That's just not you, Allie. You're a woman of action. And you need to go to him, work things out with him, together, the two of you...."

Maybe Rhia was right.

But deep in her heart, Alice didn't think so. Alice thought that Noah needed time to figure a few things out.

She was giving him that time.

At least that was what she told herself.

While she waited.

And did nothing.

Thank God for her horses. Without them, it all would have been too much to bear. She gave her days to them gratefully, rising long before daylight to be the first one at the stables, not going back to her villa until sunset.

On the last Wednesday in October, she woke from her restless dreams even earlier than usual. She went straight to the stables and tacked up the chestnut mare Rosanna to ride. She'd just set the saddle well forward on the mare's fine back when she heard it: the soft rhythmic rustling of a broom brushing the floor.

Her heart roaring in her ears and her gloved hands suddenly trembling, she turned.

He was there at the edge of the shadows, tall, strong, golden. Wearing battered jeans, an old sweatshirt and worn Western boots.

His name filled up her throat. She hesitated to let it

out, struck silent by the absurd certainty that he was only a fantasy brought on by her own desperation and longing, that he would vanish as soon as she dared to acknowledge him with sound.

She made herself say his name anyway. "Noah?"

He dropped the broom. It clapped and clattered against the stone floor. And then he was lifting his head to face her. He tried on a smile that didn't quite make it. In those blue eyes she saw hope and fear and so many sweet, tender questions.

And love.

She did. At last. She saw his love.

He made a noise, a tight, tortured sound. And in a whisper, he said, "Alice." He held out his arms.

It was enough. It was everything.

With a soft cry, she covered the distance between them in swift strides. He scooped her up and she grabbed on tight.

He turned them in a circle there in the darkened stable, so early in the morning it still felt like night. His cheek, rough with morning stubble, pressed to hers—at first.

And then he turned his head just that little bit more. Their lips met in a kiss that told her all the things she needed so desperately to know. A kiss that promised tomorrow.

And the next day.

And all the days after that.

On Friday they flew to Los Angeles.

They took a suite at the Beverly Hills Hotel and made love for hours. When they finally fell asleep, exhausted from jet lag, pleasure and happiness, they slept until the middle of the following day.

At three in the afternoon, they stood on a palm-tree-lined street in the pretty, hilly neighborhood of Silver Lake. He showed her the Spanish-style house that his parents had owned, where he'd lived until the money ran out after his father died.

"It's a comfortable house," he said. "Built in the 1920s and big for that era. Four bedrooms, two baths. A great house to raise a family."

She linked her arm with his and shaded her eyes with her other hand. "You loved it here."

He nodded, his gaze on the house where he used to live. "We were happy. Safe. Until my father died, I honestly thought no trouble could touch me—or maybe I didn't actually think it. It was simply true. A fact of life. But then one morning, he kissed my mother goodbye, walked out the front door and fell off a roof two hours later. Everything changed."

She leaned her head against his shoulder and wished she could think of something both helpful and profound to say. All that came was, "It's so sad. And scary…"

He tipped her chin up and kissed her, just a tender brush of his mouth across hers. "Come on."

They got back in the car and he told the driver where to go next.

Twenty minutes later the car pulled to the curb on another street, where the houses were smaller and more run-down, with barred windows and doors.

They got out and stood on the sidewalk by the car, beneath a beautiful tree with delicate fernlike leaves. "A jacaranda," she said. "We have them in Montedoro, too."

He pointed at the house across the street, a small stucco bungalow painted a truly awful shade of turquoise. The paint was peeling, the doors and windows barred. A battered chain-link fence marked off the tiny bare yard. "One bedroom," he said. "One bath. My mother slept on the sofa. Lucy had the bedroom. There was an extra room, very small, in the back. I had a cot in there. I hated that house. But not because it was so ugly and cramped. It just… It always felt empty to me. Empty and sad. Well, except for Lucy. She was like a bright ray of light, even when she was so sick and I was sure we would lose her like we lost my dad."

"So, then, it wasn't *all* bad."

"Bad enough," he said gruffly, still staring at the turquoise house.

She reached up and guided his face around to look at her. "It means so much to me that you've brought me here."

He turned to her fully then, there beneath the lacy branches of the jacaranda tree, and he gazed down at her steadily, his eyes like windows on the wide-open sky. "I love you, Alice." He said it softly but firmly, too. Without hesitation and with no equivocation. "You are my heart, my life, all the hope for the future I didn't even realize I was looking for. I want you to marry me, but if you're not ready, I swear I can be patient. I can wait as long as you need me to."

She put her hands on his chest, felt his heart beating strong and steady beneath her palm. "Oh, Noah…" Across the street, a woman with long black hair pushed a stroller in front of the house where Noah used to live. Two boys raced past in the middle of the street, laughing and bouncing a ball between them. She thought that it wasn't such a bad street, really, that there were people in the small houses around them who loved and cared for each other, who looked to the future with hope in their hearts. She whispered, "I was so afraid you wouldn't come to find me."

He laughed then, but it was a ragged, torn sort of sound. "Me, too." He took her by the shoulders and met her eyes again. "The love thing. Talking about it, saying it out loud… It's hard for me."

She laid her hand against his cheek. "It will get easier. Love is like that. The more you give, the more you have to give."

"Think so, huh?"

"I know so."

"Hannah got fed up with me," he confessed. "She told me off, said I was scared to love you and I'd better get over myself and deal with my fear before you got tired of waiting for me."

She shook her head and dared a smile. "It would have taken a long time for me to get that tired. But I'm glad you came sooner rather than later."

"I gave some thought to what Hannah said…"

"And?"

His mouth twisted wryly. "It's old news."

"Tell me anyway."

He glanced up into the ferny branches of the tree, then down at the cracked sidewalk and finally into her eyes again. "My parents, that's all."

"They made you afraid to love? But how? From all you've told me, they did love you, very much. And they loved each other.…"

He lifted a hand and stroked her hair, his touch so sure and steady—and cherishing, too. "I know. It doesn't make sense. They loved each other absolutely. Even I knew that, and I was only a kid. But my mother was never the same once he was gone. She let everything go.

She was like a ghost of herself. She was…just hanging around, waiting for it to be over."

"Oh, Noah. Are you sure? Did she say actually that?"

"No, of course not. But she didn't have to. It was there in her face all the time. That faraway look, a bottomless sort of sadness. The day we lost her, I think she knew what would happen if she didn't get to the doctor. But she wouldn't go. She wanted to be with my dad. It was where she'd wanted to be all along."

Alice started to speak.

He put his finger against her lips. "I realize I'll never know for certain that she let herself die. I realize she did the best she could and that we survived, Lucy and me."

"But you've been afraid. Afraid to love so much…"

He nodded. And then he bent and he kissed her. It was the sweetest kiss, tender and slow.

When he lifted his head, she said, "Don't be afraid. Or if you are, do it anyway. Love me anyway."

"I will," he replied. "I do."

And then, slowly and clearly, she said, "Yes, Noah. I will marry you."

He looked so startled she almost laughed. And then he demanded, "You mean it? You will?"

"I love you. And yes. I will."

He stuck his hand into his pocket and came out with the ring he'd offered her that first time they made love. When she shook her head in wonderment, he explained, "I've been carrying it around with me all along, just in case. It got to be like a talisman. I kept it on me even after you left California."

"Noah, I do believe you're a complete romantic."

"Shh. Don't tell anyone. Let it be our secret."

She gave him her hand and he slipped it on her finger. It was a perfect fit. "I love it," she whispered. "I love *you*."

They shared another slow and tender kiss.

Then, hand in hand, they turned for the waiting car.

\* \* \* \* \*

*A sneaky peek at next month...*

# Cherish™

**ROMANCE TO MELT THE HEART EVERY TIME**

## *My wish list for next month's titles...*

**In stores from 15th November 2013:**

❑ Snowflakes and Silver Linings — Cara Colter

& Snowed in with the Billionaire — Caroline Anderson

❑ A Cold Creek Noel & A Cold Creek Christmas
Surprise — RaeAnne Thayne

**In stores from 6th December 2013:**

❑ Second Chance with Her Soldier — Barbara Hannay

& The Maverick's Christmas Baby — Victoria Pade

❑ Christmas at the Castle — Marion Lennox

& Holiday Royale — Christine Rimmer

**Available at WHSmith, Tesco, Asda, Eason, Amazon and Apple**

## *Just can't wait?*

*Visit us Online*

You can buy our books online a month before
they hit the shops! **www.millsandboon.co.uk**

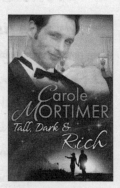

# *Wrap up warm this winter with Sarah Morgan…*

## *Sleigh Bells in the Snow*

Kayla Green loves business and hates Christmas.

So when Jackson O'Neil invites her to Snow Crystal Resort to discuss their business proposal… the last thing she's expecting is to stay for Christmas dinner. As the snowflakes continue to fall, will the woman who doesn't believe in the magic of Christmas finally fall under its spell…?

### 4th October

## www.millsandboon.co.uk/sarahmorgan

# Come home this Christmas to Fiona Harper

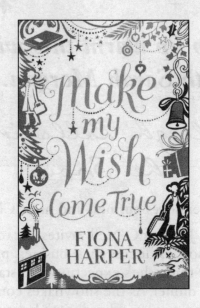

From the author of *Kiss Me Under the Mistletoe* comes a
Christmas tale of family and fun. Two sisters are ready
to swap their Christmases—the busy super-mum, Juliet,
getting the chance to escape it all on an exotic Christmas
getaway, whilst her glamorous work-obsessed sister,
Gemma, is plunged headfirst into the family Christmas
she always thought she'd hate.

**www.millsandboon.co.uk**

# *Meet The Sullivans...*

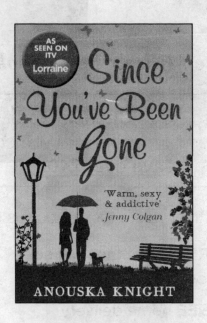

# *The World of Mills & Boon*®

There's a Mills & Boon® series that's perfect for you. We publish ten series and, with new titles every month, you never have to wait long for your favourite to come along.

---

## *Blaze*®
*Scorching hot, sexy reads*
4 new stories every month

## By Request
*Relive the romance with the best of the best*
9 new stories every month

## *Cherish*™
*Romance to melt the heart every time*
12 new stories every month

## *Desire*™
*Passionate and dramatic love stories*
8 new stories every month

M&B/WORLD3